Anti-Aging Cream

A Novel of Finding Yourself, Starting Over, and Trucks

Gallagher Green

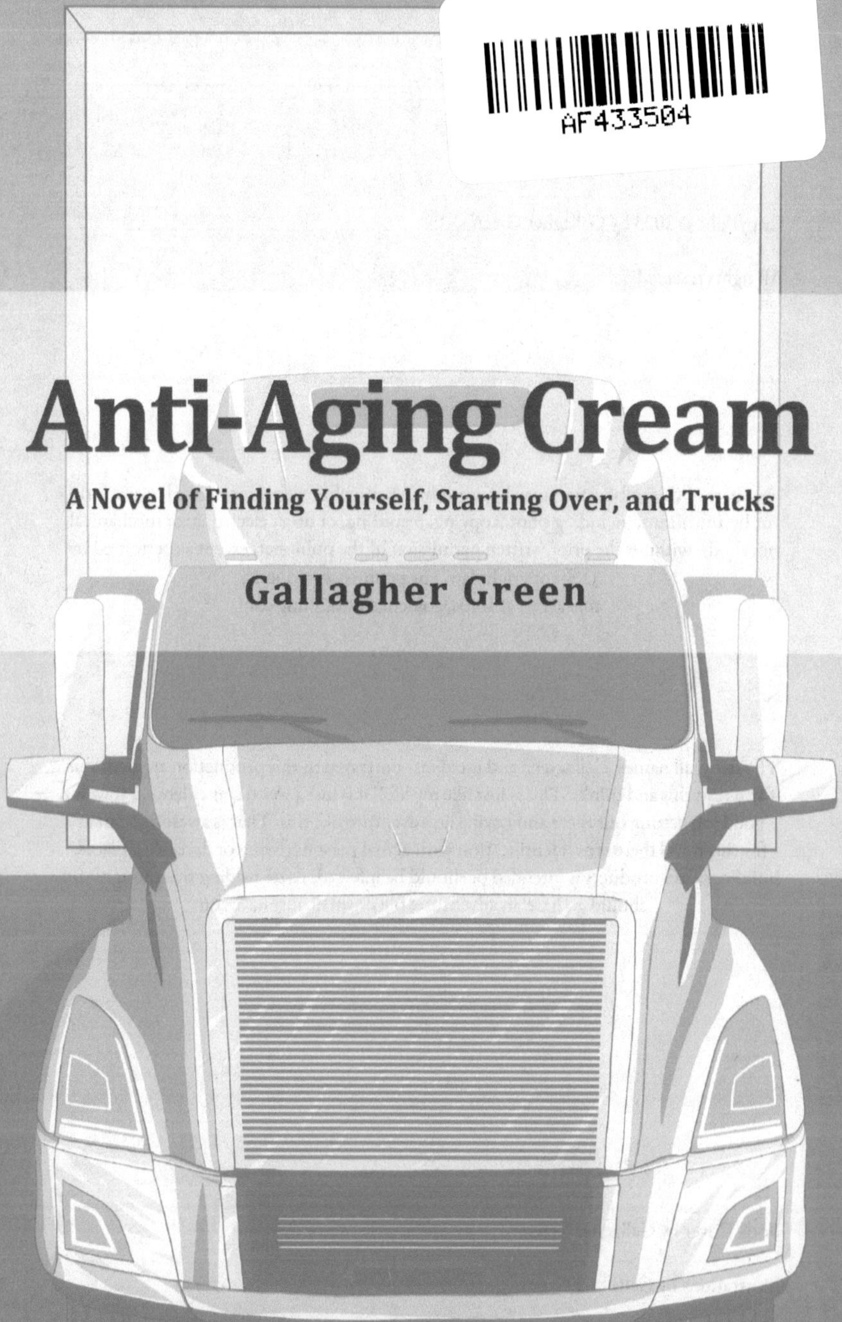

The story, all names, characters, and incidents portrayed in this production are fictitious.
If you read this and think, "This is just like my life!" it is just a weird coincidence. However,
good job getting out there and having an adventure like this. That is awesome! But as
for this novel there is no identification with actual persons (living or deceased), places,
buildings, and products is intended or should be inferred. After reading this though, you
should go have an adventure; big or small, just have fun.

Book Cover by Gallagher Green

Illustrations by Gallagher Green

First Publication 2023

Contents

Contents

1

Highwayman

Here I am, forty-three-years old, standing on the side of a high-way, with onc small bag, no money, no car, no husband, no home, or even a life for that matter. I mean nothing... less than nothing. Less than I even had a half-hour ago, which is more than I thought I would have a half-hour ago.

A half-hour ago, some man was holding a gun on me and I thought I might lose my life, or be raped, beaten, kidnapped, or any number of horrible things... maybe even all of them. All of them does seem a bit excessive, but that is the world we seem to live in, and the kind of luck I seem to be having.

It seems to be getting hotter with every step, and I am really starting to wish I had asked for my bottle of water, but I will just try and remember to do this the next time. But, I'm not dead of heat stroke yet, so I will just keep walking.

I watch car, after car, after truck, after bigger truck fly past, no one seeming to even notice me, and I am wondering whatever happened to southern hospitality, when suddenly a black truck with a large red stripe running up the hood and cab pulls over, and the man in it rolls down the passenger side window. "Ya broke down?"

"You could say that," I say with a small laugh.

He is slow speaking, seeming to take his sweet time while I roast in the sun. "Anyone come'n?" he asks. I notice he has been; and is looking everywhere but my eyes. "I can take ya if you need," he continues

"My husband is on his way. He is coming from that way"—I nod up the highway in the direction I was walking—"and I thought I would just walk a bit and meet him sooner." He just stares for a second. "I might as well get my daily exercise in, right?" I say with a laugh, but he doesn't.

"Aw-right, good luck to ya then," he says. "It's hot though, here." He chucks a can out the open window, and by the act of some miracle I manage to catch it. "Nice catch."

"Thanks," I say as he gives a one-finger wave and speeds off, leaving me in a nice little cloud of black smoke. Something about him just didn't seem like he was worth the chance. I might have just been too hard on him, or maybe it is because I just don't feel like trusting anyone, especially men. Nonetheless, one's like this gentleman, who didn't even hide the fact he was trying to look through my clothes. But he did give me this nice can of light beer.

How much farther until I come across something? I wonder as I continue walking, holding the cold can of beer to the back of my neck. Possibly the weirdest thing someone in Texas has ever done with a can of beer on a hot day, but I hardly ever drink, and have never liked the taste of beer.

I look up slightly like I have so many times in my life; like I have since I was old enough to know how, and start to open my mouth to pray, but stop. I have done this several times a day my whole life, every time my life seemed to go wrong, or when something was wrong with someone I knew. And here I am. "I'm done with that..." I say to the heat that seems to really be getting to me.

My feet are starting to really hurt and they are hot; I can feel the pavement's heat seeping through the soles of my shoes. "Maybe it's better than I remember," I say with a sigh, crack the can open, take a drink, and instantly have to stop myself from spitting it out. It tastes as awful as I remember, but it is still halfway cold, and it is wet. Not sure it will help my being thirsty in the long run, but right now I would drink nearly anything.

A car is suddenly beside me, quiet enough that I didn't hear it pulling up. I smile at the woman driving and wave. Only then I remember I am holding the can of beer... and I just waved with it, sloshing a generous amount of beer on myself...

I am grateful that her car doesn't leave me in a cloud of smoke as she speeds off. "Damn it!" I say, throwing the still mostly full can into the ditch. "Don't cry," I tell myself, breathing in a sharp breath. "You don't need that on top of everything." I look around, realizing that I am truly talking to no one, that I have no one... and start crying as I continue walking.

It feels like such a long time, but finally I see it, a rest stop. There is only one semi truck parked along the wide drive idling loudly. *Maybe I should ask him for help?* I think walking past the semi, *I don't think I should,* figuring a truck driver would probably be no better than the beer-drinking truck guy. So I just B-Line for the women's restroom; hoping it isn't utterly filthy, and that there is no one waiting to attack me in there. It isn't like there is security of any kind.

I open one stall door, then the next, and the next... and the next, *What is wrong with people?* I wonder swinging the door shut, feeling sorry for whoever cleans these places. "Praise God," I say, seeing that the last stall is... useable. The sinks are clean; other than the paper towels that were too hard for people to throw away, those are all over. I wash the beer off my hand first and then my arms and face. The water isn't cold, but it is cool, and I realize I am starting to feel dizzy.

I look in the mirror; which isn't as reflective as I thought it would be, and take a deep breath, feeling a little better. "Well, at least with all of this going on, you're not thinking about the other thing," I say to my reflection, and think briefly about the other thing. Staring at myself, wondering how I didn't know sooner, why I didn't let myself know sooner, and if I even know now. "You might just be making excuses, or maybe you are just crazy or something." I take another deep breath and smile at myself in the mirror, then stop when I see what the smile looks like.

"You'll be fine, just get to the next town and you can figure it out from there," I say to the mirror me, and splash some more water on my face, "You got this," I reach for a paper towel, "You gotta be kidding me?" I say, checking the other two towel dispensers, both as empty as the first. "Well, that seems about right." And I wipe my hands dry on my shirt, just like I always told my kids not to do.

I stand at the water fountain outside and drink as much of the warmish water as I can, knowing I need to stay hydrated, wishing I had a water bottle of some kind. But I don't, so I start walking again as a semi-truck suddenly gives a hiss and a jerk as it slowly starts to roll. *I wonder if this is some sort of punishment from God?* I think as the sun beats down on me, and I start to list the sins I know I have committed and the ones I may have committed.

The semi-truck stops with another hiss and jerk as I walk in the same direction as it. As I come up from behind it, I notice the entire width of the bumper on the trailer is lined with those fake balls rednecks hang on the bumpers of their trucks, but the right side of the bumper is lacking a few pairs from being equal with the other side. Then I get close enough to read the long, bold print bumper sticker, *"Piss this bitch off and yours will be hanging here,"* with an arrow pointing to an empty spot on the bumper. I can't help but laugh when I see this and read it again while looking over the nearly full row of balls swinging from the bumper.

I am wondering what kind of truck driver would have this on their trailer, when I hear a voice say, "You walken?" I look up from the balls to see a Black woman standing on the bottom step of her semi, holding onto the chrome handle on the side of the cab, her black hair blowing slightly in the hot, furnace breeze. *She's beautiful...* my mind instantly says, like it does too often. But, my mind isn't wrong.

"Yeah."

She just stares at me for a few seconds as I walk closer. "Why? It's like a hundred degrees out."

"It's a long story, but I'll be fine. I'm just going to the next town," I say, like I completely got this under control, not like I was about to pass out in a public restroom only a few minutes ago.

"That's nearly fifteen miles."

"Fifteen miles?" I say, feeling defeated.

"Yeah. Where are you from?"

"San Antonio."

"That's nearly a hundred and fifty miles from here." I will give her credit. She is spot on with her distance guess. She's a trucker for sure. "Why are you clear out here walken?"

"My car broke down," I say plainly.

"You don't have a phone?"

"No one to call."

"Yeah, that's a problem. You want a ride then?"

"That would be great," I say, glad I didn't have to ask.

"No problem," she says, stepping off the truck's step and onto the ground. She is a good amount taller than me, and it seems that most of that height is legs; which I try not to stare at.

"Thank you so much," I say right as I hear a loud vehicle, and look to see the same black truck with red stripes up the hood and cab. It's the man that gave me the beer and creeped me out. I told him my husband was coming to get me, and I wonder what he might do if he sees I lied. Quickly, I jump forward the few feet between this woman and myself, using her as a hiding place, or maybe a shield? I hadn't realized just how scared I was of that man until now, as his truck roars past.

"I'm sure you're a great person, but... I'm not really looking for... that." I look down and see where my hands are. "Not that I'm not flattered, bu—"

"I'm sorry," I say, pulling my hands off her and quickly stepping back, feeling my face heat up. "I really didn't mean that. I would never—"

"It's fine. I've been felt up by worse people than you," she says with a laugh and a grin. "So, who was that? An Ex?"

"What?"

"The guy in the pickup. You were hiding, right? Or am I so sexy you couldn't keep your hands off me?"

"No, never—I mean yes, you are... But no, I wasn't—" I stammer, getting very flustered, and start to feel dizzy again.

"Calm down. I was just yanking your chain." She smiles in a very disarming and comforting way.

"The guy offered me a ride earlier, but—"

"He made your skin crawl."

"Yeah. So I told him my husband was coming to get me," I say.

"If you were worried about him seeing you, don't be. I have a spot on that bumper just for him," she says with a wink that makes me smile, and I feel better. "Well, circle around and climb in. It's too goddamn hot to stand around talking out here."

2

Truck Ride

As I pull the handle of the semi's passenger side door, I am surprised at how clean it is inside. and how far it is up to the seat. I sit down on it and swing the door shut, looking down out the window. "Higher up than you thought, isn't it?" the woman says.

"Yeah, it really is."

"You'll get used to it, and once you do... damn, you feel powerful." I can't help but smile at this. *I am really starting to like her*, I think.

"If the seat is hard, the adjustments are on the front and side. The person who bought the truck new was a husband and wife driving team, so they had the good seats put in on the driver and passenger sides. Which means there's a shitload of buttons on them. So, just buckle up and play around with them."

"Okay, thanks," I say, pulling the seatbelt on.

"No problem. Off we g—" she pauses, sniffing the air. "Is that you that smells like beer?"

"I thought I washed it off."

"Was too much beer the reason your car...'*broke down*'," she says with air quotes.

"What?" I say, unsure of what she is insinuating.

"Did you have a few too many and run into a sign or ditch, or something?" She smirks.

"No! I would never. I hardly ever drink, and never enough to be drunk."

"So, beer-scented perfume... nice." I am getting the feeling she is never serious.

"It is not."

"Well, I'm going to get driving. You can straighten your story out and then tell me later." She laughs as the semi starts rolling forwards.

"Wait, you don't have to shift?" I ask, looking at where I thought there would be a shifter.

"Not these days. I used to drive a manual, but all the trucks are going to automatics."

"Why?"

"They are easier to teach new drivers; which is good since there is always a shortage. But they are also way more efficient on power and fuel," she says, pulling out onto the highway, watching in the mirrors.

"I guess that makes sense." I stare out the windshield as we go down the highway. "Oh my goodness, I never introduced myself," I say.

"Oh, I guess we did skip that part. Well, I'm Anna," she says.

"I'm Mary. It is nice to meet you."

"Nice to meet you too," she says, laughing a little.

"What?"

"Nothing, you're just a bit old-fashioned."

"Oh... Well, I am old, so that makes sense," I say, wanting it to sound like a small joke, but it comes out sounding depressed.

"You aren't old," Anna says, glancing over at me. "You look about the same age as my sibling, Evelyn. How old are you?"

I hesitate, but figure there is no reason to not tell her. "I'm forty-three."

"Yeah, you're a year younger than them. I'm thirty-five, the baby of the family. I have a brother who is two years older than Evelyn. Mom says they were both really pissed when I was born," she says, laughing.

"I'm the oldest of my family. I have five younger siblings."

"Holy fuck. That must have really sucked." I can't help but laugh a little, because it did.

"Yeah, at times... okay most of the time, it really did. Probably why I agreed to get married. I figured if I was going to raise kids, they might as well be mine." I realize that I am now just volunteering information for some reason. "So, how much farther to town?"

"It's only like fifteen minutes now. Where am I taking you?"

"Wherever is easy enough for you to stop, I will figure it out from there," I say. Having no idea how I will figure this out, knowing that I really am in trouble.

We sit in silence for a little while. "So, you get your story straight yet?"

"What?" I say, feeling a little panicky, wondering if I did or said something.

"On why my truck smells like beer?" She grins.

"Oh, that."

"What did you think I was talking about?"

"Nothing," I say too quickly. "That guy, the one in the truck—"

"Okay," Anna interrupts, "That was a pickup. If it don't got at least ten gears and air brakes, it ain't a truck," she says, and I get the feeling this is a real pet peeve of hers.

"Okay, pickup. But the guy that offered me the ride tossed a beer to me before driving off, and I don't like beer, never have. But I was thirsty and decided to drink it—"

"And got so tipsy you dumped it on yourself." She laughs.

"No, I wasn't drunk!"

"I'm joking, it was one beer. Of course you weren't drunk. You are so easy," she says, shaking her head as she laughs at me.

"I just dump some on myself, and then threw it away," I say quickly before Anna jumps to more conclusions to use to *"yank my chain."*

"Alright, I will believe you," she says, winking at me; like it isn't the truth. But I don't say anything because I just don't want to. "Sorry if I am giving you a hard time," she says, seeming to notice my tiring of it, "I am just in my truck all day and most nights for days on end, so when I do have someone around, I talk a lot."

"That's fine. I can understand that. I know the feeling of having no one to talk to."

"Oh?" she says, glancing at me with a raised eyebrow, and I realize I am saying too much again. "Your husband wasn't much of a talker?"

"Oh, he never stopped."

"But he didn't listen, did he?" she says, no longer joking.

"No, he never did. I just stayed home, so what would I have to say that he would want to hear?"

"No girlfriend?"

"No, I've never had a girlfriend. I dated Justin in high school and got married at nineteen. So I never did... that."

"Um... I just meant a friend to talk to. I didn't mean—"

"Oh, of course. I knew that," I say quickly, my face suddenly feeling really warm. "I had a good friend, but I don't anymore."

"That can happen. I've lost friends myself that I thought would always be friends. It fucking sucks... Sorry." Anna says this and sounds like she really means it. She is the first person to show me any empathy at all. "Are you okay?" she asks, glancing over at me, and I realize I have tears running down my cheeks.

"Yes, I'm fine. And thank you," I say, wiping the tears away.

"So, you mentioned having kids," Anna says, seeming to be hunting for a happier subject for me.

"I do, two. My son Aaron is twenty-four, he just graduated college this spring as an engineer. He's also engaged."

"That's great," Anna says.

"It is," I say, and continue, "My daughter, Angela, is twenty-two. She's going to college to be a teacher."

"That's really great."

"It is," I say, proud of how well they have done.

"Are you on your way to visit them?" Anna asks.

"No... no, I'm not. They're back in San Antonio."

"I'm sure they miss you," she says, like people do. It's like saying, *"You'll find someone"* or *"There are lots of good jobs out there"* or *"It will be okay, the treatment will work this time..."* it is just what we say, not completely meaning it, or even knowing if it is right for the situation. They are lies we tell each other all the time.

"No, actually, they don't. I was never a good mother. Yes, I tried. But I was never close to them. It just didn't happen, and Justin was a natural. So I was quickly overshadowed, and then they took his side and were perfectly fine with my leaving."

Anna is silent. I wonder what she will say to me. Then she just says it straight out. "Wow, sounds like they inherited their dad's 'piece of shit' gene. I have a cousin like that." I instantly start laughing, not having expected this at all.

"I guess you might be right. I hadn't thought of that."

"Well, the only alternative is you're a shitty person and mother," she says, and looks at me; longer than I like given she is driving a semi down the highway at nearly eighty mile-per-hour. "And I'm pretty sure you're not. Not from where I'm sit'n at least."

"Thanks... You're the first person to be on my side. And you don't even know me."

"Well, maybe we should fix that. You think?" she says as I see the town I will be getting out at ahead. She turns on her blinker as the exit approaches, checking her mirrors.

"I don't think we got time for that," I say as her truck drifts softly into the exit lane, knowing that I will be climbing out in a few minutes.

"Maybe," Anna says, decelerating. "Do you have any friends or family here?"

"No," I say, feeling like we have already covered this.

"How much money do you have on you?" I just look down. "Shit, you don't have any, do you?" I shake my head, still looking down. "Do you even have a phone?"

"No..." I say, feeling ashamed.

"Okay," she says, turning her truck into a lot that is half full of other trucks where there are fuel pumps, a mechanic's shop, a restaurant, and a hotel. The truck stops with a jerk, and she sets the brakes with the hiss of air. "Now, tell me what actually happened," Anna says, turning sideways in her seat.

I take a breath. "I lost everything in the divorce, but I got to keep some money I had saved back. So I decided I would just leave and figure out where I was going while driving; I just wanted to leave it all behind. But as I was driving, I saw someone walking, and I thought I should do the right thing and give them a ride since it is so hot."

"You got carjacked?" Anna says, shocked.

"He had a gun... But he was actually kind of nice—"

"Oh, he wasn't rude, that's a relief."

"Well, he was pleasant, and he could have done much worse to me than just take my car and stuff. I really wouldn't have been able to stop him."

"Shit..." Anna sighs. "Yeah, you're right. It could have been worse," she admits.

"And he let me keep my purse, just not my phone or money—"

"How much money?"

"There was about five hundred in my purse—"

"Oh shit," she says with another sigh.

"But I had eight thousand in one of my bags..." I admit, but hate having to.

"Holy fuck..." She stares.

"Everything I had to start over."

"Why didn't you have me call the police sooner?" Anna says, pulling out her phone.

"Don't!"

"Why not?"

"Because both cars were in my husband's name, and I didn't get one in the divorce. So I technically stole it from him."

"He would have turned you in for car theft?" she asks, seeming to think no one would be such a jerk.

"Justin texted me and said he knew I took it, and if it wasn't back by that evening, he was calling it in as stolen."

"That fucking asshole!" I can't help but smile at her anger over this.

"Yeah, I even bought the car myself with money I made working part-time for my... a church." I correct. "But it was in his name, because he filled out the paperwork at the dealers."

"Let's drive back to San Antonio so I can beat that mother-fucker's ass. I'm going to have his balls hanging in the empty spot on my bumper!" I laugh when she says this, and fully believe that she is willing to do it.

"It doesn't matter now—"

"You are too good of a person," Anna says, and I think she might be right.

"I didn't respond to his text before I got held up, and if I turn the car and my money in as stolen—"

"They'll know you stole the car from your ex... Damn, you are fucked," she says, as she thinks about it. "So, in short. You have no money, car, phone, or place to stay?"

"Yeah... Who would have known that I would suddenly end up homeless at forty-three?" I say, my voice cracking.

"If you don't mind a bit of a cramped sleeping space, you can stay with me longer if you want. I mean, it doesn't matter to me, but I don't think you have a lot of options at the moment."

"You really mean that?" I ask, not believing that she would be willing to do this. "But I can't even pay for food, and I don't even have a change of clothes."

"Oh, don't worry about that. There are other ways to pay... and you won't need much for clothes," Anna says, slowly looking me over, and I try to cover myself with my hands even though I am fully dressed.

"I don't... Um I can't... you see I've never—"

"Joking," she says, interrupting my stammering, and I'm not entirely sure what my stammering was about to agree to. "You gotta stop taking everything so seriously." She smiles.

"Right, sorry."

"You just need to loosen up. But that was also a bit too mean of me, sorry, too much time away from company makes me not think so well."

"It's fine," I say.

"Come on, you still smell like beer, and I really don't want to get pulled over with the inside of my rig smelling like that. Let's get you showered off."

"The moment you've been waiting for." Anna stops and stares at me, then starts laughing.

"Yes! You are finally getting it."

"I'm not joking. I saw how you looked at me, and now you want me to stay."

"Um..."

"Just yanking your chain. Now, who's too easy?" I smile.

3

Truck Stop

I walk across the parking lot with Anna, and she seems to stare at every truck we pass with interest, like she is shopping. "So, are you in the market for a different truck?" I ask.

"No, why?"

"You're just staring at them like you are."

"I just got my truck a few months ago. But, it's always fun to look. How about you?" Anna asks.

"What?"

"Which truck do you like the best?"

"Oh, I don't know anything about them."

"You don't have to, just go by looks," she says.

I look around as we walk. Most of the trucks are white, but the ones that aren't are all sorts of colors, vibrant and shining like they are new. "Why don't cars come in these colors?" I ask as much to myself as anyone.

"Thank you! I have been saying this for years. Cars are all the same boring factory colors. If you don't custom paint them, they suck!" I get the feeling this is another pet peeve.

"That one"—I point across the lot—"is really nice."

Anna looks. "I should have known a Texas girl would pick a Peterbilt with horses painted on the side of it," she says, and I can't help but giggle. It is so weird, I don't remember the last time I giggled about anything. I must have been a teenager. "What are you all giggles and smiles about?" Anna asks with a smile that tells me she is enjoying this.

"It's just been a long time since anyone called me a girl."

"Sorry, I should have asked what your pronouns are," she says, and she is serious about this.

"Pronouns?"

"Yeah," she says, and looks at me, noticing my look of bewilderment and complete confusion on what pronouns have to do with this. "You have no idea what I am talking about, do you?"

"No, I do. It just isn't a question people ask much around here, or discuss."

"We can talk about it later. We have a lot of hours ahead, and it's better that we save conversation topics."

"That makes sense."

"So, what do people normally call you?" she asks.

"Friends called me Mary, but mostly it is 'Miss,' 'Ma'am,' or 'Mrs. Murphy', it has been a long time from the years of 'girl,'."

"God, Texans have no imagination," she says as a man walking past glares at her, but Anna doesn't even seem to notice. "I mean, calling someone 'Miss' or for fucks sake, 'Mrs. Murphy,' is so boring... It is like you can't just use your own name, that you are just something owned by your asshole husband."

"I hadn't thought of it that way."

"Just my thoughts on it," she says as she pulls the door of the building open, holding it for me. "Let's get you something else to wear."

"I still don't have money," I remind her.

"Don't worry about that. The price of crappy truck stop clothes is well worth keeping that smell out of my truck."

"I don't smell that bad."

"Yes you do, you're just already used to it," Anna says, walking towards the corner of the store.

"This place is huge," I say, turning a half-circle to see everything.

"They have everything you need, except a selection. You pretty much have to deal with whatever they have," she says, half hollering it back, since she didn't stop to wait for me.

"I'm not picky," I say, taking a few quick steps to catch up.

I glance at a few things on my way, and get to the racks and shelves of clothing as Anna is already looking through them. "Just get whatever you need," she says, turning to a shelf to look at the clothes in bags.

I look through the rack of T-shirts; something I have never worn much, but there doesn't seem to be any blouses; not that I see at least, and I really don't want to ask. Most of the t-shirts have logos, some I recognize as brands of trucks, and others I don't recognize. Then I notice a fifty percent off sign. They are mostly T-shirts. "What is this?" I ask, holding a shirt up against myself. There is a picture of what looks like a truck part on it, and the words *I'm ready to go* in bold print.

Anna turns and looks at it for a second, stifling a laugh. "That's a fifth-wheel."

"What's that?"

"A fifth-wheel hitch, it's what holds the trailer to the truck," Anna says, seeming to question my intelligence.

"I know what a hitch is, I just didn't know that it was called a fifth-wheel," I say, draping the shirt over my arm, and start looking some more.

"Are you going to actually get that?" she asks, raising an eyebrow.

"Yeah. If I am going to be riding with you, I should at least have some truck-related clothes, and it's even on sale," I say with a smile, since this is the perfect mix.

"You are going to wear... that?"

"Yeah... Why?" I ask, her grin telling me that I am missing something.

"You don't get it, do you?" I shake my head slowly. "Look at the picture." I turn the shirt around, holding it at arm's length as I look at the picture. "What do you see?" she asks, with a smile.

"A fifth-wheel hitch," I answer, now knowing the name.

"It is an open hitch," she says, pointing at the picture.

"What's that mean?" I ask, and she sighs. It seems that she is no longer questioning my intelligence. She knows I'm an idiot.

"And it says 'I'm ready to go.' So, you are telling every trucker; or person that knows what a fifth-wheel is, that you are ready, to, be... hooked up."

"Ready to be hooked up?" I think looking at the shirt, and the second it takes for my mind to get there is way too long. "Oh... oh my goodness!" I say, and slam the shirt back onto the clearance rack. "Why would they even sell that?"

"Because it's a truck stop, not some fancy clothing outlet. And that is what the clearance racks always are. They are either three-extra-small, seven-extra-large, or crap like that. Funny to look at, but no one will wear it. I know from experience," Anna says, turning back to the shelf.

"You know? What, do you have one of these?"

"Naw, but Evy got me something similar once for Christmas as a joke."

"Evy?" I ask, looking through the plain solid color shirts in the four-pack bags.

"We have always called Evelyn, Evy."

"That's cute," I say, smiling, because it really is cute.

"Guess so," she says, seeming to not completely agree.

"Why don't you wear the shirt she got you?" I ask.

"Not she, they."

"What?"

"Evy is non-binary," she says. "This your size?"

"What's that?"

"Plain cotton panties. It's all they have. We'll have to stop somewhere else later for a better selection."

"I know that. And yes, those are right," I say, grabbing the package from her.

"Non-binary," she continues, without my having to ask again. She opens her mouth, but stops. "You know, let's discuss this in the truck later. Not sure it is something to discuss in a Texas truck stop," she says, dropping her voice to a whisper. I glance around at the other people around, and having been a Texan my whole life, I understand this isn't the best place to talk about some things.

"Right, another driving topic then. What about the shirt Evy got you?"

"It has an air horn on it and says 'Want me to blow?' Well, judging from those red cheeks, you get that one," she says with a quiet laugh.

I don't say anything, and just focus on finding the right size of sports bra; all they offer, and they too are in a four-pack. Then I go over and look through a rack of jeans, seeming to be the only type of pants they sell. "These sweatpants are your size, aren't they?" Anna asks, holding out a pair of sweatpants, also in a plastic bag, but there is only one pair in a bag for the pants.

"Oh, I didn't know they had those. I just saw the jeans," I say, realizing I will have to live a life in cheap sweatpants until I can pay my own way. "Yeah, those will fit."

"Great. Did you find some jeans yet?" she asks, poking through the jean rack.

"I will just get the sweatpants. I hadn't seen them before."

"You're getting some jeans, you gotta have some real clothes. I just thought the sweatpants would be something to sleep in. I mean, I really don't care what you wear, I'm a t-shirt and underwear person myself—"

"No," I say way more vehemently than needed. "Sweatpants are perfect. I honestly hadn't even thought of something to sleep in."

We look through the jeans until I find my size, and we get four pairs. "You have never worn the shirt in public?" I ask.

"What?" Anna says, looking at me.

"The shirt Evy got you."

"No," she says with a little laugh.

"You scared?"

Anna eyes me. "What's making you so... daring?"

"Just thought someone with a row of fake balls on the back of their truck would have—"

"More balls?" she says flatly.

"I was going to say guts. But if you would rather use that word, fine."

"You've been around me less than an hour, and you're already getting weird... I must be rubbing off on you." She's right, I wouldn't normally do this. But, I normally wouldn't do a lot of things. *Maybe jail does change you?* I wonder. *Or maybe Anna is more of a friend than anyone else.*

"Just saying." I smile and turn towards the register, my arms full of everything.

"Big talk coming from you."

"Says the person that doesn't wear the shirt."

"Fine, I will under one condition," she says from behind me.

"Oh yeah, and wha—" I am interrupted by something hot pink being thrown on top of the pile I am holding.

"Turns out, they have more colors than just the black you found," Anna says, and I don't even have to ask to know it is the fifth-wheel hitch shirt.

I follow the sign that points towards the showers as Anna takes the clothes she bought me back to the truck; with the exception of what I am going to change into. There doesn't seem to be very many other people around, at least not in this area. Maybe I will luck out and the showers will be empty, or maybe they are all individual rooms. *That would be nice,* I think with a little hope as I see the door marked *'Women's Showers'.* Pushing on the door, it squeaks slightly as it swings open. I walk through the little L-corner that keeps people from seeing in, only to see what looks like a standard locker room, more gym than high school though.

There is only one other woman; who looks to be in her mid-sixties in the room, and she is just zipping up her bag. "Hello," I say politely as she walks past, and she just looks at me, not saying anything, like I did something to her. It feels like everyone seems to hate me these days. I don't even have to know them, and they still hate me.

"Oh, excuse me," I hear a voice at the same time as the door gives its little squeak, indicating its opening, but I don't hear a response. I look in the direction of the door, and a younger woman; maybe mid-twenties, walks in with a duffle bag. "What a bitch," she says to herself, but out loud as she looks back towards the door.

"Hello," I say, hoping that this time it goes better.

"Howdy." It does go better, and I am glad I said something. "What's her deal?" she asks.

"I don't know. She doesn't seem like a very friendly person," I say with a smile. Sitting down on the long bench, I start untying my shoes.

"Her problem, not mine," she says brightly. She seems like one of those unnaturally bright people. She drops her bag on the other end of my bench and pulls off her shirt while continuing to talk. "So, are you a trucker, RVer, traveler, or vanlifer?"

"I'm riding with a... friend that is a trucker," I say, not meaning to have paused before saying friend like that, but it is so new. Pausing sounded odd, like there is something I am hiding. *What if she thinks I'm gay, or something?* I wonder, not sure how she will react to the idea of a gay person being in here with her. *Not that being gay means someone would try something. I never would, not that I am gay. But if I was, I wouldn't try anything, even if I was attracted to her... She is pretty, and seems kind...* I snap out of this line of rambling thoughts, as I realize I am staring at her as she drops her bra on the bench with her shirt and is unbuttoning her pants.

"That makes you a trucker," she says, not seeming to notice the pause in my answer, or my staring at her.

"How bout you?" I say, quickly undoing the buttons on my blouse, feeling like I need to catch up so she doesn't think I am just here to watch or something. *Do people do that? Come to places like this to watch?* I wonder, because I feel like it is something that someone has done at some point in time.

"Vanlife!" she says, with so much pride that it makes me smile. Considering she is now nearly completely naked in front of a stranger while saying this makes it very impressive, and I find myself more than a little envious of that pride and happiness in her life.

"That must be interesting. Do you like it?" I ask, laying my bra on top of my shirt on the bench and try not to think about it. I have always hated public showers, ever since the first time in school. I always feel a lot of anxiety and get extremely uncomfortable. But now? Now it is time to get past it. The last few months have done nothing but prove the ways I have been living my life weren't working. *So, maybe this isn't working either,* I think.

"I love it. It is so interesting." She seems to truly mean this, she looks happy. "It is hard at times too. I have to work seasonal jobs and I also do some online work. But it doesn't take as much money with no rent or utilities to pay," she says.

"If I was younger, I might give it a shot. It sounds like a nice change," I say, standing up and unbuttoning my slacks.

"You're never too old. So, if you decide to try it, just do it. I mean," she continues, now completely naked, but it seems she is waiting on me. At least I get that feeling. "My family thinks I'm bat-shit crazy, my dad thinks I'm throwing my life away, and my mom started crying when I told her." She laughs. "I am pretty sure she thinks 'vanlife'"—she air-quotes—"is code for a life of endless drugs and sex with someone different in every town."

"I am sure she just worries," I say, and realize that is what someone like her mom would say. *I am tired of being that,* I think. "Sorry, I shouldn't say that, it is kind of a natural response. But... she should trust you. You're an adult," I say, stepping out of my panties and dropping them with the rest of my clothes. And I don't feel too anxious. Maybe talking is really keeping my mind off of the fact I am standing here naked next to a stranger.

"Yes... Thank you," she says, seeming to truly appreciate this response, and that makes me happy.

Then she looks down, but at me, and my mind starts to panic. *Is she one of those people that comes here to look at others? What should I do? Should I say something?* "Do you have flip-flops?" she asks, pointing a finger at my feet.

"What?" I ask, a little flustered and very confused.

"Flip-flops or sandals, something to wear in the shower."

"Oh, I didn't think of that. This is my first time using a truck stop shower," I say, looking down at her feet that are in blue flip-flops, and making sure I keep my eyes from wandering up her very smooth legs.

"Yeah, you want something. Lord knows what kind of shit you can't see is on those floors," she says, turning to her bag. "These places are fine, but I just don't trust that they are cleaned that well, or that often."

"I hadn't thought of that," I say, wondering if my socks would help, or maybe something else. I think of lots of strange ideas for feet covering, and look around the empty room with the idea in mind of finding something, and to keep myself from staring at this beautiful; and very naked young woman, who is bent over while looking through her duffle bag.

"Here you go," she says, turning around with a smile, holding out a pair of blue flip-flops like hers, still held together with the plastic binder; showing they are new. "These are the extras I carry, in case something happens to my pair, or I step in something so gross I just throw them away."

"Really?"

"Oh God, you don't even want to know the gross things I have stepped in."

"No," I say laughing, "I mean, can I really use these?"

"You can have them. They are super cheap."

"I can pay you," I say, and instantly realize this means asking Anna for money. I am still not used to having no money at all.

"No, you're not paying. Let's call them a gift. By the way, I'm Alesha. And welcome to life on the road. Either by van or big-rig, you will love it!" she says with a smile. I take the flip-flops, thinking she might just be right. Because I am really starting to love it, and it hasn't even been two hours.

4

Shower Talk

I hang my towel on the hanger outside the shower's entrance and look at the metal box next to it. It has a quarters slot and even a credit card slot, and it reminds me a lot of the controls at a car wash. "I kind of expect this to have a soap, rinse, and wax setting on it," I say as I drop the quarters Anna gave me into it.

Alesha starts laughing as she drops quarters into the control box of the shower next to me. "I never thought of that, but you're so right, it is like the same as a carwash." I don't know why, but it makes me feel really good when she laughs.

I step into the shower as the water starts, and I think about this. I realize I never made people laugh at home, even when I said something I thought was funny. Sometimes Deb laughed and would say I was funny. But I was always comfortable with her. I had always trusted her, it's why I went to her first. "Pro tip!" Alesha says over the noise of the water, her voice echoing outside the shower curtain, "Do your hair first. Washing some soap off in the sink isn't bad if you run out of time, but washing hair conditioner out in the sink is a bitch."

"Oh, I didn't think of that. Thanks."

"And if someone walks in, they think you shower in the sink. Trust me, awkward."

"Is that experience talking?"

"Maybe..." she says, and starts laughing again, and it makes me so happy.

"How long have you been traveling in your van?" I ask, liking the conversation. Which I never have liked talking to someone while I was showering before. But before now that was either the kids when they were little, bugging me about something, or Justin complaining about who knows what. When in both cases, I just wanted to be alone for that short time in the shower. It was time I wasn't cleaning, cooking, working at a part-time job, or dealing with any number of other little things that no one else ever noticed. Unless they weren't done, that is.

"Almost a year," she answers.

"Wow. Was it something you have always wanted to do?"

"A little. Well, I honestly started following this girl on the internet who posted vlogs about her vanlife, and I thought it looked really cool. I originally was going to do this with my boyfriend..." She pauses for a few seconds, seeming to be thinking, or maybe rinsing and unable to talk, it's hard to know. "We planned it out, I sold my car, bought the van and used the money from whatever else I had to sell to convert it. I did luck out, and the person who owned the van before me had started converting it, and had set up all the electrical and a few other things, so that helped a lot!" she says, and I am getting the feeling she loves talking about her van. She's proud of it, because it is something she did, something she built.

"Did your boyfriend help convert it?"

"A little, but he wasn't good at it, and tried to show me how to do everything, even though he didn't know how to do it. I was the one that did all the research. He never researched anything, but he still knew what was best." There is no question, this is a hot-button issue for her.

"I can understand that. My husband would come home, and then tell me how to wash the dishes, or act like I was cooking something too long. When I had been doing it every day for over twenty years!" I say and realize this seems to be a hot-button issue for me too.

"Oh my God, what is with them? You just want to tell them to go fuck off!"

"I should have," I say, as much to myself as to Alesha.

"I curse God every day for not making me a lesbian so I would never have to deal with a man again," she says, laughing.

"I know, right?" I say, laughing weakly, and feeling awkward. "So, he changed his mind on the plan?" I ask, wanting to get back to the original subject.

"Only after I gave up my lease, sold everything that wouldn't fit in the van; which was pretty much everything I owned, and quit my job. Then he says 'I'm not sure this is a good idea'," she quotes him in an exaggerated stupid voice. "So that's when I told him to fuck off, and just left. Me and my van... that's all I need." When Alesha says this, it is lacking the enthusiasm of before, that undying happiness and joy is gone. That's when I realize why she is so friendly and talks so much. She's lonely. It is only her day in and day out. This was supposed to be a life with someone she thought she loved, but now it is just her.

"You're brave..." I suddenly say. "I wish my daughter was like you... I wish I was like you." I hear her water turn off; my water turns off. "Is that it? Is time up?" I ask, looking at the nozzle, glad I just finished washing off the last of the soap.

"Yeah... That's it," she says, her voice sounding weak and tight, now the only sound in the locker room. Alesha clears her throat. "Did you finish?" she asks.

"Just barely," I say, sliding the curtain back enough to get my towel, hearing her pull hers all the way open. So, I do the same. I am trying to get past these old thoughts of mine; and it isn't like we haven't both seen it all by now.

"So," she says, sounding a little more chipper, but she seems to be trying harder to be chipper this time, "how long have you been trucking?"

"About thirty minutes. Not including the time I have been here at the truck stop," I say, and she stares at me with her towel on her head, in the middle of drying her hair. "I know, I'm some veteran." I laugh.

"What the fuck happened where you already needed a truck stop shower only thirty minutes in?" she asks.

"I didn't expect that question," I say, laughing. "Well, I needed the shower after my long walk in this heat, before Anna offered me a ride."

"Break down?"

"Carjacked. Gun to my head, stole everything I own." She just stares at me wide-eyed, towel still on her head.

"Maybe my mom was right, and this is too dangerous," she says. "I am definitely not telling her about it, though." This makes me laugh. As a mother, I know I would not want to hear about it if I were Alesha's mom.

I proceed to tell her the story of the carjacking and my walk while we dry off, and I try not to look at her... too much. The times I do look; just a little, they are fleeting, and I really don't know why I do. It makes me think of my youth, sneaking looks at the other girls, in class, at the pool, in the changing room. After I married, I forced myself to stop such childish behavior, learning that thoughts like this were sinful and not tolerated by man or God. But now? Now that my marriage and the God I knew from church seem to be a sham, things seem different again. I look at Alesha as she drops the towel after drying... but just a little.

"How can you be in such a good mood?" she asks after I finish my story of the day. "I would be bawling my eyes out after a day of fucking shit like that."

"Oh, I cried a bit for a while. But it was really almost funny—"

"How could that be funny?" she says with a smile, that seems to question my sanity.

"After the last month or so I have had, it just felt like... I don't know," I say, thinking about it.

"I know what you mean, that moment when life can't get worse, and then it gets so much worse."

"Yeah, that's it," I say, pulling on the new jeans that are stiff and uncomfortable. But they fit, so that is what matters. I notice that Alesha puts on the same clothes she was wearing when she came in, but shoves her underwear into her duffle bag, along with her wet towel.

She grins when she notices my watching this, and I quickly look away, too quickly. "What's the point? I'm just going back to my van to change. Too much trouble to bring clothes in with me... I'm lazy."

"I was actually thinking that if you live in your van and work from there, you can wear whatever you want all the time. That must be really nice."

"Yeah... it really is," she says, seeming happy that I get it. "To be honest with you, there are days I only wear my panties, or just a robe," Alesha says.

"I bet that it is nice..." I say.

"Yeah, it is. As long as I know no one's around. Otherwise you have a good chance of someone pounding on your window wanting to know why you are parked there... The only time that ever happens is when I am more or less naked. Clothes on, no one ever chooses to show up then," she says, laughing.

"Well..." I say, deciding it is only fair I share something, "I once read in a magazine; in the area where readers write in, and this woman said she liked to clean her house naked, vacuuming and such. She said it was something that made her feel a little free while still getting housework done, and that everyone should try it—"

"Did it end with wild sex with your husband when he came home early?" she asks with a big smile, seeming to hope this is the story ahead. I however, involuntarily grimace at the idea and try to erase the mental image from my mind.

"Heavens no. But, the kids were in school at this point, and I thought 'why not'—"

"I have a feeling this ends bad," she says, laughing quietly.

"I am cleaning the living room, and the doorbell rings, scaring me half to death. But, instead of just staying quiet, I yell 'be there in a minute,' half in a panic, like I have been caught. Well, it takes me well over five minutes to get all my clothes on—"

"All of them? Why all of them?"

"I don't know. My mind was all over. So by the time I get to the door, it is someone with a package that just needs signed for. He is grinning ear to ear, because I took so long and he knew something was up—"

"He thought you were stashing the neighbor in the closet." Alesha laughs.

"I know he did!" I say, laughing with her. "I was so embarrassed I never did it again."

"But see," she says, "every time, that is when someone chooses to show up. It's crazy!"

"I guess that is a high point of being a nudist. You just don't care." She starts laughing really hard at this idea.

"Maybe we should both be nudists, it would just be easier!" She laughs.

"And you living in a van, think of all the space you would save, no longer owning clothes." I point out, and she laughs even harder.

"You are so right! But maybe you should wait a few days before you tell Anna you are going nudist in her truck," she says, and now I'm the one laughing harder than I have in years as we walk out of the shower room together. "Can we exchange phone numbers?" Alesha asks, her laughter calming down.

"No..." I say and she stares at me blankly, looking shocked. "That guy stole my phone!"

Only by the grace of God do the two of us make it to a nearby bench, before we collapse onto the floor with hysterical laughter. People walk past and stare, which only makes it all funnier. "Um..." I hear, and look up through tear-filled eyes to see Anna staring at me, unsure what is going on and who my best friend is next to me; who is currently beating her duffle bag with her hand as she laughs.

"Oh, hey," I say to Anna as I wipe the tears from my eyes.

"What the hell happened in that shower?" Anna asks, raising an eyebrow.

"What didn't?" Alesha says, elbowing me as she jokes.

"Anna, this is Alesha—"

"I'm Mary's shower buddy."

"Is that a thing?" I ask, looking at her.

"It is now!" she says as we start laughing again.

Anna stares for a second. "Did she get you to smoke, or vape something?" Anna asks.

"No, no," I say laughing, waving my hand at her. "Alesha, this is Anna. The woman that saved me."

"It's nice to meet you," Alesha says excitedly, and stands to greet Anna properly.

"It's nice to meet you too," Anna says, and just lifts her hand to shake Alesha's hand when Alesha hugs her. I have to try very hard not to laugh at Anna's expression as this happens.

"Is she freaking out as much as I think she is?" Alesha asks, and I burst into laughter. "Sorry," she says, stepping back. "I was just joking."

"That's... Fine," Anna says, seeming unsure of what else to say.

"I'm going to find a pen and paper so I can get your number," I say, standing.

"Oh, right, no phone," Anna says. "I can just put it into my phone if that's okay."

"That's fine by me," Alesha says and reads her info off to Anna. "Oh, I just thought of something. I have my old phone in my van. It isn't great but it worked last time I used it. You might as well take it. You can at least use it at free Wi-Fi spots."

"Really?" I say, amazed that so many people are willing to help me, and I can't help but wonder why I didn't have people like this earlier in my life. "Do we have time?" I ask Anna, knowing we need to get back on the road.

"I'm ready to head back to my van. I know where it is. It won't take a second."

"Fine by me," Anna says, and the three of us start walking towards the doors.

Alesha's van is a large full-size one with a tall roof so she can even stand in the back of it. "This is my home"—she slides the side door open—"it was originally a delivery van," she says.

"It looks great," I say, surprised at how clean and organized it is inside.

"Don't sound so surprised," she says. "You thought it would be a disaster, didn't you?" She looks at me.

"Well, maybe. You just don't seem like that organized of a person."

"Hey!" Alesha says, laughing at my honesty.

"You're the one that was too lazy to put on her underwear after your shower," I say, and Anna looks at Alesha like she is seeing if she can see something through her clothes. I know she can't though... I tried.

"Okay, you do have a point," Alesha admits. "But this is different."

"It's like the sleeper of a truck," Anna says. "If you aren't clean and organized, it will drive you crazy and you won't make it two months before you quit."

"Exactly! I read about this before I started vanlifing it."

"I guess that makes sense," I say, thinking about it.

"I'll get that phone," she says, moving some things around in her van. "I bet you are the type to keep a perfect house all the time," she says as she digs through a storage container.

"Yes, I am very much that way."

"I figured that too," Anna says.

"It was how I was raised," I say.

"Were you raised like it was your job as a woman?" Alesha says, turning around.

"I guess you could put it like that," I say, knowing it is correct.

"Did you have younger brothers?" Anna asks.

"Yeah, four—"

"Holy shit," Alesha says.

"She has five younger siblings," Anna says to her.

"Oh God, your life must have sucked." She says this just like Anna did when she found out.

"Did your brothers ever clean the house, cook meals, do dishes?" Anna asks, getting back on point.

I don't have to even think, it was always just me. My sister being the youngest and never helping with much of anything, spoiled for the most part by everyone. "No... It was just me."

"That fucking shit sucks," Alesha says.

"Yeah, it really does," Anna agrees.

"Here you go," Alesha says, holding out the phone as she steps out of her van. The phone looks really nice to me, better than the one that got stolen.

"I don't know how to thank you for everything," I say and hug her, because I really want to.

"It's just a phone," she says with a small, tight laugh.

"You know what I mean," I say, and she squeezes me tighter. The hug is long enough that Anna starts looking awkward, but it doesn't feel long enough for me and Alesha. But it has to come to an end.

"It was nice meeting you," Alesha says, holding out her hand to Anna, who seems happier about this than the hug. "And you better message, call, text, or something the second you get that thing figured out," she says, smiling at me.

"I will. You can count on it," I say.

Anna and I walk towards her truck in silence most of the way, until Anna breaks it. "So... what was that long thank you and goodbye for? Come on, tell me. What happened in the shower room?" She says this, sounding like she is half joking, and half wanting to know.

"It was really nothing... She's just had a hard time of it too, and that's hard when you have no one to tell." I should know, my whole life has been not talking about things with people. *Maybe if there had been a stranger for me to talk to in the shower room, things would be different,* I think, and continue thinking about it as I pull myself into the truck.

5

On the Road

I stay quiet as Anna focuses on navigating her truck through traffic, working back towards the highway. I just look out the window, not at traffic or anything else, I just look at nothing in particular. No, I actually think about Anna and Alesha. *How did I not get the chance to be like them while I was young? How did I let myself fall into a life I never wanted?* "You motherfucking bastard!" I blink out of thought as Anna yells this and I am jerked forward as she stomps the brake for a second.

"What? What happened?" I ask, looking around.

"That asshole cut me off!" she says, more than a little mad.

"Maybe they didn't mean to." She shoots a sharp-eyed glance at me. "Or maybe they did do it on purpose, I really don't know," I say, feeling very nervous.

"I got them now." Anna smiles, glaring through the windshield as we pull up behind a pickup that is stopping at a light that just turned red.

"Are you okay?"

"I am now," she says, her smile never stopping.

"What are you doing?" I ask as she stops so close behind the pickup I can hardly even see it. "You aren't getting out, are you?"

"Why would I do that?" she asks, with a slightly evil look as she pulls a lever on the dash down, and I hear a loud hiss as she holds the lever down. "You ever seen the movie 'Duel'?" Anna asks as she taps the throttle of her truck, making it lurch slightly and shake as the engine roars. It feels like she is holding the leash tight on some monster as it pulls, trying to get to that pickup and rip it to pieces.

"No... I haven't," I say with a swallow.

"That's probably for the better," she says, looking over at me with a grin as she stomps the pedal harder. "Do me a favor, reach up and pull that twice." She nods at a loop of rope hanging from the ceiling. I am pretty sure I know what it will do, and I'm not disappointed as I pull the loop, resulting in a deafening blast of the truck's air horn, and I can't help but smile at the sound.

Anna lets go of the lever on the dash, and it snaps back into place. At the same time, the pickup takes off from the light; even though it isn't quite green yet, turning onto the highway on-ramp. Luckily, the light has turned as Anna stomps the throttle and wheels the truck onto the on-ramp behind the pickup. I am surprised at how quick her truck accelerates. "Lucky for us, I have a light load," she says, seeming to have read my mind.

"Is it really lucky?" I question, and she laughs, seeming to enjoy this way too much. "What is your plan here?" I ask as she stays as close as she can to the pickup.

"These assholes buy these big expensive pickups, and then think they're king of the fucking roads... But that's my title."

"You're scaring me..."

"Don't worry. If I wanted him dead, he would already be dead," she says, and reaches up and pulls the loop of the air horn with a big grin.

I hold on as I watch the speedometer climb over nine-ty-mile-per-hour. "How fast are you going to go up to?"

"Not much more. Hold on though, I'm going to hit the brakes hard in just a second," she warns as we go up a hill.

"What?"

"Just trust me," she says, getting even closer to the pickup, and pulls the air horn again, holding it longer this time. The pickup starts pulling away from us, and must be doing close to a hundred. "Hold on!" Anna says, letting off the throttle and stepping on the brake. Not too hard, but hard enough I am pushed against my seatbelt.

The pickup is over the hill and gone. "Why did you do that? What was the point in all of that?" I say, sounding much more annoyed than I thought I would.

"Wait for it," she says, so I am quiet and don't say anything else.

We top the hill at just under the speed limit, and there is the pickup; pulled over with a highway patrol sitting behind them with their lights on. I stare in amazement. "Man," Anna says, "this is only a sixty-five, so that ticket is really going to hurt."

"How did you know?"

"I have run this highway more than a few times, and all us truckers know that there is always a cop waiting just on the other side of that hill without fail. So, when I saw his tag was from Oklahoma, I knew he wouldn't know the area, so I just encouraged him to speed." I stare at her, not sure what to say, and then burst into laughter.

"That is so great," I say, laughing. "And I have wanted to pull the rope on an air horn my whole life."

"It was the first thing I did when I got into a truck. It was a childhood dream," she says excitedly, "and doesn't it feel so powerful?"

"It really does." I agree, smiling at the memory of pulling it from only a few minutes ago. "I need to get this phone working. I gotta tell Alesha about this."

"While you fool around with that phone, I'm putting on a podcast. That okay?"

"Of course, it's your truck," I say as I hold the power button on the phone until it turns on.

I stare at the screen as the phone comes to life, its lock-screen popping up. I swipe the lock and it opens, glad there isn't a password Alesha forgot about on the phone. But the phone is loaded with apps. She didn't reset it. *But why would she? She hadn't planned on giving it to some stranger... no, to a friend,* I think with a smile.

While some woman on the podcast starts her interview with someone about something to do with bodies, I notice the icon for the photo gallery. I tap on it, and it opens to a whole bunch of photos. I glance over at Anna, feeling like I am looking at dirty photos or something, but she is looking at the highway ahead.

I start looking through the photos, including photos of her ex-boyfriend, and friends, all of them out having a good time together. But the photos are all dated to over a year ago, the only new photos are selfies that most likely went on social media, along with photos of sunsets, and meals. The type of photos people take to show others how great their lives are. But there is nothing that shows the bad days, nothing showing her life in between the smiling selfies and perfect sunsets.

"Are you looking through her photos?" Anna says, and I jump, feeling caught.

"She didn't clean them off," I say, and tap the folder of photos from the text app. They are only photos sent by friends, and seem to have dwindled off to only a photo a week at most, instead of the dozen a day she was getting.

"Isn't that a bit of an invasion of privacy?" she asks.

"She is really all alone..." I say, looking at a photo of her looking so happy with friends.

"That's the life you choose when you travel like that," Anna says.

"But I'm worried about her."

"You just met her."

"That doesn't mean I can't worry about her. She never stopped talking in the shower room, even taking the shower next to me so we could keep talking... She needs someone in her life to talk to."

"I knew your kids were assholes," she says out of nowhere, and it is like a slap. My kids and I may not be on the best terms now, but they are still my children.

"What?" I ask defensively.

"You said before that you were worried that you were just not a good mother. Well, you are all worried about a girl you barely know. You are acting like her mother, worried, and wanting to take care of her."

"I just worry about people."

"My point is. If your kids are asswipes, it wasn't your fault. No chance," she says, and I just stare at her and blink hard a few times as my eyes start to sting. "I'm sorry, I didn't mean to upset you. I just mean—"

"No, you didn't..." I say with a smile, that isn't very impressive. They never are when you're trying not to cry. I listen to the podcast for a second. "What is this about?" I ask as the man describes how human bodies rot, and how you can donate yours.

"Oh, it's the science podcast Oligies... You do believe in science, don't you?" she asks with mock seriousness, making me smile and laugh a little.

"What if I said I didn't, then what?"

"I would kick you out of my truck right here and now."

"What? You wouldn't try to convert me?" I say in surprise, putting my hand over my heart.

"I ain't some bible-thumping Sunday Christian. I don't give a fuck about changing minds. I'm not your teacher, I'm your truck driver," Anna says with all the seriousness in the world, and I can't help but laugh at her.

"Sunday Christian? Never heard that one," I confess.

"My grandpa used to say that. He said it is the Christians that go to church every Sunday, but then try and stiff you on their bill, cheat, or treat people like dirt every other day of the week. But come Sunday, they are back in church praying, smiling, and telling people how they do the Lord's work," she explains.

I think about that for a second. "He is right. I know a lot of people like that... I might be like that," I say honestly.

"What, you a churchgoer? I mean, it's fine if you are. I know that they aren't all bad, ninety-eight percent of them just give that two percent a bad name," she says with a smirk, and I can't help but laugh, even though I think she just insulted me.

"I grew up going every Sunday at a minimum—"

"What if you were sick or something?"

"Then I would listen to the service over the phone."

"Damn, that is devotion," she says, now truly serious.

"It was just the way I was raised, and I continued it with my children—"

"Maybe you are a bad mother." She smirks again.

"Yeah... I may be."

"I'm sorry, I shouldn't have said that. I don't know when to shut up sometimes," she says.

"That's true. But—"

"Ouch," she interrupts.

"I don't think I did my kids any favors. It made them close-minded adults. Like I said, I was a 'Sunday Christian.' I might have gone to church all the time, but I had lots of sinful thoughts... Things that weren't Christian at all."

"That ain't it. You were devoted to a fault maybe, but I have the feeling you were always a good person. And 'sinful thoughts'," she says with air-quotes, which worries me as her hands aren't on the wheel, "just means you were thinking for yourself. It doesn't mean that there was anything wrong with it. You seem to be way too hard on yourself."

"You might be right," I say, thinking about it. "I got so used to everyone being hard on me, that maybe I didn't notice when I started doing it to myself."

"That's it. The world keeps fucking you over so much, you don't even notice when you start fucking yourself."

"Isn't... that what I just said?" I question.

"Well, yeah... But you're a trucker now, so you need to sound like one."

"Do all truckers swear like that?"

"I don't know. I haven't met all of them. But I do. So I am going to say yes." I smile at this, because it really does make sense.

"Maybe you're right, and it is time I stop fu, fu... Sorry, can't say it." I sigh.

"All in good time, all in good time." She smiles, and her smile makes me happy.

6

Sleeper

I stare at my phone. It doesn't have a phone plan but I use Anna's phone as a hotspot for the internet. I go to my social media and send a message through it to Justin, telling him to call the police because I don't have his car. I don't mention that I had it to start with, that isn't something he needs to know at the moment.

I look out over the parking lot of trucks as the sun starts to set and hear a car door slam the same second the driver's door of the truck opens. "Can you take this?" Anna asks, handing up the pizza box.

"Of course," I say, taking the box. "I didn't know they deliver to trucks like this."

"Yeah, as long as they can find you easily, they are cool with it," she says, pulling herself into the truck.

"Do we just eat here?" I ask, not really sure where you eat while in a truck.

"You can, but I was going to put something on TV. If you want to watch with me, just go back to the sleeper. I'm going to close the curtains."

"Okay," I say, taking the pizza into the sleeper, surprised at how big it is. But, there is only one bed, it is a double size bed; or at least close, I figure I will just sleep in my seat up front.

Anna pulls curtains in place over the windows that nearly blacken the entire inside of the cabin, until she hits a light switch on her way back. "Here," she says, folding down a table from the wall. "Is a soda fine?" she asks, opening the door of a little refrigerator I hadn't even noticed.

"Wow, this is really set up nice," I say, setting the pizza on the little table.

"The truck companies have gotten really good at designing these sleepers. They are really nice to stay in," she says, handing me the can of coke and then opening a cabinet to take out some napkins. "It makes life a lot easier."

"I can see that," I say, looking at the TV, which is larger than I would have thought.

"Find something on TV"—she tosses the remote on the bed next to me—"while I change, I can't stand lying around in bed wearing jeans." She says this as she starts unbuckling her belt. *Should I turn around, or close my eyes?* I wonder, but Anna doesn't seem to pay any attention to me, sitting only a few feet from her, so I turn on the TV and try to act like I couldn't care less. When I actually want to look nowhere else.

I scroll through the shows on the TV as I glance at her from time to time, watching as she pulls out a small clothes hamper; throwing in her jeans, t-shirt, and bra. *Stop that, what's wrong with you,* I tell myself and look back to the TV. I glance up slightly and see the perfect reflection of Anna standing there half-naked as she pulls a shirt and pants out of a drawer. *Don't look,* I tell myself, but can't seem to stop and I continue watching as she pulls on a pair of sweatpants and a T-shirt. I look back at the TV.

"You find anything?" she asks, dropping onto the bed.

"Oh, not yet," I say, feeling flushed and warm. "You pick, it's your TV."

"Okay, if you say so," she says, taking the remote that I hold out to her, looking me in the face. "You look warm."

"Do I? I guess it is a little warm," I say, feeling uncomfortable and guilty.

"It is a bit warm in here. The temp control is over there"—she points—"lower it a bit." And I do. "Oh, and your clothes are in that bag. So you can change whenever," she says, as I notice the bag on the floor.

"Thanks again for all of this," I say, pulling out the sweatpants and a t-shirt.

"Don't worry about it. The day I'm not willing to help someone, you can just put a bullet in my head, because I'm worthless," Anna says, and this makes me smile.

I put my hand on the hem of my shirt to pull it off, but pause, seeing Anna sitting there looking at her phone. *This is no different than the shower room, and I was completely naked in there for a long time*, I think. *Then why are you just standing here?* "Oh, sorry," Anna suddenly says, having noticed my hesitation; or more like my completely freezing. "You can change up front. The curtains are blackouts, so no one can see through them. Just slide the sleeper curtain shut."

"Thanks," I say, walking towards the front. "Sorry."

"Don't be sorry," she says as I slide the sleeper curtain shut. "I grew up playing a ton of sports in high school, so I really got used to the whole changing room scene."

"Oh, I never did play sports," I say, as I pull my shirt off and feel very aware that Anna is just on the other side of that curtain. Sure there are who knows how many strangers just outside the truck, behind the other curtains, but my mind doesn't think about them... it thinks about Anna. "What did you play?" I ask, hoping a conversation will make this less awkward.

"Volleyball, basketball, and softball. I sucked so bad at softball though, but I was good enough for them to keep me around," she says with a laugh.

"You really liked sports then," I say, feeling more awkward than before now that I am talking to her while nearly naked.

"I lived and breathed sports. God I love them," she says, and from the sound in her voice, she really does.

"Why didn't you go to college and play?" I ask, now feeling like I need to continue the conversation.

"I said I loved sports, I didn't say I was good enough to go anywhere with it," she says, laughing more, not seeming to be bothered by this.

"It seems like you are pretty okay with that."

"Well, I would have loved to go pro in something, or play college at the least. But I always knew I would never be good enough. I had to practice all the time just to keep up with the girls who only practiced half as much as I did. Just how it goes, it was a lot of fun though."

"I guess that's what matters," I say, pulling my t-shirt on and feeling better that I am covered.

"Yeah, it really is."

I take a deep breath, hoping my unexplained—or unexpected—nerves aren't showing on my face as I slide open the sleeper curtain. "You find something to watch?"

"Yeah, you like old rom-coms?"

"I haven't really watched very many of them," I admit, sitting down on the bed with a good amount of distance between us.

"Really? Why not?" Anna asks.

"Well, normally—"

"Ooh, just set the pizza here between us," she says, so I do.

"Normally," I continue, "I didn't watch much TV during the day, and my husband watched what he wanted in the evening, since he had been at work all day—"

"But didn't you say you worked?"

"Well, yeah, but—"

"Then you had as much right to it as he did. Shit, if you also made the meals when you got home from work and kept the house clean, then you deserved to watch what you wanted even more." I stare at her, realizing she is knocking down everything I was taught growing up, and that she is right. My life had never been fair.

"I guess that's true... But now I can watch," I say with a smile.

"I'll get you caught up on everything you missed out on," Anna says, taking a slice of pizza.

"I hope you do," I say, feeling like the words have a different meaning than I intended, so I just take a drink of my coke and grab a slice of pizza.

I sit on the bed, eating pizza and laughing at the funny points in the movie, thinking that I wish I would have been watching these earlier in life. Would I have married Justin if I had experienced this adventure in love? I know it is fiction, like the novels I hide at the back of my e-reader's library, an e-reader that is now in the hands of my carjacker. *If the police catch him, and take the car back to Justin, he or one of the kids might look through the e-reader's library—* "You okay?" Anna asks, interrupting my thoughts.

"Yeah, I'm fine. I just remembered my e-reader was in my bags in my car. I normally read before bed. That's all," I say, knowing I can't tell her the rest of it.

"Oh, that sucks. Sorry," she says.

"Not your fault." I smile and look back to the movie, taking another slice of pizza.

We keep watching, making our own comments and views on the characters and their relationship, pointing out their mistakes that we can easily see as the viewers. We laugh and say how stupid they are for the misunderstandings. Once the pizza is gone and the box is back on the table, I move closer to the TV to see better and closer to Anna without noticing it. Until the couple in the movie are together, and they start stripping off their clothes as the sex scene quickly progresses.

I suddenly notice that Anna and I have both gone silent as we watch intently, and at the same time... I notice how close I have moved to her. I swallow involuntarily and pray she didn't hear it. And as I watch the naked man and woman, I find myself glancing at Anna, comparing her body to the woman's on the screen. Then I force myself to keep my eyes on the screen, knowing that it would be bad if Anna sees me intently staring at her while the most explicit sex scene I have ever seen plays out in front of us.

Finally the scene ends, and none too soon... or maybe too soon, I'm not really sure. "Damn, I forgot how steamy that scene is, not a good choice," Anna says with a laugh.

"Oh..." Is all I can manage to say.

"Yeah, it makes me remember how much trucking sucks. It's been a long time since I had a scene like that in my movie, if you know what I mean," she jokes, looking over to me. "Damn, looking at you, I would also say it was a bad choice." She laughs.

"I... don't... I mean, didn't watch movies with.... stuff like that. It's not... um—"

"Got it. It was probably all football, or shows with cops, and movies with machine guns involved in them, right?"

"Yeah. And westerns."

"Oh, of course. You're a Texan. How could I forget westerns," she says and I laugh a little, but I want more. Laughter, I mean. "I'll try to pick shows that won't get you all turned on every night. Don't want to drive you mad." She grins, and something about her grin just makes me happy, and drives me a little mad. *Why hasn't anyone else ever been able to do that?* I wonder.

"Oh, don't worry about me... I'll be fine."

"Well... I need to get up early and get on the road," she says, stopping the movie. "I always go for a short walk before bed, and stop by the restrooms to brush my teeth and stuff. Wanna come?"

"Sure, sounds great."

"Not to mention we could both use a walk in the night air to cool down," she says, flapping her t-shirt with one hand, and fanning her face before bursting into laughter. And I can't help but do the same.

I slip my shoes on and climb out of the truck, Anna climbing out after me. The cool night air is really refreshing, even with the faint scent of diesel in the air from the other trucks coming and going or just idling. "This is actually much nicer than I thought it would be," I say, looking at the trucks under the dim lights of the lot.

There are a few people here and there, some walking like Anna and myself, others sitting on benches or leaning against trucks talking, laughing, and enjoying the night air. "Yeah, it is. It is also nice to stretch your legs and get some fresh air before bed after spending the day sitting."

I notice another man and woman walk past laughing and having a good time, and another couple with two little kids. "There are more couples than I thought there would be, and families. I thought trucking was the single man's game."

"You sexist conservatives never move out of the nineteen-fifties," Anna says, looking at me with a little smile, and I realize she's teasing me. I haven't been teased by a friend since high school. Deb had a little, but it wasn't really her thing. Justin would tease me, but it always seemed like he was the only one who thought it was funny; or his friends did, and I just laughed along feeling picked on. But I don't feel picked on when Anna teases.

"Would some nineteen-fifties lady have watched that movie scene? I think not."

"You got me there... The way we both stared unblinking at those two going at it... I think we're both 'lonely'," she says with air quotes, making me laugh. Air quotes seem to be another thing she likes to do. "Wait, you were married not long ago—"

"What, you think you can't be 'lonely' when you're married? Trust me, you can be," I say, and feel like I'm not sure this is a subject I want to broach at the moment.

"A lot of couples are driving partners as well," she says. I am surprised that she doesn't ask more about what I just said. *Did she notice I didn't want to talk about it?* "Or their partner just rides along, even with kids. I wouldn't do that though."

"Why not? It would be nice having the people you love close all the time," I say, thinking how nice it would be to have your family always there.

"Trucking is dangerous. Between weather, terrain, mechanical failure, and other drivers that are idiots on the road. It isn't if, but when you will get into a wreck. People think trucks always come out safe because they are big, but that isn't true... You don't take someone you love with you on a job like this, and you also don't take dangerous routes if you have someone you love waiting."

"Oh, I never thought of it like that," I say, realizing how much sense she makes.

"Not to mention that trucks aren't set up to keep kids safe, you can't even strap a car seat down. I see people doing the stupidest shit, thinking it will keep their children safe in a wreck. But I know the smallest wreck, and those kids are dead—"

"People like that shouldn't be allowed to have kids."

"Right? They are too stupid to own a goldfish," she says.

"Glad you are responsible."

"Thanks."

"Then again, you did chase a pickup down earlier today... Yeah, maybe I should rethink that responsible comment," I say, as she starts laughing. *I did that,* I think, smiling.

"You have a point. And I've been in two decent wrecks."

"Really?"

"Yeah. I walked out of both of them. One was pretty close though. That's why I have this truck, totaled the last one."

"Wow... Glad you weren't hurt."

"Thanks," she says. She doesn't seem to want to talk more about it, so I don't ask.

We don't say much else, we just get ready for bed and then walk back. Anna types a text out on her phone as she walks, and I see responses pop up, but I don't look or ask who it is. I wonder if it is the person that she loves that keeps her from taking risks. I am pretty sure she isn't in a serious relationship, but that doesn't mean there isn't a man out there somewhere she is involved with.

We climb back into the truck and I sit down in the passenger seat, feeling around for whatever lever reclines it. "You staying up a little longer?" Anna asks, stepping back into the sleeper.

"No, I'm shot."

"Me too," she says, glancing back at me, then pauses, looking at me as I feel around the seat. "What are you doing?"

"How's this thing recline?" I ask, not looking up.

"Are you sleeping there or something?"

"I don't want to bother you," I say, looking up at her, and she stares at me with that grin again, and I can't help it, I grin back.

"You are not sleeping there, and you won't bother me at all," Anna says.

I get up from the seat. "Well, I'm not su—" I stop mid-sentence as she pushes a release; or something, and lowers a second bed. "It has a bunk bed?" I ask, my mouth hanging open in surprise, like she just opened a door to another room.

She turns and starts laughing when she sees my face. "What? You thought I was going to have you share a bed with me?"

"I didn't know there was a bunk bed."

"Well be glad, cause there wasn't much chance of me sharing my bed with you," she says, giving me a little slap on the arm as she jokes. "Oh hell, I wouldn't have been able to let you sleep in that seat, I would have caved." She laughs. *Why did there have to be a bunk bed?* A part of my mind deep down whines. *What am I thinking that for?* I wonder, and wonder if the stress of the last month has driven me insane.

"This is great, thanks."

"Can you get up there?"

"Yes, I can get up there," I say, but not really sure if I can.

"I am fine with sleeping up—"

"I got it," I say, and put one foot on the lower bunk and grab onto the frame. Giving it everything I have, I start pulling myself up, and I feel like I am going to make it. Then I seem to be slowing down, and I'm not sure I am going to make it. Suddenly there is a hand on my butt pushing me, and I roll onto the bed. My face feeling warm from Anna touching me, even though it was just so I would make it onto the bed. "Thanks," I say, stifling a girlish giggle that I should have outgrown over thirty years ago. But suddenly there it is, making me hide my face and bite my lip. *What is wrong with me? Is this a mid-life crisis?*

"No problem. It wasn't the smoothest bunk climb I have seen, but you made it."

"I'll have you know, this is my first time climbing or sleeping in a top bunk," I say, feeling a little proud.

"Really?" Anna says, seeming truly surprised.

"Yeah, I never had a friend with one as a kid, and I never had one. So, this is a first." I smile.

"Lots of firsts for you today."

You have no idea, my mind says. "Yeah, it really is. And I thought I was past the age of having first anything," I say.

"First off," she says, holding up a finger, "you are never too old. Second, you aren't old. So stop saying that."

"But I am—"

"Nope, not while you are with me," she says, and I feel really happy at hearing those words. And I don't feel old.

I look over the edge of the bunk to say something, just to see her toss her sweatpants on the floor next to her bed. *So, she just sleeps in panties and a t-shirt,* I think, and bite my lip again, remembering she told me this at the truck stop. I completely lose what I was going to say.

"Oh," Anna says, looking at me as she sits on the edge of her bed, "if you have to go to the restroom, the flashlight is over there," she says pointing at a flashlight in a holder on the wall.

"Okay, thanks," I say and stop looking over the edge, feeling like I was staring at her legs; because I was.

"Lights out then," she says, and the cabin goes dark.

"Can I ask a question?"

"Sure."

"Why do you trust me to stay with you? You know nothing about me." I ask this, unsure why I want to know.

"Well, you picked up a stranger on the highway; something no one does. And after he steals everything you have, you were thankful to him for letting you keep a few tiny things, and for not hurting you. Sorry, but being thankful for that is fucking insane." I laugh, but it comes out more like a giggle, I can't help it. "So I have no question about how good of a person you are."

"Thanks... But that's why you trust me?" I say, feeling like I only got a half answer.

Anna is quiet for a moment, and I start to wonder if she is going to answer when she does, "And... maybe Alesha isn't the only one that's lonely," she says this quieter, no humor or joking sound to her voice like before.

"Well... I guess that means there are three of us in that club then..." I say, swallowing hard, but Anna doesn't say anything. Then there is a sudden bump in my mattress of Anna giving it a little kick, and I instantly smile big.

"I also figure there is a good chance you are completely insane, and how can I pass up having that in my truck with me?" she says, right as I wondered if she was asleep.

"Coming from the madwoman who ran someone down for cutting them off."

"Hey, he had it coming," she says, laughing quietly.

"Excuses," I say, laughing with her.

I lie there staring at the ceiling; or more like the darkness. I just stare, smiling to myself. "You won't believe what Sarah told me in gym class today, she thinks Bobby Davis has a crush on her," Anna stage whispers in the dark.

"What?" I say, giggling, and she starts giggling.

"Doesn't that seem right though? This does feel like a slumber party, or a sleepover."

"It really does," I agree. "But Bobby is totally into Jessy."

"Oh my God... Shut... up!" Anna says, and I burst into laughter.

"Thanks... This is actually the most fun, and the happiest I have been in a long time," I say, because I feel like she should know.

"Me too, Mandy."

"My names Mary," I say, not sure what to think.

"Oh, right, sorry. Mandy was the woman I hauled around last week," she says, trying to stay serious. But we both lose it at the same time and are back to hysterical laughing.

After several minutes of tear-filled laughter, we finally calm down to a normal level. "Now I'm not even tired," I giggle, and the giggle is starting to feel like part of who I am now, like trucker Mary giggles. It's her thing.

"Same," Anna says. "Aw fuck it." I hear and then something lights up the sleeper. It's the TV. She moves it up; apparently it is on an adjustable arm. *This truck just keeps getting better.* "We might as well finish the movie."

"Okay," I say, moving closer to the edge of my bed to see better.

"Just try not to get too turned on up there and disturb the downstairs neighbor."

"Same," I say, giggling.

"And if we both end up turned on? God help us," she says plainly, and hits play as I start laughing again.

7

Haul'n Ass

With a lurch, I wake up and realize it was a literal lurch as I bounce slightly on my bed, instantly remembering I'm in a truck. *Anna's truck,* I think with a little smile as I look at the ceiling and the net-type thing over me and my bed."

As I lie there, I think about yesterday, talking, and last night. *Do I have a crush on her? You're too old for that. Stop fantasizing about people,* I tell myself with a little internal sigh. *But... does a fantasy really hurt anything?* I wonder as I start to think about Anna and me, and—"You wake yet?" Anna calls back and I jump, feeling caught, because I am, even if she doesn't know it.

"Yeah," I say, taking a deep breath as I feel my cheeks; and the rest of me, feels warm suddenly. "I just woke up."

"There are buckles on that thing like a seatbelt, careful not to get tangled and fall getting down," Anna says, and I can't help but smile at her explaining this. *You need to get a handle on yourself,* I think, wondering why my mind is getting so out of control, and why I am smiling at everything.

"Okay," I say, finding the buckles. I move the net of wide straps aside, making sure my foot or hand aren't caught up in them, and then look off the bunk trying to find the best way down. The truck seems to sway and bounce much more than it was when I was lying. *Or am I swaying?* I wonder watching everything move around me.

"You need help? I can pull over—"

"No," I say too quickly. "I'll be fine." I turn around and lie on my stomach, sliding off the edge until my feet touch the bottom bunk.

I sigh in relief as I start to step down. *That went better than I thought it would*, I think, proud of myself.

"Bridge!"

"Wha—" I just start to ask when the whole truck lurches and I make a stumbling fall the rest of the way, and right as I think I am okay, the truck lurches again. But this time it feels like the cab is going to come off the truck, and that I might be air-born.

"Fucking bastard!" I hear Anna cuss as I hit my head on the top bunk, fall and bounce off the mattress of the bottom bunk before hitting the floor of the sleeper. "You okay?" Anna asks, sounding concerned.

"Yeah... I'm fine," I say as I pull myself up, and try to find out if I lied to her or not. "What was that?" I ask, sitting down in the passenger seat after an unsteady walk to the front of the truck.

"A bridge. A shitty bridge, but a bridge."

"Oh..." I say, not realizing the bridges could be so rough. "Are we near a rest stop?" I ask, hating to say anything.

She pokes at the display mounted on the dash. "Looks like about ten minutes. If that's too long, it's pretty desolate out here, I can just pull over," she offers.

"No, I can wait," I say, and once again hope I'm not lying, but I really don't want to pee on the side of an old highway. I touch my head and feel a small bump forming.

"You hit your head?" she asks, glancing at me.

"It's fine." I notice how high the sun is. "What time is it?"

"Almost noon."

"What? How could I have slept so long? You should have woken me up."

"Why? It's not like there is anything going on, and you must have needed the sleep."

"Actually..." I say, thinking about it, "That was the best night's sleep I have had in a long time. How long have you been up?"

"Oh, I also overslept, but I stayed up too late," she says and I remember the movie ending and us falling asleep well before midnight. "I got up just after seven."

"That's early."

"Normally I'm rolling by six, so that was sleeping in, and why we will have lunch in the truck, sorry."

"No, I'm the reason you are running behind. If I can help with lunch or something, just tell me," I say, knowing there is nothing I can really do.

"Thanks, I might take you up on that and have you make me a sandwich later. For now, you might want to change, I doubt you want to go into a gas station wearing that," she says, glancing at me.

"Right," I say, getting up and walking back to the sleeper, pulling the curtain shut. "Where should I put my clothes that need washed?" I ask, laying them on the bed as I take them off.

"Just throw them in the hamper. But we won't be washing them until tomorrow, so don't toss anything in you'll want tonight, or you'll be digging them out later," she warns.

"Okay." I continue changing, which proves difficult when everything moves and sways. But, after far too long, I am done, and make my way back to the seat. I hear a notification ding, and I don't think much of it, then it dings again.

"That must be you, because it isn't me," Anna says.

"Oh, right," I say and take the phone out of the holder where it was still charging. I turn it on and see the notification.

Alesha: Hey.

Alesha: How's it going?

"It's Alesha," I say.

"Who else would it be?" she asks.

"I did set up my social media, it could be someone else," I say. "But, you're right, no one else would be messaging," I admit.

Me: Good morning.

It isn't a second before she replies.

Alesha: Morning? Did you just wake up or something?

Me: It isn't noon yet.

Alesha: Overslept, didn't you? hahaha

Me: I couldn't sleep. LOL

Alesha: I get that.

I feel a little bad about lying, but I don't want her to know I slept that long, it just isn't something you should do.

The truck starts slowing; I look up to see a gas station approaching. Anna pulls in alongside the pumps for semi trucks. "At least there isn't some dumbass in a pickup parked here fueling up because they think they're cool," she mocks, and I smile, unable to not enjoy her hate of drivers that annoy her.

"Back in a minute," I say, throwing the door open and climbing down. I don't run into the store, but I walk faster than normal, that's for sure. And thank God the stalls weren't all occupied, because I might have just had to sneak into the men's room. I will have to remember to limit how much I drink in the evening, and no more coke with dinner.

I walk out of the bathroom and see Anna getting coffee. "Get whatever you want," she says, walking past me towards the restrooms.

"Okay," I say, feeling like I need a coffee even though I slept forever, but I do decide to get decaf; not wanting to be the reason we have to stop again.

My phone gives a notification sound as I snap the lid on the coffee cup. I lean against the counter and pull my phone out of my pocket, surprised that I am still connected to Anna's hotspot signal.

Alesha: How did you sleep?

Alesha: Because it was a truck, not being weird. hahaha

Me: That does sound weird. LOL I slept well. I think I was more tired than I thought.

Alesha: omg after your day, not surprised.

Alesha: Tanks full, gotta get going.

Me: Okay, bye.

Alesha: Where are you at?

Me: A gas station fueling up.

Alesha: No silly. WHERE are you?

I smile at this, laughing to myself as I start to respond, and then realize.

Me: I don't know where we are. LOL

Alesha: Still in TX?

I think about it, and look out the windows at the front of the store, with nothing outside to tell me anything.

Me: I don't know what state we're in. LOL

Alesha: LMAO

"You ready?" I look up and see Anna walking towards me.

"I know this is dumb. But what state are we in?"

"We're halfway through Oklahoma." She doesn't make any jokes, she doesn't make fun of me for not knowing. She just acts like it is a perfectly normal question.

"Thanks," I say, smiling more than I mean to.

Me: I asked Anna, and she said we are halfway through Oklahoma.

"But," Anna says, picking up her coffee, and mine since I am texting, "we'll be in Lincoln, Nebraska by tonight."

"Really?" I ask, surprised.

"You bet, we'z haul'n ass today," she says, making me laugh a little.

Me: She says we'll be in Lincoln, Nebraska by tonight.

"You want a donut or something?" she asks me, stopping at the glass pastry case.

"Oh no, I stopped eating those years ago."

"Really? Never?"

"Well, when you get—"

"If you say old I am leaving you here," she warns, pointing the donut tongs at me.

"Well, I do need to watch my health."

"One won't kill you. I haven't had one in months, but today, it just sounds good." I cave and pick one.

I climb back into the truck with the coffees and donuts while Anna finishes up fueling the truck. I sit in my seat waiting as my phone's notification sound goes off.

Alesha: Holy fuck, that's a lot of miles.

Alesha: TTYL

Me: Bye.

While I have my phone out, I decide to check and see if Justin ever looked at my message, hoping he did so I don't have to call him about the car. But the message is grayed out, and I can't go to his profile. I go to my contacts and see that everyone that I might have considered a friend has done the same, including Aaron and Angela.

"Hey, you okay?" Anna asks. I look up to see she is in her seat and staring at me with concern.

"What?" I ask, feeling confused, and I don't know why I feel this way.

"You look upset. What's wrong?" *Am I that transparent? Or can she just see through me?* I wonder.

"I just found out that everyone I thought was a friend has blocked me, and so have Aaron and Angela... I know they took their dad's side, but I thought they would at least want to stay in contact with me a little," I say all at once, and am more upset than I thought I would be. "Sorry, I should have kno—" I stop as she is suddenly hugging me, and I am more confused than ever before. But I instantly feel better, knowing I have her, if no one else.

"They are just mad and being stupid. They'll come around," Anna says close to my ear, so close I can feel her breath.

"Thanks..." I say, and breathe in her hair, her scent. Then the hug breaks. Anna is back in her seat and I already miss her against me.

"And it's a fact that kids don't stop being stupid teenagers until their mid-twenties in some cases," she says matter-of-factly, and I can't help but laugh as I wipe my eyes. "How bout you tell me what happened while we drive?"

"Okay... Thanks," I say, moving around in my seat a bit to get more comfortable.

"Oh, before we start, why don't you adjust that seat to your liking?"

"Okay," I say, feeling like I am saying it a lot, but words seem hard to find at the moment. I move the different knobs on the seat, when my seat makes a hissing sound and raises really high.

"That's the air ride, and you can also lower it... if you want," Anna says with a smile that conceals a laugh. I adjust it again and it makes a louder hissing sound and I find myself nearly sitting on the floor. With that, we both start laughing. After a few minutes, I have it just right. "And unlock the slide."

"What's that?" I ask, sounding almost as confused as I feel. "Why do seats have to be so complicated?"

"Because it's good." She laughs. "Here, I'll get it for you," she says, leaning against me and reaching down to a lever on the seat. I try not to breathe, because I know my breath will betray me. There is a big part of me that finds these little moments of a childish crush fun. It makes me feel younger, and I guess there is no reason I can't enjoy a little bit of fun. Because that's all it is... Not that I would object to more. What are you saying? Don't ruin a good thing, "Enough is as good as a feast," I remember the quote, trying to keep myself grounded as the middle-aged woman I am.

"You're all set," she says, smiling at me.

"Thanks," I say, my voice sounding a little different.

"With it unlocked, the seat will slide with bumps. Much better for your back," she explains, as she starts pulling the truck out of the station. But I am just glad she didn't noticed the sound change in my voice. "So, what the hell started all this?"

"Right. It's a long story."

"You better hurry. We only have six or seven hours before we get there," she says, and I laugh. I laugh far too much and am far too happy for a stupid joke that isn't even that funny. *What am I going to do?*

I take a moment to kinda gather myself. "So, I wasn't a very good wife—"

"Stop right there."

"What?"

"You aren't putting yourself down in this story. Maybe things weren't mutual between you and your husband, but no taking the blame."

"Okay," I say with a little pang in my chest because Anna doesn't even know the story yet, but is already on my side. "We got married young, and it seemed that it just wasn't a good idea,"

"A high school sweetheart that didn't hold up to time?" she asks.

"Um... Kinda," I say, not wanting to get into that. "Anyway, I thought he might be cheating on me, and I thought it might have been going on a while. But I gave Justin the benefit of the doubt, and I tried harder to make things better for him... To do whatever he liked—"

"Really?"

"It was how I was raised. If something was wrong in a marriage, it is the wife falling short in the relationship—"

"If he is a cheating asshole, the wife must not be a good enough screw. Makes perfect sense," she says, completely serious, and I can't help but laugh a little... which makes her smile a smile that I can't look away from, that I don't want to look away from.

I blink when I realize I am just staring at her not saying anything. "Yeah... That is actually pretty close to it. But when I found a make-up compact in his car between the seat and center console, I couldn't ignore it anymore—"

"Good for you. What did you do?"

"I'm going to tell you if you let me, that is."

"Sorry," she says.

"So I went to my best friend, Deb. I have known her over ten years. She and her husband had been good friends of mine and Justin until three years ago when she and her husband got a divorce, and he moved. Her divorce seemed more mutual. She said they grew apart, but I'm not sure about that. It just seemed like she was—"

"Are you getting off topic on purpose?" Anna asks, glancing at me.

"Not on purpose, sorry."

"Stop apologizing."

"Right, sor—" I stop myself abruptly.

"You have a problem." She smiles, shaking her head.

"So, I went to Deb and told her I had suspected something for a long time, and showed her the compact I found. She said to wait a few days, and she would help me get more evidence, so he couldn't just deny it."

"Sounds like a good plan."

"But, a few days later I get a registered letter in the mail, I open it up... and it was a petition for divorce—"

"Seriously? Before you could even confront him? What the fuck?"

"You sound as confused about it as I was. I thought it was the weirdest timing in the world, and I was in shock over it all. I never thought that would happen. So I tried to call Deb, but got her voicemail; but she worked, so I wasn't surprised. I thought about calling one of my siblings, but I couldn't get myself to, and I wasn't going to drag my kids into it."

"God, you have to start thinking about yourself."

"What?"

"You are always so concerned about everyone else. This could have been considered the worst day of your life, and you were worried about bothering other people with it. For God's sake, think about yourself above others for two seconds." Anna almost sounds angry about this.

"I hadn't thought of it like that, sorry.... Oh, I don't mean to, sorry—I mean sor—" And Anna starts laughing.

"You are so messed up," she says, glancing at me. "Back to the story."

"So, I decided to just wait, but it wasn't even noon yet. So, I called him."

"That had to be hard."

"Better than just waiting."

"Good point."

"He said things just weren't working for us anymore, and that I knew this too. He wasn't wrong. I knew something was wrong, and I knew I wasn't happy. So, I asked him if he was having an affair, and he said yes. So I hung up without hearing anymore and decided I would pack some things and stay with Deb for a day or two until I found a room somewhere. But I just couldn't stay in that house with him."

"Shit, who could?"

"As I'm packing my bags, I start carrying them out to my car, so I will be gone before he is home from work. But he came home early."

"Of course he did," she says, and I love how she doesn't have to wait to the end to know whose side she's on. *I hope it stays that way,* I think.

"Justin starts saying that he will leave, that I'm not going anywhere, and starts taking my bags back in the house while I try to carry them back out, and—" I notice Anna is shaking slightly, like a slight vibration. "Are you laughing?" I ask, instantly smiling with a little giggle.

"I'm sorry, but I just have this scene playing in my head of you two carrying bags back and forth, and it looks really funny," she says, now laughing.

"Well, you will love this next part," I say, laughing as I now think about how this must have looked. "Justin and I get into a screaming fight. It was the first time I have ever screamed at anyone. So we are in the house and I am putting my makeup, skincare, and such into a bag. When he asks where I would even go, and I say I will stay with Deb a few days. He gets quiet and asks if I have talked to her, and I told him no, but she will be fine with it. That's when he tells me that he and Deb have been sleeping together for four years—"

"Holy fuck! Your best friend was screwing your husband?" Anna says, looking at me longer than she really should since she is driving.

"That's when I realize that she told Justin I knew and stalled me until he could file for divorce—"

"That fucking bitch!" Now Anna is angry as she hits the steering wheel with her fist. "Who the hell does something like that? That is just horrible. I can't believe someone could be so awful. Next time I'm in Texas, I'm running her down." I'm not sure she is joking about this, and it makes me smile, and I like her more than maybe I should for it.

"Thanks... But this is where I messed up. I started screaming at him again, and apparently one of the neighbors called the police when we were fighting outside; we had also left the front door wide open with our bag-carrying thing. I got so mad, and when he told me to 'shut up and listen' I threw what I had in my hand at him... It was a one-quart glass jar of anti-aging cream, and I hit him square in the face right as the police walked into the house—"

"Oh shit. Did you hurt him? I feel like it probably wasn't enough."

"It broke his nose, two front teeth, and knocked him out... He also got a mild concussion when he hit his head on the bathroom's tile floor."

"Holy fuck, maybe I'm wrong, that's pretty good," she says, laughing. "You should have played ball, you have an arm of gold!" Anna punches me light on the arm, laughing even more.

"But, I got arrested for assault."

"Damn, didn't think of that. And the two cops saw it... that's bad."

"Yeah... I was lucky and my son bailed me out. But made it clear he wanted nothing to do with me—"

"That's why everyone took his side," Anna says, now getting it.

"Including the judge. But, since I was listed as abusive after that, the court waived the mandatory wait time for a divorce petition, so it was all over very quickly. It still isn't final, but will be soon."

"So, you got nothing because of all of that?"

"Pretty much just my clothes, and the money I had set aside in cash they didn't know about. But that's now gone too."

"Your lawyer couldn't do anything?" she asks.

"I didn't try hard, because Justin said if I didn't fight anything, then they would make sure I didn't go to jail—"

"That is horrible of him! You should have hit him a few more times with that jar," she says, more upset than me, which she notices. "Why aren't you madder?"

"Well, I didn't want to go to jail. I was also glad I'm just out of the marriage. I never thought I would be. Actually... what Deb did was worse. That was... is hard for me."

"She's out of your life now, too. It's all good now. We're going to have a great time," she says, smiling at me, more sweetly this time.

"Thanks. I don't know what I would do without you," I say, and instantly feel awkward about it.

"You would just be walking a lot more," she says with a wink that makes me laugh. "That was some good anti-aging cream," she says, glancing away from the road to me.

"Oh..." I say, not sure how I will react if she compliments my looks.

"Yeah, it worked great. You used it, and now you are single, traveling the country, and having movie-night sleepovers. It's like it turned you into a goddamn teenager again!" Anna says. We both start laughing so hard that I start to wonder if we should pull over.

8

A Full Day

The scenery doesn't seem to change much as we pass from Oklahoma to Kansas, but Anna says it will get better the farther north we go. I manage to remember the password to my ebook account which is still tied to Justin's bank account, and he doesn't have the password to the ebook account. I think about buying a few hundred books, but then decided it would be smarter to read the books I already own.

So, I read as Anna listens to podcasts of all kinds; she seems to have an endless supply of them and in every subject imaginable. I put my phone down and stare out the window.

"Is the podcast bothering you?" Anna asks.

"Hmm..." I say, looking over at her. "Oh, no it isn't at all. My eyes just get tired of reading on a phone screen."

"I get that. Just didn't want to bother you."

"I've read through a thousand TV shows and sports events playing in the background, all while Justin would be telling me to watch this or that... He never got that I really couldn't have cared less. Sorry, I'm not starting on that," I say, feeling like I have unloaded enough on her.

"Care if I put on music?"

"It's your truck. Why are you even asking?" I say with a smile.

"Okay, but it probably isn't what you're used to," she says like a warning. Then she starts playing the album, and it is very different from what I had expected. But something about it is refreshing from what my kids had listened to, and Justin's country music that I never liked.

"She has a beautiful voice."

"She does," Anna says, seeming to really appreciate that I notice this.

After several more songs I find myself truly enjoying the music. Something about her voice, and the emotion she sings with is moving. I've listened to songs in church, and even some Christian music, but none of it spoke like this. "You okay?" Anna asks, and my head snaps over to her, feeling like I forgot where I was. "You okay?" she asks again, and then she glances away from the road, reaching over wiping a tear off my cheek that I didn't know was there.

"Yes, sorry—"

"Don't."

"Right," I say smiling. "I didn't expect that song to..." I pause, not sure what exactly it did.

"Yeah, that song's called 'Lucky' and it is good for making people realize stuff... All her music is," Anna says this like something about the song pulls at her as well. We are both quiet for a while, Anna most likely reflecting on the song, the same as me. But, I am also thinking about the feeling of her finger on my cheek. How can I not think about it?

The album ends and we are but silent a bit longer than is comfortable. "So, can I ask a personal question?" Anna asks.

"Of course."

"Did you want to get married?" she asks. "I mean, you just didn't act like you did when talking about everything earlier."

"I thought I did back then, but now? Now I realize that I thought I did because everyone else wanted me to."

"This didn't come up while you were dating?" she asks.

"We didn't date."

"Are you serious?"

"My parents didn't think it was proper. So, we had the church youth group. There were a lot of members, and we did something every week."

"So, it was like a big group date?" Anna asks with a raised eyebrow.

"No, it... Actually, I hadn't thought of it like that. But it kind of was like a group date with about seventy people, plus some adults chaperoning."

"Wow, that is one big group date. Man, if you could have ditched the chaperons, that could have been one hell of a good time," she says with a smirk.

"Oh no, that is not something I would have done," I say, feeling embarrassed at even the thought.

"Don't know till you try." She smiles at me. "But we're getting off track."

"Yes. So, Justin went to my church and school, and I never really paid any attention to him. But he was popular and good in sports, and everyone said how good-looking he was. So, when—"

"Wait. Did you think he was good-looking?"

"Well, I guess I never noticed it. But I was young—"

"You married the guy, and you weren't even attracted to him? So, you obviously didn't love him either." She says this last part with so much pity, I don't think she means to... but it's there.

"No, I didn't. I told my mom and friends. But, they said I was lucky he liked me, that every other girl in school would jump at the chance to marry him, and that love comes later—"

"Fuck them!" Anna says, seeming angrier about this than she did about my breakup. "That is manipulative fucking bullshit... God-damn, that pisses me off!"

"I wasn't the only one this happened to, and he was kind. That is more than some end up with. So, that was a blessing, and I never complained because of it, 'enough is as good as a feast'," I say, re-membering the quote I have always liked. I look over to Anna, who is taking short looks at me; the closest she can get to a staring glare while driving.

"You have to stop that. You need to give a fuck for your own life. Enough is not as good as a feast. The person who came up with that shit used it as a way to starve the people below them while they feasted. Every time you defend these fucking assholes by finding the little good things in them, you are condoning their behavior while belittling yourself," she says glancing at me. "You do it all the time! You were thankful that beer-drinking redneck didn't kidnap you. You were grateful to an asshole that held a gun to your head and stole everything you owned, because he didn't kill or rape you. You're grateful your cheating scumbag of a husband who took your life from you and turned your own kids against you didn't beat you." I feel myself getting angry as she lists these things off. It is like she is stripping away everything I have been taught and told my whole life... what I have been my whole life. "They used you and left you homeless with no regard for you... Yet you are thankful—"

"I'm not thankful, I hate them! But it's all I have left. It is the only tiny bit of hope I have. If I can't be thankful for what little things I can find, then I have nothing left... Nothing!" I say, voice cracking, eyes stinging. "I don't know what else to do. I don't know how I am supposed to keep going... I've never been on my own, I have no idea what to do, and I'm scared... So, I can't let myself think of the bad things."

"Yes, you can. You can't hide from them anymore," she says, leaning over from her seat, reaching far enough to take my hand. She pulls it towards her enough to continue holding it while she drives. "I'm sorry that I was so blunt. But, you deserve better, and now that you can make your own choices, I don't want you following that same shit they told you. You can't keep focusing on the good parts of the bad things in your life, because those are still the bad things."

"I never thought of it like that."

"So, when something's shit, call it what it is, shit," she says, and something about this makes me smile a little as she squeezes my hand lightly. I don't say anything, but she keeps holding my hand, and I feel safe. She is like the part of me I have been missing my whole life, the part that was kept from me. I don't know if that is a friend, or more. But I know it is what I have never quite had before.

It is a little while before Anna taps play on another album. It is clearly the same artist, but her sound is much different. I think about reading more of my book, but I just can't seem to get myself to. So

I just watch out the window, the scenery slowly changing. I find myself looking at the other vehicles on the highway, because I can look right into their cars from my high seat in the semi.

I feel like I have been set apart from all the other people while riding in the truck. I feel important, and even a little proud. I can understand why some people love driving truck and never want to give it up, and I wonder if Anna's this type of person, if this is what she loves, or even likes doing. "Do you like driving truck?"

She turns the music down. "Naw, I've never liked it."

"Really?" I say, surprised. "You seem like you do though."

"I just try to make the best of it," she says plainly.

"Why do you do it then?"

"It pays good. I did really bad in school since I only focused on sports, and I didn't want to spend a fortune on community college to end up with a job I hated; that would most likely pay shit. So, I got my CDL and started driving."

"How long are you going to drive?"

"I guess I had all these questions coming," she says with a small laugh. "Well, I wanted to quit a year or so ago. But I keep putting it off for some reason. It's fine though. I'm glad I put it off." She says a bit wistfully, which makes me smile.

"Why?" I ask, really wanting to know what gives her that sound in her voice.

"Oh, well... Since I stay in my sleeper, and don't have rent or even a car, I really save a lot of money up quick," she says. But she doesn't have that sound to her voice, and I'm not sure why.

"That's nice," I say, not sure what else to say. "Think you will keep driving then?"

"I guess... Don't really have a reason to quit. I mean I have a job if I do, but I might just try to retire early into that job... I don't know yet."

"That's nice you have a job waiting," I say.

"Evy and I have been buying houses. It's where all my money I make here goes," she says.

"Oh, are you going to sell them?"

"Someday. But for now, we rent them out by the day—"

"Like Airbnb?"

"Yeah, we rent out through them and other similar companies. We tried doing regular rentals, but people kept trashing them, and everyone was so impossible to work with. So we gave up on that one."

"Sounds like a good business," I say. We continue on, the truck swaying lightly with a lolling motion. "I wonder what I'm going to do?" I say absentmindedly, having not thought about it much until I hear Anna's life plans.

"What do you mean?"

"I can't just keep riding around with you. I have to find a job and a place to stay."

"Without an address or money, you are really in trouble. I can loan you enough to get set up though," Anna says without hesitation, and I am astounded that she would even offer this.

"I could never ask you to do something like that. It is too much."

"Well, I would though... I like you." I feel my heart squeeze at these words, like she just confessed her undying love for me. "If you want..." she says, but hesitates, "you could also get your CDL."

"And drive truck?" I say, surprised that she would even think I could do this.

"I know you are more than capable," she says, like she was reading my thoughts. "There are lots of jobs, not just long haul. And I can help you study, teaching you as I drive, and you can use my truck for the driving test." I think about this, completely unsure.

"I don't know... This is something I have never considered before," I say.

"Once you pass. If you want..." she says with more hesitation, "we could be driving partners." This snaps me out of thinking. It is something I can't believe Anna even said, and I wonder if I misheard her.

"What?" I say, thinking I must be misunderstanding something.

"I can only drive for so many hours, not only for safety, but legally. And if you drove with me, we could trade off," she explains, and I feel my heart catch, because it is what I thought. But, is it something

I should do? I feel like I would be doing it for the wrong reasons. "Well, it's just an idea. Think about it," she says after a moment of my hesitation.

"I will think about it," I say. And as we drive Anna puts on another podcast, while I think about the idea, fantasize about the idea, and feel like I am betraying her kindness and trust as my mind thinks of what living in the truck would be like in my dream world.

It seems that I can't think about anything else, even as we pass through Kansas; areas that are far more beautiful than I thought Kansas was. But I don't seem to enjoy it, because I can't stop thinking about Anna, and everything suddenly seems a little awkward between us. We hardly say anything until we are pulling up into the parking lot of the Lincoln, Nebraska truck stop, and Anna shuts the truck off.

"Sorry if I said something wrong," Anna suddenly says, still sitting in her seat, seatbelt on, staring out the windshield. "I didn't mean anything. I was just trying to think of something for you... Can't have you homeless," she says with a weak laugh.

"No, you didn't say anything wrong. I really can't believe how kind you are... I also just feel overwhelmed by everything," I say. It isn't a lie. I just might not be overwhelmed for only the reasons Anna thinks.

"That's why I didn't mean to pressure you. And you can stay with me as long as you want, and I mean that."

"Well, maybe I will just ride around in your truck for life," I say as a joke.

"Okay... I mean, other drivers have a dog or two always riding with them. So, maybe I should just keep you around for company," she says with a smile that makes me laugh. And I think how I might just do that, just stay with her, keeping her company. *If I got an online job, I could actually do this. It wouldn't have to pay much*, I think, realizing this could actually be a thing.

"Well, tomorrow is a new load, so we better get some rest," she says.

"Oh, where are we going?" I ask, and saying *"we"* feels odd, but in a nice, warm way.

"We're going to LA, baby." Anna smiles.

"Really?" I say, feeling excited.

"You bet. Why don't we go find something to eat, and then come back here and watch another movie."

"A sleazy movie?" I ask, joking.

"For you... you bet." She grins and winks, making me laugh. I actually kind of hope it is another movie with a smutty scene or two.

9

Getting Close

We walk the two blocks back to the truck, after having eaten too much at a Thai place that was better than I thought it might be. We don't say much as we walk, but just enjoy the evening air; which is much cooler than what it had been in Texas last night. Part of me has trouble believing how far we have traveled in just one day.

I think about my past and realize that in a few days, I will have traveled farther than I have in my entire life. Before, I had only vacationed outside of Texas a few times. I can't help but smile to myself, because I am changing my life. And I am doing it in my forties. I had thought it was too late for me to be able to change anything.

"You want to take a shower before we turn in?" Anna asks.

"Yeah, that sounds good," I say, and start getting my clothes together. I grab my night clothes so I won't have to change again; Anna does the same.

We walk through the truck stop. This one isn't as big as the last one, and it seems almost deserted. The few people we do see look worn out and like they are half asleep, and even though I just sat there all day, I feel the same way.

"Showers here are like fifteen or seventeen bucks, so we'll just share one," Anna says as we turn down a hallway.

"What?" I say, not sure how to respond to this. *Now she wants to share a shower?* I think, confused about what's going on.

"Yeah, they are really expensive. But, it's for forty-five minutes. So, I'll just wait outside until you're done, then I'll take a quick one," she explains, and I feel a wave of relief, because I am just not ready for that. I'm not sure how this will work, since the last shower was just a locker room, and the showers didn't cost near so much.

I follow her into a hallway with four doors on each side, and I see that the showers are in their own rooms. This explains why they cost more and give you more time. "Okay, I'll be quick," I say, turning the door handle.

"Take your time. I'll knock if you are running out of time, but I don't take long to shower at all," she says, leaning against the wall and taking her phone out.

I walk into the little room, closing and locking the door behind me. The room is about the size of an average bathroom, including a sink, mirror, toilet, and small changing bench. I hurry and undress, neatly folding my clothes and placing them on the bench. I think about Alesha chattering away the last time I was doing this. Being in that shower room with her seems like it was a lifetime ago, not yesterday. I slip on the flip-flops she gave me and decide I'll text her when I'm out.

As I start washing myself, my mind starts to think about sharing a shower with Anna, fixating on what that might be like. "Lord help me," I say to the water, and continue showering, forcing my mind to other things.

"That was quick," Anna says as I step out of the room.

"Yeah, I didn't feel like a long shower."

"You do look tired. Here"—she holds her keys out to me—"go back to the truck. No reason for you to stand around in a hallway all wet," she says.

"Okay, thanks," I say, taking the keys.

"Oh, take my phone too," Anna says, holding it out.

"Why?"

"So there is internet in the truck. I don't need it, and I won't be far behind you."

"Thanks," I say, taking her phone. And I can feel this little nagging part of me that would rather wait outside the door for her, but I know that is just being foolish, and I start my way back to the truck.

There is this eerie feeling about walking back. It is the surreal feeling of not belonging. Not that I am just out of place in the truck stop, but that I am out of place in the world, that I am just walking through it without experiencing it in almost an out-of-body way. I don't like it, it just feels wrong, and as I step outside in the parking lot, it isn't any better.

I start wondering what I am really doing with no plans, and fawning over a woman I hardly even know. I stop, noticing a *'Help Wanted'* sign in the truck stop window. *Maybe I should just try to get a job here,* I think, wondering if this is a better option. I keep thinking about the sign as I open the door of the truck and climb in, but decide I should text Alesha, maybe ask her thoughts.

Once the door of the truck is closed behind me, I feel better, almost like a homey feeling; even though I have only been here for a day and a half. But the time doesn't seem to matter, I just feel like I exist inside the truck, that I just belong here. *Or is it that I want to belong near her, and not the truck?* I shake that thought from my head, knowing it isn't going to help.

Sitting down on the bed I take out my phone.

Me: Just used the flip-flops. Thanks again.

Me: And the phone, thanks.

The screen shows that she has seen it, but there is no indication she is texting back. So, I lie back on the bed and realize it is still unmade from this morning. I stand up and start pulling the covers off when my phone rings. It's Alesha. "Hello?" I say, answering it within the second ring.

"Hey," Alesha says cheerfully. "I thought I would just call. Seemed easier than texting a million times."

"I thought young people didn't talk on phones and only text?"

"Young people? God, don't say that, it makes you sound old," she says.

"I am old."

"Yeah, I guess so," she says, and then starts laughing a few seconds later. "You thought I would say 'no, you're still a young woman,' or something, didn't you?"

"I kinda did. That's what Anna would say."

"What's her opinion about this?" she asks, clearly wanting me to ask her.

"Oh, she's still in the shower. I'm back in the truck waiting," I explain.

"Waiting, waiting for what?" she says with mock insinuation.

"No, I mean to just watch something on TV," I say, feeling defensive.

"Cool, that sounds fun," Alesha says, with a bit of a change in her tone, no longer joking. "So, how do you like it? Being a trucker?"

"It's nice, I just read a lot today, and we listened to music, talked some," I say, not sure what else to say.

"That sounds like the average day of riding. It sounds nice though. You two get along well?"

"Yeah..." I say, and realize how I said it, like a dreamy-eyed teenager. "So far it seems like we get along," I say, trying to recover from that.

"Cool..." Alesha says this like she is thinking at the same time.

"How was your day?"

"Nothing interesting, really. I just finished a video session, and am getting things in my van put back into place. That's also why I'm not texting. I can talk to you while working."

"I didn't know you did videos."

"Oh, yeah... It's just a little side income. They're nothing you'd find interesting," she says, and the way she says it gives me the feeling she doesn't want me to ask about it, so I don't.

I hear the door open. "Just me," Anna calls from the front.

"Sounds like Anna's back, and I need to get something to eat. So talk later?" Alesha asks.

"Yeah, and you can call whenever, I'm not really doing any-thing," I say, as Anna notices I'm on the phone.

"Enjoy your movie night girl," she says, "And don't do any-thing I wouldn't do," she jokes.

"What would it be that you wouldn't do?"

"Actually... not much. So, that might have been bad advice..." she says, exaggerating her thinking this over. "Yeah... don't follow that advice at all." I laugh at her seriousness about this.

"Okay, I won't. Good night," I say, smiling.

"Night!" she says, making kissy sounds at the phone and then hangs up.

"Why are we not doing what Alesha would do?" Anna asks.

"Oh, well, apparently there is nothing she won't do."

"Hmm, noted," Anna says, and looks at the bed, which is completely stripped down. "What happened to that?"

"I was remaking it when Alesha called," I say, and start making it again.

"Really?"

"It is just making the bed. You should do it every morning," I say, straightening the fitted sheet and pulling it tight.

"I normally just pull it straight before I go to bed. It's just going to get messed up again," she says in the same way my kids did when I would get on them about not making their beds.

"You sound exactly like my kids did."

"Don't compare me to them," she says, sounding offended. Which in turn makes me look at her offended, because even after everything, I am still their mother. "Sorry, I just don't get how anyone could turn on you," she says sincerely, then helps me with the top sheet, and I smile at this. "Nope, not the blanket," she says as I reach for it. "I want to curl up in it while watching the movie. So no point in bothering with it." I do as she says, because she has a point. "Now find a movie, I picked last night."

It takes me a little while, but I settle on another romance. "Have you seen this?" I ask before starting it.

"Nope, looks good though. Hey, maybe there will be another steamy scene or two," Anna says, elbowing me lightly with a smile. We watch the movie, sitting side by side. The movie is good, but I'm not sure it is as good as last night's. It seems slower, or maybe I am just more tired.

"Here," Anna says, handing me one corner of the blanket as she pulls it over herself, and I do the same.

We watch sitting together under the blanket, and as we both seem to get sleepier, we move closer together. But I don't overthink it. I don't have the feeling of a crush overtaking me like before. I just feel happy that I am here next to her, that I am here, in this truck, watching a movie that I wanted to watch; even if it is boring. Because they are things I have never done in the past. *I'm going to do it, I'm going to get my CDL,* I think, as a final decision as my eyes start to feel too heavy.

I wake up to the feeling of hair in my mouth; not a lot, but it doesn't take much. It takes a second for me to realize it is Anna's hair that is choking me, and that she is on her side, still asleep next to me. I'm not sure what to do, so I just lie still, staring at the bottom of the top bunk that I should be in. "Good morning," I hear Anna say next to me with a yawn.

"Good morning," I say, feeling guilty, like I did this on purpose. "I guess we fell asleep."

"Yeah, guess so... What time is it?" she says reaching for her phone. "Just before eight, that's not too bad."

"No," I agree, as though I know her time schedule.

"Well"—she sits up onto the edge of the bed—"I better get her started warming up," she says, standing and walking up to the front. I pull the blanket a little tighter and wish she hadn't gotten up, and pray she'll come back; but I know she won't.

The truck gives a vibrating shake as the engine cranks, then smooths out as it starts. "When do we leave?" I ask as Anna steps back into the sleeper.

"It will be a while until we leave because we are scheduled to drop this load off at nine-thirty, and then pick up our next load at eleven-thirty. So, it will be a while until we are actually on the road," she says as she starts pulling off the clothes she slept in, tossing them on the floor. I try to not look at her, remembering that I can't make this awkward. I do wish I had my phone to use as a distraction, but I don't, so I just stay curled up in the blanket.

"So," I say, feeling like not talking is making this more awkward, "I decided last night that I will try studying for a CDL... If you still want to help me with it."

"Oh my God, yes!" Anna says with way more excitement than I had expected. "This will be great. It really isn't that hard at all and I will get you setup to start studying," she continues as she starts getting the clothes she wants out, now naked, and I can't help but wonder why she wouldn't find her clothes first. "Oh," she says, turning to me, "you can use my laptop."

"You have one?" I say, having not seen one around.

"Yeah, I just don't use it much. But I will just make you your own name on it—"

"You don't have to go through that much trouble. I can just use my phone."

"No way, that would suck," she says, pulling on her jeans and sitting down on the edge of the bed. "It will make it much easier with a laptop."

"Well, okay," I say.

"I know you will do great!" Anna says as she puts on her bra and grabs her t-shirt, pulling it on. "Well, you better get dressed. We ship off soon," she says walking up to the front and slides the curtain shut without me having to ask, which I appreciate.

Climbing out from under the covers isn't what I want to do, but I don't have much choice, and they aren't quite as nice without Anna here to talk with. I look through the shopping bag that is still serving as my dresser and closet, and find what I need; which only takes a second, then change. But I don't feel as awkward as I did changing last time. Then I make the bed and put Anna's, and my dirty laundry in the hamper, folding the pajamas and putting them where they belong.

I slide the curtain open. "So, how long will it take to get to LA?" I ask as I look in the mirror, brushing my hair out, and missing my makeup.

"Um... with DOT laws, it will be two days, not including today's driving," she says, looking at the tablet mounted on the dash of the truck with a map up on it.

"That is a long way."

"Wait," she says looking into the sleeper, "did you clean in the five minutes you were in there?"

"I just picked up the laundry and made the bed," I say.

"You don't have to pick up my dirty clothes."

"They were annoying me just laying there," I say, and she starts laughing.

"Fuck, you have been picking up after slobs for too long, so you can stop. I promise I'll start cleaning up after myself," she says with a smile.

"I will need help making the top bunk. I just can't reach it."

"Hey, that reminds me. How's your head?" she asks, standing and moving close to me.

"Oh, it's just a little bump, it will—" She lays her hand on my head, and I feel a little warm again.

"Ouch, that is a pretty good bump." Anna sounds truly concerned.

"It's fine, really."

"Well, tell me if you need aspirin or ibuprofen, I have some."

"Okay, thanks."

She suddenly leans forward and kisses my head. "There, now it will feel better." She laughs. "Let's go get some coffee, something for breakfast, and hit up the restrooms before we leave," she says, turning to open the curtain over the driver's door and the door itself. I just stand there, trying to bring my heart rate down to something more normal. Not that if I had a heart attack, I wouldn't die happy.

10

A Trucker's Breakfast

The coffee selection is surprisingly good in the truck stop; since it is a smaller one. I had expected two options, black, and yesterday's black. But instead they have a dozen different kinds, so I get a caramel with cream; decaf, of course, since I don't know when the next rest stop will be.

I hold my coffee while waiting for Anna, and stare at the selection of breakfast sandwiches and burritos, all of them making my stomach turn at just the smell. "Get one if you want," Anna says from behind me.

"Oh, heavens no. Justin liked them, but the idea of food sitting in the open air being heated by light bulbs kind of makes me feel sick. I mean what kind of per—" I turn around to see Anna staring at me with a breakfast burrito in one hand and a large cup of coffee in the other.

"You were saying?"

"Well, I just mean, I don't like them. They just aren't breakfast to me."

"They have egg and ham... Well, this one does."

"But it's still a burrito."

"Let me guess, breakfast to you is eggs, bacon, and pancakes," she says.

"Yeah, that's a good breakfast."

"Then you want that one"—she points at a burrito under the light—"it's eggs and bacon, wrapped in a pancake." I actually have to press my lips together, thinking I might gag.

"I'm fine, thank you," I say, my voice betraying my feelings towards the burrito.

"I get it. You're too fancy and upper-crust for my working-class breakfast," she says, acting upset.

"Yes. Everything about it, just awful... and sad. I'm just so used to my truffle omelet, with gold leaf garnish served by my personal chef. It's just hard for me to slum it with your waffle burrito," I say, waving a hand at the breakfast selection under the glowing lights as Anna laughs.

"Pancake, not waffle." She laughs.

"Actually," a man with a store employee shirt says, "that one is waffle." He points at some type of burrito wrapped in bright paper.

"Ooh, really?" Anna says, interested. "What's in it?"

"It's strawberry, blueberry, a syrup frosting wrapped in a Belgium waffle. So, it's really not that unhealthy," he says, seeming to think the mention of the two fruits outweighs everything else in it.

"I'm getting it for you," Anna says, looking at me.

"I'll get you gals a holder," the man says, going over and picking up a flat piece of cardboard that unfolds into a basket-like holder that even has a spot for our coffee.

"You really don't have to get me that," I say, but kind of want to try it.

"If you're going to be a trucker, then you're in my world now." Anna smiles at me, and I know that I am eating that burrito, rather I like it or not. But a big part of me is fine with that, if it is what makes her happy.

The same man rings us up saying. "You'll like that fruit burrito. It is even vegan, other than the egg in the waffle. If you're into that vegan thing." I can't figure out if this is some attempt at flirting, or if he is just this proud of that fruit burrito. Either way, it makes the minute it takes to pay awkward. But I always feel weird when the person running the checkout comments on what I am buying.

"So," I say as we walk across the parking lot, "why was that guy commenting so much about the burrito?"

"No idea, but it made my skin crawl," Anna says.

"Not your type?" I joke.

"Yeah, no. He couldn't have been farther from my type, in every way." Anna says this with so much emphasis that I am curious about what her type must be. Maybe she is into the buff gym addicts, or the suave, rich type of guy, I think about this, and wonder if I should just ask her. But, if I do that, then I can't think of what other types she might be into, and I kind of like leaving it unknown.

I climb into the truck first, and Anna hands me the carrying thing with our breakfast in it. Sitting down in my seat I take a drink of my coffee, and nearly choke. "Did it go the wrong way?" Anna asks as I cough.

"No, I think that was yours," I say, clearing my throat.

"Really?"

"I didn't mean to, and what is that?"

"One-quarter black coffee, three-quarters hot chocolate, and three espresso shots." I just stare at her. "What? It's good. Please don't tell me you don't like it."

"No, I was just expecting my coffee, and not—"

"Hot choffee," she says.

"What?"

"It is when you mix hot chocolate and coffee. Choffee," she explains. "Try it again."

"No, it's fine."

"Come on, give it a fair chance."

I take another small drink. "I must admit, that is actually good."

"See," she says, taking a bite of her breakfast burrito. "You gotta give things a chance. Try this." she holds out the burrito, and I just stare at it wondering when we started sharing food. I never even did this with former best friend Deb, or Justin. "Come on!" she says, thrusting it towards me. I relent and take the burrito, biting a small piece of the corner. "More than that," she says seriously. So, I take a big bite of it. "There you go." She smiles big as I chew, and actually swallow. "What you think?"

"It tastes better than I thought, and it tastes better than it smells." Not that the smell is a hard thing to beat. "But, it is too greasy for me," I say honestly.

"That's the best part."

"The grease is the best part?" I say, not sure how this could be.

"Yeah, anything that isn't greasy isn't worth eating," she says, grinning. "How's yours?"

I pick up the fruit burrito and take a bite, and there is a surprising amount of the syrupy frosting inside. "Not bad... It's actually pretty good. Really sweet though, I don't think I would call it healthy," I say, and Anna starts laughing.

"Oh God, how could that guy think anything in that place is healthy?" She laughs.

"Here," I say, holding it out, and she just leans over and takes a bite as I hold it.

"Wow, that is really sweet. But, pretty good."

"This is the last time for me though," I say, taking another bite.

"Why?" she asks.

"I'm too old to eat foods like this. I'll be dead within a year if I eat this all the time."

"Yeah," she says taking a bite, "I try not to eat this way, but it is so damn hard not to. Bite?" She holds hers out again, and I take a bite of it, even though I'm not a big fan. Something about it feels nice, sharing with someone like this, having someone in my life who wants to share with me, and that I want to share with. So I hold mine out to her, and I have what is the best breakfast of my life... Despite the truck stop food. It turns out the food isn't what makes a great breakfast.

It doesn't take long for them to unload our trailer at the first stop, and I just wait in the truck while Anna signs some papers and talks with someone from the company. And then we are off to the next stop. I don't talk, not wanting to distract Anna while she navigates the city's traffic. But it doesn't seem like long before she is backing up to a loading dock; not unlike the last one.

I lie on the bed, enjoying what time I have out of the seat while they load the trailer, seeming to take longer. I was hoping Anna would be here relaxing with me, but she is overseeing the loading of her trailer; which makes sense. So I wait by myself. After checking my social media to see if I am still block by my family; which I am, I decide to message Alesha.

Me: Good morning. Doing anything?

I stare at the screen for a second, and then lay the phone down. I am about to turn on the TV when my phone notification goes off.

Alesha: Hey girl. What's up?

Something about having her as a friend, even though we barely know each other, is fun, and I am really grateful for her. I start typing out a simple text to ask what she is doing, but then I stop and delete it.

Me: So, something happened.

Alesha: OMG, tell me. :D

Me: Anna and I slept together last night.

Something about sending this feels weird, it is something I never would have done before. But something about talking with someone I don't know is freeing; there is no judgment. I don't have to be any of the things that are expected of me. I can just be who I have always wanted to be. And I realize this is why I love being around Anna. *My God, Anna was right, that anti-aging cream really worked,* I say to myself.

Alesha: HOLY FUCK!

Alesha: Are you shitting me?

Alesha: You're joking, right?

Alesha: Wait, are you a lesbian or bi?

Alesha: HOLY FUCK!!!

I laugh as these texts pop up in rapid succession.

Me: Slow down, I'm slow.

Alesha: (A GIF of George Takei saying "Oh my" and winking)

This makes me start laughing really hard, slowing my response even more.

Me: LOL

I am glad that she holds off from texting more, giving me time to respond.

Me: I'm not joking, we really did.

Alesha: WOW!

Alesha: Was it good? How did it happen?

Alesha: Tell me everything!

I think about what to say that will lead her on longer.

Me: I thought it was good, but I really don't know.

I grin to myself and type the next part before she can reply.

Me: It was the first time I've slept with a woman.

I send this and start laughing, thinking of her reaction. But in all honesty, this isn't even a lie, I never have before last night.

Alesha: Oh wow, this is incredible!

Alesha: I'm proud of you for being yourself.

I stop laughing, and suddenly feel bad. Here she is being so supportive, and I am just yanking her chain.

Alesha: You are one up on me, I've never done it in the sleeper of a truck. hahaha

This makes me feel better. But it is time I tell her the truth.

Alesha: So, how did it happen? I want all the dirt.

And this is my perfect opportunity.

Me: We were watching this romantic movie while sitting on the bed next to each other, sharing a blanket.

Alesha: AND???

Me: Then the movie started getting boring, and we both fell asleep. I don't think either of us woke up until morning.

I send the message and it shows she's seen it, but there is no indication of her replying, until the dots start bouncing on the screen and her text pops up.

Alesha: You bitch. LMAO

When I read this I instantly start laughing.

Me: What does "LMAO" mean?

Alesha: (voice message)

I turn up my volume and hit play on a five-second recording of her hysterically laughing, so much so that I wonder how she managed to record it. Which in turn makes me laugh hysterically.

Alesha: lmao = laughing my ass off.

Alesha: You should know that. You're not that old.

Me: Yes I am. LOL

Alesha: Goddamn you for stringing me on.

Me: Sorry. LOL

Alesha: Shit you had me going. I totally thought you two fucked. lmao

Me: Sorry to disappoint you.

Alesha: Thanks though, that was the funniest thing of my life.

Alesha: Nearly peed myself, not kidding.

Me: I just couldn't help it.

Anna opens the door and climbs in. "What the hell is going on? I could hear you laughing from outside," Anna says with a smile, and I suddenly feel embarrassed.

"Sorry, I was just texting with Alesha."

"Must have been some conversation." She grins. "Well, we're loaded and ready to roll. So, get saddled up," she says, dropping into her seat.

"Okay."

Me: We're loaded, gotta go.

I climb into my seat and buckle my seatbelt. "Next stop... LA," Anna says as the truck hisses, and she starts pulling away from the loading dock.

"I can't wait," I say, and really do mean that.

As we start down the street, I go quiet while Anna looks from mirror to mirror as she switches from lane to lane, trying to get where she needs to be. I think about my conversation with Alesha with a smile, and start thinking about how supportive she was. *She was there for me with no judgment,* I think, and take my phone out.

Me: Even though it was a joke, thank you for saying you were proud of me, and being supportive.

Me: I'm glad you're my friend.

Alesha: I'm glad you're my friend.

I read this and stare at the screen, and before I change my mind, I type it out. Because even typing something out gives it weight, it brings it into reality.

Me: And yes, I think I might be a lesbian.

I hit send, Alesha sees it, and it is suddenly real.

11

So, I'm a Lesbian

There is something about studying after twenty-five years of never thinking I would study again that feels odd. But it seems to add to this feeling of being younger again. I would like to say that I am enjoying it, but reading through a PDF of everything I need to know in order to get my commercial driver's license is far from enjoyable. It is actually really boring, and the truck's gentle swaying motion while focusing on the laptop's screen is really starting to give me a headache.

I close the computer and set it down. "How's it going?" Anna asks. "You have been at it for hours."

"Have I?" I say, checking the time on my phone, seeing a huge amount of text notifications, and even two missed calls. But I ignore them, because I know they are all Alesha wanting to know what I meant by that last text; since I turned my phone to silent after sending it. "Oh, it is later than I thought. I didn't realize I had been reading that long."

"There is a rest stop up here. How about we pull over for a break and a late lunch?"

"Okay," I say.

Looking at my phone, and I know I better read through the text and respond. As I scroll through the string of texts, I see most consist of the same thing; Alesha wanting to know if I am joking, and why I'm not responding. I am about to text her back when I feel the truck start to slow and look up to see the rest stop ahead. Considering we're in Nebraska and not Texas, the rest stop looks so much like the one I walked to, it is almost confusing.

Anna pulls the truck up behind another truck, along the side of the parking area. "Well, I'm headed to the restroom. Coming?" Anna asks, unbuckling her seatbelt.

"I'm fine," I say.

"Okay," she says, climbing out of the truck and swinging the door shut behind her. As soon as she does, I call Alesha.

"What the hell?" Alesha answers after only two rings.

"Sorry, Anna was right here. And..." I pause, not sure what to say.

"So, you're serious," she says after a few seconds.

"Yeah..." I say, my eyes stinging and throat growing tight.

"Hey..." she says softly, "it will be okay. This isn't a bad thing, this is good."

"I guess," I say with a bit of a sniff, "I just don't know what to do."

"You don't have to 'do' anything. This is who you are, and you will just continue to figure things out," she says, and it makes me feel better. "Did you tell your family? Is this why you broke up with your husband?" she asks after a few seconds of silence.

"No. Well, it is partly why I never loved him, or was attracted to him. But you're the only person I have told."

"Oh, shit... I'm the first person you've told?" she says, sounding like she doesn't believe me.

"Yeah."

"Um... Thanks for trusting me." Alesha says this like she isn't sure if this is what she should say. "Well, when did it start? Have you always felt this way?"

"I have. I just never let myself believe it. Not for a long time, at least. The only crushes I ever had were on girls when I was young, but I thought it must have been something else—"

"What else could it be?" Alesha says, laughing a little, which makes me laugh.

"Well, there was a man a few years older than me in my church when I was about sixteen, and I remember overhearing my parents talking about him. He was attracted to men, but they said he just needed to get married, and that would solve it. That he just needed a wife."

"What happened? Did it work?" Alesha says, sounding like she knows the answer already.

"I honestly don't know. He got married, and they moved a few years later."

"I feel sorry for him and the woman that married him," she says, sounding truly sorry for them. "Is that what happened to you?" she asks after a moment of silence.

"No one ever knew about me. But it is in a way. In school I only had a few crushes and they were on girls."

"Like little crushes? Because a lot of girls have small crushes on girls, that don't amount to anything. I did, and I'm straight," she says. "Not that I mean this is you, I just mean—"

"No, it's fine, I know what you mean," I say with a smile at her, trying to clarify, and I hear a sigh of relief on the other end. "But, no. These weren't little crushes. But I always thought I just really wanted them to be my best friend. I remember this girl in my class. I thought it would be so great if we were friends, I couldn't stop thinking about her. Thinking back now, I was head over heels in love with her."

"Sucks you couldn't go for it," Alesha says. "I have a question."

"Sure."

"Did you check me out in the shower room?" I can tell she is smirking by the sound of her voice, but I am still instantly flustered, feeling so embarrassed.

"No, I didn't, I wouldn't, I... I—" I stammer before she cuts me off.

"Relax," she says, laughing. "I thought I noticed you checking me out, but I just thought it was because I'm pretty fucking hot." *She isn't wrong there.* "But now the cat's out of the bag."

"It wasn't that I was—"

"You don't need to make excuses. To be honest, I would have been insulted if you hadn't," she says, and I don't know what to say to this. I still am not used to someone like this, someone who is so open and comfortable about... everything. "And I know this is making you very uncomfortable, and that you hate the idea that I know you were looking at me while I was naked. But would it help if I said I looked at you?"

"Um... I... um—" She starts laughing really hard.

"I am saying all of this because you had it coming after you screwed with me earlier. Not to mention texting me that you're a lesbian, and then leaving me hanging for hours," Alesha says. I think about it, and start laughing, because this is complete payback.

"Now we're even," I say.

"Yeah, that sounds good," she says as I see Anna walking back across the parking lot.

"Anna's coming, I gotta go."

"Oh, why?"

"Because I don't want to talk about this in front of her," I say, watching her get closer and closer.

"You should just tell her... She's not homophobic, is she?"

"No," I say, a little offended at even the idea.

"Then just tell her. Unless you have a crush on her or something," Alesha says laughing, but then stops as I am quiet, once again unable to speak. "Wait, do you?"

"I gotta go," I say.

"You have a crush on Anna! Holy fuc—" I hang up on her, and switch the phone to silent a few seconds before Anna opens her door and climbs in.

"Whatcha doin?" Anna asks.

"Oh, just talkin' with Alesha a bit."

"Glad you have someone to talk with. Let's eat, I'm hungry," she says, stepping back to the sleeper. I glance at the lock screen of my phone and see a text.

Alesha: What the fuck!

Alesha: You're crazy.

Alesha: And mean! lmao

I smile at this and slide the phone into my pocket. "So, what are we having for lunch?" I ask, stepping back into the sleeper.

"Ramen," she says, pulling two plastic ramen containers out of a cabinet. "You like it, don't you?" she asks.

"Yeah. I think so... it has been a long time."

"I'll start it. You find the last thing you remember in the movie before we fell asleep."

Slipping off my shoes, I climb onto the bed and start searching through the movie to find our place, which doesn't take as long as I thought it might; but the soup doesn't take long in the microwave; that I'm not sure I even noticed she had before. We sit in silence, slurping at our soup as we watch the movie.

"You know," I say, "I think I am starting to realize why we fell asleep watching this last night."

"I know, it is just so boring," Anna agrees.

"Sorry, I should have picked something else."

"Don't know till you try, and there are a lot of sucky movies and shows out there."

"Here," I say, stopping it, "you find something else."

"Okay, let's see if I can do better... Actually," she says looking at me, "I'm throw'n in a crappy sitcom rerun, and you are choosing again tonight." I don't know why her looking at me when she says this means something to me, but it does... more than it should.

"Why? I already tried."

"Well, you should get a second chance. And we don't have time for a full movie now, and I don't want to screw up tonight's movie," she says with another smile at me.

We watch a rerun I have actually seen, and Anna has seen more times than she can count; according to her. But it is good, and funny. It is nice having a meal sitting next to her on the bed, and we both manage not to spill any soup. Which is good, because Anna apparently did this in her last truck, and she said she was never able to get the soup smell out. But she also hadn't used baking soda to clean it. Baking soda would have taken care of it.

After lunch, I make a trip to the restroom before we leave and call Alesha while I do. "What the fuck?" she says answering, "You have a thing for Anna?" she asks before I can say anything.

"Yeah..." I say, not sure what else to say.

"Like a little crush or what?" she asks, completely serious.

"No, it's not a little crush."

"Fuck... You really like her then?"

"Yeah... I really like her."

I can't seem to keep my mind on studying after telling Alesha everything, and now it just seems different. They say something doesn't truly exist until you give it a name, and I feel like this is what has happened. I wonder, think, and try to decide what I should do, or if I should do anything at all. Anna listens to another podcast while my mind runs circles, and I stare at the window. Not at the things outside the window, but at the reflection of Anna.

Thinking back, I remember the different girls in my life. I look back on them, now knowing why. Janet, the girl I sat next to in Home-EC. She was this pretty, sweet, kind person that everyone liked. She was good at things like sewing, and would try to help me when I had trouble. But I was always mad at her, and once remember pulling my hands back when she touched them to show me something. Now I know, it is because I liked her. And I remember being very upset when a girl in grade school didn't want to be friends with me. Even though I had lots of friends, I wanted her more than anyone. Now I know why.

I think about all these things. There are so many. I started thinking about these things a couple of years ago, but now... now they seem more pressing. Part of the weight has been lifted off of me by telling Alesha, I actually feel much better with someone to talk to honestly. But there is a new weight, not as heavy as the last, but it is there. It is the weight of some deep down part of me, the part of me that is the true me wanting to live, to be happy. But this means I need to tell people, I need to tell Anna.

"You're quiet," Anna says, pausing her podcast. "You alright?"

"Yeah... Yeah, I'm fine."

"You just seem a little off," she says, and I love that she can tell when I am a little off after knowing me such a short time.

"I'm... I'm just trying to figure out some things."

"I can understand that. It's hard."

I think for a second, *Maybe I can do this in stages, letting it come forward slowly.* "I have just started realizing a lot of things about myself over the last year, and read some books, and some blogs about other people that felt the same way. It's funny how I spent over forty years not understanding things that seem obvious now. And ever since I found out about Justin cheating with Debra, I feel like I have been someone else my whole life, and for no one at all." I spill all of this out, not meaning to say so much at once. But, it's out now.

Anna nods her head. "I can't relate entirely to that, but I can a little. For a long time I wasn't sure what my deal was either... Like, I knew I was different from the other kids, but I didn't know why. Evy and I are really close, and they're a lot older than me. But we didn't talk about everything. They didn't tell me; and our parents, they were transgender until they were like twenty-six," Anna says.

"Oh, that's right, you mentioned that," I say, having forgotten it.

"Yeah, and so I kind of found myself in a type of denial. I mean, I figured that there was no way I was bisexual, because the odds of me and Evy both being queer seemed impossible to me. So first I said I wasn't, then I said it would pass, then I finally realized it was who I was. But I was pretty fucking miserable for a long time." She looks over at me and I am just staring at her. I don't know how to react. I was going to slowly tell her I'm gay over maybe several days, or a week. But now? Now I have no idea what I should do.

"Are you okay?" she asks. "You don't have a problem with my being bi, do you?" she asks, sounding a little defensive. Which is understandable with my reaction.

"No, not at all," I say quickly. "I just wasn't expecting that... I had no idea."

"I used to wear a big sandwich sign that said 'I'm bisexual', but it got in the way of my driving truck, so I had to let it go," she says, completely serious, making me start laughing.

"Sorry, I didn't mean it like that. I guess I was just caught off guard... I'm not really sure," I say, feeling embarrassed.

"It's fine. I was just giving you a hard time. And I know that for me it was nothing like what you are going through, so I don't mean to act like I know." She says this so thoughtfully, always, always so careful not to belittle what I am going through.

"Well..." *I'm just going to do it. Waiting now will just make it harder. Be braver. That's the new me, right?* I think and take a breath. "Your story is close."

"Oh?"

"My realization last year that made me start reading was, that... I..." I pause, taking another deep breath, "I'm a lesbian." Saying this, I instantly hold my breath and stare out the windshield, like I don't want to know her reaction. But after a second, I look over to see her staring at me with her mouth hanging open. Suddenly an alarm of some kind starts squealing, and she snaps her head back to the road, steering the truck back into our lane.

Then she looks at me again in quick glances, still in shock by this sudden confession. "You're serious? You're a lesbian?"

I think for a second, "Well, I was going to wear a big sandwich sign—" Anna burst into laughter at this, and I feel like this might be okay. Even though I have a crush on her, I really just don't want to lose her as a friend.

12

What Does This Mean?

We're both quiet for more than a few minutes, that feel very uncomfortable; to me at least. It isn't like everything has changed, well everything has. But not in a bad way, just an unexpected one. It is still more than enough to leave both of us a little unsure of what to say.

"So..." Anna says slowly, "we're making good time." I can't help but start laughing at this.

"Yeah, I guess we are," I say, and the silence returns.

"So, you think being a lesbian screwed your marriage up?" Anna suddenly asks.

"What?" I say, stunned by the bluntness.

"I just figured it is probably something you have thought about, so I might as well just bring it up."

"Well, I would rather not talk about that now," I say, not even wanting to think about it.

"Cool, I get it," she says, and we sit in silence again. "Did you have a thing for your friend, Debra?"

"What?" I ask, looking at her. "What is with these questions?"

"I'm bored, and we're stuck in here together, and I kinda want to talk about it."

"A little when I first met her, but she's not my type," I answer.

"What's your type?" Anna instantly asks.

"Truckers!" I say just as fast, and she starts laughing.

"Seriously though, what?" she asks after she stops laughing.

"I am still trying to figure this all out. I honestly don't know my type," I say, even though I have a thing for one trucker, I know that much.

"That makes sense. Tell me when you find out though."

"What's your type?"

"I really don't have one."

"You don't have one? After asking me?"

"Well, I don't really just fall for people right off the bat. And I never just fuck the closest pretty person that shows any interest. I'm not the one-night-stand type of person. I need more of a relationship first."

"That's nice. It seems like so many people are the type that have one-night stands these days," I say.

"It isn't just 'these days,' people haven't changed. People; mostly women, are just more free to do things like that now," she says.

"That's true. It doesn't seem to matter like it used to."

"How about you? Are you the one-night stand type?" Anna asks.

"Well, I don't think so. But, I really don't know. I was always married to Justin, and I never cheated—"

"You should have. Damn, you missed your chance to screw Deb first." This makes me laugh at the idea of this, because I hadn't really thought of it.

"Oh, I don't think so—"

"Wouldn't it have been great to tell him, 'Been there done her' when you found out?" she says, grinning at me as I keep laughing.

"You know, that would have been nice. Maybe I should have seduced Deb while I had the chance." I joke. "Anyway, I never had a chance to see if I am a one-night stand person. But I don't think so."

"Maybe we should sign you up for a dating app. Find you a one-nighter while we're in LA."

"I'm not sure if you're serious or not," I honestly say.

"Fifty-fifty," she says with a mischievous smile.

"I think I'll pass. But maybe next time."

We are silent for a little bit again, until I go back to studying, and Anna turns back on her podcast. Everything seems like it always has. Nothing feels awkward or wrong, and I feel a wave of relief move over me.

I slide the curtain shut on my side, closing off the view of the highway rest stop, not that it is much to see.

"What are you doing?" I ask Anna as she wraps her seatbelt around the pull handle of her door and buckles it.

"Just wrap yours through like I did and buckle it," she says, and I do. "It is a handy trick when you are parked somewhere like this for the night, just to make sure no one gets in."

"We locked the doors," I say as I click the buckle in place.

"And someone that even halfway knows what they are doing will get around a door lock in less than a minute. But no one will get that undone," she says, opening her door, which only just opens before the seat belt pulls tight.

"Wow, I never would have thought of that."

"I don't worry about it when I spend the night at a truck stop, since there are lights, cameras, and other truckers coming and going all night. But out here on the highway in the middle of nowhere, I don't take chances."

"That's understandable," I say.

"I'll start dinner. You find that movie you're supposed to pick," Anna says as we walk into the sleeper.

"Okay," I say, unsure what I will pick. "I'm going to change first, though."

"Good idea," Anna says. I look through the plastic bag my clothes are still in, as Anna starts shedding her clothes, which makes me happy because it feels like nothing has changed. I really didn't know for sure if things would change, but I didn't know they wouldn't either. "I don't know about you, but even though I just sit there, I always feel grungy at the end of the day."

"You're right," I say, sliding the curtain shut behind me as I step into the front. "I really do feel like I need to change at the end of the day. Why don't you just wear whatever you want while driving? No one is going to see you," I ask, tossing my clothes on the seat.

"The same reason I don't clean house naked."

"You tried driving your truck naked?" I ask, pulling on my sweatpants and t-shirt.

"No." She laughs as I open up the curtain. "I just mean that you never know what will happen."

"Oh, that makes sense," I say, thinking about the story I told Alesha about my attempt at clothesless house cleaning.

"I have tried driving in sweatpants or something like that, and it just felt wrong. Not sure why, but I just need to be in jeans while working," she says, opening up the refrigerator.

"I guess I can understand that. I always got dressed, did my hair, and put on at least some makeup every day. Even if I had no plans to leave the house. It just felt right," I say, turning on the TV.

"I used to wear makeup, but I stopped because it is too much of a pain to clean off on the road. I have some if you ever want to use it though."

"Really? Thanks. Some carjacker is wearing mine right now," I say, making Anna laugh at the idea. *I like making her laugh.* "Are you cooking a frozen lasagna in the microwave?"

"Yeah," she says, punching in the time.

"Can you do that?"

"No, but I thought I would do it anyway," she says as I glare at her. "Yes, I've done this, and it works fine."

I scroll through movies I have never seen with no idea what looks good. "What about this one?" I ask.

She looks over. "You never seen it?" Anna asks, raising an eyebrow.

"No, why?" I ask, getting the feeling that I should have, for some reason.

"You've never seen Notting Hill?"

"No, why?"

"Because it is kind of a classic in rom-com movies."

"So, you've seen it?"

"Yes, yes, I have seen it!" She laughs.

"Then I hate to play something you have seen."

"Wrong, we're watching it. You'll love it!"

Anna is right on both accounts. First the microwaved lasagna; and bread, are surprisingly good. And second, Notting Hill is really good. Sweet, romantic, and funny. Nothing in it not to like, and sitting next to Anna under the blanket as we watch makes it even better.

The movie finishes in its fairytale ending, and we are soon staring at the menu with nothing playing. "You like it?" Anna asks.

"Yes, I loved it."

"I personally don't think you can go wrong with Hugh Grant or Julia Roberts, and together, you know it is going to be good. Plus, they are both pretty damn cute."

"They are great. Julia Roberts is cute, and he is a great actor," I say.

"But not cute?" she questions, looking at me.

"Well... I mean, he's fine I guess. And I'm sure most people think he is handsome, but—"

"Handsome? Hugh is way past handsome."

"Okay fine, I'm sure most people think he is a stud."

"Much better."

"But he really isn't my type—"

"Well, you are a lesbian," she says with a smirk, and I feel my cheeks grow warm. "Are you blushing?" Anna asks, amused.

"I'm still not used to talking about it. It's still weird."

"So, you don't find Hugh attractive at all?"

"I guess not... Sorry, I don—"

"Why are you apologizing? This actually proves rather conclusively that you are a lesbian, because if Hugh doesn't do it for you, no one does."

"Thanks," I say, laughing a little because she is probably right.

"I mean that accent alone... fuck," she says, leaning her head back against the wall.

"Should I go up front and leave you and Hugh alone for a while?" I ask.

"Maybe... I'm not sure yet," she says, thinking about it, before we both start laughing.

"We better get some sleep," I say.

"Very true."

"Well, let's see if I can make it into the top bunk today," I say, standing.

"I'll stand backup, just in case," Anna says, standing.

"I appreciate that."

"You know, another high point of you not being into Hugh in any way. If we ever happen across him broke down on the side of the highway, I have a better chance with him if you aren't competing for him as well."

"Really? You think this is a possibility?"

"You never know," she says.

"Isn't he a little too old for you?"

"You're spoiling the fantasy. Why would you do that?" she says in a begging voice.

"Sorry, I didn't mean to," I say, smiling at her, laughing again. I find myself loving how much I laugh around her. "So, do you fantasize about finding attractive celebrities stranded along the highway often?"

"Oh, you have no idea," she says with a grin. I prepare myself for my climb into my bed, grabbing onto the sides. "Not just celebrities though, the idea of finding anyone like that stranded is a pretty constant fantasy."

"Oh..." I say, suddenly feeling very aware that she found me stranded on the side of the highway. But I tell myself this doesn't mean I am, or ever will be part of that fantasy. "I guess that makes sense."

"Here, step in my hands, I'll boost you," she says, clasping her hands together in front of herself.

"You sure?"

"Yeah, come on. It will be easier." I do as she says. "Upsy daisy," Anna says, partly lifting me as I use her hands as a step.

"Thanks, that was much easier," I say, pulling my covers over myself.

"So, what's yours?" she asks.

"My what?"

"Your fantasy. You know one of mine, so it is only fair." I hesitate about this. "Now no backing out," Anna says sternly. I look over the edge of the bed to see her toss her sweatpants on the floor as she climbs into her bed, and suddenly all I can think about is a fantasy. But I'm not going to tell her about that one.

"I don't know. It's hard for me," I say, and think about it. "I guess..." I pause, thinking about whether or not I should actually say it, but I might as well. After all, I am trying to be a new me, no longer hiding. "I guess it might be, being with a woman. No one in particular, but not a stranger or someone I didn't like," I clarify quickly. "But I have never even kissed another woman, so I feel like... I don't know..." I say, feeling like I am rambling without knowing my point of this.

"You feel like you need to prove you're a lesbian. That having not kissed, had sex with, or been in a romantic relationship with a woman means you might not be," Anna says, and she is completely right, understanding exactly what I wanted to say, but couldn't.

"Yes, that's it."

"It is one of the shitty things queer people still have to deal with. It is like we have to prove what we are, and until we do, we aren't who we say we are. Straight until proven otherwise," she continues.

"Yes, it is really unfair."

"So, if your fantasy is as simple as being with a woman you are attracted to, then that's fine," she says.

"Thanks," I say somewhat quietly, feeling awkward.

"But now that I think about it, that is more like a goal. Or maybe even just something going to happen in the future. A fantasy needs to be more unrealistic, something that will never happen; even impossible."

"You think so?" I ask, knowing that Anna is now joking around to lighten the mood. She doesn't seem to like things to be serious for too long.

"Yeah. So, maybe instead of just one person, you should want to be with an entire sports team or cheerleading squad. Ooh, maybe the Sunday school teacher," Anna says, seeming to really enjoy coming up with replacement fantasies for me.

"I was the Sunday school teacher."

"No shit? Fuck, you were so prim and straight-laced."

"I taught years ago, and I am still prim," I tell her. I like to think I'm not completely void of my upbringing.

"Says the lesbian on the top bunk whose fantasy is sex with any willing woman she comes across."

"I told you, I have standards," I say, unable to not laugh, because maybe I'm not so proper anymore.

"So, if you're the teacher... Then maybe a student then. Just the two of you. She comes to you needing help understanding why lust is a sin, and yo—"

"Stop it!" I laugh.

"Yes, and then the student says, 'I try but I ca—"

"I mean, you stop it," I say, laughing hard.

"Okay, fine. But it was just about to get good."

Oh, I know it was, I think. "I don't care," I say, still laughing.

"Since you were never attracted to your husband, it must have been a nightmare when it can to having sex with him," she says, and I wonder why I like her being so straightforward about this.

"It wasn't great... Actually, it was quite horrible. But I didn't really know why back then. I thought it was something else that you just got used to as your marriage progressed."

"Did it?"

"I am homeless, lying here talking about fantasies with you. What do you think?"

Anna starts laughing. "Damn, you are really starting to loosen up."

"It never got easier. I'm sure this was a big part of why he started having an affair... I guess I can't blame him for doing that."

"Like fuck. You're doing it again. You are blaming yourself for the shitty actions of others. Fuck him for treating you like that. If he had a problem, he should have talked to you about it, or suggested seeing a couple's therapist. But going out and just cheating on you with your best friend? That is a fucking asshole move."

"You're right," I say, thinking about it. "He never told me there was a problem. How was I supposed to know? I'm—"

"A lesbian," she finishes for me.

"I wasn't going to say that," I say, laughing. "I was going to say, I'm not psychic."

"Oh yeah, that is true," she says, also laughing.

"But you're right. I couldn't even figure out myself. How was I supposed to know what he was thinking?"

"Right?" Anna agrees.

We lie there for a few minutes, and I think about this a little more in-depth. "Thanks."

"What for? That Sunday-school teacher fantasy?"

"No," I say, giggling. "It has been nice talking with someone about all of this. I never have, and it is really nice."

"Glad I can help... And thanks for talking. It has been great having someone around to talk with. I don't think I realized how much I missed it."

"Seems like it worked out for both of us," I say.

"Yeah, a lucky fit."

"Good night then."

"Good night, sweet dreams," she says, and it makes me smile.

I lie there thinking, staring into the pitch-black of the sleeper. I think about telling Anna, and her telling me. About what we have been talking about, her fantasy of picking up someone on the side of the highway, and the fantasy she gave me. I can't help but wonder, *Did Anna ever go to Sunday school?*

"Are you still awake?" Anna asks in the softest whisper ten or fifteen minutes later. Seeming to be very careful not to wake me if I am asleep.

"No," I say softly.

"You're thinking about that Sunday school student, aren't you?"

"Oh, shut up," I say, as she burst into laughter.

13

It Happens to All Truckers

I stretch my arms over my head and look out the windshield, then close the laptop, setting it on the floor between the seats. "How's my student doing?" Anna asks, and I feel my cheeks warm slightly because of that darn fantasy she came up with.

"Oh, it's going fine... I think. I guess I won't know until I try the practice test."

"And until you actually get behind the wheel."

"Okay, that scares me," I say, because it truly does.

"It's easy. Just like driving a large car," she says with a smile.

"Really?" I say with hope, thinking that maybe I am just over-thinking it.

"No, it's actually nothing like that."

"Why would you say that, then?" I ask, laughing.

"I don't know. Guess I'm just bored."

"I am glad that my gullibility is a source of entertainment for you."

"Yeah, thanks," she says, and she actually sounds like she really does appreciate this.

I look out the window for a bit as we sit in silence, but it doesn't seem to be awkward. As I think about this comfort between us, I realize that even last night talking about sex and fantasies, I didn't feel awkward. Maybe a little, but not like I did before, not like I would with anyone else. It gives me the giddy butterfly feeling people talk about, but I had never experienced... until now.

"Hey," I say, suddenly thinking of something. "I thought we would go through Colorado."

"I decided it was better to just stay north."

"Isn't it slower this way?"

"Since when did you start learning route times?" she says, glancing at me with a smirk.

"I just searched our route on my phone and saw there was more than one way."

"It is faster, but only by a few hours. And I-70 through the mountains is brutal as fuck. So, if you overheat your brakes you have to stop and have them fixed; which isn't cheap, and that takes way more time than just staying north. Plus, there is a good chance of brake failure, and that isn't fun."

"Have you had it happen?" I ask.

"I-70 is what ate my last rig."

"Really?"

"I had a full load when my brakes gave out. But I was lucky, and it happened soon enough I was able to catch a runaway."

"A 'runaway'?"

"It is somewhere to kind of wreck on purpose, like a safe wreck place. That doesn't make sense, but you'll learn about them," she says. "But the one I hit was like a long dirt and gravel road up the side of the mountain. I was going about ninety when I hit it—"

"What did you do?"

"Held on and tried to keep the bastard under control, prayed like hell that I wouldn't go up and over the other side."

"What do you mean?"

"It isn't unheard of to hit the top of the hill on some of those and go over the other side, and when that happens you've got a high chance of rolling all the way down; and if that happens, you're fucked."

"Oh my goodness, I had no idea."

"Anyway. My rig jackknifed part way up, laid over and went into a barrier. I walked away, but totaled all of it. Not a good day."

"You were okay, so it was a very good day," I say, overwhelmed with emotion at even the idea of anything happening to her.

"I guess."

"No, it was. I can't imagine something happening to you. I don't know what I would do without you," I say, and suddenly feel like I might have said too much, because I did.

"Thanks..." she says somewhat quietly. "I'm not really sure what I would do without you either."

We both just sit in silence, things feeling a little different for me, and I wonder if things feel different for Anna too. We switch into mundane chitchat for a while, and it seems like we both avoid any topics that could lead to more meaningful, intimate conversation. But it still doesn't feel awkward, but more like neither of us is quite sure where what we said will take us.

How does Anna feel about me? Does she "like" me? This question gnaws at me as I sit in my seat staring at the computer, but unable to actually get any studying done. *What about me?* I think, wondering if what I am feeling for Anna is more than a crush. After all, it isn't like I have a lot of experience in this area. I was hardly able to recognize a crush as a teen, so why should I be any better at understanding anything now that I am in my forties?

We stop for a lunch break before we get to Las Vegas and watch another sitcom rerun. It is just easier than starting a movie we don't have time to finish. Anna is worried traffic might be bad where the highway goes through Vegas, but we luck out and it isn't bad. "How do you like Vegas?" Anna asks as we pass iconic casinos and hotels.

"It's fine."

"Fine?"

"It is interesting seeing these places I have always heard of and seen on TV and Movies. But Vegas has never been my type of place," I explain.

"I'm the same way, never been my scene. But it is too bad it's the middle of the day. It looks so much different at night with everything lit up."

"I can see that," I say, looking out the window.

"How about LA?"

"I am actually looking more forward to seeing LA."

"I have always liked going there. I never have time to actually see it, but someday I will."

"You should just make time," I say.

"Yeah, I would like to go to Magical Land."

"Really? I have always wanted to go there someday, I have wanted to forever," I say.

"Me too."

"I wanted to take the kids, but Justin said it was too far, and it was pretty clear that I wanted to go more than him or the kids. So, we never did."

"That's why he is an asshole. Because he should have just taken you and left the kids with someone. That's what I would do."

"Too bad I didn't marry you," I say, not really sure why.

"Yeah, you really should have. Although, I would have only been ten years old when you got married. So it is really your fault for not waiting for me to grow up."

"You're right... I should have waited. But, nothing to be done now," I say with a laugh.

"It's not too late, look!" Anna points out the windshield. I look to where she is pointing and see a sign for a chapel. "It's like a sign from God. We can get married now!" she says, laughing.

"Well, I guess we could." I laugh.

"Too late," she says as we pass the exit ramp to the chapel. "We'll think about it and maybe stop on the way back through."

"It might be too early for us anyway, better we wait," I joke.

"Actually, I know you better than some people I have known for years," she says, glancing at me.

"Yeah, you're right. I feel like I know you rather well too," I say with a smile, and things feel a little too serious again. Anna notices this time as well. I can see her look a bit tense.

"It would be worth getting married to me in Vegas just so you could send those wedding photos to your family, or maybe just introduce me to your kids as their new stepmom," she says, making me laugh at the thought. But something about it feels like she is hiding behind the humor.

"That would be funny."

"And what a way to come out to them."

"It really would be," I say, picking my phone up and swiping it open. "I want to tell Alesha about this. She will love the idea."

"Just wondering," Anna says, no longer joking, "when are you going to tell your family?"

"Oh..." I say, having thought of this, but largely avoided it.

"You don't have to answer, I didn't mean to pressure you. I shouldn't have asked. It isn't my business—"

"It's fine," I say, not wanting her to feel bad for asking. "I don't know... I've thought about just not telling them. It doesn't..." I pause, swallowing the lump in my throat. "It doesn't seem like I will be seeing them, so it doesn't seem like it matters. And, I don't know if they need to know. Does it really matter?"

"Well, it might not seem like it now, but I bet your kids will come around one of these days. Once everything calms down, they will see everything with a more clear perspective."

"You think they will?"

"Yeah. People always get caught up in the moment when something bad happens, and they don't look at the whole picture. They just side with what's easy and straightforward, and that normally isn't the truth or right," she says. "As for coming out to them, that's your choice, no one else's. And I know some people don't ever come out to their family, but some also find that they almost have to deep down. So, just do what feels right to you."

"Thanks," I say, appreciating what she's said. "I really don't know how they'll take it. But I don't think they will take it well."

"That's another thing. If you do tell them, tell them for you. You can't worry about what they think. This is about you, and if they can't see that, then fuck them." I can't help but smile at this. "And we can always just get married in Vegas and post the photos online and tag your church or something, that really is an option," Anna says, now back to joking, but I like it.

I text Alesha about Anna's marriage idea and everything else, but she doesn't respond. I look out the window, but the landscape has changed to desert; which is nice, but starts to look the same to me quickly, so I go back to studying. I do seem to be remembering what I have read, so that is something.

The next several hours seem to pass slowly, but I assume that it is like this sometimes when driving truck. "You see that mountain up there?" Anna says.

"The one straight in front of us?"

"Yeah, that's Mt. San Antonio, and just on the other side of it is LA."

"We're really that close?" I ask, surprised.

"It's just over an hour to stop for the day," she says, sounding happy about it herself.

"That's great. Where do you go next?"

"Already wanting back on the road, and we haven't even gotten there yet. Slow down, Mary," she says with a smirk.

"I was just wondering."

"We are headed home."

"Home?"

"New York, the next load is a straight-through run."

"Is that better? Or would—"

"Did you hear that?" she interrupts, and I can tell that she is listening and very serious.

"Hear what?" I ask, listening, but I don't know what for.

"Maybe it was just a bad spot in the pavement," she says, and I can see her relax. "Sometimes, bad pavement will sound lik—"

suddenly there is a loud explosion from the front of the truck and the passenger side drops. "Fuck!" Her arms go tense on the steering wheel, holding it hard to one side.

"What is—" I'm interrupted as the hood of the truck starts violently bouncing with an extremely loud noise, like the engine is trying to beat its way through the hood. I can't form words, and just hold onto the seat as tight as I can, unable to look away.

"Shit, shit, shit!" Anna says, pulling the cord for the air horn as chunks of the front fender start flying through the air, bouncing off the windshield and cab. Something large; a few feet long, sails through the air, hitting the windshield just in front of my side. The windshield shatters in front of me, and cracks streak through to Anna's side. "Son of a bitch!"

I look over to see how hard Anna is fighting the truck, not to keep it in our lane, but to keep it on the highway. Somehow she does it. She keeps us from slamming into the center divider, and from careening off the highway, where I am sure the truck would have rolled over. But we come to a stop with a jerk of the cab, and a thick smell of burning rubber in the air.

Before I can say anything, Anna has her seatbelt off and has the door open. I wonder what she is doing when she pulls a large fire extinguisher from behind her seat and disappears. Suddenly that smoke smell of burning rubber is all I can think about. So, I pull my seatbelt off and climb out of the truck as fast as I can, thinking the truck might be on fire.

Once I am on the ground, I look and see Anna just standing there holding the fire extinguisher. "Oh my God..." I say, half in shock as I stand next to her, staring at the truck. The entire fender and part of the hood are gone, ripped completely off. The tire is mostly gone, only some shreds holding onto the rim. "What happened?"

"The mother fucking tire blew out," she says, not looking away.

"And did all of this?"

"Yup. When they fly apart they rip everything in their way to shreds, and can even catch fire. Damn, this was the last thing I needed."

"At least we're okay, and no one was hurt. So, we can be thankful for that," I say.

She slowly looks at me. "You never change, do you?"

"Oh right, I forgot... Damn it!" I yell, kicking a piece of tire hanging from the rim. Anna instantly starts laughing hard.

"There might be hope for you yet," she says smiling. "Now, I'm going to get this mess pulled a little farther off the highway, you can wait here," she says, setting the fire extinguisher down and turning to walk back around.

"Hey."

"Yeah?" she says, stopping and looking back at me.

"You were incredible," I say, and she smiles, everything seeming to not be so bad. We are both okay after all.

14
Everything Happens for a Reason

I take a picture of the truck's damage, once Anna has moved it farther off the highway, and type out a text while Anna sets emergency reflectors up around the truck. I caption the photo, *"First truck wreck"* and send it to Alesha.

"I'm going to go get what debris I can out of the highway, back in a few minutes," Anna says, putting on an orange reflective vest like construction workers wear.

"Let me help."

"You shouldn't. It's dirty and dangerous."

"Please, let me help. I want to," I say.

"Okay," she says, pulling another orange vest out of the truck and handing it to me. "Watch out for cars though. People don't pay any attention, and even if they do, they couldn't care less about you."

"Well, that makes me feel good," I say, trying to sound hurt as we walk up the highway.

We walk along the shoulder, pulling anything on the highway off to the side, waiting for traffic; which luckily isn't too bad. "I should have asked sooner," Anna says as we each grab an end of a large chunk of what used to be part of a wheel well, "but are you okay?"

"Yes, I'm fine. I didn't get hurt," I say, not sure why she looks worried.

"I know you weren't hurt. But that got really dicey, and it scared the shit out of me. So, I just want to make sure you're okay."

"Thanks. It was a little scary, but I really wasn't worried. I knew we would be okay," I say as we drop the piece by the shoulder.

"You're not going to say God was protecting us, are you?" she asks, raising an eyebrow.

"Well, not that God wasn't watching over us—"

"I knew it—"

"But," I say, interrupting her, "I wasn't worried because I knew you could handle it... and you did."

"Really?" she says, tossing a piece of tire tread off the road. "Because I wasn't so sure."

"Well, I was," I say and walk out to the center divider to get a large piece of tire before she can say anything. I don't know why, but I don't want to hear her response. Grabbing the piece, I carry it back across. When I toss it down, a sharp pain grabs at my hand like tiny razor-sharp teeth. "Ouch," I involuntarily say, shaking my hand. I look at my hand and a line of red droplets appear, very much like something bit me. Anna doesn't notice any of this as she drags another piece of something off the pavement, and I don't say anything.

"Is that everything?" I ask.

"Yeah, I think so," she says, wiping the sweat off her brow. The heat is quite unbearable, but luckily I am a bit used to heat; having spent my whole life in Texas. "We'll start dragging it back in a second. I want to call a wrecker and get them on the way," she says, taking her phone out as we walk farther away from the highway. I take my phone out and see Alesha responded. I am close enough to Anna to have Wi-Fi from her phone's hotspot, so I will be able to respond.

Alesha: OMG Are you okay?

Alesha: What happened?

Alesha: What, did you die? hahaha.

Alesha: I will never forgive myself if you are actually dead.

Alesha: Where are you? Are you okay?

I smile reading these.

Me: Yes, I died. But I will tell you what happened anyway.

She instantly texts back.

Alesha: lmao.

Me: We are both fine. We just blew a tire.

Alesha: Just blew a tire? That must have been one pissed tire, because it bitch slapped the fuck out of your ride.

I can't help but start laughing when I read this, because she is completely right. Anna just glances at me with a grin as she talks on her phone.

Me: LMAO.

It's the first time I have ever texted that, but it feels good because I really am.

Me: Nearly had a heart attack when a piece of tire broke the windshield in front of me.

Alesha: F U C K!

Alesha: I would have peed myself.

Me: How do you know I didn't?

Alesha: lmao.

Alesha: I'm dead.

Anna hangs up her phone.

Me: Talk later. Need to drag debris back to the truck. It's everywhere.

Alesha: Shit, that sucks.

Alesha: ttyl.

Me: What's that mean?

Alesha: OMG It means talk to you later, lmao.

Me: Oh. ttyl.

"So," Anna says as I shove my phone in my pocket, "the wrecker said it will be two hours before they can get out here."

"Then what?" I ask, not sure how any of this works.

"They will tow us to LA and fix the truck. I will call my insurance and another truck to haul our load so it isn't late," she explains.

"Sorry all this happened," I say, picking up some of the debris we had set on the shoulder, and start walking towards the truck.

"I knew it was your fault, you popped my tire on purpose," she says as she drags a large piece behind her.

"I just couldn't help but do... whatever it is to a semi-tire that makes them do that."

"How detailed," she says as I laugh.

We keep carrying and dragging pieces back, leaving anything that isn't very big, and it doesn't seem like it takes too long before it is all in a pile next to the truck. Then we climb back into the truck to get away from the heat, but the truck is already stifling hot inside.

"Didn't take long to heat up in here," Anna says, turning the sleeper's air conditioning on.

"I'm so sweaty, I'm going to change," I say, grabbing some fresh clothes as she dials a number on her phone. I step up front, closing the curtain behind me. I hear her talking to someone who sounds like another truck driver on the phone as I close the curtains in the front of the cab, which feels odd in broad daylight. Changing quickly, I use my dirty shirt inside out to wipe the sweat off myself, wishing I could take a shower, but it will at least keep from getting my fresh clothes instantly sweaty.

"—I'll let you know, thanks," Anna says, hanging up the phone as I open up the curtain and close it behind me to help keep out the heat. "I got a friend who is going to meet us at the shop to take my trailer to unload," she tells me.

"That's good," I say, dropping my clothes into the hamper.

"Is your hand bleeding?"

"What?" I say, looking at my hand, where it is still stinging. "Oh, it looks like it is. But it's nothing."

"What happened?" she asks, taking my hand, and I feel myself go slightly stiff with her touch.

"Something on a piece of tire caught my hand. It really is fine though," I say, feeling stupid that I wasn't more careful.

"It must have been the wires."

"Wires?"

"Yeah, the steel wires that make up the belts of a tire. They are nasty bastards that are really sharp, and it hurts so bad when they poke you. Does it hurt?" she asks, looking into my eyes, still holding my hand.

"A bit," I say, feeling like the words are hard to get out of my mouth.

"You shouldn't have helped," she says with concern.

"But I wanted to help you," I say, still looking into her eyes, noticing that they are a beautiful gray. But, I think her eyes would be beautiful no matter the color.

"Let me clean it up for you, sit down," she says, turning and opening a cabinet, and I sit down on the edge of the bed, things feeling different again. "Okay," she says. Kneeling down in front of me, opening a little first aid kit. With an alcohol wipe in one hand, she takes my right hand, and gently wipes the dirt and grime from picking up the debris away. Then swabs the cuts and tiny punctures with peroxide. "You really did get it good. I'm sure it must hurt. I hope this isn't burning too much." Anna says this as gently as her touch.

"It doesn't, thank you."

She spreads a thin layer of antibacterial cream on, and places a small gauze pad over it. Anna softly squeezes my hand as she wraps medical tape around it, pressing the tape down as she goes with soft strokes. "Is that too tight?"

"No," I say, a bit nervously, tucking my hair behind my ear with my other hand. Still holding my hand, she reaches up and sweeps my hair behind my ear on the other side.

"You should wear your hair back more," she says, her hand still beside my face.

"You think so?" I say, with a noticeable waver in my voice.

"Yeah, it's really pretty back. Not that it isn't always pretty," Anna says, her voice having the same waver as mine.

"Thanks... You are too," I say, not really making sense. But I don't think that matters as I suddenly feel like I am on the edge of something, something that will change my life if I step off of it. I know that I won't be able to undo it. But, I don't care. I am tired of not stepping forward for myself, I am tired of not exploring my life, and I am done with playing it safe. For once I am doing what I feel is right for myself, even if there is no coming back from it.

"Thanks..." she says, and we seem to be closer than we were. And I realize, I'm not the only one that has moved closer, and that I'm not the only one willing to step off this edge. We both jump back as there is a pounding knock on the cab of the truck.

"Fuck," Anna says, almost sounding out of breath, and maybe disappointed.

"Who is it?" I say, as though she would know.

"I bet a million dollars that it's a cop. Stay here, I got it," she says with a smile before I can say anything. Then turns and pushes through the curtain.

I stare at the curtain, hear the door open, and her saying something to someone, then climb out of the truck; the door closing behind her. I fall back onto the bed, staring at the ceiling; that is actually the bottom of my bed. Breathing a little hard, my heart beating like I have been running. *Is this it? Is this what it feels like?* I wonder about this feeling I have never felt, never even come close to feeling with Justin. *Is this what it feels like to truly want to be with someone? Well, I know who I can ask.*

Me: Are you there?

I send the message to Alesha, unsure what else to do. But feeling like she might be able to help me. If nothing else, I feel like I need to tell someone, because I suddenly feel scared, but I don't even know what it is I am scared of.

To my relief, she texts back in less than a minute.

Alesha: Am I where? I don't know if I am there until you tell me where I am supposed to go. But do any of us know where we are truly going? It's a deep question. I will think about it and get back to you.

I smile at her stupid response, that is clearly just her annoying me for fun. But I ignore it, knowing I probably don't have time to waste, that Anna will be back soon.

Me: I think Anna likes me.

Alesha: In the "she wants to do you" way?

Me: Do you have to say it like that?

Alesha: Soooo... That's a yes?

Me: Yes. And I don't know what to do.

Alesha: You're freaking out, aren't you?

Me: A little.

Alesha: Hahaha.

Alesha: What happened?

Alesha: Tell me why you think she likes you.

Alesha: In the biblical sense. ;)

Me: Very funny.

Me: I cut my hand (nothing serious) while picking up the debris from the truck off the highway, and she was cleaning and bandaging it. Then something changed and we were about to kiss when a cop knocked on the door. Wanted to text you while she is outside.

I send this and within a few seconds, the phone rings with a video-call. "Hello?" I say, answering.

"Okay, tell me again," she says.

"Okay, but quiet, I don't want her to hear, and I am hanging up when she comes back."

"I totally get it, I don't want... to get in the way," she says, bouncing her eyebrows, but I ignore it.

"I could have bandaged my hand myself, but she did it, and was so gentle—"

"Sexy," Alesha says, and I'm not sure if she is being serious or not.

"Then we kind of started looking into each other's eyes, and then..." I trail off, feeling uncomfortable telling it to someone, wondering if I am breaking Anna's trust. Texting hadn't seemed like this.

"Who made the move, you or her?"

"What?"

"Who went for it?" she asks, like this is some basic question, and I feel like I am too old for talks like this.

"We both leaned forwa—"

"You both went for it at the same time?" Alesha says, wide-eyed, and I just stare at her. "Holy fuck, that's like... Yeah, this... this might be going somewhere," she says like she is thinking out loud. "Big question. If the fuzz hadn't showed up, would you be making out right now?" Alesha asks this with her mouth hanging open, seeming very excited by the question.

"I don't know..." I say, looking down away from the camera. But remember, I am trying to be more forward and honest. "Yeah, I think so." She instantly squeals so loud that I quickly clap my hand over the speaker. "Quiet," I say, and she stops.

"Okay," she says, eyeing me through the screen. "If you were making out, would you then have gone for it?"

"What?" I say, surprised she would blatantly ask this. Well, maybe not that surprised. She is a bit like that.

"Would you go all the way? Or at least part way?"

"I don't know," I say honestly, because I really don't know.

"Do you want to?" she asks, moving closer to the camera, intently staring. It is an odd feeling having someone stare at you like this through a camera.

"I don't know... I guess."

"Oh my God, you do want to screw her?"

"I didn't say that. And why are you so interested?" I ask.

"I'm bored, and my sex life sucks. Moving around constantly and living in a van makes it hard, and I have to live vicariously through you. So get busy with Anna and then tell me about it."

"You're not gay, are you?" I ask, wondering if everyone I suddenly know is bisexual or a lesbian.

"No, I'm straight. But like I said, my sex life sucks. Beggars can't be choosers. So tell—" I hurry and end the call, as I hear the door of the truck open, knowing that Alesha will be annoyed. But knowing it will annoy her makes me a bit happy.

"Is everything okay?" I ask Anna as she pulls back the curtain.

"Oh, it is so nice in here," she says, waving her shirt back and forth, and looking very sweaty and so hot... in both meanings of the word.

"Was there a problem? It seemed like it took a while."

"No, he just wanted to make sure we didn't wreck or hit someone. He was happy; well, as happy as a highway patrol ever is," she smirks. "That we cleaned up the debris. He didn't even check the load, but he just kept standing there, like he had nothing better to do. And it is hot as hell out there, but I can't really tell a cop to fuck-off," Anna says, and things seem more normal. *Maybe it was just the heat, and it won't come up again,* I think, and am not sure if I like that idea or not.

"Glad he's finally gone then. Why don't you sit down and cool off? I'll find something on TV."

"Good idea, but I'm going to change out of these sweaty clothes," she says, getting out some fresh clothes.

I turn the TV on to find something to watch and prepare myself at the same time for her to start stripping off her clothes like she always does. Then she steps into the front and closes the curtain. And I now know without question... things have changed.

15

L.A. Baby

I stare out the window at what is Los Angeles. A place I have always wanted to see in person. And even though this isn't the main; glamorous part of the city, it is still great. I watch it all pass by my window from the backseat of the tow truck, while Anna talks trucks and what all hers needs with the driver.

When he arrived, I was surprised how he didn't say much at all about the damage, making me think it is more common than I would like it to be. I can't help but wonder how I would have reacted if I had been the one driving, and if I am actually suitable to be a driver. I was going to ask Anna, but after that moment in the truck, I haven't been able to get myself to say much of anything. We just turned on some more reruns and didn't say much else.

Something about this change still worries me, but I think the thing that is worrying me is that I won't pursue it, that I won't take the chance. I keep telling myself that I will no longer act like I have all my life. But when Anna came back into the sleeper after that cop left, I could have walked straight up to her and kissed her, but I didn't. I didn't even say a word. I just acted like nothing happened at all.

The tow truck turns into a huge lot with trucks and trailers parked here and there, and a massive garage. "We'll get your rig unhooked. You can head on over to the office and get things sorted. Once it's unhooked, you can get what you need out," the man says.

"Sounds good," Anna says, and we climb out of the tow truck. "So," Anna says as we walk across the parking lot, seeming to want to fill in the silence, "how did you like riding in a tow truck?"

"Well, it was nicer than I thought."

"They really are nice trucks."

"I thought I would be stuck sitting in the middle of a single bench seat next to some sweaty guy the whole time. So, I'm just happy that it had a back seat," I say.

"How old did you think the tow truck would be?" she asks, looking at me with a grin.

"I don't know. I just didn't know what to expect," I say, laughing a little, and glad that Anna brought this up. It makes me feel better.

"The driver's real nice too," she says, glancing back at him as he is doing something with the truck.

"Yeah, he did seem nice," I say, thinking if I can remember anything he said that wasn't truck related. Anna stops outside the door to the office and stares at me for a few seconds with a grin. "What?"

"I mean he's hot."

"Oh..."

"You didn't notice?"

I look back over at him and watch for a second. "I guess I just didn't pay much attention to him." *Because my mind was on other things, and still is,* I think, looking back to Anna.

"He isn't really my type," Anna says, and I realize how relieved I am, like she was going to abandon me for tow truck guy. "But, I did notice him."

"Everybody said Justin was good-looking, and I was with him for over twenty-five years and never saw it."

"You make a fair point."

"I wonder what Alesha would think of him?" I say, like an out-loud thought.

"I bet she would flip out," Anna says, looking at her phone. "Here, send her this," she says as my phone buzzes.

I look at my phone and open the text she just sent me to see several photos of the tow truck driver. "You took photos of him?" I say in a hushed voice.

"I took the pictures of the truck to send Evy, and he just happens to be in them as well."

"Yeah, in every one of them. I thought he wasn't your type?" I say, feeling more annoyed than I have any right to. Anna and I aren't... anything.

"He isn't. But, he's Evy's type," she says with a wink, and pulls open the door to the office.

I walk into the office behind Anna; and even though it is perfectly clean, there is still a smell of grease and diesel in the air. There is a woman in an office chair behind a counter who talks on the phone while typing and looking at a computer monitor. There are some parts sitting behind the counter on some dirty-looking rolling table that I am pretty sure explains the smell.

Anna sits down on a vinyl stool at the counter. There are three of them, and they have brands of parts and oils printed on the vinyl. I sit down next to her and notice they are the type that swivel. The woman only glances at us with a smile, but she is clearly in the middle of something.

It sounds like she is trying to locate a part. So I forward Alesha the photos of the tow truck driver real quick while we wait.

I sit on the stool and rotate to the side, looking around the room. The walls have shelves with model trucks on them, a chrome bull-dog, and other knickknacks. There are also some trophies for truck shows, and a truck pull, along with photos of the events. Then I notice a large calendar with two women; a blond and a brunette posing against a polished semi truck with chrome wheels, they are both wearing what might be called bikinis, but I personally feel like they are lacking in coverage to be considered as such. Even though I have always hated these types of calendars, I must admit I would be disappointed if there wasn't one hanging in here, because it just fits the rest of the decor too well.

Then I notice something about the calendar I almost missed. "So, is it the blond or the brunette that has you so interested?" Anna asks.

"What?" I say, looking at her.

"You're the one staring," she says with a grin, having noticed my staring at the calendar.

"Neither."

"Then, what... the truck?" she asks.

"It's the fact it isn't January," I say, "And I am wondering why it has never been turned."

"Maybe they are the best in the lineup," Anna says.

"Wrong," the woman behind the counter says, hanging up the phone. "That is just how useful paper calendars are. I don't think we have gotten past January in years..." she says, thinking about it.

"That does make sense," I say, looking away, even though it is still bugging me that it isn't kept up to date.

"So, you the ones with the rig they just dropped?" she asks.

"Yeah, Anna Ginkans," Anna says, and I realize this is the first time hearing her last name, she never told me.

"Alright," the woman says, "from the list Adam gave me, we can have everything by tomorrow morning. Unless another problem turns up, but I doubt it would be anything that would change the timeline. So, it looks like noon, the day after tomorrow is the estimate right now, and I'll let you know as they start into it."

"Alright, that sounds good to me," Anna says.

"You're lucky that we aren't more busy," she says, holding out a tablet with a stylus, and Anna fills in a few things.

"Well, I really appreciate it," Anna says, handing the tablet back.

They exchange a few more pleasantries and then we are back outside in the heat. "So, now what?" I ask.

"We find a place to stay, and I'll call us a car. We can get our things together in the truck while we wait," she says.

The truck is stifling hot inside, so we grab everything we might need and shove them into whatever bags are available, including what perishable food there is in the refrigerator. Anna also has a gym bag she packs enough clothes, and most of the dirty laundry; with hopes of a washing machine at wherever we are staying.

"Holy fuck it is hot in there." Anna gasps as she climbs out of the truck behind me. After we both decide that it is too hot to wait in the truck.

"Just awful." I agree. "So, now what?"

"I guess find a hotel."

"I am going to owe you so much money," I say with a sigh, not sure how I will pay it back.

"Stop worrying about that," she says, looking seriously annoyed that I keep bringing up the topic of money.

"Sorry," I say, and she glares at me. "Right... Sorry for that... sorry."

"I give up on you," Anna says with a sigh. "Just sit your ass down"—she pats one end of the gym bag as she sits down on the other—"and have a pop," she says holding a coke out to me.

I take the can and sit down, right against her. It is very warm out to sit so close, but I don't say anything. "I guess we'll just watch movies tomorrow?"

"What?" she says, glancing up to me from her phone.

"Tomorrow, since we will have nothing else to do."

"We're in LA with no plans at all. Nothing to do. No jobs, no work, no nothing," she says, grinning at me.

"Okay... So, is there something you want to do?"

"Yeah, but I'm not telling you. Right now, we are booked at a Hilton, and a car is on its way," she says, and smiles at me.

"A Hilton? Don't feel like you need to get somewhere nice for my sake."

"Maybe you are cool with a dive motel. But I have been in the sleeper long enough, that I deserve to be a princess for a while." This makes me laugh.

"Yes, you do."

"Thank you." She smiles. "And you'll have your own your bed on the ground." She says this as a joke, but it feels more like she wanted me to know that we aren't sharing a bed.

"I have only slept up there twice."

"It's a top bunk... twice is two too many times," she says, taking a drink of her coke.

We sit in the hot parking lot for a few more minutes without saying anything. It is the moments of silence that are hard, those are the moments that are strained. Everything is fine as long as we just keep talking. *If I only had something to talk about*, I think. *I should ask how Evy is doing. I don't really know anything about her... I mean, them,* I think, correcting myself mentally.

"So," Anna says right as I open my mouth to ask about Evy, "sorry if I made things awkward earlier in the truck. I think the heat and stress of everything going to shit had just gotten to me."

"Um... Yeah... It was the same for me," I lie.

"So, let's just forget it happened. I didn't mean anything by it," she says, looking down at her can of coke while she swirls the bottom of the can in circles. "You're a great friend, and I don't want this to screw things up," she says, and downs the last of her coke.

"It won't, and thank you. You're also a great friend," I say, and down the rest of my can of coke.

"Nother pop?" she says, holding a can up for me. "It is the nice thing about not being on the road."

"You have a good point there," I say, taking the can and cracking it open. My phone dings, and I check it to see a message from Alesha; not that there is anyone else that would be messaging me.

Alesha: Holy shit!

Alesha: You tie him up, I can be there in a day.

Me: So, you also think he is attractive?

Alesha: Goddamn you.

Alesha: This is so unfair.

"Well," I say, looking over to Anna, "Alesha agrees with you on the tow truck driver," I say, glancing around to make sure no one is within earshot.

"Told you." Anna smirks. "And Evy also asked about him after I sent them the photo."

"So, I guess that makes me the odd one out," I say.

"No, it doesn't. You gotta stop acting like you're the odd one out for not wanting to fuck every hot guy we come across."

"Right." I think for a second. "I hope this gets easier soon."

"How many years were you hiding your sexuality?" Anna asks, knowing the answer. "You can't undo decades of thinking in a few weeks, months, or even years."

"I'm sure you're right."

"Once you're making money and things are going better, you should think about finding a therapist to talk to. Might do you a lot of good working past a lot of the shit that has been crammed into your head."

"I hadn't really thought of it. But... maybe you're right."

"And if you still have trouble figuring things out, and being comfortable with another woman, then we'll just hire you a nice escort," she says matter-of-factly, taking a sip from her coke.

"An escort?"

"You know... a prostitute."

"I know what an escort is," I snap at her, keeping my voice down. "Even someone old like me knows that." I take a drink of my coke.

"You're not old, not even close."

"I'm not young," I mutter.

"Stop it," she says, elbowing me with a laugh.

"Fine... I'll try," I say, and we sit in silence for a moment or two.

"I just realized something," Anna says with a mischievous smile.

"What?" I say, unsure and not trusting her.

"You never said no to the idea of getting you an escort." She smiles big.

"It was implied," I say, staring at her.

"Yeah, sure it was," she says with a wink.

"Yes, it was."

"I had other plans for tomorrow," she says, looking off into space, like she is talking to herself. "But maybe this would be better."

"Haha, real funny."

"I'm going to start looking," she says as she swipes open her phone.

"Real funny, you can stop now," I say, laughing a little, giving her a little push. We sit there for another minute or so.

"What do you think?" Anna asks, rotating her phone my way.

"About wha—You are actually searching escorts?" I say, wide-eyed as I stare at a photo of a woman who is more or less naked.

"Your type?"

"Will you stop it?" I say, looking away from the phone.

"Okay, fine," she says, closing the page, "I just thought we might as well get some prices"—she sticks her phone into her pocket—"Aww, your cheeks are turning all red." She laughs.

"You are an awful person."

"Come on, I was just joking. You need to stop being so stuffy. You're no better now than you were when I picked you up." This gets my attention, because I have never liked people calling me stuffy.

"Yes."

"What?" she asks, puzzled.

"From what I saw... Yes, she's my type," I say with my chin held high, deciding I won't let Anna be right this time. She looks at me surprised, and then grins.

16

Hotel Surprise

I step into our room and swing the door shut behind me. I look around as I set my bags down; which are literally plastic bags, which seemed to confuse the woman at the front desk. But I don't blame her. There probably aren't too many people that check in with plastic shopping bags in place of suitcases. Once Anna explained that our truck broke down, this seemed to make them more sympathetic than annoyed.

"So, this is a Hilton room," I say to no one, as I slip my shoes off and walk across the room. I look at the two queen beds. A big part of me is disappointed that there wasn't some mistake in the booking, leaving us with only one bed we would have to share. But, of course, there were no mistakes and we have our own beds. "You should have known that wouldn't happen," I tell myself. *You have been reading those stories too much,* I think. But, the beds are so close that there isn't even enough room to stand between them, so that's something at least.

I already told Anna that I was going to take a shower first thing, feeling like I need it like never before, after the heat of cleaning up the debris on the highway, and sitting outside the truck waiting for our car to pick us up. So, she said I could take one first, and she would go do our laundry in the hotels laundromat.

Opening the door to the bathroom, I freeze at the site of the enormous bathtub, it is one with jets and the digital spa controls. I run my hand over it, having only seen them on TV and in movies. I wonder why Justin and I never stayed anywhere this nice the few times we did go somewhere. But instead we always stayed in what was most likely the cheapest place he could find, always saying that we just needed a place to sleep, nothing more. But now, now that I am here and running my hand over the *"more"* he said we didn't need. The more I know that I want and deserve that *"more."*

However, I only have about an hour before Anna will be done with the laundry. I swing the bathroom door shut and start the water running into the tub. It fills as I quickly undress and step into the shower to wash the visible sweat and dirt off. The water runs off my skin with a faint tint of brown, and I wonder if I have ever been this dirty.

It doesn't take as long as I thought it might to figure out the controls to the spa bath, and it is wonderful. "This could be a vacation by itself, who needs to go anywhere else?" I sigh as I lean back and close my eyes as the water bubbles and foams around me.

"You in here!" I suddenly hear, with a knock on the bathroom door. I jump, sloshing water over the side of the bathtub.

"Yes. Don't come in!" I yell back. "Who is it?" I say, not even sure who knocked.

"Who is it?" Anna says. "It's me... Are you expecting someone else? You didn't hire that escort, did you?"

"No. I just didn't hear you well at first."

"I'm not coming in," she says as I hear the door handle moving. I look to see it open just enough so she doesn't have to talk through the door.

"Are you done with the laundry?" I ask.

"Yeah, it's been nearly an hour and a half."

"Oh..."

"Did you fall asleep?" she asks with a little laugh.

"I think I did. This bathtub is incredible."

"Really?"

"I'll be out in a minute."

"Okay," she says, and I hear the door close.

I get out, towel off, and then put on one of the hotel robes. There are even slippers which are more comfortable than I thought they would be. "Just wondering," I say, walking out of the bathroom, "why are we going somewhere tomorrow? This is pretty nice." Anna just smiles, staring at me. "What?" I say, feeling like she didn't hear anything I just said, but is distracted by something about me.

"It's nothing. You just have a towel wrapped around your head."

"So?"

"It's just... really cute," she says before looking away to pick up her phone. But it seems like that is just an excuse to look away.

"Oh... well, I just always do that to dry my hair. Justin always said it was silly, and I should just use a hairdryer."

"Just another reason he's an asshole with the IQ of a fucking cabbage." This makes me smile. "But trust me, tomorrow will be great."

"Okay..." I say, turning on the huge TV.

"And we're in LA" Anna says walking into the bathroom, swinging the door shut only about three-quarters of the way. "We're not spending it sitting in a hotel room, no matter how nice it is."

"I guess you have a point," I say.

"Damn straight I do," she says as I hear the shower turn on, and my mind is instantly thinking of her standing in that glass shower. I look for a movie or something on the TV, but I still keep thinking about her in there, wondering if she will soon be in the bathtub. I bite my lip as I wonder, *What would happen if I went in there and kissed her right there in the shower. If I got up right now and went in there, leaving my robe here... what then? What would Anna do? Was it just the heat of the day earlier when we were in the truck?*

"You find something?" I blink and look over to see Anna standing there in a robe, drying her hair.

"Oh... nothing yet," I say with a swallow, knowing that I seem to have another fantasy to add to my seemingly always-growing list of Anna-based fantasies. "You're not taking a bath?" I ask.

"I thought about it. But I thought I would watch a movie with you," she says, sitting down on my bed next to me, instead of on her own bed. "Oh, and why is the bathtub so big?"

"I figured that was just the way places like this were," I honestly say.

"Well, yeah. But why a spa jet bathtub big enough for two, when the beds are separate?" she says, pointing at her empty bed. I look over at it, and then back to mine.

"I guess that's true. They must not have planned separate beds when they built the room," I say. But my mind can't stop thinking about the fact that the bathtub is big enough for two, and that Anna noticed. I also wonder why I didn't notice, but I was pretty happy at the idea of just taking a bath, so I guess I wasn't thinking about other things.

"Anyway, let's find that movie."

We sit on my bed with the covers pulled up and watch another romantic comedy, like nothing ever happened earlier today. At least that's the way it seems, and the way Anna acts. But I wonder if it is just that, an act. Because I notice my heart is beating quicker than it was last night as we sat together watching a movie, and I pray that my acting is good enough that she doesn't notice, because I don't want to lose her, even if she is no more than a friend.

"I love that one. Have you seen it?" Anna asks as the credits start rolling.

"Maybe a little bit of it when I was a kid. It seemed a bit familiar."

"My dad loves the classics, so I have seen Holiday a couple of times. But I can never get enough of Grant and Hepburn," she says.

"They are great," I agree. "The old movies have such a great quality to them that new movies just don't have."

"Yeah, they do. I think a few new movies have it, but it is hard to find," Anna says, picking up her phone. "I'm starved. You feel like some pizza?"

"Sounds great. I am hungry now that you mention it."

I flick through movies while she places an order to have it delivered, not sure what to put in next. "Alright, it will be here soon."

"So, where are we going tomorrow?"

"Well, I wanted it to be a surprise," she says, turning to me, suddenly looking excited, "but I can't stand it." She has the biggest smile on her face.

"What is it?" I say, laughing at her overwhelming excitement.

"I got us tickets to Magical Land tomorrow!" I just stare at her for a second.

"What?" I say, knowing I must have misheard her.

"First thing tomorrow morning, I am taking you to Magical Land," she says with a big smile. And I'm in shock by this. No one has ever done anything like this for me.

"Are you kidding?"

"No, I'm not that mean." She laughs. "Your annoying positivity about the truck blowing a tire made me realize that maybe this was the chance we have both been waiting for to see Magical Land. Plus, it really sucks that all those years, no one would ever go with you or take you." I just stare at her, unsure of what to say. "Are you crying? I didn't mean to make you cry."

"No... sorry," I say, wiping my eyes with the sleeve of my robe. "But no one has ever done something this nice for me."

"And that's why they're all assholes." She smiles.

"You're right, and that's why this will be better. Before, I would have been trying to watch the kids the whole time, and Justin would have been in a bad mood; because he always was when we did things he didn't like—"

"Asshole," she interjects.

"But now there won't be any of that if it is just me and you," I say, feeling so happy about this. So happy that I am single, it is the first time I have felt the realization that I can do what I want.

"You suddenly look very happy... What is it?" she asks with a smirk, knowing me well enough to know I am thinking of something.

"I'm just realizing how great it is to be single, to do what I want." Anna smiles big, excited for me. "I have an idea to make the trip there a little more fun."

"What?" Anna asks suspiciously.

"I'm going to wear that shirt with the fifth-wheel hitch on it you got me." I grin.

"No way? You really are?"

"It is something I wouldn't have even considered before. But I'm doing it."

"Then I will wear the shirt Evy got me," Anna says.

"You brought it?" I ask.

"Yeah, it was in with my other t-shirts, and I just grabbed all of them since I don't have that many."

"This is going to be great!" I say, grabbing Anna and hugging her. I don't know what it is like for Anna, but it is awkward and uncomfortable for me. But I am so excited I just don't care.

It's seven thirty in the morning and the air is only slightly cool as Anna and I stand at the front of the line to get into Magical Land, with more people forming a line behind us, most are tired-looking kids, and even more tired-looking parents. I hope that time will pass quickly as we stand here, and that none of the kids will start whining or crying.

"How are you feeling?" Anna asks me. "It seemed like you didn't sleep too well last night."

"I feel great, but I didn't sleep very well. I take it you didn't either?"

"Not really. I think I was too excited about coming here."

"Me too!" The little girl in a tutu next to us yells excitedly. Her mother doesn't even look up from her phone, and I hate her for not enjoying her child's excitement. It makes me wish my kids had wanted to come, or had ever been excited about anything like this with me next to them. I think about what I would have been like, standing here like this mother with Aaron and Angela when they were the age of her little girl, with this bubbling, overwhelmed excitement.

I am surprised as Anna instantly squats down to the little girl's level, smiling big. "I have always wanted to come to Magical Land. I have been dreaming of it," Anna says to the little girl.

"I have wanted to come my entire life," the little girl says like this has been an utter eternity, and not four years. "But I am finally here, and—"

"Stop bothering the woman, Sweetie," her mother says, finally glancing up from her phone.

"Oh, no. She isn't bothering me at all," Anna says with a smile. The woman replies with a quick meaningless smile and continues with her phone.

Anna just continues talking with the little girl, and then the little boy behind them joins in. They talk about Magical Land, their favorite characters from the Magical movies, princesses, and everything in between. But Anna isn't just talking with the little kids to entertain them; she is excited and passionate about the conversation. She is making this a magical day they will always remember before they are even in the park.

Watching how wonderful Anna is with the two children, how natural she is with kids, how kind and loving she is, I realize that I am completely in love with her. That she is someone I want to always be with in every way.

17
Magical Land

Once we walk through the gate and are actually in the park, I am amazed at how extraordinary it is. The amount of detail is incredible. I find myself staring at a trash can, because it is made to perfectly blend into the scene, not looking like a trash can at all.

"If you're done staring at that trash can, I have a plan," Anna says, laughing a little.

"It is so perfect though, it is actually pretty."

"Yeah, you're right. But the plan."

"Okay, what's this plan?" I say looking at her.

"Let's hit as many of the popular rides as possible before the crowds are bad—"

"So, we are just going to run through the park?"

"Let me finish," she says, slapping me on the arm. "If we do that, then we can enjoy the aesthetics and less popular rides after the crowds are here. This way we aren't waiting in line for thirty minutes or more for those rides."

"That is actually a really good idea," I admit.

"Then get your butt in gear," Anna says, jerking a thumb at the fast-growing number of people coming into the park.

"Where first?"

"Just follow me," she says, turning and walking in a very direct way.

"To the end of the earth," I whisper.

"What?" Anna says, glancing back.

"Didn't say anything." I smile.

We hit one ride after another, only having to wait a few minutes at most. Riding our favorites two or three times while the lines are still short, and we are both as overexcited and ecstatically happy as any child in the park. Adults stare at Anna and I as we hold on to each other laughing so hard that we can hardly stand, and we don't even know why we are laughing, we just are.

Anna is right though, with every ride we exit there is a very noticeable increase in the amount of people in the park. Our being at the front when the gates opened made all the difference; plus the advantage of not having slow-walking children with us. But, after an hour, it feels like we are no longer ahead of anyone, so we slow down to a more comfortable pace as the heat becomes more noticeable. We also start going into the little shops to look around. We don't buy anything, but it is still fun and lets us cool off.

"Do you like rollercoasters?" Anna asks me as we stand, staring at a very large one.

"I don't know... I've never been on one," I say, somewhat in awe of the impressive piece of steel engineering that twists and turns in seemingly impossible ways, made even more amazing when a short row of people rocket past spiraling into the air in one of the coaster cars. "But... I think I might just do it."

"Seriously? This one?" Anna says. I look at her, and she is staring at me like I have lost it.

"Yeah."

"I know that you are wanting to be a new you, and stuff. But you don't have to prove it by doing this," she says, like I am being pushed into this.

"I want to."

"You will have to on your own," Anna says.

"What?" I say, disappointed.

"Sorry, I can not do roller coasters. I have always hated them."

I think about it for a second before saying, "I understand, but I am doing it anyway."

"Okay, I'll wait to drag you off after then," Anna says with a grin. And we walk over to the line, which isn't very long. I wonder if a short line is a bad sign, but I'm doing this. I will not turn back.

A man and woman behind us argue in a playful way; obviously a couple, they look to be in their early twenties. "I am not doing it," the man is saying as the woman pulls on his hand. I notice the rings, and wonder how long they have been married.

"Come on, it will be fun," she whines while laughing.

"No way. They make me sick, I will puke everywhere," he says, laughing with her, but serious about not going.

"But I don't want to go alone," she says with disappointment as she stops pulling on his hand.

I suddenly have an idea. "You can ride with me," I say to them. "Anna won't go with me," I say, gesturing towards Anna.

The woman looks at me for a second. "Really?"

"I've never been on one, and it would be nice riding with someone else."

"I've only ridden on little ones. But I want to ride on this one so bad," she says.

"What if you puke on her?" the man says.

"I won't, I'm not you," she says with a mean playfulness.

"What if you puke on her?" Anna repeats to me.

"I won't, I'm not you," I say in the same way as the young woman starts laughing.

"Come on, let's leave these chickens behind," the woman says, looping her arm through mine like we are old friends and steps into line with me. "The chicken bench is over there," she says, pointing at a bench next to the exit of the rollercoaster.

"Have fun, and no whining to me if you get sick," the man says.

"Yeah, same goes," Anna says.

I watch them walk off together, talking. "She your girlfriend?" the young woman asks.

"What?" I say, feeling knocked off balance. "Oh, no. She is just my friend."

"Oh, sorry. Just thought you were."

"No, it's fine," I say with a smile, not wanting her to worry. "I'm Mary."

"I'm Madison. And I will really try to not puke on you," she says with a smile.

"I'll do the same. Have you ever been to Magical Land before?"

"Nope, first time. But I have always wanted to come, for like my entire fucking life."

"Me too," I say.

"I wanted my friends to come, but they couldn't make it," she says. "So, you're lucky you're here with your friend."

"I really am. I hope your friends can come next time," I say as we are suddenly next up in line. "Are you ready?" I ask her.

"Hell yeah," she says, and her happiness makes me excited.

We get into our seats; they are close together. The worker pulls the padded bar over our shoulders, and there is no going back. There is a light beside the track that looks like the lights I have seen on drag race starts; I remember them from when Justin would sometimes watch races on TV. It is easy for me and Madison to see because we are in the first seat.

There is a long beep, and the first amber light lights up. "Does this take off fast?" I ask Madison as the second of the four lights turns amber.

"I don't know," she says as the third light lights up amber. "I think it goes up a hill fir—" She doesn't have time to finish what she is saying before the fourth and final light turns green and we are both pushed into the backs of our seats as everything around us turns into an instant blur. It feels like someone is sitting on my chest. I want to look over at Madison, but I can't seem to move my head.

I start to think this might have been a big mistake when the force against me lessens, but we haven't slowed down, and now we are going straight up. All I can see is the clear blue sky. Until I am suddenly staring straight down. I hear screaming and look over to see it is Madison next to me, and I can't tell from the look on her face if it is good or bad screaming.

The roller coaster moves so fast that it all feels like a blur and is hard to even see where we are or what is next. But the one thing I do know is we are going higher, and higher, until we peak and are suddenly going slower as we go around a gentle curve. "Are you okay?" Madison asks me.

I look over at her. "Yeah, I'm fine. You?"

"I think I will be fine... Oh, wow," she says, looking ahead, and you can see across the entire city. It is a beautiful view. It feels like one of the highest points in the city. But then it dawns on me, *If we are this high up, there is only one way down,* I think right as I see the track in front of us disappear. "Oh, fuck!" Madison screams as the feeling of the ground disappearing hits us, the feeling of falling.

Somehow, even with the padded bar-type harness over our shoulders holding us in our seats, I feel like Madison is wrapped around me, holding on like a drowning cat. And as we plummet straight towards the ground, I scream with her... or at least I think I do. I'm not sure if it is me screaming or not, but I can't exactly spend the time or energy to figure it out.

Then we're suddenly pulling out of the drop, and are pushed into the padded bars, stopping as fast as we took off. Then we slowly roll forward and stop at the platform. "Are you okay?" I ask her.

"Yeah... yeah, I'm okay," she says, not sounding completely okay. "If John asks, it isn't bad at all, okay?"

"Same if Anna asks," I say.

"Deal," Madison says as the bar lifts for us to get out.

"So, you don't want to go again?" I ask with a smirk.

"Fuck no... It was really a bad idea," she says quiet enough that her husband won't hear, since he and Anna are standing close as we walk out.

"You lived," Anna says with a smile.

"Of course," I say, like it was no big deal at all.

"Yeah, it was great," Madison says.

"Great?" her husband questions.

"Yes, John, it was great, because I'm not a chicken like you," she says.

"You didn't scream or freak out?" he says.

"No."

"Then what's that?" he says, pointing behind us.

Madison and I turn to see a big screen with a photo of the roller coaster car dropping off the final huge hill, Madison and I right there in the front car, screaming our heads off. And the photo explains how Madison was clinging onto me. It is because I met her halfway, as best I could. We were both grabbing onto each other the best we could while screaming, and I never even knew it.

"Oh, well, I am buying a copy of that," Anna says, stepping up to the counter.

"Me too," John says.

"It's not what it looks like," Madison says, still trying to save her pride. "You are supposed to scream on roller coasters."

"That is way more than just screaming," he says, laughing. There is a good amount of more cussing from Madison, but there is no stopping him from buying the photo. And I don't even try to convince Anna of anything, because I just don't care, I did it and that's all that matters to me.

Anna and I walk away together as John and Madison head in the other direction. "So," Anna says, walking closer to me than is needed, "you actually did it. You went on one of the scariest roller coasters in the world."

"What?" I say, looking at her.

"John told me that after you were already on it."

"Wow, I didn't know that..." I say, thinking about it.

"But you actually did it"—she leans even closer so the swarms of children don't hear—"you crazy mother fucking bitch," she says, smiling. Her breath is warm against my ear, and despite the heat of the sun... I love the feel of her warmth. I bite my lip and think about what else I should take chances on.

We continue on, going from ride to ride, attraction to attraction. Taking shelter from the heat every so often in one of the shops, and we continue this until the sun starts to set. "Are you as tired as I am?" Anna asks.

"I'm getting close. I guess running around an amusement park for ten hours will do that."

"Yeah, I guess it does," she says with a smile. "Come on, there is one more ride I wanted to save for last."

"Really? What is it?"

"Not telling, just follow me," she says, and I do without asking any more questions. It isn't long before we are staring up at a massive Ferris wheel. I had seen it in the distance earlier in the day; given its size it would have been hard to not notice it, but I had forgotten about it.

"We can watch the sunset from it," Anna says.

"Oh, I never thought of that."

"Let's go before everyone else gets the same idea... I want a car to ourselves." I just nod to this and follow her to the Ferris wheel. We step into the car of the Ferris wheel, and the operator closes the door behind us.

"Is it air-conditioned in here?" I ask, noticing that it is a very pleasant temperature inside.

"I think it is," Anna says as I sit down on the seat, and Anna sits next to me instead of across from me.

"How long does it take to circle?" I ask.

"It circles once and takes twenty minutes. So we should get a nice long view of the sunset," she says. The sun is already sitting just above the ocean surface.

We sit in silence, just looking out the window. We both take short videos of the view, I send mine to Alesha, and Anna sends hers to Evy. "Can I ask you a personal question?" I ask as we approach the top.

"I thought we were past asking first?" She grins at me.

"Do you want kids? I mean, you were just really good with those little kids this morning," I add quickly, seeing the sudden change on her face at the strange question.

"Um... Well... I, of course, have thought of it a little. And I have always liked kids." She says this with a smile, almost like remembering a memory that hasn't existed. "But... I really don't think I will ever have any myself."

"Oh, I see."

"Why do you ask?" she says, knowing it wasn't just because of the little kids this morning.

"I guess I was just thinking, and I know that you are about that age—"

"Actually..." Anna interrupts. "Honestly, I never wanted to do the single mother thing. I was too scared to raise kids by myself—"

"You have family," I say.

"There is no fucking way Evy is going to help me with something like that, and Mom and Dad are past the helping with kids' age," she says with a laugh at even the idea of it. "Anyway, it was never something I was really disappointed about or anything. And I wasn't going to get married just to have kids. That's just not me."

"That's good you don't regret it," I say as we both stare at the sun setting over the water, as we look out over the top of the city. "It is really beautiful."

"Yeah, it is," Anna says softly.

We sit in silence as we lower slowly toward the ground, and it is a comfortable silence that almost feels warm as it wraps around us. "Looks like we are back on the ground," I say, as the car is only a few feet from the platform.

"Yeah... we are. Too bad, I really didn't want to come back down," Anna says with a hint of disappointment in her, the same disappointment that I feel in myself.

The man operating the ride opens the car door, and I notice that there isn't a line, only a few people. "Is there any way we can go around again?" I ask.

"Sure, no one else is really wanting on anyway," he says, walking slowly beside the car with the door still open. "Enjoy the lights. Most people miss out on the night view." He smiles and closes the door.

"Thanks," Anna says.

"I thought it would be nice too. It is so peaceful, just watching the view with you... it's really nice.

"It is... And it is so much better than an evening in the sleeper," Anna says with a tired smile.

"Are you tired?" I ask.

"I am, and this damn Ferris wheel seems to be rocking me to sleep," she says with a soft laugh.

"Why don't you lie against me and watch the view?"

"Okay," she says, gently lying against me, her head resting on my shoulder. I softly lay my head against hers, like it is the most natural thing in the world, and with every breath, I breathe her in.

We are nearly at the top again, and the city lights are surprisingly beautiful. Something about it just makes me know I need to say it. "Anna?"

"Yeah?" she says softly.

"I... I think, I'm falling in love with you," I whisper. She doesn't say anything, or move... until she does.

She slowly moves, sitting up. Anna looks me in the eyes, her face in the deep colored contrast of the colored lights on the outside of the Ferris wheel car, and she just stares into my eyes, not saying anything. I lean closer to her, and she doesn't move closer, but she also doesn't move away. I am calm, and something just feels right as our lips touch.

I kiss her, then she leans into me, kissing me back. The Ferris wheel, the lights, Magical Land, and the city of LA disappear from existence as I kiss someone I am in love with for the first time in my life. I know this from the feeling inside of me, a feeling I never felt with Justin, a feeling I have waited my whole life for, that I gave up on so many years ago. A feeling I even doubted at times existed.

Our kisses turn from new and gentle to passionate as fireworks start bursting in the air, lighting up the dark sky in reds, yellows, and blues. Even though they are Magical Lands' scheduled fireworks display, it feels like they are just for us. As I feel Anna tug lightly at my bottom lip, I never want the Ferris wheel to stop, the fireworks to end, or time to move forward. I want this moment for the rest of my life.

18

First Love

"I bet it was great, wasn't it?" the Ferris wheel operator says as he opens the door of our car with a smile.

"Yes, it was, thanks," I say, unable to stop from giggling a little as Anna and I step out of the car. "Good night."

"Good night to you two, too," he says, seeming very happy, and something about it makes me think that he knows.

Anna and I walk in silence through the crowd that is working their way towards any of the shops that sell food. "Do you want to eat here, or get something to take back?" Anna asks me.

"Oh, let's get something to take back. If that's okay with you?"

"It would be great. I think I have been sitting in a truck too long, my feet are really tired... But, I am now kind of awake otherwise," she says with a smile, and takes my hand in hers as we walk. It doesn't take as long as I thought it might to walk out of the park, and even though it is dark. The city sidewalks and streets are so well lit you would never know it was night.

"How about Italian?" I ask as we approach an Italian restaurant.

"Do they do takeout?" I point at the takeout sign in the window. "Oh, guess they do," she says with a laugh, and then kisses me. My cheeks instantly turn warm. Anna smiles and laughs. "That little kiss makes you blush?"

"I didn't mean to. It... It's just different here," I say as some people walk past.

"You're right, it is. But it makes you look so cute," she says. Smiling, as I am pretty sure I blush more. "Come on, let's order some dinner," she says, holding the door open for me.

We decide on lasagna and bread, and the person at the counter says it will be five or ten minutes. Part of me is surprised it's not going to be a longer wait, given how many people are in the restaurant. We sit down on a bench just outside the door to wait, and my phone gives a ding. I pull it out, knowing that it is Alesha.

Alesha: OMG, I wish I was there.

"Alesha is jealous," I say, not looking up from my phone. "I mean, of the view, in the video," I add quickly.

"I knew that's what you were talking about," Anna says. "Evy's the same. Though, they said it isn't worth putting up with Magical Land for it."

"Evy really doesn't like that place, does sh—they?"

"Nope, they say it is nothing but misogynistic propaganda for gender role enforcement."

"Isn't that a little much? I mean, there are quite a few characters in their movies that are gay," I say.

"I am astonished that you even know that," she says, looking surprised. "Did your church have a 'burn the children's movie night' or something?"

"Haha, really funny. My church never did that... probably because they didn't know about the characters," I say, as Anna starts laughing hard. "Because there were members that definitely would have done that. But, I knew from my research while I was trying to figure out my own things. One article leads to another, and I always liked Magical Land stuff, so I read them."

"Okay. But," she says, "it's only the newest characters that are queer, and not evil. All the old ones were always the evil villains."

"That's true..." I say, thinking about it.

"And name me one trans character."

"Yeah... Evy might be right," I say and look at Anna. "Does this mean I shouldn't like Magical Land?"

"I still like them, and they're getting better. Evy just doesn't think it is happening fast enough. But, it was hard for them growing up with no role models, never having a character on TV or in a movie that they related to... It really sucked." Anna says, sounding like it hurts her that Evy didn't have this, that they struggled so hard to find their place.

"I'm sorry that it was so hard... I know that it isn't the same, but I can relate a bit to that. My parents wouldn't allow anything with a gay character to be played in the house."

"You had it worse than Evy or me. We might have been confused and had trouble figuring things out, but our family was supportive. You didn't have that, and I can't imagine."

"Thanks... But, things change," I say, and this time I kiss her.

"I bet our food's about done. I'm going to use the restroom, and then I will grab our food on the way out. Here"—she holds out her phone—"take my phone so you have Wi-Fi."

"Thanks," I say, sticking her phone in my pocket as she pulls open the door to go back inside.

Me: The day was wonderful.

The indication of Alesha texting instantly pops onto my screen.

Alesha: That was so nice of her to take you.

Me: It was.

Alesha: Are you sure there is nothing there?

Alesha: Between you two.

I think about it for a second, *She's my best friend, and this is what best friends are for,* I think as I tap out the two words.

Me: We kissed.

Alesha: WTF!!!!!!!!

Alesha: How?

Alesha: Like, when?

Alesha: Was it just like a small kiss?

Alesha: An in-the-moment thing?

Alesha: Why aren't you responding?

Me: Because you won't give me a chance!

Alesha: Sorry, I'll wait.

Me: We were on the Ferris wheel.

Alesha: The Ferris wheel? I'm sorry, is this a 50s high school romance?

Me: Fine, I won't tell you.

Alesha: Sorry, (mouth zipped shut emoji).

Me: I also told her I am falling in love with her.

Alesha: Holy fuck.

Me: Was that a mistake?

Me: Am I moving too quick?

"Hey, you ready to eat?" I hear Anna say from behind me, making me jump. "Oh, sorry, I didn't mean to scare you."

"No, it's fine, I just didn't hear you," I say, sliding my phone into my pocket as it dings again with Alesha's response.

"You can get that," Anna says.

"Oh, it's just Alesha. I'll answer it later."

We walk down the sidewalk, not saying anything. "What have you told Evy about me?" I suddenly ask, just wanting to know for some reason.

"What? Oh... I guess just the normal stuff. We're close, but we don't just tell each other everything. I'm sure Alesha knows more about me than Evy does about you."

"I don't... I haven't told her everything about you. I mean I—we do talk about you a little, but just in passing," I say, feeling embarrassed.

"Oh dear God," Anna says, looking at me, "you've told her everything, haven't you?" She stares at me.

"Not quite everything..." Anna keeps staring at me. "Okay, yeah... Pretty much everything," I say quietly, feeling ashamed.

"Shit, you can't lie, can you?" she says with a smile, knowing that she now has something on me.

"I can lie."

"Oh really? Then what was that?"

"I just can't lie to you."

"Oh..." Anna says, her whole expression changing.

"But I didn't tell Alesha things to gossip... You know how new this all is to me. I just needed someone to talk to, and ask for a little advice. I really—"

"Hey, I don't care that you tell her about us. She's your friend." I feel relieved with these words and her smile. "Besides, it isn't gossip if it is what's happening with you."

"I guess you do have a point."

We walk another half block before Anna stops and looks at me sincerely. "But you can also just ask me if you aren't sure about something, I understand, and whatever it is, it's okay. Also, I don't know exactly what our relationship is. But, I'm not going to push you in any way. I want you to go at your own speed. Tell me if you ever aren't ready for something or if I'm moving too fast. I don't want to do that." I just stare at her. It is the kindest thing she could have said, and it makes me love her even more.

"Thank you. I will do that, and tell me if I am ever going too fast or something."

"Don't worry, I am fine and am okay with whenever you are ready." She smiles, and I know what she means.

We get back to our room and instantly start a movie as we sit down at the end of my bed; since it is more directly in front of the TV, and start eating our dinner. Having only eaten some small things while at Magical Land, we are both starving.

"We should eat at that place tomorrow for lunch," Anna says after we finish eating. "That was really good. So much better than microwave lasagna."

"It was good," I say. "Well, I'm going to go take a shower. I feel surprisingly dirty after an entire day in the sun and heat."

"Alright," Anna says, pausing the movie and picking up her phone.

It feels good to be out of the clothes that smell of sweat and whatever the mystery smell of the amusement park is that I don't want to ever think about. I run the shower on the cool side, and the water feels nice, dissipating the remaining heat of the day that my body was holding onto. But as the water runs over me, I think about the day, and it feels like it has been several days, not just one. But there isn't a second of it that doesn't make me smile like a child in an ice cream shop.

Even the roller coaster; maybe it most of all. Not only was it actually fun, but it is something that I am proud of, something that I can tell people about. Someday I will tell Aaron and Angela how their mom; a person they think is so predictable, rode one of the scariest roller coasters in the world.

I dry myself, put on my robe, and wrap my hair with a towel. "You aren't asleep?" I ask as I walk out of the bathroom, seeing Anna in the same place, but now lying back.

"Nope"—she sits up—"I am surprisingly not that tired. I guess I was just tired of walking. Anyway, I'm taking a shower. I'll be out in a bit, and we'll finish the movie."

"Okay," I say as she stands and walks to the bathroom, but she stops next to me, and gives me a kiss. As she closes the bathroom door, the fact we are in the same room, our beds being so close, becomes very real.

I grab my phone, remembering that I haven't checked to see what Alesha texted back.

Alesha: I don't know if you are moving too quickly, it depends on you and Anna, what she is like?

Alesha: You are leaving me hanging again.

Alesha: Why do you have to tease me?

Alesha: Bitch. ;)

I smile at her text, because it was awful of me to leave in the middle of a conversation like that.

Me: Okay, sorry. We were walking back to our room and had a quick dinner.

It isn't a second before she has seen the text, and my phone instantly rings. I answer it quickly.

"Hello?"

"I thought it would be easier to call. I'm in the middle of putting everything back together for the night," she says, and the changing volume of her talking tells me she has me on speaker again.

"That's fine, thanks," I say, sitting in a chair at the far side of the room, so I am farther from the bathroom; not wanting Anna to hear. "Anna's in the shower, so I don't have too long."

"Okay, to the point, then. I personally don't think it is a mistake to tell someone you are in love with them, even if you have only known them for ten minutes."

"Really?"

"Yeah, why wait? Better to just put yourself out there, and if you fall flat, get up and keep going. It's better than not knowing."

"I guess you have a point," I say, thinking about it.

"So, are you going to sleep with her tonight?"

"What?" I say, nearly dropping my phone. "I have only known her for like four days."

"You are looking at this all wrong."

"How am I looking at it wrong?" I ask, confused.

"First of all, it is all about how you and Anna feel. If you have known each other ten minutes or ten years before you have sex, it's always your choice, and not set by a predetermined amount of time." This does make sense, in a way. "Also, how long would you say an average date is?"

"I don't know..." I say, thinking about this, trying to figure it out like one of those word math problems that I never got right. "I guess if you have dinner, and see a movie... Three hours?"

"Close enough. That might actually be on the long side. And in a movie you are watching the movie, you really aren't that connected," Alesha says.

"That's true."

"Now, we'll say you and Anna have known each other for four days. That's ninety-six hours. We'll say forty hours of that was sleeping. So, you two have been together constantly for fifty-six hours. At three hours a date, that is equal to... eighteen or nineteen dates, more or less," she says matter-of-factly.

"I hadn't thought of that," I say, a bit in shock.

"It is no wonder you have fallen in love with her. You two know each other better than most people when they get married. Plus, you have even seen each other at some very stressful times, and that makes a big difference."

"I never thought of that. But you are right."

"Plus, being in such a tight space in that truck, that is also something most wouldn't be able to handle."

I hear the shower turn off, since Anna hasn't closed the door all the way. I don't know if she did this so I could hear when she was coming, or if this not closing doors all the way is a thing with her. "Anna is coming, so I have to go. But, thank you so much. I feel much better."

"Not moving as fast as you thought, are you?" Alesha says with a smug sound to her voice.

"No... No, I guess I'm not moving fast at all."

"Are you going for it?" she asks.

"Like I would tell you," I say with a smug sound myself.

"Ooh, you are going for it aren't you?"

"Gotta go."

"I know you will tell me later."

"I have to go," I repeat.

"Hey," she says, in a way that makes me pause, and not hang up. "Just do what you and Anna feel like you want to do. Don't think about all the shit people in your past have told you, or would think. Fuck them, this is your life now. Remember, you're the badass bitch that rode a badass roller coaster, even when no one else would."

"You're right, thanks," I say, happy I have her.

"Okay, good night."

"Good night," I say back.

"You better tell me what the fuck happens, first thing in the morning!" I hear her yell as I hang up.

"Are you on the phone?" Anna asks, walking out in her robe.

"Oh, Alesha just called. I'm off though," I say, typing out a short text.

Me: I will.

Me: P.S. Nice math skills. :)

Alesha: Thanks.

Alesha: And no one uses P.S. when texting. Hahaha

"What?" Anna asks as I laugh at the text. "Sorry, not my business."

"Oh no, it's fine. It's just, apparently, you're not supposed to use 'P.S.' in texting."

"Hmm... I do. Why wouldn't you?" Anna says, thinking about it.

"I don't know. This is just what Alesha said. I will ask her later, but I don't want to get into it now," I say, setting my phone down with a soft click of its case on the wooden table.

"Yeah, that does seem like it would be a can of worms with her." She says this as I step closer to her. "What is it?" Anna asks, and I know she is unsure of my moving so close.

"Thanks... Everything about today was a dream come true."

"Oh, it was nothing... And I have always wanted to go too, and it was so much fun with you. It would have sucked if you wouldn't have been there. So, thanks for going with me." Anna looks into my eyes as she says this. The last few feet between us disappears, and I kiss her.

But this time it's different. I move my hands up the soft robe until my hands are in her hair; wet from the shower, my fingers tangle into it as I feel one of her hands at the small of my back as the other one traces up my spine making my muscles pull tight. There is no asking if we are ready. We both know that there is no question, and I wonder how long we have both been waiting for this. I don't know how Anna feels, but I feel like I have been ready for this for the entire forty-three years of my life.

"I was clean on my last test," Anna says, "and haven't been with anyone since." She stares intently into my eyes as she says this.

"Me too," I say, in a heavy breath. "After I found out about him cheating on me, I got tested."

My hands move down without me even noticing, and pull the knotted belt of the robe loose. Gently, slowly, the robe slides down her shoulders as I kiss her neck. Anna lowers her arms from me so the robe can fall away, and somewhere between lying and falling, she is on the bed as I follow her down. She touches my body as I am over her, kissing down her collarbone. For the first time in my life, I have never wanted to be with someone so badly in every way. There is nowhere else I would rather be, and no one else I would rather be with.

As I feel her skin, smell her scent, close my eyes as her fingers brush against me. I realize this is the first time I have wanted to be with someone. I'm not scared, I don't feel sick or disgusted, I'm not forced or obligated because it is my role or job in the relationship. But this is the feeling of wanting to be with someone, the feeling of passion, of being with the person I want to be with because I love her. *Is this my true first love?* I ask myself as my muscles tighten under her kisses, and know she wants to be with me as much as I want to be with her.

Anna's breasts rise and fall with quickening breaths under me. There is no fantasy in the world that can compare to this moment and the moments to come. Why would I need a fantasy in my mind, when I have Anna right here... in my arms?

19

Close

Anna's hair tickles my nose as I wake up lying tight against her, her body warm against me, and it seems too good to be true. I think of last night, and it doesn't feel like a dream, or hazy. It is vivid, bright in my mind. Like taking the first breath after a life of drowning, I will never forget even a second of being here.

She starts moving until she rolls over and is facing me, her eyes open as she smiles at me. "I thought you were awake," Anna says with a giggle, for some reason unknown to me.

"I am. How did you know?" I ask, smiling back at her, giggling as well, for the same unknown reason she is giggling.

"Oh... that's not important," she says. Her giggling turns to laughter as she kisses me.

The kiss finally breaks. "How did you know?"

"You don't want to know."

"Tell me."

"You snore." I stare at her. "Just a little, and it is quiet, and so cute," she says quickly.

"I do?"

"Justin never mentioned it? I figured he would have been the type to say something."

"Oh, he never would have told me. He's a heavy sleeper, no matter how much the kids cried as babies, he never woke up once," I tell her.

"That must have pissed you off."

"It used to. But I really can't find it in myself to care about it now... I wonder why?" I ask, running my fingertips down her side to her thigh.

"Who knows?" she says, looking into my eyes.

"So, did my snoring keep you up?"

"Why are you bringing that up now?" She laughs.

"I don't want to keep you up."

"You aren't. Your snoring isn't all the time, and it has always been really cute."

"Always?" I question.

"Yeah," Anna says, with a look that makes me feel stupid for missing something, but I don't know what it is. "Your bed over there isn't that far away, and neither is the top bunk. Not to mention we slept together the night before last."

"Oh, right. I guess I hadn't thought of that," I say, feeling stupid.

"What, you thought you only snored after sex or something?" she says, laughing.

"No..." I say, feeling a little embarrassed. "I just hadn't thought about me possibly keeping you awake."

"Well, you definitely did that last night, but it wasn't from snoring," she says kissing me again, but this time on the side of my jaw, and continues kissing her way to my neck as I naturally lean my head to the side taking in a deep steady breath while her hands find their way across my body.

"It turns out the architect that designed this place was right," Anna says, glancing over at me. "This two-person spa jet bathtub was a great idea."

"It was a great idea," I say, lying next to Anna as the water foams around us.

"I am glad you suggested spending the morning here," Anna says, laying her head back and closing her eyes. "I wonder if I can get one of these installed in my truck?"

"We'll have to ask the shop when we go pick up the truck."

Anna laughs. "That would be worth asking just for their reaction."

"I just thought of something," I say.

"What's that?"

"Did those stupid t-shirts work, but just with each other?"

"Holy fuck, you're right," she says, sitting up and looking at me. "Those goddamn slutty trucker shirts got us. I didn't know they were that powerful," she says, laughing, and I laugh with her. But, something hurts when she says this. I am the one who started the joke, but now the idea that this was just a sexual tension release or something, and nothing more, makes me feel a little sick. But I won't ask more from her. I don't have the right to ask for more than she wants to give.

"We will have to be careful where we wear them."

"Yeah, we really do," Anna says as her phone starts ringing. She grabs it, having set it within reach when we got in. "Hello, this is Anna Ginkans," she answers. "Okay, great to hear. Thanks, bye."

"Truck ready?" I ask.

"It will be done by one-thirty, and we can pick it up whenever. So, I guess we'll have lunch at that Italian place, load up, and then head for New York."

"Sure you don't want to just stay here permanently?" I ask, playing my fingers across her stomach.

"Umm... I wish I could, that would be... 'nice' feels like too much of an understatement. But I don't think that is in my budget." Anna breathes these words only a few inches from my face.

"Then when is check out?" I whisper, moving my hand as the water continues bubbling around us.

"We have a little over an hour."

"Then we better not waste it," I say with a long kiss as I lean against her.

Anna pulls back with a small, deep gasp, like a swimmer coming up for air, saying, "How have you... you become..." her breath sharpens, "this... this... like this in a... a," she breathes in, her voice turning thin, catching, "few days?" Her arms wrap around me, not to hold me, but to hold on.

"It wasn't just a few days," I say against her neck. "I have been ready for this, wanting this, needing it my entire life. I'm just finally awake..."

"Oh... oh, okay. I gue... I..." she tries to say, but her words seem to lose their reason and purpose, and just don't matter anymore.

I sit in the sleeper of the truck, waiting while Anna is getting our load situated. I stare at my phone screen, reading through the few dozen texts from Alesha wanting to know what happened. Since I have neglected her for the entire day; partly because I'm not sure what to say, and partly because until we checked out of our room, texting her back was the last thing on my mind.

Me: What are you doing?

Alesha instantly sees it, and the bounding indicator dots hardly even start before the text pops up on my screen.

Alesha: WTF! Where have you been?!!

Me: Sorry.

Alesha: Whatever. What happened?

I stare at this, suddenly unsure of what I should say. Everything about this just feels awkward and weird.

Alesha: Are you okay?

I can feel a tone change in this.

Me: Yes, I'm fine.

Me: Sorry.

Alesha: Stop apologizing.

Alesha: I should apologize. I've been pressuring you, and I shouldn't have done that. I'm sorry.

Reading this means more than I thought it would. Knowing that she noticed and is actually concerned about me.

Alesha: Are you happy?

This makes me laugh, because it is an underhanded and kind way of asking the same question.

Me: I also didn't text back sooner, because I am tired. I didn't sleep much last night, and spent the morning in the spa bathtub.

Alesha: Didn't sleep well?

Me: Never even made it to my own bed.

Alesha: OMFG.

Me: What?

Alesha: Oh my fucking God (sighing emoji).

Me: Oh, thanks.

Me: That bathtub was wonderful, and so nice after time in the truck.

Alesha: I bet it was. Sounds nice.

Me: Did I mention it was one of those big two-person spa baths?

Alesha: That sounds really great. I am so sick of truck stop and gym showers.

Alesha: Wait, OMG!

Alesha: So, I guess you will tell me all, just in a subtle, nondirect way. lmao.

Me: I guess so.

Me: Anna told me I could tell you whatever I wanted. But I'm just not good at that.

Alesha: That's fine, but I'm always here in case you need to talk about it in extreme detail. ;)

Me: What is with you young people? LOL

Alesha: You're not that old. You're just conservative. Hahaha

Me: Probably true.

Alesha: At least it was true. I think you might be kicked out of the conservative club after last night. lmao

Me: And most of the morning until checkout.

Me: Also, they can keep that club.

Alesha: DAMN...(Shocked emoji)

Alesha: When you go for it, you go big. I'm sooooo jealous.

Me: You're straight.

Alesha: I am. But that doesn't mean I can't be jealous.

Alesha: And it has been so long. I am starting to get desperate.

Me: don't get too desperate.

Alesha: I won't, don't worry.

Alesha: I can just fantasize about you and Anna now.

Me: Don't say that. It's weird.

Alesha: Would it help if that guy that towed your truck was in the fantasy as well?

Me: How would that help?

Alesha: Seems like him being there would help me.

Me: You have a problem.

Alesha: Don't worry, it's just a fantasy. It's not like I am going to get all of you into a hotel room and make it happen for real. I'm not you. LMAO

I stare at this and realize she's right. I lived out a fantasy. I didn't even know this could happen, and am not sure what to think about it.

Alesha: You still there? Was that too far?

Me: No, it wasn't. LOL

Me: But you make a good point. You can fantasize about us. I would feel guilty tonight if you had nothing, and I have Anna next to me.

Alesha: You bitch. (Red angry face emoji)

Me: LMAO.

Alesha: Look at you cussing... kinda. LMAO

Alesha: I gotta go. Sorry again if I got pushy. If I ever get pushy, just tell me to fuck off.

Me: It's fine, don't worry. I should have let you know something sooner.

Alesha: No, you should have taken a video.

Me: I'm leaving now.

Alesha: LMFAO.

I manage to figure out what the "F" is for in this one without having to ask. It makes me laugh; how she is always making jokes to lighten things up.

Alesha: Seriously, though, congratulations.

I stare at this and think about it, because I hadn't thought of it being something like that. But in a weird way it is such a big deal, having all of this happen in a matter of days, after having resigned myself to my old life, knowing that I would never be with someone that I actually loved, or ever wanted to be with. *It's a shame I'm not real religious anymore, because it all feels a little like a miracle,* I think.

Me: thanks.

Alesha: I would send you a card, but I'm not sure where I would get a card for this.

Me: Me either. I'm sure someone out there sells them, though.

Alesha: I will see what I can find. TTYL

Mc: Bye.

The mountains are beautiful as we drive through them leaving LA, but it seems like it isn't long and we are out of them and into the desert, which gets tiresome quickly. They haven't exactly changed in the few days since we drove through going to LA. "It's nice being back on the road. Don't you think?" I ask.

"Not as nice as the hotel and Magical Land, or the amusement park. But, yeah, it is nice being back on the road."

"What?" I ask, confused about what she means, then I get it.

"You are so cute when you turn all red like that," she says with a laugh. "I was just joking. I didn't mean to embarrass you."

"I know you were. And you're right, that was more fun than trucking."

"Hey, maybe we'll luck out and break down in Las Vegas for a few days. There is a Ferris wheel there that is a half-hour ride. We could have a lot of fun in a half-hour," Anna says, glancing at me with a seductive glint in her eyes.

"That's true, we could. But, I hate for you to have the expense of another breakdown."

"You have a point. There is probably a cheaper option for semi-public sex," she says, thinking.

"When did it turn into... that?"

"I'm not sure... I thought it was your idea?" Anna looks at me.

"No, I never said anything about that. Wait, you're okay with the idea of that?" I say, staring at her.

"I don't know... are you?" she asks, glancing at me again with a certain look.

"No!"

"I'm just playing around. I know you never mentioned it," she says, laughing.

"I'm not sure. You seem pretty into the idea."

"Well, maybe it can go on your bucket list," Anna says.

"That's not something I would really put on a bucket list, if I had one."

"Wait, you don't have a bucket list?"

"No, not really," I say.

"That needs to change. You have to have goals to shoot for."

"Okay, I will think about it," I say, not wanting to say that if I would have had a bucket-list, she would have checked all the boxes off yesterday and this morning.

I catch up on my studying for my CDL while Anna listens to a podcast, but I feel like I have to read everything twice before it sinks in. Not that the podcast is distracting me, but the slight feeling of euphoria seems to still have a hold on me from yesterday and this morning. It is like I can't stop fantasizing about it, even though it just happened.

There is also an increased feeling of longing towards Anna, something that I thought might lessen after being with her, but it has only grown stronger. So, now I know, it wasn't infatuation or sexual tension. But, the more I focus on reading, the more I get my mind off of the *"What ifs?"* that keep running through my head.

"I guess I'll pull over for the night," Anna says. I look up from the laptop screen to see that the sun is just starting to set.

"I didn't realize it was that late."

"You've been at it for a while, and it isn't too late. But I thought it would be better to get a fresh start in the morning, since today wasn't a good start." I look at her and raise an eyebrow. "You know what I mean," she says with a laugh.

We get everything settled after parking at a rest stop, and Anna starts microwaving something for dinner while I get out some sweatpants and a fresh T-shirt.

"Oh," Anna says as I start changing. "I guess now you don't mind changing in front of me." She smiles.

"Yeah, I guess not," I say, feeling a little self-conscious, which seems stupid.

"Are you getting nervous?" she asks.

"No, I'm fine"—I pull on the sweat pants—"I'm not getting nervous."

"Okay, just thought it looked like you might be a little bit," Anna says, standing up and kissing me before I can pull my t-shirt on.

As Anna starts undressing herself to change, I sit down on the edge of the bed, but this time I don't have to steal glances at her in the reflection of the window. I can just watch. "You are seriously going to just watch me?" Anna asks with a giggle.

"Why not? Does it make you nervous?" I ask with a smile.

"Well, no... But I'm definitely not used to it."

"You are normally by yourself, so of course you're not used to it," I say.

"Normally by myself, that kinda hurts."

"Sorry."

"That's okay. Later I'll just make you kiss it and make it better," Anna says as she pulls her t-shirt on and sits down next to me.

I look down at her bare legs. "Aren't you forgetting something?" I ask.

She follows my line of sight, looking at her legs. "I've always been a t-shirt and underwear person. The sweatpants were just because you were here, but I thought you wouldn't mind now." She looks at me, and a smile spreads across her face. "You like my legs, don't you?"

"Oh, they're very nice legs."

"Thank you. And you've probably never tried just a shirt and underwear, have you?"

"No, I never have." Anna just stares at me with the same smile. "You're going to make me, aren't you?"

"Sure am. You wouldn't make me feel like the odd one out, would you?"

"Okay, fine," I say, standing up with a sigh.

"You don't have to act like it is so horrible," she says, laughing as I pull off the sweatpants I just put on. "Now, that's much nicer, isn't it?"

"I guess," I say, not sure. "I just feel colder."

"Let me help you warm up then," Anna says, grabbing my hips. Pulling me against her, she wraps one arm around my hips and slides her other hand under my shirt, lifting it enough to kiss my stomach. "How's that?" she asks between kisses.

"Umm... I love that," I say as the microwave starts beeping.

"Son of a bitch." Anna sighs, leaning back away from me. "Did that warm you up enough for now?" she asks, looking up at me, her arm still around my hips.

"Not as warm as I would like to be, but I'll survive," I say, looking down at her and would give anything for her to not stop.

We start another movie while we eat dinner. It is just another romance. "I was going to say that I can still sleep in the top bunk. This bed isn't that big, and just because we.." I pause, not sure what we are yet, "doesn't mean we have to sleep together," I say, setting my empty plate on the little table.

"That is sweet of you to say. I appreciate you not wanting to be pushy. But I'm not going to fuck around with you, and then send you away to that shitty top bunk after I'm done. If you want to stay up there, then that's fine. But I personally would rather have you down here with me," she says, kissing my cheek, and sets her empty plate on top of mine.

"To be honest, it isn't that uncomfortable up there. But getting up and down is terrifying," I say as Anna laughs. "And I am so scared I will roll off in the night."

"You poor thing," she says with a soft smile, giving me another kiss on the cheek.

"Then, I think I will sleep down here with you," I say, kissing her back, but not on the cheek. "Why don't we turn the movie off? We'll finish it later."

"I really don't care if we finish it or not," she says, quickly turning the movie and the TV off, tossing the remote to the side. "I did say I would warm you up after we ate."

"True, and I am still cold..." I say as if we actually need an excuse.

20

New York Bound

I wake up to the feeling of Anna's skin against mine for the second time in two days, and I am starting to think I could really get used to this. "You awake?" Anna asks.

"Yeah. You?" I ask as she laughs quietly from behind me.

"Maybe," she says, kissing my neck.

"Oh... You better not start that," I say, closing my eyes with the feeling of her lips on my skin.

"I won't," she says with a sigh that is somewhere between disappointment and pleasure. "I do need to get past you to start the truck warming up."

"Does that mean I have to move?"

"I can climb over you. But I'm not guaranteeing anything if I do that."

"I hate to take the chance, so I will just move. I need to make a trip to the restroom anyway."

Anna starts the truck, and we both get dressed and go to the restroom. "So, I forgot to ask. Where exactly in New York are we going?" I ask as we brush our teeth in the rest-stop sinks. Which is something I never thought I would ever do.

"We drop our load off at Rochester. But Evy and I are from Ithaca, and they are out on the edge of the city."

"Oh. What about the houses you rent out?"

"Most of those"—she stops, spitting into the sink—"are about ten or fifteen minutes outside of town along the lake."

"Lake?" I ask, and wash my mouth out. I look over to see Anna staring at me with her toothbrush hanging out of the corner of her mouth. "What?" I ask, not sure what I said that would make her stare at me like this.

"Ithaca sits on Cayuga Lake... One of the Finger Lakes? Oh God, please tell me you have heard of the Finger Lakes?"

"Of course I have."

"Well, I wasn't sure for a few minutes."

"If you grew up there, did you go to the city much as a kid?" I ask as I start brushing my hair.

"City?"

"Yeah, New York City. I have always wanted to see it but nev—" I freeze as she stares at me again. "What now?"

"How close do you think Ithaca is to New York City?"

"I don't know..."

"It's over two hundred miles."

"Really?" I say in surprise.

"New York isn't that small of a state. I don't know why people always act like the whole state is just the one city," Anna says, sounding annoyed.

"Sorry. So, I'm not the first person to make this mistake?"

"Pretty much everyone that isn't from New York thinks this."

"I'm really sorry," I say again.

"Don't be. And, now you know," she says, giving me a quick kiss. "Ooh, minty."

"You're using the same toothpaste," I point out.

"Yeah, but it tastes better on you."

"It does? Let me check," I say and kiss her back. "You're right, that does taste better on you."

I continue reading as Anna drives; the days seem long and I wonder how Anna ever stood this by herself. But, she still seems very content with her work, not seeming to mind staring out the windshield for hours at a time. I can't help but wonder how driving together affects relationships.

"So, how long will we be in Ithaca before the next job?" I ask, when we are only about four hours from Rochester.

"Three days before my next load," she says, and something about the way she says it gives me a bad feeling.

"That isn't very long. You can't take more time than that?"

"Being stuck in LA cut into my time off. Not that it wasn't totally worth it," she says, glancing at me with a smile. "But, I will be going on the next run alone."

"What? Why?" I ask, with a wave of disappointment hitting me.

"I don't want to go without you, but the load goes to Canada, and I figured you don't have a passport on you."

"Oh... No, I don't have one," I say, looking at the floor of the truck. "Why didn't you say anything sooner?" I ask, looking at her, feeling a little mad that she is just now telling me this.

"Before I figured you would just stay in my room at Evy's, and just hadn't gotten around to mentioning it. But then... I kinda forgot about it—"

"You just forgot about it?"

"I'm sorry..." Anna says, noticing my growing anger, that is actually disappointment. "But I haul to Canada all the time. So, I just didn't think much of it."

"How long will you be gone?"

She doesn't say anything for what seems like way too long, and I feel my heart fall and my stomach hurt because I know it isn't going to be good. Anna sighs, like she doesn't want to say it. "Two weeks."

"Two weeks?"

"It is because I haul from one town to the next, like we have been." I look out my window, feeling betrayed, even though I don't have that right. We aren't in any type of relationship that gives me the right to be angry about this. At least this is what I tell myself as I feel tears slide down my cheeks. "I scheduled these hauls before you were riding with me," Anna says, and I know she is trying to make it clear that she didn't do this on purpose. But it just points out how little time we've been together.

"It's okay... I understand," I say, still looking out the window. "I'm sorry for acting like this. I know this is your job and you don't have a choice in it."

"I did fuck up by not telling you sooner—"

"You kind of did."

"Hey," she says with a little laugh, trying to make things a little lighter again. "Let's face it. It's actually your fault."

"My fault?" I say, looking at her.

"Yeah, you have been keeping my mind on only one goddamn thing lately."

"I guess that's not wrong," I say, laughing a little. "I've been pretty one-track-minded myself."

"No kidding there," Anna says, looking at me with insinuation. "You know, I am about due for my break. How about I make my shitty mistake up to you... Or, at least try?"

"You don't need to make up anything to me. You really didn't do anything wrong. So, don't worry about it."

"Thanks..." she says softer. "So, I guess I'll just go on a walk or something with my break. Since I don't need to make anything up to you now."

"Well, you might owe me a little bit of an apology. I mean, if it will make you feel better."

"It will make me feel a little better. But I think it will make you feel a lot better."

"So, did that do anything to make you feel better?" Anna asks. Sitting on the edge of the bed as she pulls her shirt on over her head, and I just lie on the bed without a stitch of fabric on. Even the blanket and top sheet are a wad crammed in the corner; having gotten in our way.

"I'm not sure... I think I feel a little too good. So I will have to pay you back a little tonight," I say. Sitting up, I straddle her from behind, wrapping my arms around her as she sits on the edge of the bed, and kissing her neck. *When did I become like this?* I wonder, because it is so out of character from how I would have acted just a few weeks ago. *But I don't care what I used to be like, I like being like this,* I think as I bite her earlobe, gently tugging on it.

"God..." Anna says in a moan. "If you do that, we'll never get there."

"Okay," I say, stopping, "I don't want you to be late for the drop-off."

"Thanks, sorry. Trust me, I would rather have a sexy, naked woman toying with me than hauling a load. But the sooner we're done, the sooner we'll be in a real bed again."

"This bed's not bad."

"It isn't, but," Anna says. Turning around and kissing me hard, pushing me down as I lie back with her over me, and my head hits the back wall of the sleeper. "See, there isn't enough room for what I want to do to you."

"I see your point," I say with a giggle as she moves off of me. "But that hurt." I get up, rubbing my head where it barely touched the wall.

"I'm going to the restroom again before we take off. You coming?" Anna asks.

"Good idea," I say, and start picking my clothes up from the floor.

After getting dressed, we walk back towards the restrooms. I notice how dim it seems, and that's when I notice the dense dark clouds. "Looks like we will be driving in the rain soon," Anna says, looking around at the sky, and as though queued by her words, there is a rumble in the distance.

"It sure feels like it. The air is very muggy and still."

"It is," she says, "and you can smell it."

"I have always loved the warm rain smell and feeling right before a storm."

"Me too!" Anna says. "But I didn't grow up in tornado territory. I think I would be terrified every time a storm started to build."

"Oh... I never thought of it like that," I say, thinking about it as we both stand in the parking lot staring at the clouds, the rumbles of thunder getting closer.

"Really? You never thought about that before?"

"Well, I guess I just grew up with tornado watches and warnings being a yearly thing. They were always just normal, so I never thought much of it. Does that make sense?"

Anna stares at me for a few long seconds. "No! That doesn't make any sense. It isn't like growing up around them is going to keep them from killing you."

"Maybe it does. I am still alive after all." I smile at her.

"That is some top-tier logic."

"We did go into the hallway of the house if there was a warning, and it was close," I say.

"You went into the hallway..." She stares at me again. "As an alternative to what? The patio?"

"Well, it isn't that uncommon to stand outside and look to see if you can see them coming."

"Them who," she says, seeming confused. "Holy fuck. By 'them'"—she air quotes—"do you mean the tornado?"

"Yeah."

"Oh my God. How stupid are you?"

"I didn't do it. Justin used to, but I made him stop. People in other tornado states like Kansas, Oklahoma, Missouri, and Arkansas do it too." I say like this will help, and I'm not sure why I think this.

"What is wrong with everyone?" she asks, her mouth open.

"I thought everyone knew about this."

"No... Why would everyone know this?"

"Not sure," I say, thinking about it. "Well, now you know." I smile.

"Yeah, that there are more stupid people than I thought out there."

"Now you really should have known there are a lot of stupid people."

"Very true, I should have known that one," she says as a big rain-drop hits the pavement in front of us. "Oops, looks like we stood around too long and are going to get rained out."

"That's okay," I say as more drops start hitting as we reach the door of the restroom. "If we get drenched by the rain, I'll just have to help you get changed out of your wet clothes."

"I feel like I have maybe unleashed something into the world I shouldn't have."

"Oh, I'm not sure about that. I think it is more like..." I pause, not sure about what I am going to say.

"Making up for lost time?" Anna says, filling in my blanking.

"Yes. I'm making up for lost time."

"Well, I'm glad I can be there for you to make up this lost time with... Or maybe on?" I laugh at this.

"I think it is both."

"I think you are right," she says with a laugh.

"You know, now that I think about it. Today was the first time I have ever just had sex in the middle of the day like that," I say.

"Really?"

"It isn't exactly like I pushed or encouraged Justin for it. So, that was the first time."

"Did you like it? The time of day, I mean," she says with a little giggle.

"I could get used to it."

"Well, I'm willing to help with that... If you want."

"I'm going to hold you to that."

"You better," Anna says with a grin as the rain starts pouring outside. It pounds against the metal roof of the building.

"Wow, it's really coming down out there," I say in a raised voice so she can hear me.

"Yeah," Anna says, looking up at the ceiling. "We better hurry." She looks at me.

"Hurry, why?"

"Because I said I would help you get used to it. And there is no way we won't be soaked by this rain. So, we are probably going to need time to help each other... change." She says this and the instant feeling of anticipation tells me that maybe she did unleash something in me, because I have never looked so forward to getting drenched in a thunderstorm in my life.

21

Evy

It rains steadily as we drive through Ithaca, like it has been since the rest stop. Even after the extra time it took to... change, it was still raining. We drove in the storm for the rest of the way, the rain only let up as we pulled into Ithaca. "Well, from the looks of it we might get all wet from the rain again, so we should probably take a hot shower to warm up once we get there," Anna says.

"As much as I like that idea. I doubt Evy will think much of us doing that."

"It's my house too. And they can just get over it."

"I'm not going to go off and have sex with you the second after we show up at your sis— sibling?" I ask, looking at Anna, not sure if this is right.

"Yeah, sibling."

"Sorry, it just sounds awkward."

"You'll get used to it," Anna says.

"Anyway. I'm not going off to have sex the second we get to your sibling's."

"What if we give it fifteen minutes and then say we are really tired from the drive? And my room has its own bathroom with a shower," she adds.

"I am tired... So, maybe it wouldn't be that bad, and she—they probably expect us to be tired," I say.

"See, it's not a bad plan. And you don't have to feel bad. You will have plenty of time to get to know Evy. And once you do, you'll realize you are much better off blowing them off for sex... or almost anything else, for that matter," Anna says.

"That's really mean."

"What? You would rather sit around on a couch making small talk with your siblings than take a shower with me?"

"Okay, I see your point," I say, laughing. "But my siblings are much more of a pain."

"Older sisters always say that."

"We have good reason," I say, glancing at her.

"Why do I get the feeling that was directed at me?" Anna says.

"Only part of it."

"I am having second thoughts about letting you shower with me," she says, glancing at me.

"No, you're not."

"Yeah, you're right," Anna says, swinging the rig wide to pull into a large semi-sized driveway at a really nice-looking house.

"Wow, is this it?"

"Yeah. You like it?" she says, looking at me with a smile, as she pulls the parking brake knob with the instant sound of releasing air that I am now used to hearing.

"It is beautiful. It is a Victorian, right?" I ask, staring out the windshield at the light blue two-story house.

"Close. It's Edwardian."

"Oh," I say, as though I know the difference. "I have always loved these houses."

"I bought it some time ago. But Evy is half owner because they are fixing it up inside, bit by bit."

"That is great."

"It is a lot more work than I thought it would be, so I am pretty sure I screwed them royally on that deal," she says with a laugh.

"It doesn't seem like you feel that bad about it," I say, raising an eyebrow.

"I really do, honest," Anna says.

"Oh, really," I say as thunder rumbles somewhere in the rain.

"Whatever," she says with a smile, then turns the truck's engine off and leans over, kissing me. "Let's go in. I'm actually a little excited for you to meet Evy."

"Really?"

"Yeah, I think you two are going to get along well," she says.

"Okay then," I say, opening my door and climbing out. I walk around to the front of the truck. "The rain has stopped." I look up at the sky.

"I don't think it is going to last long," Anna says as the sky lights up with lightning. "Oops, I forgot my phone. Go ahead, I'll be right there," she says, walking back around to her side of the truck.

I start walking towards the house, which is a little way off from where the truck's parking space is; guessing there used to be a house next door, but it is now an empty lot that Anna must have bought for a parking spot. I am just crossing the regular driveway when a woman with blond hair tied in a short ponytail to one side comes out of the house looking annoyed. "Hello," I say, unsure of who I am talking to given she is white.

She stops and looks at me for a second with car keys in hand. "Hello..." she says, seeming unsure herself. "Wait, you're Mary. When did you two get here?" she says, looking past me, I look over my shoulder and see Anna starting towards us.

"Just a few minutes ago," I say. "Yes, I'm Mary." I hope that she'll say who she is.

"It's nice to meet you," she says, brightening, stepping forward and hugging me. When she steps back she notices I am still confused. "I'm Evy... Anna neglected to mention that I'm not Black, didn't she?"

"Yeah, she kind of did."

"That explains why you had that 'why is the stranger hugging me?' face." I can't help but laugh at this. Evy is a lot like Anna.

"I should have figured it out quicker," I say.

"Hey, Sib," Anna says, walking up, seeming happy to see Evy.

"What the fuck's wrong with you, you moron?" Evy says.

"What did I do?" Anna asks.

"To start, you didn't text me when you got to town—"

"Forgot," Anna says.

"And you didn't tell her that I'm white, so she thought I was some rando hugging her."

"Oh, yeah... Forgot about that, too."

"You are such a fucking dumbass, Annabel."

I look at Anna, a little surprised. "Annabel?" I question.

"You didn't tell Mary your name is Annabel?" Evy asks.

"No..." Anna whines like a child. "I hate it... I didn't want her to even know," Anna says, still whining.

"I like it," I say, smiling at her.

"I knew you would, and that's why I didn't want to tell you," Anna says, almost pouting.

"You never grow up. You're still the same whiny little bitch you've always been."

"I am not," Anna says, still whining. And I am starting to get the feeling that this is Anna when she is around Evy. She is like a pouting child that is being scolded, and it is so cute.

"Well, I gotta go," Evy says.

"What, you're leaving?" Anna says, looking truly disappointed, and I am thinking that abandoning Evy after fifteen minutes for shower sex wasn't going to happen, because no way Anna would leave Evy's sight after so little time.

"Yup, goddamn fucking shit has hit the fan at the lake house," Evy says, looking annoyed again.

"What's wrong?" Anna asks.

"The water alarm sent me a notification. The basement is getting too wet. And this son bitch rain isn't helping, and it is just getting ready to hit us."

"Do you need help?" I ask.

"Yeah, we aren't doing anything," Anna says.

"Naw, I'm sure it is just the motherfucking pump again. They're pieces of shit, so I have an extra one I will just swap it with," Evy says, and it is clear that they are someone that cusses the more frustrated they get.

"Okay," Anna says. "We will just wait for you then."

"Yeah, sure," they say, eyeing us skeptically. "Just keep it in your room, I don't want you doing things on my couch or something."

"I would never—" Anna starts.

"Oh yes, you would," Evy interrupts.

"Whatever. You better go before the whole place floods," Anna says as raindrops start falling.

"No shit. If I never come back, it means the motherfucker shorted out and electrocuted me."

"Be careful," I say.

"Yeah, turn the breaker off before you touch anything," Anna adds.

"Yeah, yeah," they say, waving us both off as they start towards their car. "I'll be fine, I'm too goddamn unlucky for something to kill me. That bastard up there enjoys fucking with me too much to let me die," Evy rants, and then climbs in their car and pulls out of the driveway.

"So, what did you think?" Anna asks me as Evy drives off.

"They were very nice," I say with some hesitation.

"Cusses a lot, don't they?"

"So much," I say as Anna starts laughing.

"Yeah, Evy always gets like that when they are mad or frustrated about something."

"I guess it is better than keeping it bottled up," I say.

"True."

"So, you want to give me a house tour... Annabel?" I say, biting back a smile.

"Oh, I knew it! Please don't start that."

"Start what... Annabel?"

"You better stop."

"Make me stop. Because I think Annabel is a cute name," I say, taunting her.

"Make you? I think I can do that," she says, reaching out and pulling me against her. "We do have the entire house."

"Except the couch."

"Yes, except the couch. But..." Anna pauses, "I have never wanted to have sex on a couch so much in my life, until Evy said that."

"I know... What is that?" I ask.

"I think it is 'don't push that button' syndrome."

"The couch is forbidden fruit."

"Then maybe we should stop standing out here in a storm like a Texan in a tornado, and go try some fruit," Annabel says, biting at my lower lip, and I am amazed at the difference in her when her sibling isn't here.

As we step onto the porch, the rain goes from a drop here and there to a solid shower; the wind picking up at the same time. We hurry through the door, rain following us in, propelled over the span of the porch by the wind. The storm door slams behind me as soon as I am through. "Wow, we barely made it," I say looking out the door.

"Yeah, it looks like the storm is here, and it seems much more pissed off than the storm earlier."

I close the door, which muffles the now-driving rain outside, and I turn around to see the entry room of the old house. "It is beautiful," I say, taking it all in.

"Come on, I'll give you the ten-cent tour."

"That would be great," I say, slipping my shoes off. Anna notices and does the same. "I don't want to get anything on the floors."

"Yeah, Evy is always complaining when I don't take my shoes off," Anna says.

We start across the room as a crack of lightning sends white light through the windows, filling the room. The resulting thunder close behind it is so loud the windows rattle, and it hurts my ears. Anna screams. I just stare at her for a second and start laughing. "It's not funny. That scared the shit out of me," she says.

"Sorry, I just wasn't expecting you to scream. It was cute," I say giggling.

"So glad my light heart attack amused you."

"Sorry I laughed," I say, giving her a small kiss.

We continue on, and just walk into what is now being used as a living room when everything goes dark. "Oh, you have got to be kidding me..." Anna says.

"Storm must have gotten the power somewhere."

"Yeah, I guess so. This really sucks."

"Does it? Being stuck in an old house, the power out, a storm outside. There is only one thing to do in a situation like this," I say, able to see now that my eyes have adjusted.

"Get murdered?"

"What?"

"Killed by ghosts?"

"No," I say laughing. "I thought it was romantic."

"Oh... Really?"

"The sound of rain and thunder is always romantic."

"Then I have the place for you. Follow me," Anna says, grabbing my hand and pulling me along, and my heart skips a beat. She has never taken my hand like this, and something about it just makes me happy. It's a feeling I love almost as much as I love her.

"Where are you taking me?"

"My room," she says. "Wait, that sounded way to high school."

"I never had that happen in high school, so I liked it."

"You would," she says with a laugh.

"Hey, what's that mean? Annabel."

"You didn't?" Anna stops, looking at me and I just smile at her. "I am so going to let the ghosts murder you."

"I'll take my chances, because I just like calling you Annabel too much."

"Well, I'll get you back later," she says, continuing to lead me up the stairs. Anna opens a door in the surprisingly dark hallway, leading me into a room, and closes the door behind me.

"So, this is your room," I say, walking around it, looking at the few decorations.

"It's pretty plain. I'm not here enough to do anything else with it."

"That's fine. After all, I'm not in here because I want to look at your décor," I say as Anna walks over to two doors. "Is that a closet?" I ask.

"Hell no," she says, pulling the doors open, revealing a large balcony. "How's this for a romantic place during a storm?"

"Oh wow, it is wonderful," I say walking over to her. The wind has completely died off, but the rain is still pouring down in sheets. "No chairs?" I ask, looking around the empty space.

"I have always meant to get one of those loungers or some chairs, but never got around to it," she says, and I am starting to get the feeling that Anna truly has no life outside of her truck. Even there, she doesn't have much of a life, not like she deserves to have.

"That's fine, I understand," I say, not sure what else to say and not wanting her to feel bad.

"So, we could just lean against the wall?" she says, with a laugh teasing her tight lips.

"Maybe just lie on the floor."

"Aren't you turning into quite the wild thing," she says laughing, as I giggle at the idea. "Wait, I have an idea. I'll be back in a second," Anna says going towards the door.

I sit down on the edge of Anna's bed as I take my phone out.

Me: Anna has a really nice house. But there is a big storm outside, and the power is out.

I send the text to Alesha and see that I don't even have a signal since Anna isn't close enough with her phone. I sigh, looking at the screen, then put my phone on the bedside table and lie back on the bed, closing my eyes for a second. Even though it has been a long time since Anna has slept in this bed, I can still almost smell her on the blankets.

"Are you sleeping? Or just sniffing my bed?" I hear Anna say and jump as my eyes shoot open. "That's the reaction of a bed sniffer," she says.

"I was not. You just scared me," I say, sitting up.

"I know you weren't, I was just joking," she says, tossing a bag; kind of like a gym bag, on the balcony floor. "You did look like you were about asleep though."

"It was just really nice lying there, listening to the rain and thunder outside."

"You'll love this then," she says, opening the bag.

"What is that?"

"An air mattress. Evy used to go camping sometimes, and still does when they find the time. Thank God they have a pump for it that isn't electric."

"Yeah, I bet that takes a long time to blow up by mouth."

"Yeah, but I bet you would like to watch that," she says with a mischievous smile.

"I would. You would look so sexy blowing up that mattress, all out of breath, sweat dripping down your face, lips puckered..." My own breath changing as I say this.

"You better stop, or we'll never make it as far as even trying to air this up."

"Okay, I'll stop," I say, now laughing. Anna attaches the hose of what looks like a large bicycle tire pump to the flat mattress, and starts pumping, going up and down with the handle. "Oh... this is better than watching you blow on it."

Anna pauses, looking over her shoulder. "Enjoy the view, because I know I will when I make you take a turn in a second," she says, and goes back to pumping. Something about her saying this makes it more exciting, even though there is nothing to be excited about. I mean, I've had sex with her, seen; and touched, every inch of her. So I'm not sure why this is exciting. But, it is.

I reach over and grab my phone from the bedside table, turn off the sound, and take a video. Laughing to myself, because I will torment her with it later. At least, that's what I tell myself. "Okay, your turn," Anna says, turning around, her face with little beads of sweat gathered here and there. I ignore them though, and take over pumping the handle, up and down. "You were right, this is nice."

"Glad you're not disappointed."

"In you? Never," she says, and this makes me happier than it should.

It doesn't seem like it is more than a few minutes until the mattress is full. "It seems like you did too much. You should have let me take over sooner."

"I got to see you looking all cute, pumping that pump, and that's all I wanted. I didn't want you to do all the work. This was my idea after all, so I should do the work."

"Still..." I say, feeling bad.

"Let's get the blankets and pillows," Anna says as she starts pulling things loose from her bed, and I hope Evy is gone for a long time. Because I'm no longer in the mood to sit around visiting with anyone.

22

To the Sound of the Rain

"Oh my God!" Anna says, grabbing me.

"If you are that scared of lightning, why don't we go in?" I say, laughing a little as she clings onto me with both hands wrapped tight in my shirt.

"Lightning injures and kills a lot of people, you know that, right? It can travel for miles, and ball lightning can even travel through walls."

"Then let's go in."

"No, I'll be fine... Sorry," she says, loosening her grip on me.

"Don't be sorry. If you are scared of lightning, you are scared of it, nothing to be sorry about."

"That's sweet of you to say," Anna says, kissing my cheek.

"I'm scared of snakes," I tell her.

"Um... Texas has like a million snakes that want to kill you. So, it would be stupid not to be scared of them."

"Good point. We do have a lot of poisonous ones."

"Venomous," Anna says.

"What?"

"Venomous. They have fangs that inject their victims, so they are venomous. If it was their bodies that were dangerous to predators; like dart frogs, then they would be poisonous," Anna explains to me.

"Okay, I'll try to remember that," I say, not sure why this is relevant.

"Sorry, I start vomiting up crap I hear on podcasts when I want to think about something else."

"Stop apologizing. Who do you think you are, me?" I smile at her. "Here," I say, moving her head to my shoulder, "just close your eyes and listen to the rain."

"Okay," she says, doing as I say.

"This is so nice... lying here with you," I say, closing my own eyes.

We just lie quietly, the rain falling at a steady pace; not a downpour, but more than a shower. With the occasional rumble of thunder, making it perfectly peaceful. The cool damp breeze causes us to huddle close together under the blanket. I hear my phone's notification go off from the side table in the bedroom where I left it. "Is that your phone?" Anna asks me softly, a little dreamlike.

"Sounds like it."

"Do you want to get it?"

"Not really," I say, not opening my eyes, and my phone goes off again.

"Are you sure?"

"It's just Alesha, she's fine."

"Okay," Anna says, right before her phone's notification goes off.

"Is that your phone?" I ask.

"Sure is. And that's Evy's notification sound, I better check it," she says, sighing.

"Okay, if you have to," I say, and kiss her as she looks up at me. "I love being here with you."

"Same," she says, kissing me back, but this kiss has much more to it. It's a kiss that wants to go places. Her phone's notification sound goes off again. "Fuck..." Anna whines, pulling back from the kiss as I try to follow her, not wanting it to end. "They better have something good to say," she complains as she pulls the covers back, climbing off the air mattress.

"What does Evy want?" I ask as Anna walks back, sitting on the edge of the bed and handing me my phone.

"They said it has gone south, and not sure when they will be back," she says, typing a reply.

"Do they need help?" I ask, opening the messenger app.

"Just asking," Anna says, staring at the phone's screen. "Nope, Evy said they got it, and to either fix dinner ourselves or order something."

"Okay," I say, setting my phone on the floor next to the mattress, and then crawl across, sitting down behind Anna with a leg on each side of her.

"What are you doing?" she asks, looking over her shoulder at me.

"What do you think I'm doing?" I ask, moving her hair aside and kissing her neck. She starts to turn around, but I wrap my arms around her to hold her in place. "Where do you think you're going?"

"I guess nowhere," she says, giggling as I move my hands down and bring them up under her shirt.

"Darn straight, you're not going anywhere." I pull Anna's shirt up and off, throwing it through the doorway and onto her bedroom floor. It barely hits the floor before I am unhooking her bra while still kissing her neck.

"Someone is in a hurry," she says, giggling again as she moves her arms, letting her bra slide past.

"Do you want me to slow down?" I whisper against her ear as I move my hands down and unbutton her jeans.

"No..." she says, lulling her head back against my shoulder. "I don't want that."

"Good. Not that I would have slowed down, even if you wanted me to." Anna rolls her head to the side for a hard sideways kiss as she lifts her hips, and slides the jeans off her hips as she works the pant legs down until she kicks them off.

"Fuck," she says through a noticeable change in her breathing, "thunderstorms really make you wild."

"You think so?" I ask, tugging at her panties.

"Yeah... I think so."

I hold her now naked body tight against me as I kiss neck, jaw, mouth. Enjoying the feel of her body under my hands when she suddenly pulls away, standing up. "I didn't say you could go anywhere," I say, as she turns to face me, her body only lit by the dim light of near nightfall during a thunderstorm, and I want to tell her how beautiful she is standing in front of me, but I can't find the words.

"Oh, but it's my turn now," Anna says as a prolonged flash of lightning illuminates her as she steps close to me, grabbing my shirt, yanking it off me. It is a matter of seconds before I find myself completely exposed to the cool, wet wind of the storm blowing across my skin. But it is far from cooling me down in the slightest. I stand up, not letting her stop me, and kiss her as I pull her body tight against mine. I turn us until we have turned enough, and I push Anna down onto the bed.

I straddle her, sitting on my knees over her lap. Reaching down, I pull Anna up to a sitting position, and she buries her face against me, her hands squeezing my sides. I can't stop myself from letting out a quiet moan as my body tightens with an involuntary response to the touch of her lips on my skin pulling at me. Suddenly we are both lit in a pale yellow light that spills from the open double doors, the power having come back on. But neither of us says anything, because other than being able to see each other better, we really don't care.

I move Anna back from me just enough to make her stop. She looks up at me. The light's sharp angle creates an equally sharp contrast on Anna's face as she stares up at me. "You are so beautiful. But," I continue before she can say anything, "this is about you. So I need you to lie back."

"Why's this about me?" she asks, not to give me a hard time though, she just wants to know.

"Because I want to, because..." I stop myself just before I say *I love you,* because I am suddenly scared to say it. "I want you. I want to make you forget about the lightning... and everything else that scares you." Anna doesn't say anything, she just moves back on the bed until her head is on a pillow. But she never breaks our eye contact. *Something about this time is different,* I think, as I start kissing my way up her body. This time it isn't just sex like before, this time something is different, changed, better... scarier.

We can only hear the light rain outside the covering of the balcony, the dark making it impossible to see. The lightning and thunder have also moved on, leaving us huddled tight together under the blanket, neither of us sleeping; who could sleep after that? The light from Anna's room, still spilling over us.

I roll over under the blanket and against Anna, laying one leg over her so I can be as close to her as possible. I kiss her breast softly before laying my head on her chest as it slowly rises and falls, and I can hear the steady thump of her heart. *I want to tell her. I want to tell her how I feel, that I love her.* "What are you thinking about?" Anna asks, her arms coming around me, hands clasping as they rest against me.

"More like wondering," I say, not moving or looking at her. But I know she is looking at me.

"About what?"

I close my eyes for a second, listening to the steady beat of Anna's heart and the rain. "What is this?"

"What?"

"Us... What are we?" I ask, scared to hear the answer.

"Well, this is your first same-sex experience. So, I guess we are just enjoying something together, something that is new to you." Anna says this almost clinically. And I feel my heart fall slightly.

"Oh..."

"Why?" she asks, sounding a little concerned.

"No, that's what I was thinking, too. This has just been really nice..." I say, knowing that I can't say more than this, not now. "Thanks for everything. I really was in trouble before you found me."

"You would have been fine. But, I'm glad we found each other. I've never enjoyed being around someone this much."

"Really?" I say, moving off of her, and we both sit up, the blanket falling away.

"Yeah," she says as we turn. Facing each other, we wrap our arms loosely around one another, holding each other up. "It has been a lot of fun." Something about the word *"Fun"* hurts. *Is that all this has been, "fun"? Just something we both enjoy*? I wonder.

"Yeah..."

"Are you okay?" she asks, seeming concerned again.

"Yes, yes, I'm fine. It has all just been... a lot."

"Are you sure? I don't want anything to make you unhappy," she says.

"You're sweet." I smile.

"Well, I just..." she pauses for a second, thinking. "I don't know... I think... No, I know that I—"

"Evy, there you are!" We both hear, and turn simultaneously to see a man in well-dressed casual clothes standing in the middle of Anna's room staring at us as we sit in the middle of the air mattress, still very naked. I'm not sure who is more surprised, him or us. "I'm sorry!" he says, turning away as soon as his mind starts working enough to do so. Which is the exact amount of time it takes for my mind to snap out of the same shock and snatch up the blanket to cover us.

"They aren't here!" Anna calls after him as he goes out the door.

"Yeah... Yeah, sorry!" the man calls back.

"I'll be down in a second!" Anna calls. "Are you okay?" she asks me quietly.

"Yeah, I'm fine."

"That's Evy's boyfriend, Nathan," she says, answering my next question before I can ask it. "You look a little pale. You sure you're okay?"

"Yes, I'm fine. I just wasn't expecting someone to walk in," I say truthfully. But some of the paleness is due to our conversation just before, and what it clarified. That we are having fun. Or at least, Anna is. But I can't expect her to want more out of it than that. I didn't exactly ask her any details about her feelings towards me when I pulled her robe off in that hotel. I was perfectly happy skipping right over figuring out our relationship and moving straight to sex.

So why should I expect more? I should just be grateful that I have a kind, loving person I can trust myself to be with.

I follow Anna downstairs after a five-minute shower and fresh clothes, knowing that I am going to feel very awkward as soon as we are downstairs. "I am so sorry," Nathan says the second we walk into the kitchen. "I didn't know you were back in town, Anna, and that you had a girlfriend." Just thirty minutes ago, I would have felt giddy at hearing someone say I am Anna's girlfriend. But now? Now it just hurts, because we aren't. I know this now. "Oh, are you not," he says, backtracking, seeming to have noticed the look on my face, or maybe Anna's, if she too reacted how I did.

"Calm down, Nathan," Anna says, sitting down at the kitchen table. "Don't worry about it. We weren't actually doing anything at that moment, and it ain't like you saw something you've never seen before." He looks more embarrassed at this, and I feel more embarrassed about this. "Dude, you're blushing. Please tell me after all this time you have actually seen Evy's boobs." I am getting the feeling now that Anna is just tormenting him.

"Anna, stop it," I say, slapping her on the shoulder. "I'm Mary," I say to Nathan.

"It's nice to meet you"—he holds his hand out—"I'm pastor Nathan Claassen," he says as I shake his hand.

"Oh yeah, I forgot to mention that he's the pastor at Evy's church," Anna says with a sardonic grin, and I am starting to wonder if I did something wrong to her, or if Nathan did. Because I feel like she is punishing us.

"Oh..." I say, not sure what I am supposed to say to a pastor after he sees me naked in bed with another woman.

"I stopped by—" he says.

"Because you needed to be fruitful with my sibling?" Anna interrupts, making it clear it is him she is punishing. *Wait, did Anna say Evy's church? Evy goes to church?* I wonder as I think of Evy, a person who cusses and swears more than anyone I have ever met. Not to mention is non-binary, something my church would have never approved of.

"Because," he continues, ignoring the comment, "Evy was supposed to be at a study group tonight."

"They had a sump pump quit in one of the houses, but then texted and said things went south and would be late," Anna says.

"That was a while ago," I say, looking at the time on my phone.

"I'm sure Evy is fine and will be back anytime. Why don't you make yourself useful, preacher boy, and help me make dinner?" Anna says this more like an order than a question.

"I'll help," I say.

"Nope. You're a guest. He's just here to eat our food, so he can at least help cook it."

"Anna, don't say that," I say.

"It's fine," Nathan says. "I am used to it. She has been pissed ever since my brother and her broke up."

"That has nothing to do with it," Anna says defensively, and now I am getting the feeling that she would rather he hadn't brought this up.

"He's fine. Just in case you were wondering," he says, and I wonder if this wasn't a serious relationship. I am a bit annoyed that he would bring this up while I am standing right here. But remember that I am just something for Anna to... have fun with.

"Too bad," Anna says. "I was hoping that fucking asshole got himself killed."

"It wasn't that bad," Nathan says.

"Oh, let's let Mary decide. She might as well know what the fuck this is about, and it would be nice to get the opinion of someone that isn't some cisgen, white, male preacher that thinks everyone should be forgiven." I realize that Anna has now dragged me into it, and I wonder why I have to play judge.

"Really? You are going to describe me like that?" Nathan says, starting to lose his calm demeanor.

"Why? Were any of those wrong?" Anna asks, looking at him hard, and he doesn't say anything. "When we started dating, he knew I was bi and said he was fine with it. Then, after a year together, he says how he is glad he was able to 'straighten me out'." I stare at her, knowing how much this must have hurt her.

"He didn't mean it like that," Nathan says, trying to make it not sound so bad, which makes sense, since this person is his brother.

"Really?" Anna says looking at him, "Because I don't remember you being there, and I think I would have remembered you being there since we were both naked in bed when he said it." She looks back at me. "So, apparently he thought that being bi was just like a phase I was going through, and that his fucking me for a year had cured me."

"I'm sorry," I say.

"Why? You didn't do anything," Anna says.

"I just know how much that must have hurt you."

"Thank you. And it really did," she says, looking at Nathan, who looks like he knows he has been wrong. And also looks like he is tired of being the one that catches all the anger that is directed at his brother. "To give him credit, he was good, not as good as he thought he was, though. And God, he was nowhere near as good as you." She says this offhandedly, glancing at me, not seeming to realize what she just said. I don't say anything either, and try not to react. But I don't think I pulled it off. "Anyway, in short. I dumped him, and it made me sick to think I spent a year of my life with someone who thought they could fuck the queer out of me."

"He was young and stupid," Nathan says.

"On that subject. Tell Mary about your coming over to our house to try to see if I would talk it out with him. Tell her how that went." He just looks annoyed; but not surprised, so she looks at me. "He came over to 'help' and instead hooked up with Evy."

"It wasn't like I didn't know them. We knew each other really well."

"Sunday school, right?" Anna says.

"It doesn't matter where we met, and we also went to school together growing up," he says. And I get the feeling they are moving onto another argument without the first one ending.

"I'm home!" I hear Evy yell from the front door. "Someone come and help me out!"

"I'm coming dear!" Nathan calls back and instantly heads in that direction.

"So, do you two always fight like that?" I ask after he is out of the room, and quiet enough he won't hear.

"More or less," she says, like it is no big deal.

"It sounds like you and his brother were serious."

"We were."

"I am sorry you went through that."

"Thanks. Can't imagine what your break up must have felt like," Anna says.

"I actually don't think it was as bad as yours... I had never loved Justin, and he had stopped loving me a long time ago. So it was over long ago, it just took us a while to end it. You loved him though, and didn't know there was even a problem," I say, taking her hand.

"Yeah... I really was in love with him," she says, hugging me.

"Let's fix some dinner," I say, our arms still around each other.

"Oh, by the way," Anna whispers, as we still hold each other. "I wasn't lying," she says. I start to wonder what she means when she kisses my neck and her hand slips under my shirt, caressing the small of my back. I know then what she means, and I feel my face grow warm as I blush.

23

Employed

I lie on the bed and stare at the ceiling, holding my phone. Anna hasn't come in yet, and must be talking with Evy. So, I look at my phone for a second and then tap call.

"There you are," I say, as Alesha answers after a half dozen rings.

"Yeah, I'm here," she says, with a yawn. "I was just dozing while watching TV."

"Oh, didn't mean to bother you."

"Stop it, you're fine," she says. "What's up? You don't sound very chipper for someone who has been doing... well, Anna."

"Haha, very funny."

"You do sound down though, something happen?" Alesha asks.

"I found out that... we're apparently just having fun," I say, and something about it gains weight as I say it to Alesha.

"Wait, you and Anna?"

"Yeah."

"But, like, how do you know that?"

"She told me," I say plainly, trying not to let my emotions get control.

"She told you that?" she says, sounding like she can't believe it.

"So... I guess I was wrong," I say, my voice cracking a little.

"Okay, tell me what happened. Like, everything." So, I do. I tell her every detail I can remember. I even tell her how it seemed like so much more than just sex this time. Alesha just listens, giving me the space to talk. She doesn't interrupt, say any crude jokes, or judge me for thinking my relationship with Anna was more. Because now that I hear myself telling all of this to Alesha, I sound like a juvenile fool who fell for the first person who gave me any attention.

"I feel like a fool," I tell her.

"Don't say that. Everyone does this—"

"In grade school."

"For fuck's sake, will you stop making everything about goddamn age? Falling for someone has nothing to do with age, and I still think you have a chance with her," she says.

"Really?"

"Of course. It seems to me that she likes spending time with you. I have had physical relationships that were only about having someone to screw. And for me, they never wanted anything to do with me otherwise. We met up, got it on, and that was it," Alesha says.

"Really?"

"Yeah. So, I wouldn't give up yet. Just don't push her on it. I would just have fun and see where it goes."

"Okay, thanks," I say.

"Hey, anytime. After all, you are the only exciting thing in my life," she says, making me laugh a little.

"I need to get to bed. It's been a long day," I say, feeling really tired.

"Me too."

"One of these days I will call without a problem," I say.

"I like to have a bit of your drama. I have missed the drama of my friends after I went van-life."

"So, now I'm drama?" I ask, laughing.

"Yeah, but your drama is so good."

"How is it good?"

"It is all sexy and fun. It is really hot at times," she says, breathing heavily into the phone.

"Real funny." I laugh.

"Well, it is," she says, laughing as well.

"I'll let you go now. Thanks, you are a great friend."

"Oh, I know," Alesha says smugly.

"But you can really be a—"

"Say it! Say it!" She eggs me on as I laugh.

"A bitch."

"You said it!" she yells into the phone, laughing hysterically.

"You are such a bad influence," I say, laughing nearly as much as she does.

"We bitches always are," she says, suddenly serious. And I can't help but wonder how she can go from hysterical laughter to serious like that.

"Okay... On that note, good night," I say.

"Good night, love you," she says, and it makes me happy hearing it from a friend, knowing they mean it.

"Love you too," I say happily, and hang the phone up.

I stare at the blank screen for a minute, just smiling and feeling better. Because Alesha is right, I will just go one day at a time and see what happens between me and Anna.

After several more minutes and no sign of Anna, I turn out the light and pull the blankets close. The room is still full of the storm's cool, damp air, but it makes it a consuming comfort that pulls me into an instant sleep. I'm not sure how much time has passed when I feel the bed move slightly, and a soft kiss on my cheek right before a warm familiar body cuddles tight against mine.

I sit at the kitchen table by myself drinking some coffee, knowing Anna got to bed late. I didn't want to wake her up by just lying in bed awake, and for some reason, I felt like being by myself for a little while. So, I sit at the table staring at the wall and drinking my coffee, as my mind runs through things between me and Anna like I am planning an attack strategy.

I feel like I am trying to win her, I think with a sigh. After everything with Justin and Debra; not to mention losing Debra as a friend. Also, losing my kids on top of that. I feel like I'm not sure

I am ready for something else. *What if I spend all this time trying to get her and then lose in the end? I'm not sure I can take that... I'm not sure I can take losing anyone else.*

As I stand at the counter pouring another cup of coffee, I stare at a jar with a candle in it. It is the same size and color as the jar of anti-aging cream I hit Justin with. I pick the jar up, rolling it in my hand and start to laugh, thinking of Anna saying that the jar of anti-aging cream worked so well that it was turning me into a teenager. It is suddenly really funny because here I am at six-thirty in the morning, unable to sleep because I am worried about if a girl does or doesn't like me. "Forty-three years old... with teen drama," I say to the candle as I slowly shake my head. *I know what I am going to do,* I think. With the haze of my early morning doubt gone, I set my freshly filled coffee cup down.

I walk up the stairs as quietly as a can, and softly open and close the bedroom door; careful not to let it slam. I slip out of my clothes; having already dressed, and slide under the covers. "Is it morning?" Anna asks, her eyes hardly even opening.

"It's very early. Go back to sleep," I whisper.

"Okay..." she barely says as she burrows herself tight against me, her head resting on my breasts. I kiss the top of her hair and close my eyes. Because Alesha was right, if I am going to have a chance of this changing, I need to just be with Anna.

"So," Anna says as I open my eyes, her gray eyes staring into my blue, "you came back."

"I did... I was halfway out of town with your truck and decided stealing it was wrong," I say as she starts laughing.

"Oh, like you could drive my rig."

"Hey, I've been studying hard and paying a lot of attention to your driving. So I could drive your truck," I argue, laughing with her.

"Okay, maybe you're right. You are a very fast learner... I can attest to that," Anna says, laughing. "Different note. You were wearing your sweats—"

"Pajamas."

"Stop trying to make them sound better than they are," she says. "Anyway... You were wearing your sweats last night, so"—she picks up the covers to look at me—"why are you now only in panties?"

"I couldn't sleep earlier, and got up at about six—"

"That's early."

"What? You never get up that early?"

"Not when I'm off work," Anna says, which is a good point.

"So, I got dressed, went downstairs and made some coffee. But I decided to come back later."

"Did you feel odd sitting in someone else's kitchen by yourself, or did you just miss me?" she says with a big grin.

"Both," I say honestly. "Actually... More of the latter."

"Good answer," she says, kissing me.

"I can smell something cooking. I bet breakfast is being made."

"Most likely, Evy has always been the good host type."

"You're not?" I ask.

"I'm more of the... 'Lock my guest in my room and keep them as a sex toy,' type," she says with air quotes.

"So, you've done this to other people?" I ask, raising an eyebrow.

"Umm... Do I have to answer that?"

"Actually, I think I would rather not know."

"Good choice," she laughs. "But I honestly haven't done that... too much."

"Okay, whatever," I say, knowing she is just giving me a hard time. "Let's get dressed and go help with breakfast."

As I start to get up, Anna grabs my wrist, pulling me back. She rolls over, swinging her leg over me, so she now sits over my hips. Holding my hands down, our fingers lace together as she kisses me. "I think we should stay here," she says, kissing my jaw and neck in the way she has found that I will do anything for.

"Five minutes," I say with a smile.

"Umm... Ten," she says, letting go of my hands, sitting upright just long enough to pull her t-shirt off and toss it to the floor before lying down against me again.

Her one hand grabbing mine as her other runs down my side. "Okay"—I breathe in with a quiet moan from her touch—"ten... minutes."

Twenty minutes later, we walk down the stairs together, and I am glad that I went back earlier this morning, for multiple reasons. I do wonder what a purely physical relationship is like, not knowing what the differences are, having not experienced them. But I have also never experienced a relationship of love and romance either. *I guess I will figure it out as I go,* I think as we walk into the kitchen. *I wish Alesha was here; I bet she could tell me at a glance.* This thought makes me smile with a small laugh.

"What?" Anna asks, looking at me.

"Oh, it's nothing."

"I know what it is... I'm that good." She grins.

"That is true," I admit, in a whisper.

"Whatever it is you're talking about, please stop," Nathan says from the kitchen table.

"I'd continue in detail. But, I know Mary wouldn't like that," Anna says, and I like that she thinks of my feelings.

"You have good timing," Evy says, turning around from the griddle. "All the work is done."

"Sorry, Ev," Anna says, once again the doting little sister kissing Evy's cheek. "Are you doing better today?"

"Yes, I am doing better. At least, I smell better," Evy says.

"So," I say, sitting down at the table. "What happened? I kind of missed it," I ask. Because all I heard was lots of cussing and swearing as Nathan helped Evy upstairs dressed only in their underwear. They didn't come down for dinner until sometime after I went to bed. So, all I know is something bad happened while Evy went to fix the sump pump in the rental house.

"Well, it turned out that the water alert the alarm in the basement had sent me wasn't from rainwater, and the sump pump had quit," Evy says, setting a large stack of pancakes on the table as Anna gets plates and flatware for everyone. "It was because the mother-fucking sewer backed up, and all that shit plugged the pump."

"Oh no... What did you do?"

"Turned off the power down there and waded in," Evy says, noticing the gut reaction look on my face. "It isn't like I wanted to. But I didn't have a goddamn choice, had to get the pump working."

"That's why you left your clothes outside," I say, it now making sense.

"Yeah, those are trash. And I'm pretty sure that fucking pervert neighbor across the street took pictures."

"Sweetie," Nathan says, "he's in his eighties."

"Your point being?" they say, looking at Nathan. "He has never liked me, and has always liked staring at me... Or any girl or woman that walks past. You can be old and still be a pervert." Nathan doesn't say anything else, seeming to know Evy well enough to know when it isn't worth arguing with them about something.

"So, what are you going to do next?" Anna asks.

"I have to hire a hazmat cleaning crew. Insurance will cover it, but not all of it. So I will have a shitload of work to do myself."

"Sorry I'm leaving in a few days, Ev," Anna says.

"We'll get it," Nathan says.

"It's fine," Evy says. "It's keeping up with cleaning the rest of the fucking houses between customers that will be so goddamn hard." Their increase in cussing is like a stress indicator.

"I can handle that," I say with hesitation as I cut my pancake with my fork.

"That's nice of you, but I won't even get a start on fixing the damage until after you and Anna are gone, and I can clean the hou—"

"Oh," Anna interrupts. "Mary is staying here, since she doesn't have a passport and I'm going to Canada." Nathan and Evy stare at Anna.

"You didn't tell Evy?" I say, staring at Anna now too.

"Kind of forgot," she says, smiling at me, as I glare at her.

"I can stay somewhere else," I say to Evy, who doesn't look as confused or annoyed as I was expecting.

"It's fine," they say. "There is plenty of room, and I'm used to my stupid little sis doing things like this."

"Hey!" Anna says with a mouth full of pancake. I just look at her. "Okay, sorry. I'll try not to do it again."

"But," I say, "I am happy to help clean houses. Cooking and cleaning are the only things I really know how to do."

"I can think of a few other things," Anna says, grinning at me.

"If you really don't mind, I could use the help, and I'll pay you," Evy says.

"You don't have to pay me. You are already letting me stay here. That's enough payment," I say.

"We'll pay you," Anna says. "We need the help, and you have to have a little money."

"So, it's settled," Evy says. "I'll start showing you the ropes, and you're all set."

"Thank's, that will be great," I say, really liking the idea of working. I look over to Anna, but she is typing on her phone, she lays it down as my phone vibrates. I glance at it and see the text is from Anna.

Anna: I will have to give you a physical before I can actually employ you.

Me: I'll make an appointment.

24

Away from Her

"I can't believe you already have to go," I say, looking up at Anna. She brushes my hair to the side, staring down at me as my head rests on her breast.

"It seemed to go really quick—"

"It was only three days," I say shortly, feeling angry about it again.

"I know, I'm sorry... It didn't help that Evy had you start training, I mean they could—"

"They needed my help, and when I'm hired for a job, I'm going to do it. Don't blame them—"

"Well, don't blame me."

"Sorry. I didn't mean to blame you," I say with a sigh, staring up at the ceiling. "How long before you leave?" I ask, not looking at her.

A faint glow of a phone screen appears. "Two hours. But I have to get the truck warmed up. So I can stay in bed about another hour before I have to start getting ready."

"Then it is two weeks..."

"Yeah..." Anna says, and I know she feels bad about it. And I haven't exactly made it easier for her. I know she doesn't like trucking, so it isn't very nice of me to make her feel worse. It is her job, and I have no right to interfere with that.

I move to lie beside her, putting my arms around her. "For some reason I never expect your eyes... Something about them being gray I never expect," I say, looking into them.

"Do you like them?"

"Of course I do," I smile. "Doesn't Evy have gray eyes too?"

"Yeah."

"Yours just seem... more vibrant, I think."

"My dad's eyes are brown, and Evy's dad's are blue. But Mom has gray eyes, and they must be some damn powerful genes, because Evy and I both got them."

"I'm glad you got her eyes. They're beautiful."

"So are yours."

"Mine are just blue."

"They're not 'just blue' they are your blue, and I love them." My heart skips a beat with her words being so close to saying she loves me.

"Thank you," I say, kissing her. "What should we do with our hour?"

"I don't know... It is really nice just being here with you, though."

"It is..." I say, the feeling of her body against mine feeling like home.

"Then let's just stay like this," Anna says.

"Okay... But you better not fall asleep. I'm not losing my last hour with you to sleep."

"I won't," she says with a quiet laugh that I can feel, and I want to tell her I love her, but I'm still too scared. I had hoped that she would say something to me, but here we are, lying in each other's arms, less than an hour before she leaves... and nothing has been said.

The truck's air horn gives two short blasts, and I wave as Anna drives away. "You okay?" Evy asks, standing beside and just a bit behind me.

I turn around to them. "Yeah, I'm fine," I say with a smile.

"Uh huh..." they say, looking at me for a few seconds. "Well, reckon we better get to work then."

"Okay," I say as Evy turns, going back into the house as I follow, feeling a bit empty.

"You know she really likes you, right?" Evy says, not turning around as they walk into the kitchen.

"I know..." I say. *But I want to know if it is more than just liking, I want to know if she loves me!* I want to cry out. But I don't, because why would Evy know? It is a question I should have asked Anna.

"Hot cereal sound good? I got blueberries to go with it."

"Sounds great, thanks."

Evy and I spend the rest of the day vacuuming, washing bedding, and getting houses ready for the next guest. It is a long hard day's work, but I wish it hadn't ended because at least when I was scrubbing toilets or vacuuming carpets, I wasn't thinking of Anna. Now that I sit in Evy's car. They play some music that sounds vaguely familiar, I just stare out the window and wonder where Anna is by now.

Evy turns the music down to a background level. "It was a full day. You doing okay?"

"It wasn't that bad," I say, trying to sound brighter.

"Normally, it isn't this bad. So don't worry about when you are doing this on your own while I am working on the lake house."

"Okay. But I'll be fine. I used to help clean the church at times as well," I say, and look back out the window as the houses outside become more frequent as we drive back into the city.

"You love her, don't you?"

"What?" I say, my head snapping around.

"Come on. I haven't seen someone so lovesick since middle school, when my best friend's boyfriend moved away," they say, with a grin that reminds me too much of Anna.

"Am I really as bad as a middle school girl?"

"I actually think you might be worse," Evy says, laughing a little. But they aren't being mean. I cringe a little at the thought of my acting like this at my age. "It's great that you feel that way. Most never get to fall in love later in life, they just give up... Or are lucky like me, and still have the person they love."

"He seems very nice," I say.

"He is great... We've been together a long time now, but it doesn't seem like it. Every day is still..." they pause, thinking of the word, "exciting."

"That's nice. I didn't have excitement with my husband at any point in our relationship." I laugh.

"That sucks."

"It's fine," I say, waving it off, because I really couldn't care less about anything to do with Justin now.

"Were you excited when you met?" Evy asks.

"Oh my goodness. I instantly had a crush on her. I was so nervous, but comfortable... Does that make sense?" I ask, looking over at Evy, and they glance at me with a small grin.

"I was talking about your husband," they say, their grin growing a little bigger, and my cheeks suddenly feel warm as embarrassment fills them.

"Oh... No, it wasn't like that."

"Really? Why did you get married then? Did he knock you up or something?" I look at them, and realize Anna has told them nothing about me. Evy knows nothing about me at all, and I feel a small sharp pain in my chest, because I have been dying to tell everyone everything about Anna since the second I met her.

"It's a long story," I say as we pull onto our street. "Can I ask you something?"

"Shoot."

"I do like your sister a lot. Actually... I do love her." I take a small breath. "So, do you think she loves me? I mean, as more than a friend."

"Fuck, this is like middle school," they say, laughing a little, but I don't laugh. "Sorry, just joking." Evy thinks for the next block and doesn't say anything until the car is parked in the driveway. "I'm going to be honest with you, because I think you are like me in your old age, and you want it straight." This makes me smile, because I think they are right. "I honestly don't know."

"Really?" I say, surprised by this answer. Thinking they would know since they and Anna are pretty close.

"Anna has never been good at commitment or long-term relationships. Not that she wouldn't have one," Evy says, backtracking a little after seeing some of the devastation that I am feeling, showing on my face. "But something about it has always been hard. When she and Nathan's brother Sam broke up. It wasn't just because he said something really stupid; which he did. Their relationship was falling apart before that."

"Why?" I ask, not sure I want to know that answer.

"Sam wanted her to move in. He wanted things to move forward, but she just wouldn't do it. They started fighting about it, and everything just started to go south. To be honest, I was surprised how close she is with you."

"Really?"

"Yeah. So, you might have a chance with her. But I don't really know," Evy says with kind honesty.

"We never agreed to be exclusive with each other. Do you think she will... go out with anyone else while she is on the road?" I'm not even sure why I am asking this. It is something I should be asking Anna. It isn't exactly like I can't contact her.

"Oh... I don't think she would do that. As far as I know, Anna has never been a lover in every port kind of girl. But she has also never been the type to call her older sibling to tell about the latest person she's banged." I look at her a bit blankly, not sure if this was a 'yes' or 'no'. "You really need to just talk with her. Asking me is getting you nowhere fast. Like I said, Anna seems very close to you for the short amount of time you have known each other. So, just tell her."

"Okay, thanks. And sorry for being such a middle schooler." They laugh at this.

"Hey, just so you know, if you ask about these things and Anna dumps you, I won't kick you out."

"Thanks, that means a lot," I say, laughing with them.

"I really, really need the cleaning help." They joke as they open their car door.

We go inside and shower off the day's grime. Then I tell Evy my entire story about my divorce and my coming out while we make dinner. It is nice, and actually fun telling all of it. I also tell them some about Anna and me, but not everything; not even close. Something about the time Anna and I have spent together, the things we talked about, eating in the sleeper, the truck stop shopping... falling asleep together while watching the movie. It is all just too private, something that is just for Anna and me... Also a little bit for Alesha. But she isn't Anna's sibling.

I lie on Anna's bed; that is now mine, and stare at the ceiling while doing my best to not smell her pillow or do anything else too teen-like. But it is hard to lie in a bed alone when you have only been in it with the person you love.

I look at my phone to check the time and decide I will try calling her. Not only am I now able to use the Wi-Fi in the house, but Evy stopped by their phone providers' store and added my phone to their plan. They said that they needed to be able to call me while I was working in case they needed something, but I have the feeling that wasn't the only reason.

The phone rings over and over as I listen to it, waiting for Anna to pick up. I wait until the phone goes to voicemail. Staring at the screen, I decide not to text her, because if she isn't answering, she won't be texting either. *Unless she just doesn't want to talk to you. You have been a little overbearing since you started screwing around with her,* my mind suddenly says. I know it is just my mind running away with me, but I can't help but think that it might be true.

Me: Hey, how are you?

I watch the screen hoping, praying that Alesha is around, because I feel like I need her again. To my surprise, my phone starts ringing. "Hello?" I say, knowing it is Alesha.

"Hey!" Alesha says so loud I nearly drop my phone.

"Wow, that was loud."

"That's because it is a video-call, and I am looking at a closeup of what I think is your ear."

"What? A video-call?"

"Oh God, please tell me you know what those are," Alesha says, completely serious.

"Yes, I'm not that old."

"Then why can't I see you?" she asks as I point the phone away from me. "What? Are you naked?"

"No!"

"Not that it matters, we passed that point in a friendship about thirty seconds into it," she says, laughing. And thinking back to meeting her in that shower room feels like so long ago.

"I'm not naked." I laugh.

"Then show yourself!"

"But I'm not dressed, and lying in bed."

"Why the fuck does that matter? Show yourself in the video, goddamnit!"

"Okay, fine, fine," I say, turning the camera to look into it.

"Oh my God, you look like shit!" Alesha says as I start laughing.

"Told you," I say. "Want me to turn the camera away?"

"No, you're fine. It was just the initial shock of you on camera."

"That isn't polite," I say.

"Sorry, Mom," she says, rolling her eyes. "So, let me guess. Your bed warmer is gone, and you're lonely. Am I right?"

"Anna isn't a bed warmer."

"I was going to call her something else, but I didn't think you would like it."

"Oh, and what would that be?"

"I was going to say that you were missing your fuck toy." She stares at me for a second through the camera. "Yup, you don't like it."

"No, I don't like it."

"Then you shouldn't have questioned me on it."

"Well, I won't make that mistake again," I say.

"So, when did she leave?" Alesha asks seriously.

"Early this morning."

"How you holding up? I mean, I know that it hurts like hell."

"I'm doing okay... I guess."

"You'll make it. I think this is actually good for you," she says.

"How is it good for me?"

"You need to learn to be alone. This is like the first time in your life you have been alone, right?" she says, and it is something I haven't really thought about.

"Well, after the kids went to college, and Justin wasn't really there, I was pretty much alone."

"Not the same. Not if you had that toxic asswipe of a human in your house with you. I'm sure he was always complaining or whining about something."

"How do you know that?" I ask, because he was.

"That type always does. They always have it worse than anyone else. Sure, he is running around fucking anyone that will get close to him. But he has to do it, because his life is so awful he has no choice. If you made his life better, he wouldn't have to screw your best friend."

"He actually said that the affair started because he felt deprived."

"He thinks he was deprived? Fuck, you have been deprived for over forty years!" Alesha says laughing.

"That was actually what I thought when he said this to me!" I laugh.

"I wonder..." she says thinking, "How many times a hot girl walked past, and you both looked and thought 'Damn, I want that.'"

"Oh gosh, don't say that." I laugh. "I can't stand the thought that I might have been attracted to the same woman as Justin."

"Sorry, I shouldn't have put that in your head. It was just an out-loud thought."

"Well, keep those thoughts to yourself," I say.

"Okay, I promise I won't say something like that again."

"Thank you."

"Have you talked to Anna tonight?" Alesha asks.

"I tried calling her just before I texted you, but no answer."

"So, have you two decided if you will use video-calls to stay... in touch?" she says with a grin.

"We didn't talk about it, but I guess we will talk on video-calls."

"Talk... right," she says, winking at me.

"Okay, what am I missing?"

"You know, video-calls so you don't... miss"—she air quotes—"each other so much."

"Still not following," I say, with no idea where she is going with this.

"Oh for fuck's sake, I mean video sex!"

"Oh. oh..." I say, thinking about it. "Is that common?"

"You have no idea."

"Do you think Anna is expecting that?" I ask.

"How the hell would I know? Just ask her."

"Ask her just straight out, right?" I ask, not sure I can do that.

"The way you look right now tells me half the reason you are missing her is because you have been getting it on every night, right?" I don't say anything, which is pretty much just saying 'yes' to this. "And after all, God knows what you two have done to each other, you can't ask this?"

"Okay, I see your point."

"It isn't that hard of a question. But let me know if it goes horrifically, I want to hear about that," Alesha says with a big smile.

"I will let you know," I say.

"I need to get my beauty sleep. So, you call your girl again."

"Okay, thanks."

"Anytime. I really enjoy screwing with you. Oh, and before I forget. When you lie like that and hold your phone like that, I can see right down your shirt."

"What!" I say, looking down at myself.

"Yeah, I've been looking right down your shirt the whole time."

"Why didn't you say something sooner?" I ask, folding the neck of my shirt tight.

"Because it is so much more fun to tell you later than sooner. Plus, I've already seen that pair, remember?" She laughs with a sadistic smile.

"I wonder why I have to have you as a friend?"

"All that praying for all those years just worked, God sent you me."

"Not so sure that's who sent you," I say as she bursts into laughter. "Good night."

"Good night," Alesha says and hangs up. My phone instantly dings with a text from her.

Alesha: Send this to your girl. Hahahaha

Then another message, this one a screenshot from her phone. A clear view right down my loose t-shirt I sleep in, leaving nothing to the imagination.

Me: You better delete that.

Alesha: Only after you send me a screenshot of you having sent it to Anna.

Me: Really?

Alesha: Do it!

Alesha: And I want a screenshot as proof.

I sigh, and switch to Anna's name on the texting app.

Me: Alesha took this before I knew she could see down my shirt on the video-call.

I send the text and then send the photo. I take the screenshot, and before I can send it to Alesha, Anna replies with a GIF of a cartoon character's eyes popping out of their head.

Anna: That made my night better. Are you too tired? Can I call?

Something tells me I asked Anna the question about video calling without even knowing I was. But now that I think of it, I am also sure that Alesha knew this screenshot would ask the question. I feel like she tricked me, but I also feel like I don't care.

25

Long Days, Alone

Even though it is hot and humid out, the fresh air is the most welcoming thing in the world. After spending the day breathing household cleaners of all kinds, I feel like my head is going to explode. But the fresh air instantly makes me feel better. *Too bad I don't have time to enjoy it,* I think as I carry the heavy vacuum cleaner out to the Subaru, setting it down in the driveway so I can get the hatchback of the car open.

It is an older wagon-type car that is a little dinged up and is very stained inside; which is a testament to its years of use as Evy's mobile cleaning unit. It has everything a house cleaner could wish for in it, and it is now my daily vehicle.

The average cleaning time by myself is six to seven hours, since I have to clean everything. Evy and Anna have just enough houses that need to be cleaned, that I end up cleaning a house a day, five days a week. It surprises me how often people rent the houses out for a few days at a time. Some of the people even live here in the city, but want to stay out in the country for a few days; like a mini vacation. Which is a really great idea, and I wonder why I never did this with the kids. I know the answer, but I don't know why I let Justin make all the decisions.

I climb into the car, closing the door. Starting the engine I open the music player on my phone. The stereo in the car only plays radio stations; which never have anything on, so I just turn the volume of my phone up and hit play on the same album. It is the same

AURORA album that Anna played that day in the truck. It makes me think of that day... of all those days with her.

As I drive the thirty minutes back, I decide the first thing I will do when I get home is take a bath, a long one. As I try to keep my eyes open, I just pray that I will be able to stay awake long enough to make it as far as the bathtub, or that I don't drown in there. *I wonder what we are having for dinner?* I wonder, hoping that it is done so I can eat as soon as I walk in. I would rather not have to wait any longer than necessary to scrub off the cleaner mist that has been floating onto me all day.

"That you?" I hear a man's voice call, and I know it is Nathan. He is here so much it is hard to know if he lives here or not, but he helps out a lot and is a truly nice person; I see why Evy loves him. I'm glad I have met him, because he is the kind of guy that would be great to be in a relationship with. And the fact that I haven't had a second's thought that I wish I had married him, or was dating him. Not that I was unsure, but if a seemingly perfect guy like Nathan does nothing for me, that is reassuring. I just feel like I don't need that added complication of a new sexual identity crisis.

"No, it's me... Mary," I reply, feeling like I should add my name just in case he forgot or something.

"Oh, welcome home," he says from the kitchen as I take my shoes off.

"Evy isn't home yet?" I ask, walking into the kitchen.

"They texted and should be here any minute," he says, working on something at the kitchen stove, and I am thankful he is here cooking, instead of me having to do it after a long day's work. Even though I only worked part-time for the church, it was so tiring to come home and cook dinner. I had never realized what a luxury it is having someone cook for you after a long day's work, until I started working for Evy, and they or Nathan cook every night. I do plan on insisting on doing the cooking on my days off to make it fair.

"You look worn out," he says, looking over from his work.

"I'm fine. It was just a long day. How was your day?" I ask and realize it is the same question I asked Justin every evening. He would always go off on how long and awful his day was, and that's why he was an hour or two late. I wonder if all the times he was late he was just screwing my best friend, or if it was only part of the times he was late.

"My day was fine. I visited a few parishioners and then went to the Oak River care home for a bible study. Thank you for asking." It is such a more pleasant response than Justin had ever given, even on the best of days.

"That's nice. I'm sure your parishioners appreciate your dedication. It seems that dedication like that is lacking from most these days."

"Thank you. You aren't wrong. It seems that there is a lack of dedication to faith these days."

"—Goddamn rain!" We hear with the sound of the door closing hard.

"Is it raining?" Nathan ask in the direction Evy's voice came from.

"Yeah, it's just starting. But it looks like it will set in," they say, walking in with a sigh. "If the lake house basement floods again, I swear to fuckin God, I am killing someone." They drop into a chair, looking more dirty and tired than I am, and I suddenly feel like I have been making too big of a deal about my day's work.

"And who exactly would you kill for this atrocity?" Nathan asks, raising an eyebrow as he grins.

"First of all... Don't make light of that goddamn shithole flooding. I am about to burn that fucking bastard to the ground." Part of me believes Evy when they say this. "And to answer your question... I will kill whoever is closest. I don't care if they had nothing to do with it. I will just need to kill someone."

"I will remember to stay away from you tomorrow," he says, smiling, and I think he is smiling just to irritate them.

"Does it flood because it is close to the lake?" I ask.

"The lake house?" Evy says, looking at me, "It isn't that close to the lake. It is actually farther away from the lake than any of the other houses. We call it that because I swear the goddamn thing was built on swamp ground, so the basement floods at the drop of a hat... I could kill that fuck who sold it to me. The son of a bitch told me it never flooded, never a problem at all, that the sump pump was just a precaution." I realize that I asked about a very sore subject.

"Oh, I didn't know that. Sorry."

"Don't apologize," Nathan says. "My Evs is like this every time we are in a rain stretch."

"You would be too if you were the one mudding sheetrock and painting," they grumble.

"Why didn't you hire it done?" I ask, and the look on Nathan's face seems to be screaming, *"No! Don't ask that!"* But, it's too late. I did.

"Because the asshole insurance company didn't pay enough. They paid enough for the hazmat cleaning, but not enough for the rest of the repair. So that's all me."

"Oh, I see—"

"I mean, why the fuck do they even offer the goddamn plan if they aren't going to cover it all? What the hell? I mean, I just don't know—"

"Sweety, calm down," Nathan says, and Evy stops for a second. "It's done, and we know this is what happens." He says it so softly, lovingly.

"Yeah but—" they try.

"But," he continues, "you are just stressing yourself out more. You don't need that. So, I will help you and we will just get the work done. It will be fine." Evy calms down at this. They are such a sharp contrast to each other, it is hard to figure out. They are definitely the oddest couple I have met. But it seems to work very well for them.

"You're right, sorry for getting so worked up," Evy says at a calm, normal level. "But if that insurance bastard walks in front of my car, I'm running him down!"

My eyes are closed as I lie in the warm bath, trying to find the delicate balance between relaxing and falling asleep. My phone lies close enough that I can reach it, but it stays silent. I try not to think about the fact it is staying silent. But that's okay. I understand that Anna is working, and now that she is on the west coast, the three-hour time difference makes it hard.

After forty-five minutes or so, I decide I better get out before I do fall asleep. I also have an early morning as well, so I better get a good night's sleep. But I have to force myself to get out of the warm tub, because deciding to get out and actually getting out are two very different things. My rational mind being the only part of me that is saying to get out, while my sore muscles, aching feet, and general loneliness never want to leave the calm, peaceful bathtub.

I towel myself off as the bathtub drains, and then put on Anna's bathrobe. Not only because I don't have one, but because I am pretty sure I would be wearing hers if I did have my own. My mind is just that kind of a lovesick teenager, and I have all but given up on trying to change that. I don't know if letting myself act this way will just make things worse later or not, but I'm tired of ignoring my feelings for who I love. I just want to let myself love.

Lying down on the bed, I stare at my phone. *I'll just see how her day was before I get ready for bed,* I think, tapping dial on Anna's number.

"Hey, there you are," she says brightly with the quiet rumble of her truck and the highway in the background. Hearing her voice makes me want to cry.

"I know you're still driving. I just wanted to see how your day has been before I go to bed."

"That's sweet of you. My day has been pretty uneventful, until you called that is. That's a nice highlight." I smile and feel warm at her saying this. "How about your day?"

"I literally just cleaned a house all day, nothing else. Come on, I know that something had to happen in a full day of driving, so tell me, even if it is small... I'm tired and just want to hear your voice," I say, and wonder if that is too much.

"Well, this morning when I went to leave," she says, and continues telling me about her day, all the little details of driving, stopping for fuel, and what other drivers on the highway have done. It is all the little things that no one wants to hear, or care about... Except for me. They are all I want to hear, she is all I want to hear, and I want to tell her so bad.

"You sound really tired," Anna says after I respond to her telling me about something another trucker did.

"I'm fine. It was just a long day."

"I better let you sleep then."

"I guess I should go to sleep," I say.

"You okay?" she asks, sounding worried.

"I just... need a good night's sleep," I say, lying. Because I wanted to tell her how much I miss her, want her back, and ask when she will be back, even though I already know the answer. But I also know that this will just sound needy, and I still don't feel that I have the right to put any of this on her.

"I will let you go then... Good night, sweet dreams," she says.

"Good night... Or, evening I guess. Be careful," I say.

"I will be. Don't let Evy overwork you."

"They aren't. I'll be fine."

"Okay... Bye."

"Bye..." I say with a quiet sigh. "I love you," I say a second after she hangs up. I look over to her side of the bed and lay my phone on her pillow. It feels like the closest thing to having her next to me now. "What should I do when she comes back?" I ask the empty side of the bed. "You have to tell her, if she is still interested... I have to tell her."

26

Where Did I Go Wrong?

It is good to see the sun shining brightly as I walk outside. I'm glad that last night's rain wasn't much, and that we have a couple of days until the next rain. But it is also a little depressing that I will be inside cleaning houses all day, instead of outside. It makes me miss my couple of flower gardens and little vegetable garden. It was always nice to work in them on days like this.

"No point in dwelling on it," I say to myself as I walk to my car; or Evy's cleaning car, rather.

The drive to the house I have to clean today is only about twenty minutes away, and the house is a little single-story. If it was in New Orleans, I would call it a shotgun house, but I don't know if that's what it's called in New York. It doesn't matter what it's called. What matters is that it is a small house and shouldn't take too long to clean, and there will be no stairs to vacuum, or carry the vacuum cleaner up and down; something that I hate more than anything else.

I set the carrying tote of cleaning supplies down as I unlock the door. Before going in, I look at the view from the little front porch. It is a surprisingly pretty view of the trees, with the lake peaking through them as the sun reflects off the water. I can see why people rent these houses for little vacations. I know I would.

Stepping into the house, leaving my shoes on the porch, I carry the cleaning tote to the kitchen so I don't set it on the carpet. Evy said not to worry so much, but I don't like taking a chance with the nice carpet. I walk back across the living room to go get the vacuum cleaner from the car when I step on something wet. I involuntarily let out a little scream, jumping to the side as my brain thinks of all sorts of disgusting things it could be.

But looking at the carpet, it is only slightly darker, like it is just wet. I cautiously poke at it with the tip of my toe; with the foot that already has a damp sock, and the floor is just wet. I stand there staring at it, unable to think of what could have spilled. It has been two days since the last guest, and anything they would have spilled would have dried by now. It also isn't really stained, so most likely not a drink of some kind.

Suddenly I get a bad feeling and look up, and see what I was scared I would see, a wet-looking brown circle in the ceiling directly above the wet spot on the carpet. "Oh, no... Evy is going to die," I say, thinking of them going off about insurance and the lake house last night.

I think for a second about what to do and know that there is only one thing to do. "Hey, it's me," I say into the phone.

"Hey, what is it?" Evy asks, knowing I have no reason to call, unless something is wrong.

"I am at the little house today, and..." I pause, "it looks like the roof leaked last night in the rain."

"Are you joking?" they say, knowing I'm not, but I also know they are praying I am wrong about this.

"No, sorry."

"Son of a fucker." This is more quiet, like Evy has moved the phone and is just saying this to the room.

I hear a voice in the background that must be Nathan. "What's wrong?" he asks.

"How bad is it?" Evy asks.

"I'll show you. One second," I say, and turn the video on. "See." I point the camera at the ceiling.

"Goddamnit! That's a big spot."

"What do I do?" I ask.

"I can't come. Nathan and I are already out of town to get a part for the heater in the lake house and won't be back until this evening."

"Okay..." I say, not sure what this will mean for me.

"But I will just call the crew I use for roofing. So just continue like normal, and I will let you know when the crew will be there," Evy says.

"I will start with getting the carpet dried out," I say.

"Good idea. Rent a carpet cleaner if you need to. They are great for pulling water out of carpet."

"I might do that. It's pretty wet," I say, noticing how wet my sock is.

"Thanks, I owe you."

"No problem," I say, and then hang up. I get my shoes on, lock up, and go to the nearest store that has a carpet cleaner for rent.

The cleaner does a great job pulling what water there is out of the carpet and removing any stains the water left behind. As I turn the cleaner off, my phone rings. I look at the screen and see it is Evy. "Hello?"

"Hey. So, bad news," they say. "My normal roofing crew I hire is completely booked, apparently the recent storms have been causing a lot of roof damage."

"So they aren't coming today?"

"No, and they won't be able to before tomorrow."

"Well, it isn't supposed—"

"They added rain to tonight's forecast," Evy says.

"So, what do we do?" I ask, wondering if I should put a bucket where the wet spot was.

"Are you afraid of heights?"

"Umm..." I think back to the roller coaster at Magical Land. "No, I don't think so—Wait... why?"

"Would you be willing to climb up there and paint some sealant over that area of the roof, to hold it over until the roofing crew can re-roof it?"

"You want me to fix the roof?" I say, half in shock at the idea.

"I would do it myself, but we aren't going to be back soon enough—"

"You want me to do it?" I say again.

"I will pay you so much more than normal pay. Is there any way you can?"

Hearing the desperation in their voice, I know I at least have to try. *After all, I am supposed to be trying new things*, I think. *Although, sex with Anna was a much better new thing than what this will most likely be.* "Okay, I'll try," I say.

"You are great! I will order the supplies, and you can just pick them up from the lumber yard; already paid for. There is a ladder in the garage hanging on the wall." Evy orders the supplies from the same lumber and hardware store I got the carpet cleaner from, so I only have one stop to make. They also order five one-gallon cans instead of a five-gallon bucket; which I wouldn't have been able to carry up a ladder.

I notice the spackles and splatters of the dark gray; almost black, tar-like sealant on my shoes and clothes, the same as my skin. *I have the feeling this is never going to come off*, I think with a sigh, wiping the sweat from my brow before continuing.

It isn't extremely hard work, just rolling it on with a paint roller. But I have to put layer after layer on, only guessing where the actual leak in the roof is, knowing that if I get it wrong, there will be a lot more water damage and Evy will have me killed. The only way I am lucking out with this roof repair is the roof being at a very mellow angle. So, at least I don't feel like I am going to fall off.

I dip the roller into my tray of sealant again and drop it onto the roof with a dull *splat* as my phone rings. I pull it out of my pocket and feel disappointed seeing it is Alesha, not that I don't want to talk with her, but I could use hearing Anna's voice. "Hello?" I say, answering the phone on speaker.

"Hey, what you up to?"

"Um... Just working. Why?"

"Oh, I can call back if you are working. I don't need or want anything, I was just driving and bored. So I figured I would call you," she says, and I feel a little mad that Alesha can call me while she is driving, but Anna apparently can't.

"No, I can talk while I work. I was bored myself."

"What are you doing, cleaning?" she asks.

"No, I'm not cleaning."

"Oh yeah? What then?"

"The roof on one of the houses was leaking, and the roofing crew is booked, so I am fixing a roof," I say.

"Oh yeah, right?" She laughs, clearly not believing me.

"Okay, I'll show you," I say, turning on my camera.

"Holy fuck, you are tarring a roof?" Alesha says in surprise.

"That's what I said."

"Well, I didn't think you actually meant it."

"It is going to rain a lot tonight, and Evy isn't in town today. So I had to step up." I suddenly feel really proud that I am doing this.

"How the hell did you learn how to tar a fucking roof?"

"I just read the directions on the can of roof sealant."

"That actually makes a lot of sense," she says with a laugh.

"Ask a stupid question," I say, laughing myself, glad she called. "So, what are you doing other than driving?" I ask, turning the camera around to face me.

"Damn, what is with you and flashing me?"

"What?" I ask, not sure what she means.

"I can totally see your bra through your t-shirt."

"You can!" I say, looking down at my white shirt, which now has the sealant on it.

"Oh yeah. Is your shirt soaked through with sweat?" she asks.

"I think so. It is super humid and pretty warm. I didn't know I would be doing this today, otherwise I would have worn something else."

"Well, other than me, no one is going to notice if you are on a roof," she says, making a good point.

"To be honest, I am so hot and tired, I just want to be done, so I really don't care if someone sees me."

"I would be the same way," she says.

"So, what's going on?"

"Not much, but I do have a date tonight," she says with a glancing smile at the camera.

"Ooh, that's exciting. Have you known him long? Where did you meet? Are you looking for something serious?"

"Hey, slow down. What's with all the questions?" She laughs.

"I just feel like I am the one always answering questions, and now it's your turn," I say.

"Oh, like I ever had to ask you a question. You always volunteer everything."

"Okay, fine," I say, knowing she's right, that I always just dump everything going on in my life on her.

"I met him online. We have been talking quite a bit for a few weeks, and I am going to be near his area... So, we decided to have dinner, maybe see a movie."

"You met him online? Are you sure this is safe?" I ask, not so sure about this.

"Tell me about how things turned out with your husband you met in church?" she retorts.

"Okay, I get the point," I say, and know she is right. "So, just a movie and dinner?"

"Well... Until I get a feel for him."

"And if you do?" I ask as I turn the video off on my phone, putting it in my shirt pocket so I can continue working.

"Then I feel him," she says, making me giggle against my will.

"Don't rush into things."

"Tell me, how long was it before you fucked Anna?"

"Sorry..." I say with a sigh. "Too many years of being around judgmental people has made me a little bad about that."

"It's okay. Just remember that when I tell you all the details if we do it," she says in a joking way, but I know that is exactly what she will do.

"Okay, I will remember that. Just stop pointing out my recklessness."

"Ooh, don't think I can do that. It is just too much fun," she says, laughing.

"Just tell me about internet guy already." I continue working as she tells me the story of her meeting this guy in a comments section of someone they both follow on social media, that they have just been chatting as friends until the last few days. It is nice listening, talking, and joking with her as I work. The job seems to go faster and is more enjoyable with a little company.

27

Distance

With the sudden feeling of something strangling my whole body, I jerk awake in the near dark. It feels like a dream I can't wake from as I realize my movement is restricted by something actually wrapped around me, and I am cold. It takes several panicked moments before I wake up enough to calm down and see that I am tangled in Anna's bathrobe, its belt still tied around me.

I manage to untangle myself from the robe and throw it aside. Realizing that I am cold because I fell asleep after a shower lying crosswise on the bed, on top of the blankets, and naked after the robe became disheveled. The damp air of the rain that now falls outside saturates the room... and me.

After a minute of searching in the dim gray light of the morning storm, I find my phone on the floor; having fallen at some point in the night. I crawl to the top of the bed and lie down, pulling the covers over myself. I check the phone and see it is still early. The sun must have just come up not long ago. "I should probably get up soon... I need to catch up on what I didn't clean yesterday," I say quietly to the darkness.

I stare at... nothing, as something feels wrong, but I can't place the feeling. It takes a minute or two before I realize that I fell asleep before calling Anna like I always do before bed. Picking my phone up, I swipe it open and see there is a message. I quickly tap the app, and see it is a meme from Alesha... It's funny, but it isn't Anna. "She didn't call or text," I say, staring at her name on the contact list, and the last text from me to her.

With sudden pain, I realize I am the one who calls her every night, the one who texts her in the morning wishing her a good day. But she almost never calls me, or texts, and she doesn't even reply to all my texts. I am the one making the effort to try to see if this is a real relationship, to see if she loves me like I love her. I realize that my persistence in finding out what our relationship is has worked. The answer is suddenly very clear... I'm not someone she loves. It was just physical, nothing more.

I throw the robe; her robe that lays next to me on the floor, no longer wanting it near me. I huddle in the blanket as I cry, wishing that this cold would just leave me alone, wishing I had someone next to me who wants to lie next to me, who wants to keep me warm. I just want someone to talk to, someone who is more than a friend, someone who is actually here... with me.

So, this is it... I wondered if I was actually in love, and now I have my answer, I think. Knowing now, without a doubt, I was in love. Because I have never felt as alone as I do now, knowing that I will never have the person I love next to me, keeping me warm on cold mornings.

The rain patters softly against the windshield as I drive. I decided I might as well get to work, instead of lying in bed feeling sorry for myself; I have never been that type of person. It seems like things are easier to deal with, to forget about while working. So I left early. Evy wasn't up when I left, and I honestly don't even know if they slept at the house, or at Nathan's, like they do every so often. But it doesn't matter, I don't need the *"you did a great job, thanks so much!"* pleasantries people give right now. I was just doing my job.

Something about the little house makes me hate it now. I liked it okay yesterday before I had to fix its roof, but now? Now I don't like it. I feel like it is the house's fault for my falling asleep early, and Anna's not calling. Of course, that's stupid, but I just need something to blame; other than myself for acting the fool in some love fantasy.

As I walk into the house, I hold my breath, praying that the ceiling isn't leaking. To my surprise, it isn't. Not even a drop. I can't help but take out my phone and record a video to send to Alesha, because I need to tell someone about this, tell someone that I did it, that I fixed a roof. I still hate the house, and feel awful, but there is a bit of happiness about this. It proves that I am not limited, that I am capable.

"I am doing what I want, and I don't need Anna or anyone else," I say, staring at the now-dried water spot on the ceiling. I realize I used Anna as my excuse for things. I never became who I wanted to be when I left Texas. I instantly did whatever I needed to do to be with her. "I have never wanted to drive truck... So, why was I studying for it? How could you let yourself do this?" I say, everything feeling more clear.

"If Anna wants me, then she can come to me. But I'm not chasing her, I'm not fighting for her... I'm fighting for me now," I say to the empty house, and feel like an idiot for it, but I don't care, I just needed to say it.

But it is time to get to work, the work I didn't do yesterday. I walk back to the front door and lock it, like I always do while I clean the houses. But suddenly I have an idea, something I lost the courage for a long time ago. So, I pull off my clothes and toss them into a pile on the couch. No one's around, and I want to do what I want and try what I want. If that happens to be cleaning houses naked, then I am cleaning houses naked. I can't help but laugh to myself, thinking about what Alesha will say about me doing this. *I will have to tell her.*

"You just should have taken the day off," Evy says again as we sit at the kitchen table.

"The cleaning was already a day behind, and it was already piling up. So it is better I just get it done," I say, sitting at the kitchen table, my now empty plate in front of me. It is just me and Evy tonight.

"I get that. But that is too much fucking work. You're going to overdo it."

"No, I'm not. You worry too much," I say, glad that someone does worry, though.

"What did my sister have to say about it? I bet she is pissed I asked you to do it."

"I... actually don't know. I didn't get a chance to talk with her yesterday." This seems to surprise Evy.

"Something wrong?" they ask.

"No, not really. Time zones just make it harder. We also don't need to talk every day."

"Aren't you two like... girlfriends?"

"No, we were never serious like that."

"I thought—"

"We are just friends who sleep together." I hear myself say defensively.

Evy just sits there for a minute in the thick silence. "Okay," they say, not judging.

"Sorry... I'm just really tired," I say, feeling bad.

"That's understandable. Sleep in tomorrow. I know there are still houses to clean, but you can take a little time to get enough rest."

"Okay, thanks," I say, and wonder if I will actually be able to sleep that well. My speech in the empty house about me not needing Anna or anyone else sounded good, but now it is starting to feel like what it was... just a bunch of words as empty as the house I was in. And I am sure I will be thinking about all of it all night while I try to sleep, because that's just how it works.

"Well, I'm going to go watch my K-drama and go to bed," Evy says. Until I met them, I didn't know people in the U.S. got so into watching Korean dramas. But Evy lives for them, and when I told

Alesha, she said her mom loves them. So, apparently, it is something I just missed out on.

"Yeah, I'm going to shower, and then try to actually get ready for bed before falling asleep."

"What?" they ask with a half smile, and I remember that they have no idea what I am talking about.

"I fell asleep last night crosswise and still in my bathrobe. Guess I fell asleep sitting on the edge of the bed after my shower."

"Shit, that's pretty bad. You better really sleep in tomorrow."

"I will," I say, standing. "Good night then."

"Good night to you, too."

As I walk up the stairs, I decide it is better that I text Anna, and not just ignore her, even if that is what she is doing to me. But I don't want to be that person, because maybe things haven't gone how I had hoped, but she still hasn't done anything wrong.

Me: I hope you had a good day. Mine was really long, so I am going to bed early. Good night.

I send it all in one text and then turn my phone off. I'm just not in the mood to talk with her through text or on the phone. Even though I haven't seen her in too long, I feel like I need distance from her tonight.

28

We're just...

Anna: Sorry we keep missing each other and that you are having such long days.

I read this when I first turn my phone on while still lying in bed. Having slept in was really nice, and I am glad I listened to Evy. There is also a voice message from Anna, so I turn my volume up and tap the message.

Anna: "I thought this would just be easier than texting, because you know I'm lazy after a day of driving. Anyway, sorry you are having such long days. I feel like I am the one who got you into that. Feel free to quit. Evy can find someone else, and you can still stay in my room. I do own that house as well.

On a different note, I'm still just truckin' along, so there isn't really any news. You know how it is, pretty boring. Which is good, exciting normally means something bad in this line of work. I miss you though... It feels lonely without you here... My evenings and nights are sure less exciting. Haha. But so it goes. I better go though. I have an early morning as well, so I need to get to bed. Good night... Or maybe good morning by the time you hear this. Bye."

And that's the end of the message. For a minute I thought she really missed me, but it seems that she just misses someone to screw while she's on the road. *But that's fine, I know that's all we had, and that's okay... Now that I know,* I say to myself, but I don't feel any better. I know I will once I get used to the idea of this only being a physical relationship. I might even find that I enjoy not having more than this. After all, I can do what I want with no one else to worry about.

Me: Glad you are doing well. Don't drive too much.

I send the text and decide I might as well get up. It isn't as late as it could be, but there isn't much to do just lying in bed. There isn't a TV in Anna's room, there isn't that much to do on my phone, and I would rather get something done over lying here doing nothing. At least I am making money if I'm cleaning houses.

Over the past five days, Anna and my text have become more sporadic, and we haven't talked on the phone at all. Which is fine. It seems like we have nothing to say anyway. When I talk with Alesha there is lots. We will talk for hours sometimes. But as soon as I go to text Anna, there doesn't seem to be anything I want to tell her. I feel like I am texting a stranger.

I find it a little funny because I always heard that absence makes the heart grow fonder, and it seems to have done just the opposite for us. Turning us back into strangers... actually; even worse, it has created resentment in us; at least it has in me.

As I clean houses, I swing from being mad at Anna, to thinking I might still be in love with her. From thinking she only sees me as a friend she can screw, to thinking she might actually love me. It swings back and forth in my mind until I have a headache and start to seriously question my mental health.

Where cleaning used to get my mind off of things, it now makes me dwell on them. Because cleaning the houses day after day, has made the job a robotic action. I no longer have to think about my work as I vacuum, scrub toilets, dust, mop, and everything else. I just do it. Often finishing without even remembering what I have exactly done, only seeing snippets of the workday as I drive home. But I don't think it even matters if I can just get myself to stop thinking about Anna in one way or another. Because the one thing I do know for sure is that whenever I stop thinking about her, she pops back up.

With a sigh over the entire ridiculous thing, I roll the cord up on the vacuum cleaner, and then pick my duster up out of the carrying tote to dust the corners. As I sweep it along the walls and ceiling, the doorbell suddenly rings and I jump half out of my skin, instinctively clutching my chest with one hand.

This has happened before, and it is most likely someone selling something or someone wanting to discuss religion. So I just stay quiet like I always do and wait for them to leave. But the bell rings again, and then again. "I know you're in there, Mary!" I hear with knocking, and my heart skips a beat, stops, starts, and skips a few more times, all in the course of two seconds.

"Anna?" I say, not sure how this could be happening.

"I knew you were in there," she says, and she sounds happy; but she always sounds happy. "Let me in, I don't have a key." *Thank God for that*, I think, scrambling for my clothes, which are laying in a pile on the couch.

"Yeah, one second."

"What? Why?" she asks through the door as I untangle my clothes, which weren't tangled two seconds ago. But seem to have tangled themselves as soon as I needed them.

"There is just... something in front of the door. Deep cleaning," I say, wadding my bra and panties into a ball and shoving them into my bag, knowing I don't have time to put them on. *She will know what is going on if I take too long, because I had to tell her that damn story about the first time I did this years ago,* I think pulling my jeans on, then my t-shirt, and open the door, praying my lack of bra isn't too noticeable.

"About time. What were you, cleaning under the carpet?" she jokes with that grin, her grin, and I have missed seeing it so much. But I feel so confused about all of it as every part of me screams that I still love her.

"Hey, I do my job right. I don't cut corners," I say, trying to figure out what I should do.

"Oh, I bet," Anna says, stepping in. "I've—"

"Shoes," I say, stopping her.

"What?"

"I just cleaned, no shoes."

"Wow, strict," she says, pulling her shoes off as I walk back to the couch.

"No, I just don't want to vacuum the floor again."

"So... You vacuumed the floors, then moved things around for deep cleaning so much you had blocked the door? Wouldn't you do that before you vacuum?" she asks.

"You're just a truck driver. What do you know?" I say, not answering the actual question.

"You didn't just need time to... get dressed, did you?" She smirks, and my heart squeezes tight, so tight. *God I have missed that, I have missed her.*

"So, what are you doing here?" I ask, not answering and picking up my duster, as though I can get myself to work while she is here.

"I'm just taking a day or so break before the next haul, and thought I would come and surprise you... I love annoying you," she adds, like an afterthought, or to hide something... or not hiding anything. I don't know, but I am starting to feel sick trying to figure it out.

"Oh, yeah... I should have known," I say, swiping the duster over the corners, the corners on her side of the room, the corners I have already dusted. "I kinda miss riding along," I say as Anna moves over in front of the couch, seeming to be wandering aimlessly. Everything about this is awkward and I feel like everything I am saying is meaningless, that they are just words to fill in the empty space.

"I've missed having you with me... In the truck, as well. I never thought you would love trucking so much," she says with a small laugh.

"I don't."

"What?" she says, looking at me.

"I really just don't know what I am supposed to say," I say, setting my duster on top of the other cleaning supplies, now only a few feet from Anna.

"What? Are you really that nervous?" she asks with a grin, seeming to not understand what I mean.

"I... Yeah, I guess I am." I decide that I don't want to do this. I don't want this to turn into a discussion about how I actually feel about her, because I know how she feels about me. *If I'm just a physical relationship to her, then that's what she will be to me,* I think as I now feel more in control, with the surprise of her randomly showing up having passed. So I just grab Anna and kiss her hard, not giving her a chance to say anything else. And the way she kisses me back tells me why she is here, and it isn't for a heartfelt confession of love.

Neither of us stop or slow down, and become more forceful... I become more forceful. Because, if this is what she wants, I will give it to her. As I slip my hands under her shirt, I pull it off over her head. I realize this is what I also want. I toss her shirt aside as I push her against the couch until she falls onto it and I fall with her, sitting on her lap straddling her, still kissing deep and hard. We break, and I raise my arms as she pulls my shirt over my head. "Where's your bra?" she asks, staring... not at my face.

"In my bag," I say, half breathless, as I lean forward over her.

"Oh well, tha—" she starts to say, but her words turn into a soft moan as I kiss her neck. Her stupid joke having lost its importance as we fall into loveless sex. After a lifetime of loveless sex with my husband, I told myself I would never do it again. But at least this time I want it as much as my partner does. *You just keep surprising yourself, don't you?* I think.

"I've missed that," Anna says, laughing quietly as she lies against me on the couch.

"Yeah... me too," I say, trying to not let myself feel too many emotions towards her as her body lies tight against me, her warm sweaty skin against mine.

"So, what should we do now?" Anna asks, kissing my neck.

"I personally am going to take a quick shower—"

"Ooh."

"And then finish cleaning."

"That's no fun," she says. "What about after?"

"I go clean the next house," I say plainly as I sit up.

"Seriously? But it is already late afternoon."

"Which is why I have to hurry so I can hopefully get home before eight. But given our rendezvous, it will now probably be closer to nine," I say, looking down at her.

"Sorry, I didn't mean to get you behind," she says, and I can tell she really feels bad.

"It's okay... It was worth it. I needed that."

"How early do you need to be up tomorrow?"

"I'll see what I can do. It will give me more time if you help," I say.

"Just tell me what needs done."

"Help me with that quick shower?"

"I think I can do that," Anna says, and she definitely follows through. It isn't too long before she is finishing the dusting while I clean the sinks and countertops. Anna is quick, clearly having cleaned the houses before.

We end up getting home at eight thirty, but we had an... enjoyable time cleaning. I am also starting to feel that I was overthinking our relationship, because it seems no different. Anna seems no different. But I do now realize that we have never been more than friends, who have sex when we are near. Something that is still a bit odd for me, but am getting used to as part of the new me.

29

Reconnecting

"Do you think Evy is mad that we ate so fast and left?" I ask Anna, as she lies with her head on my stomach, still slightly out of breath.

"Oh fuck, don't start a conversation about my sibling now," she says, laughing.

"I'm way older than you, so why are you the one out of breath?" I ask, laughing at her, and feeling happier than I thought I would.

"Maybe you're just not pulling your weight?" she says and moves so she can lie on top of me.

"I think you are just sitting around in your truck too much. And speaking of weight, you're heavy."

"You didn't mind me on top of you earlier." She grins.

"I was distracted."

"That's true. Maybe I should distract you again."

"I thought you might be distracted out for the night," I say.

"God, never," she says, kissing my breast. "Wait, why do you think you would be in better shape than me? You're just cleaning houses." I stare at her intently. "Okay, I'm really sorry. Not just cleaning houses, I know it is a lot of work—"

"It is a ton of work, and it is more than cleaning houses."

"Oh? What could Evy be making you do that is so awful?" Anna says half mockingly as she starts kissing my collarbone, working her way to my neck.

"One day I had to tar a roof by myself," I say nonchalantly.

"What the fuck?" Anna says, sitting bolt upright.

"What? Surprised I am more than just a house cleaner."

"Yes—I mean, no. I mean... What the fuck were you tarring a roof for?"

"The roof on one of the houses was leaking, Evy was out of town for the day, the roofer was booked, and there was more rain coming that night," I explain.

"Holy shit, they should not have had you do that!"

"Why not? Someone had to step up, so I did. And, the roof hasn't leaked yet," I say, feeling rather proud of this fact.

"That's great. But really—"

"Really what? Am I not enough of something to be allowed to work on a roof?" I say, pushing her off of me, not hard, but not wanting her on top of me anymore.

"No, no—"

"Then why can't you just say 'good job' or be happy that I managed by myself when things got hard?" I say, starting to feel really mad that she is treating me like I am a mother and housewife, and that learning; and doing something new is something I shouldn't be doing.

"Sorry, I was just surprised—"

"That's just it," I say, pushing myself off the bed. "Why are you surprised? If Evy or Nathan had done it you wouldn't be surprised. But when I do it, it's surprising! You drive semi, and I wasn't surprised. I wasn't surprised that you kept yourself alive when you told me about hitting that runaway ramp. I was impressed by your skill in an impossible moment like that. When you kept us from wrecking with that blowout, I wasn't surprised you managed that. I was amazed and inspired by your fast reactions, and knowing what to do in that split second. But I never had enough doubt in you to be surprised."

"That's not how I meant it."

"Then tell me how you meant it?" I say, but she just stares at me for a second before looking down. "Yeah, exactly. I'm just a middle-aged divorced house cleaner who could never be strong enough or smart enough to do anything more."

"No, you're not."

"No, I'm not..." I say, pulling on and tying her bathrobe. "But that's how you see me. So... fuck you," I say, slamming the door behind me. *That may be the first time you have ever said it, but I think it was a good time,* I think to myself. And actually feel really good about not just letting someone belittle me, I have had enough of that in my life.

I go downstairs, just wanting to be away from her for a little while. "You're back," Nathan says as I walk into the living room, and Evy; who is lying against him looks over to me from the TV show they are watching. Judging from the subtitles and language I don't understand, it is Evy's evening K-drama they always watch.

"Oh, sorry. I didn't mean to interrupt," I say, and turn for the kitchen. I was honestly thinking it was later than this, and that they would be in bed.

"Your house too"—Evy says, pausing the TV show—"so no reason to apologize. Sit down, if you want." Part of me wants to go sit by myself, but the rest of me really doesn't. So, I sit down in the recliner and put the footstool out.

"I'll just be on my phone, so you can go back to your show," I say.

"God, it's like having a teen in the house," Evy says, looking at me as I sit curled up in the chair, phone in hand.

"Don't be mean," Nathan says.

"Not being mean, just saying. I mean, shit, she looks like she just got in a fight with her boyfriend," Evy says, laughing, and I don't say anything. Evy stops laughing abruptly and stares at me. "Oh fuck... did you?"

"Just a disagreement," I say, not wanting to make a big deal out of it. "And she's never been my girlfriend. We've never been in a relationship." I add.

"Right..." Evy says. "So, what did she do? I know it was her fault." I'm a little surprised they aren't sticking up for their sister more.

"It was nothing, really."

"Oh, it had to be something."

"Let it go Sweetie, she doesn't want to talk about it," Nathan says.

"Well, Anna's my sister."

"And this is Mary's business," he says. Like always, he is disarming, always a peacekeeper.

"It really was nothing," I say. "I'm sure I'm just overreacting."

"Oh, Anna did do something," Nathan says.

"No question," Evy says. And I suddenly have the feeling that my personal drama is more interesting than the drama they are watching on TV.

"Why do you know that?" I ask.

"Because, whenever someone says they are 'overreacting'," Evy says with air quotes, "it means the person said something very ass-holey, and the person they said it to is blaming themselves. It is never their fault though." They say this, and I realize how many times I have told myself I am overreacting. It was the first thing I told myself when I thought Justin was cheating on me.

"They're right," Nathan says. "When people talk to me, they often think they are overreacting, and eighty percent of the time they aren't."

"People talk to you that much?" I ask.

"As a minister, I am like half therapist. Your minister wasn't like that?" he asks.

"I think he was, but I never felt comfortable talking to him." What I don't say is that I was always scared he would say I was gay. Even when I hadn't come out to myself, part of me had that fear of him finding something out about me, even if I didn't know what it was myself.

"I'm sure not all my parishioners are comfortable talking to me," he says, seeming to defend my old minister, even though he doesn't know him.

"It's because you're too damn sexy. It scares people," Evy says, smiling big at him. "Now," they turn and look at me, still smiling, "what happened?"

"It wasn't anything that major. I just told her about fixing the roof, and she couldn't get past the idea of me being able to do that."

"Why wouldn't you be able to do that?" Evy asks.

"And that's where the fight started," I say.

"Oh..." Nathan says, seeming to have the whole thing figured out.

"It was pretty one-sided," I say. "Mostly Anna trying to figure out what she said that was wrong, while I blew up at her... I really shouldn't have done that."

"If she was going to be a little fucking asshole, then she deserved it," Evy says. "You want me to go smack some sense into her?"

"No," I say, smiling, and feeling good having friends that understand my side.

"Are you sure? I'm the elder sibling, so it is allowed."

"Hon, I don't think that is allowed," Nathan says.

"Sure it is," Evy says, and Nathan doesn't bother arguing the point.

"It's fine. Like I said, we aren't a couple or anything, so it will blow over."

"You can stay on the murphy bed in the office tonight if you want," Evy says.

"Thanks, I might do that."

"Actually, I will make Anna stay in there. She's the one that fucked up, so she can stay in there."

"No, I will. Thanks though," I say.

"You are too nice. Watch this with us, and learn how you properly hold a grudge," Evy says, starting the K-drama over from the beginning.

As I watch the show, I realize Evy is right. The people in this drama can really hold a grudge. But as I think about everything that has gone on in my life over the past year, I think I have them beat in the drama department. Which leaves me a little confused about how I should feel about having such a high-drama life.

"What did you think of it?" Evy asks excitedly at the end of the show, which doesn't surprise me. They have been trying to get me to watch a K-drama with them since I got here.

Nathan looks over at me. "Don't feel obligated to say you like it," he says, seeming not so impressed himself. *He watches them because Evy likes them, and he just wants to be with Evy,* I think, and wonder if this is what couples who truly love each other do.

"I really did like it. I was a little lost, but it was better than I thought it would be."

"Yeah," Evy says, "you are kinda coming in at the middle of things."

"I also need to get used to subtitles," I say.

"I have never been good with subtitles," Nathan says. "I am just too slow."

"But you try," Evy says, leaning against him with a big smile, looking so happy that he tries for them.

I am about to say something when my phone gives a notification sound, but it isn't the normal sound of the text app I use. I tap the power button to show the notifications and it is a social media, personal message. I recognize the avatar photo immediately, not to mention the name. "You okay?" I hear Nathan ask, I look up to him, and I feel blank and a little scared.

"What is it?" Evy asks.

"Aaron just messaged me."

"Who?" Nathan asks, and the look on Evy's face says they also didn't know. It is when things like this happen that I remember how Anna told Evy nothing about me.

"He is my son. Neither him nor my daughter have talked to me since the divorce..."

"Oh..." Evy says. "You going to reply?"

"I better make sure nothing is wrong," I say, knowing this sounds ridiculous after they made it clear they wanted nothing to do with me. But I am his mother, and I need to know he and Angela are okay.

"Okay," Nathan says, and neither of them says anything else. They just hit play on a sitcom rerun.

I open the app, feeling more than a little nervous, praying that he didn't decide to message just to chew me out about something. It is the last thing I need tonight. I have really had my fill of everything.

Aaron: Hi Mom, I hope you are doing okay. Sorry I didn't message sooner, it has been hard here. A lot going on, and a lot I didn't know before. I'm sorry I didn't listen to your side of things sooner. Can I call and talk?

I stare at the message for a minute and realize I'm crying. "I'm going into the other room to use the phone," I say.

"Okay," Evy says, not asking about the message. It is something I really appreciate.

Me: Yes. Is now a good time?

I text as I sit down at the kitchen table. I stare at my phone for a moment, wondering about the conversation we might have... and how much I should tell him. My brain runs through non-existent questions and scenarios until the message shows he's seen it, and a second later, the app rings with a call.

"Hello?" I answer.

"Hi, Mom," the shaky voice on the other end says.

30

Unexpected

"How are you?" I ask my son, not sure what else to say, or what I should say. With all the thoughts that have run through my head since this all started, this conversation was never one of them, and now I wonder why.

"I'm doing good... How about you?"

"I'm fine... I've been staying busy," I say, feeling like it is important that he knows I am not just sitting around doing nothing.

"Oh, that's good. So, what have you been doing?"

"I have a friend with a bunch of rentals; rent by the day, vacation-type houses, and I have been cleaning for them."

"That sounds like a lot of work."

"It is. But I don't mind it."

"That's good..." He seems to be thinking for a second. "I can't think of anyone that owns rentals like that around here, what's his name?" I can't help but scoff a little at Aaron's assumption that only a man would own properties like this.

"You don't know them. I'm in New York."

"You're in New York City?" he says, and now he no longer sounds like he is making small talk.

"No, New York is a whole state. I'm in Ithaca, on the edge of town, actually."

"How did you end up there?"

"It is where my friend lives, so I just came with her, and her sibling hired me to clean."

"What friend? I don't remember you with any friends from New York," he says, sounding almost angry.

"I met her while traveling, she gave me a ride, and—"

"Wait. You met this person hitchhiking?"

"Yes," I say plainly.

"Mom, do you know how dangerous that is?"

"Tell me what my options were then?" I say calmly, and he is silent. He knows that I was left with nothing, and that no one; including him and Angela, would talk to me. "I left Texas because I had no reason to stay. Beggars can't be choosers. So when Anna offered me a ride, I took it."

"None of this is like you. This isn't wha—"

"No," I interrupt. "What I was before wasn't like me. This isn't a mid-life crisis, this is the first time in my life I am being myself," I say, and realize I am telling this to my son, feeling awkward. But it needed to be said.

"The police found your car," he says, more quietly.

"Your dad's car," I correct.

"Don't start," he says, reminding me a lot of Justin.

"He made that very clear when he told me he would call the police, even if I was the one that had it." He's quiet again, and I wonder if his dad told him this part of the story.

"Your stuff was in the car."

"How odd," I say, thinking I will continue to act like I didn't take my car.

"It was all your clothes and some other things," he says, and I notice he doesn't mention my money. *So, the carjacker found it before dumping my car,* I think. "Your e-reader was in there." The way he says this tells me what he will say next. "There were some... some books on there—"

"Yes, I'm gay." I just say it. I know that he saw the novels and self-help books about coming out, about understanding the feeling of finding out you are queer. "I have been my whole life," I add, not wanting him to think I just *"turned gay"* all at once, like our church likes to tell you you will.

"Is... is this why things didn't work with Dad?" I have to stop myself from laughing, because it is too perfect that he already thinks this is what the problem was.

"No... That was his four-year affair with Deb."

"But maybe—"

"I wasn't there for him?" I say, knowing this is the general direction of what he is going to say. "I was willing to live my life for what he wanted. I never said a thing against him. Everything was his decision. So, don't think that he has any right to use me as his justification." Aaron doesn't say anything else about it, and I wonder what he is thinking.

"Are you coming home?" he asks.

"I am home," I say, feeling my throat get a little tight.

"But, you won't come back?"

"I will visit you and your sister. But I have nothing there to move back for. You know that..." He doesn't say anything. "You and Angela are grown. You don't need me around for help. And I want to get a fresh start... I want to live how I was never allowed to live."

"So... you are going to start dating..." he trails off, not seeming to be able to get himself to say *"women"*.

"I already am..."

"Oh..." he says.

"I need to go. It's getting late here, and I have to work early."

"Oh, right... time zone difference," he says.

"Tell your sister to call me, or at least message."

"I will. But she's pretty mad," he says.

"I understand," I say, not really understanding why she would be so mad at me.

"I'll let you go then."

"Call me again. I love you," I say.

"Okay, I will... bye," he says, and hangs up.

I stare at my phone's blank screen for a second, then look up to the now-dark living room. *Evy and Nathan must have gone to bed,* I think. I stare at the doorway to the nearly dark room and wish Anna was standing in that doorway. Standing there to ask if I am okay, to listen to me, to wrap her arms around me and kiss me, telling me it will be alright. But she isn't, and knowing she is just up the stairs. Her being so close but still not here makes it so much worse.

Sitting in the driveway after a long day's work, staring at my phone before getting out of my car. I watch the screen, thinking there would be a notification by now from Aaron, or maybe Angela. But I know it is Anna that I am waiting for deep down, because some stupid part of me just won't let her go. Even after the fight, I hate that she left before I got up this morning.

My phone suddenly dings, and I nearly drop it. I see the name and short text on the screen.

Alesha: What's up, player?

I can't help but smile with a small laugh. "I can't believe the girl I met while naked in a shower is the one constant person in my life," I say, staring at the screen, slowly shaking my head. *She never judges me either,* I think, and wonder if she is the only person I have ever known who doesn't judge me. I slip the phone into my pocket and open the door of my car, figuring it is better to text in the comfort of the house.

"You made it," Evy says as I walk in. "Or, more like you finally climbed out of your car." I give them a small glare as I kick my shoes off, my hands busy with a few bags of groceries. "I'm joking. I know you have had a long day, and I know how nice it can be just sitting in the car."

"Anything interesting happen today?" I ask, carrying the bags to the kitchen. I hope that they will say Anna called or texted, and I'm pretty sure Evy knows this is why I am asking.

"All quiet on the western front," they say, walking in.

"We're on the eastern front," I say, and they laugh quietly.

We both start working on making dinner; even when it is just the two of us, we make a proper dinner and don't make some frozen junk food. It seems that neither of us is much for junk food, and don't mind cooking.

"Can I ask you a personal question?" I ask, after a while of silence.

"Sure," Evy says, opening the refrigerator. "You want a pop?"

"Oh... sure," I say, and take the can of coke as they hold it out.

"What's the question?"

"Are your parents still alive?" I ask, as Evy starts laughing. "What?"

"I just wasn't expecting that," they say, still laughing. "Shit... Yeah, they're in Florida."

"Florida?"

"Yes, land of the old people. And someday, you and I will also have to migrate there... It is national law," they say seriously, making me laugh. "Why do you ask?"

"I was just wondering. You don't talk about them much, and Anna doesn't either."

"They aren't big phone call people, so it is mostly text and email. They also don't have much as far as news, so there isn't much to talk about."

"Oh, that makes sense. It isn't my business, anyway."

"Then why did you ask?" Evy says, looking at me, and they are right.

"Your parents were divorced, right?"

"Mom and Dad were never married, but they were together for several years," they say.

"Was he around much as you grew up?"

"Oh yeah, he was around so much that Anna called him dad too. God, that made some awkward shit some days. You should see the look on old ladies' faces when they think your mom has two husbands." Evy laughs. "There have been times I could go for having more than a few guys," Evy says with a quiet laugh, and I think they might be serious.

"Glad he was around. That's nice."

"It was. It seems like no one pulls that off... So, you really don't have a reason for asking?" Evy says, eyeing me.

"No, just wondering."

"Are you sure you aren't trying to figure out why Anna is pushing you away all the sudden?" I feel my cheeks start to get warm. I look down at something, acting like I am doing something for dinner, when I really just feel like I have been caught. "It's fine, I get it. And I don't know if it is something to do with our parents, or something that is just an Anna thing. But I think you have two options," they say, and I look up at them. "You can either wait and see if it resolves itself. Or... move on. I know I wouldn't blame you for moving on."

"Thanks..." I say, feeling better, and feeling that I might have two people that are always here for me, and don't judge.

"After all, you are getting old as fuck. And you're so late coming out. You just have way too many women to screw to catch up, and so little time."

"I don't think that's the issue here," I say, unable to not laugh a little at this. "And I'm not interested in that."

"Oh... right," they say with an exaggerated wink.

I drop onto my bed after my shower and grab my phone. I heard the notifications go off a few times while I was showering, but they are just Alesha.

Alesha: You dead?

Alesha: Or are you banging that supermarket chick?

Alesha: Sorry for that last one. That sounded WAY too much like a guy text. Hahaha.

Me: Supermarket chick was so good, I died. So, yes, I'm dead.

I smile to myself as I send this.

Alesha: LMAO

I laugh, not at my joke, but at what she has turned me into. And that I can make people laugh. It feels great.

Alesha: Is the deli woman at the supermarket still hitting on you?

I think about what I should tell Alesha. She is the only person I have told about this. The only person I know who could help me figure out if the woman was being friendly or hitting on me. I decide I might as well tell her.

Me: Her name is Jennifer.

Alesha: Did you finally get a look at her name tag?

Me: Yes.

Me: She also entered it into my contacts with her number.

Alesha: WTF!!!

Alesha: She asked you out?

Alesha: What are you going to do?

Alesha: What about Anna?

Me: Stop texting!!!

Alesha: really excited.

Me: I guessed.

Me: I don't know if I will call her.

Alesha: Text.

Me: What?

Alesha: For fuck's sake. Don't call her, text if you want to go out.

Alesha: This isn't the 50's anymore, grandma.

Me: That's a bit mean. I'm not that old.

Alesha: You are getting hit on, and have more dates than me.

Alesha: Not to mention all the sex you're having.

Alesha: So I get to be mean to you.

Me: Don't worry, someday you will be old enough to go on dates and have sex.

Alesha: Bitch.

Alesha: Back on topic. What are you going to do? It isn't like Anna is all in or anything.

Me: I know.

I just stare at the phone, neither of us texting anything for a while.

Alesha: You're still in love with her, aren't you?

I sigh as I read this, because I know the answer without even thinking.

Me: Of course. I'm stupid that way.

Alesha: You really are. ;)

I laugh when I read this. I know she is joking, but I love that she just tells me I am.

Me: I guess I will get some sleep. Good night.

Alesha: Good night. Keep me up to date.

I lie in bed; the covers pulled up to my chin, and I look at the note Anna left nearly a week ago that is still on the side table. It says she's sorry she was an idiot, that she said those things, that she didn't tell me in person, and that she is proud of me. But it just confused me. It is such a sweet gesture, followed by no calls or texts. It seems like everything she does contradicts itself.

Thinking about this, I suddenly remember something and grab my phone, texting Alesha back.

Me: Wait, you said you had no dates. What about that guy you met online? You said meeting him went well. What about that?

I send it, and it is only a few seconds before it shows she is typing a reply.

Alesha: Oh, yeah. That's why I didn't call you. You see... My van is small, and I didn't want to wake him up.

I stare at the screen, my mouth hanging open.

Alesha: He is really tired. ;)

Me: Bitch.

Alesha: LMAO LMAO.

The next morning there are texts from Aaron when I wake up, something I wasn't expecting, but am glad to see. I open the app and my heart falls.

Aaron: Angela was in a car wreck last night. She will be okay. But can you come home?

Aaron: Just for now, I don't mean for good.

Aaron: I can pay for your flight.

I feel like I am in a half-panic, but calm myself down, not wanting to blow things out of proportion. I read through the text again, and find myself a little happy that he gets that I'm not coming back for good. But knowing my daughter is hurt makes me realize I will be there for however long I am needed, no matter what.

31

Traveling again

I run downstairs having just pulled my clothes on. Evy is in the kitchen looking tired while the coffee pot gurgles. "Good morning," they say, staring at their phone.

"I'm going to have to take time off. I am so sorry, but I have to."

They lower their phone and look at me. "What's wrong?" Evy asks, and I am sure that I look like heck, that and the fact something is wrong is written all over me.

"My daughter... Angela. She was in a... a..." It hits me in a different way as I try to say it out loud, and the words won't come out as I start crying.

I hear the screech of the wooden chair legs on tile as Evy's chair slides back, and their arm is around me, guiding me into a chair. "It's okay, take a few breaths," they say, and I do. "Okay, tell me again." Evy sits back in their chair, pulling it close to me, now holding my hands.

"She was in a car wreck last night..." I say, barely able to talk through my crying.

"Is she okay?"

"Aaron said she will be fine. But I don't know how bad it is, and I can't get ahold of him," I say, looking at Evy.

"That's good." I look at them, puzzled on why not being able to get ahold of him is good. "It is still early there, and he is probably sleeping. If things were bad, he wouldn't be sleeping," Evy explains, and they are right, I hadn't thought of it like that.

"Okay..." I say, wiping my eyes.

"Now, get something to eat real quick, then start packing. I will get your travel straightened out." I just nod my head.

I put two frozen waffles in the toaster and pour a cup of coffee as Evy taps at their phone. While I wait for my waffles, I take out my phone and start typing a text telling what is going on; copy it, send it to Anna, and then to Alesha.

My phone starts ringing almost the second I tap the power button. It's Anna. "Hello?" I answer.

"Are you okay?" she asks, sounding worried, and I want to cry just hearing her voice.

"Yeah, I'm fine," I say, walking into the living room for more privacy.

"What can I do?" she asks, as if there is anything she can do from wherever in the country, or out of the country she is.

You could be here to hold me, to tell me it will be okay... You could go with me, I think, swallowing the fast-rising lump in my throat. "No ... Evy is finding me a flight, that's all there is to do," I say truthfully, because there is nothing else that can be done at the moment. "Are you driving?"

"Just warming her up right now. I was just getting ready to leave when I got your text. I'm glad I got it before I started, since I can't check them while driving."

"Yeah, that was lucky," I say, not feeling lucky. Evy waves their phone at me. "I gotta go. Evy is waving me over."

"Okay," she says. "You tell me the second you know anything else, okay?"

"I will, thanks..." I say, and there is an odd silence.

"I'm... sorry I acted like that before. I can be really stupid at times... I really am sorry," she says.

"It's okay. I could have handled it better. Sorry, I got mad."

"It was my fault though..." I don't say anything. "I'll let you go. Keep me up to date."

"I will," I say, and want to say *"I love you"* but don't. "Bye," I say into the phone.

"Bye." And we hang up.

"Hurry and eat," Evy says.

"Did you get a flight?"

"Yeah, wheels up in an hour and a half. You have a layover of just about an hour, but you should be wheels down in San Antonio before three."

"Thank you so much. Tell me how much I owe you, I have cash," I say, knowing that a ticket this short notice wasn't cheap.

"Forget it. I owe you a lot more than that," Evy says with a wave of the hand.

"I will pay you back somehow."

"I'm telling you to forget it, for fuck's sake," they sigh. "Okay, if I go pack you a bag while you eat?"

"Oh, yeah. But I can get it."

"You need to eat and then get cleaned up. You look like shit." I laugh a little at this, knowing they are right. "Anything specific you want me to pack?"

"All I have is jeans and T-shirts."

"Yeah, why don't you wear anything else?"

"They were stolen with my car. Anna bought me all of those at the truck-stop," I say, remembering how great that day was, and I wonder why it feels like so long ago, how we can now be so distant. *I should have never told her I was falling in love with her. Maybe I would still be with her, watching movies in the sleeper every night if I had never said anything.*

"So those are truck-stop clothes? God, you have to get something else."

"I like them," I say. Evy looks at me for a second, and I feel like I let something slip out with those three words.

"Whatever. Just eat, shower, and do your hair."

"Okay," I say, glad I have them as a friend.

I turn my phone off of airplane mode as I get off the plane. The instant my phone connects to a signal its notification sounds several times in a row, but I ignore it until I find my next gate.

Sitting in a seat nearest to my gate, I take my phone out. Anna, Alesha, Evy, and Aaron have all texted. I go straight to Aaron's.

Aaron: Sorry I didn't respond sooner, I was getting some sleep. She just went into surgery for her leg. It will be awhile. She probably won't be awake before you get here.

I feel tears running down my face again from the shock of not knowing she needed surgery. But I focus on not letting myself fall apart, taking a few deep breaths. Then tell Aaron I will be there as soon as possible, and move to the next text.

Alesha: Fuck. I am so sorry.

Alesha: I am headed for San Antonio now. Do you need a ride from the airport?

I stare at this and re-read it before texting her back.

Me: If you are in the area, a ride would be great. Why are you going to San Antonio? I thought you were going west?

I check Evy's and Anna's texts. They both want to know if there are updates. I text them the little bit I learned from Aaron. Then a voice message from Alesha pops up.

"Hey, I'm driving so I couldn't text. Picking you up is no problem. Send me your flight number and I will meet you inside the airport. And I am going to San Antonio because my best friend's daughter was in a car wreck... Thought she might need a little support. Perk of living in a van." The message ends, and I feel like crying again, but for a different reason than before.

I send Alesha my flight number and time I should land, right as my flight is ready. I grab my bag and walk to the gate, glad that it won't be too long, and I will be there. I only want to make sure Angela is okay, but there isn't a single bit of me that wants to be there for any other reason.

To my own surprise, I manage to sleep for most of the flight. The long days and stress seem to have built up, and I feel a little better after sleeping. It wasn't the best sleep of my life, but it was better than sitting here worrying the whole flight. Or worse, small talk with the person next to me.

They announce we are landing, and in no time at all, I am walking through the skyway. I walk through the airport hoping I can find Alesha in the mass of people spreading out in every direction. *Why does it seem like everyone knows exactly where they are going, except me?* I wonder, feeling like I am missing some secret about airports. I realize I am better off to just call or text her to find her, than wander around aimlessly.

"There you are!" I hear, and look up from my phone just in time to be wrapped in a tight hug. "Are you okay?" Alesha asks.

"Yes, I'm fine," I say, feeling my chest tighten.

"Like fuck you are," she says. "Damn"—she steps back—"we better get you to that hospital," Alesha says, wiping away a few tears from her own cheeks.

"Thank you so much for picking me up."

"I wouldn't even think of doing anything less," she says, glancing over to me as we walk at a quicker-than-normal pace.

"I don't know what I did to deserve you as a friend."

"Just remember that the next time you want to call me a bitch," she says, grinning at me.

"That was because you were saying how unfair it was that I was dating while you had some guy sleeping next to you." I laugh.

"You still have more people throwing themselves at you than I do. Just not fair. We should at least be equal."

"Not my fault you can't keep up," I say.

"Ouch, that was mean. But I will just catch up. I have been holding back, and I will just stop casting men off."

"Oh, really?"

"Yeah, I am going to start right now," she says as I see her van come into sight. "Hey, I have a question."

"Sure."

"Is your son cute?" Alesha asks with a mischievous grin.

"Don't even think about it," I warn.

"Hey, we're adults. That's up to us."

"Question."

"Yeah..." she says, knowing I am going somewhere with this.

"Is your mom cute?" I ask, smiling at her.

"Fine, you win. Let's agree, we won't screw each other's family."

"Deal," I say as she circles the van, unlocking it.

"Oh, and try not to picture me naked too much while we are together," she says, and opens her door.

"Same!" I say laughing, hating to admit to myself that I will most likely fail at this.

I feel a lot better just talking about stupid things, instead about everything that is going wrong. I know this is why Alesha did it. She is really great that way.

Alesha turns into the parking lot after what doesn't seem like much time, but this is probably because she saw all the traffic lights as suggestions.

"Thank you so much for the ride," I say.

"No problem," she says, turning into the parking lot.

"Um... you can just drop me off at the doors."

"Yeah, I hate to be intrusive. But, I'm not letting you go in there without me. You need someone in your corner," she says, pulling into an empty parking space.

"You don't have to do that," I say, hating for her to get involved.

"Who's going to be in there?" she asks, turning her van off and looking at me.

I think for a second and realize she's right. "I know. But you have already done so much for me, and—"

"I don't keep count of things. So, let's stop wasting time by counting who owes who and get the fuck in there."

"Okay," I say.

We stand in the elevator; just the two of us as we go up to the right floor. "So," I say, feeling like talking about anything will help me not feel so anxious about everything else, "do you always drive like that?" She looks over at me.

"Something wrong with my driving?"

"Well, it just seems that you never learned about stoplights."

"They're overrated, they just slow you down," she says with a shrug.

"They are there to slow you down. Stoplight, it's in the name."

"It's like school crossings. They're like one of those information pamphlets places hand out, just a suggestion."

"What? School crossings are not just a suggestion," I say, staring at her wide-eyed.

"I'm just fucking with you!" she says, laughing. "I never drive like that, but I knew you really wanted to get here quick."

"Really?"

"Yeah, really."

"What if we got stopped?" I ask.

"I wasn't worried."

"You would just flirt your way out of the ticket, wouldn't you?" I ask, having the feeling this is something Alesha would do.

"Hey, say what you want, but it works," she says. "You wouldn't think that would still work, but men are fucking idiots and never learn"—the doors open with a ding and we start down the hallway—"so it is easy. Not to mention the fact I drive a mobile bedroom. Fuck, they're halfway there before they even get to my window."

"What if it is a woman cop?"

"It, like, never is. But if it was, then you're up to bat," she says, winking at me.

"What? I don't think that would work," I say.

"How many trips to the supermarket before the deli lady started throwing herself at you?" She raises an eyebrow, and I just stare at her.

"Mom," I hear, right as I open my mouth to say something. I look over to see Aaron coming towards me, pausing when he sees Alesha. "Glad you made it... is this your..." He tries to say quietly but falls short of saying it at all, staring at the twenty-four-year-old Alesha next to me.

"Fuck I wish," Alesha says, looking at me with *a "look"* that makes me feel very awkward, "but sadly, I'm not a lesbian. Not that she wouldn't try to convert me!" I wonder if she realizes how weird that is to say to my son, and he looks as awkward about it as I do. *This couldn't get any more awkward*, I think, right as I notice Justin standing just around the corner. Judging from the look on his face he heard it all, and it is the first time hearing It.

32
My Family... and Alesha

I stand staring at Justin, frozen, watching the look of uncertainty and confusion on his stupid face. Aaron looks like he also doesn't know what to do. But Justin doesn't say anything, so I hope maybe he didn't hear it all. It isn't that I want to hide it from him, but I don't want to have this conversation here and now.

"Oh fuck," Alesha says. "I thought they knew?" She looks at me, and I know she feels horrible for outing me to my ex-husband. Even though she didn't mean to, this just made it completely clear that he didn't misunderstand anything.

"I'm not here to talk about that," I say, knowing that I have to say something, and not wanting this to be about why we broke up. "How is Angela doing?" I ask.

"Um..." Aaron says, seeming to kind of snap out of it. "She is still in surgery, but should be out any time now. So you haven't missed anything."

"Okay, good."

"We're sitting over here," Aaron says, turning to the corner where Justin is still standing. Alesha and I follow him. I pat Alesha's shoulder with a small smile, wanting her to know it's okay, that I'm not mad at her. Part of me is actually relieved that he just knows now. I had thought about just never telling him. It isn't like he has any right to know how I live my life.

"And this is Alesha," I say to Aaron as we walk to our seats. Justin now looks furious, and I know it won't be long before he says something about it. After twenty-five years of marriage, I know Justin too well to be wrong about this. It isn't an *If* but a *When* for him to demand answers.

"I'm Aaron," he says to Alesha. "Thanks for giving my mom a ride from the airport."

"Happy to do it," she says.

"So, you live around here?" he asks, and I am almost surprised at how nice he is being to Alesha, given her first impression. But Aaron always was a nice person, who never has held things against people... Which is why it hurt so much when he wouldn't even talk to me.

"San Antonio? Fuck no... Oh, no offense. It's just not my scene," she says, realizing she may have just insulted him. "I live in my van and travel around the country."

"Really? That sounds interesting," he says as we sit down in the waiting room chairs. "I guess it was lucky you were in the area."

"She wasn't," I say, and Aaron looks at me. "She drove nearly three hundred miles to meet me at the airport."

"You really did?" Aaron says in surprise. I glance at Justin to see his reaction, but he doesn't seem to have noticed. He just stands there looking mad. I suddenly want to knock his teeth out again for acting like this while our daughter is in surgery.

"Yeah..." Alesha says with a modesty I didn't know she had. It makes her kind of cute and innocent looking. "Mary is my best friend, and I thought it would be nice if she had a friend with her."

"Well, thank you. And thank God for bringing you here for her," Aaron says, and it sounds odd. It seems like so long since I have been around someone who speaks of God like this, even though Nathan nearly lives at Evy's and is a minister.

"Hey, God has nothing to do with it," Alesha says, and Aaron's expression changes. I know he won't like this. "We should give thanks to the Ethiopians."

"Why?" Aaron says, now confused... like me.

"Because, they are the ones who discovered coffee," Alesha says, and Aaron starts laughing. I am amazed how Alesha seems to just make stressful situations lighter.

"Here is your coke sweetie," I hear and look over to see Deb holding a can out to Justin. "Oh..." she says, seeming surprised I am here. *What? She thinks I wouldn't be since Angela is my daughter? And she should naturally be here since she is a home-wrecking adulterer, lying, conniving, fucking bitch,* I think, realizing I might be more angry at her than I thought I was.

"How are you doing?" I ask her, trying to keep myself from getting angry, since that isn't why I'm here.

"I'm good. How are you?" she asks.

"I don't know until Angela is out of surgery," I say honestly, because I really feel like this is where the answer to this question lies.

"Yes, of course. I am glad you were able to make it." Deb says this like I wouldn't have bothered, like I'm not a good mother. There have been too many times I have wondered if I was a good mother. But I will not let her, of all people, act like I'm not.

"You must be Debra," Alesha says in a very friendly way with a very convincing smile, that is so convincing it scares me a little. "I have heard so much about you... And you too, for that matter, Justin. It is nice to put faces with the stories." And even with the sweet sound to Alesha's voice, I can tell by the look on Debra and Justin's faces that they know exactly what she means.

"You are?" Debra asks, not in a friendly tone.

"Oh, sorry." Alesha laughs like it was her being stupid and forgetting that part, and it is so genuine Aaron laughs a little with her. "I'm Alesha, Mary's best friend."

"It's nice to meet you," Debra says with a pleasant, fake smile.

"Thanks. I hadn't planned to be around here, but as soon as Mary told me what was going on, I drove right down to be here for her."

"That's nice," Debra says, starting to seem more irritated.

"It never crossed my mind not to. She's my friend, so I want to be there for her, no matter what. You can't do your best friend wrong, you gotta be in their corner no matter what," Alesha says, and everyone caught the meaning in that one. Justin looks more irritated, as Debra looks away and down to the floor. Aaron checks his phone. "You know, a soda sounds good. Where's the machine, Deb?" Alesha asks.

"I'll show you," Aaron says, standing.

"Cool," Alesha says with a smile, a real one. They walk off in the direction Debra came from a moment ago, and I am alone with the two of them. I know this is what Justin is waiting for, that he won't be able to not ask. I feel like I can count down to him asking. It is a reminder of how long I was with him, how many years I was with him, years that I should have spent somewhere else.

"So, that's why you were never there," he says, like clockwork.

"I'm not going to talk about this now," I say, just wanting to know if Angela is okay.

"I don't know why not. It isn't like we have something else to do," he says.

"What do you want from me? You already took everything I had. Isn't that enough?" I ask, looking at him.

"That isn't what this is about," he says.

"So... That's a no?" I say, and he looks even more angry.

"Since when? When did it start?" he asks, and I know what he means. He wants to know when the lesbian switch was flipped.

"Your affair? Only you two know that... Wait, was Deb your first? Did you cheat on me before Deb?" I ask, knowing this will plant a seed in Debra's mind... Or maybe water the seed that is already there, because I am sure she has thought of this herself. How could she not think of this?

He looks really angry now, angrier than I have ever seen him. "I mean, how long have you been a fa—"

"Finish that word and I'll kick you in the fucking balls so hard they'll pop like party balloons," Alesha interrupts with an icy tone. The stare she gives him is like a dare, telling him, *Go ahead, try me, motherfucker. See if I'm lying.*

Justin fumes as he stares back at her. "How long?" he asks again, looking back at me and not finishing the word.

"Justin... What's going on?" Debra asks, confused.

"It doesn't work like that, Justin," I say, not giving him the chance to answer Debra. "I have always liked women." Debra's eyes go wide. "But it wasn't something that was accepted in my family. So I married you because it is what they wanted, what you wanted, and I thought I would just get past it." The color drains from his face at my telling him this straight out that I never wanted to marry him.

"You..." Debra stammers, "you've always been a... lesbian?"

"Yes," I say simply, getting really annoyed that this is such a shock to everyone, now that it seems so normal to me.

"And are you..." she says, looking at Alesha.

"Nope, I'm straight... Well, I did make out with some girls at a few parties in high school... but I was like, really drunk, and I also fucked with some guys while really drunk. Guys that I totally regretted hooking up with; which is why I try not to drink much these days. Drunk Alesha gets way too wild." She laughs. "So I guess the answer still is... Yes, I'm straight." I can't stop myself from laughing at this extremely long answer.

Justin still looks furious, Debra looks more confused than ever, and Aaron just looks a little shell-shocked. I probably shouldn't have said those things with him here, but Justin didn't give me much of a chance, and Aaron isn't a child. Sometimes things just need to be said, and this is one of those times.

"Mr. and Mrs. Murphy?" a woman in scrubs asks, walking up to Justin and Debra.

"I'm Angela's mother," I say, and the doctor turns to me, looking embarrassed.

"Oh, I'm so sorry, I did—"

"How is she?" I interrupt.

"Um, she is fine. Surgery took a little longer than planned, but it went well," the doctor says with a smile.

I feel a wave of relief, but also realize that I don't know exactly what they were going to do in surgery. "What did you have to do?" I ask.

"We put an intramedullary nail in her tibia to hold it in place while it heals; sometimes people call it a rod. With the type of femoral fracture she had, and her level of activity, we decided hemiarthroplasty would be best, which is a hip replacement." I can't stop from gasping slightly when she says this, and there is suddenly an arm around me. It is Alesha. "It is actually a great way to repair a break like this. It sounds drastic, but it is a much better option for her age and lifestyle," she says with a reassuring smile.

"Thank you so much," I say, wiping tears away, not realizing that it was this bad.

"How long until we can see her?" Aaron asks before I have a chance.

"She will be back in her room soon, and then you can go in. But it will be a while before she wakes up. A nurse will come and get you as soon as she is in her room. Any other questions?" I shake my head and she pats my shoulder. "Sorry about my mistake earlier. I shouldn't have made that assumption," she apologizes, and walks off.

"Deb and I are going to go down to the cafeteria. Do you want to come, Aaron?" Justin says, like Alesha and I aren't even here. But I'm not surprised, as I have thought back over the years, and the way he behaves when things aren't going the way he wants, he has always been childish.

"I'm going to stay here with Mom," Aaron says.

"Want me to bring you back something?" Justin asks, but directs it specifically at Aaron.

"Oh, that is so nice of you," Alesha instantly says. "I am fucking starved. Grab us three orders of double cheeseburgers, with onion rings—you like onion rings, right?" Alesha asks, looking from me to Aaron.

"Yeah," Aaron says, and I nod.

"Awesome! And if they have a veggie-burger option, get one of those. I'm trying to limit my consumption of animal flesh. You know, least I can do for driving that old van!" Alesha says, laughing as she holds out enough money for this order. "If this doesn't cover it, let me know and I will make it up."

"Oh, I can pay for my own," Aaron says.

"No, I got this," Alesha says.

I can't help but find it a little funny as Justin and Debra walk off to get our order, with no choice but to get it for us with Aaron wanting something as well. I know that the last thing Justin wants to do is anything that will help me or Alesha. But Alesha seems very good at playing people, and putting them into a position where they have to go along with her.

"How are you doing? You look tired?" I hear her say, and look up to respond and see the question was to Aaron. She's right though, he does look tired. It makes me happy that Aaron seems to have calmed down about what happened between me and Justin. He actually seems more on my side than he ever has about anything; not that there were or ever have been sides... But if there was, I think he is on mine. He and Alesha also seem to be becoming friends, which is a bit odd, since they are quite different in many ways.

"Oh, I forgot. I better text Anna and Evy to tell them what's going on," I say.

"You better, they will be pissed if you don't," Alesha says, and she is right, Evy will kill me, and Anna will be... maybe annoyed? I'm not sure. I wish I was more sure about so many things with Anna.

33

Are They Friends?

I sit, waiting for the nurse to come and get us. I'm also waiting for my lunch, seeming to be hungrier than I thought. I stare at my phone, hoping that Anna will text me back, but I know she is driving and will once she gets a chance.

"I'm going to the restroom, back in a sec," Alesha says, standing up, leaving Aaron and I alone. It is the first time in a very long time that we have been alone.

"Does Angela know?" I ask him.

"Yeah..." he says, knowing what I am talking about. "Sorry, I shouldn't have done that—"

"No, it's okay," I say. "I'm not good at telling people... Sorry I told you the way I did, but I knew I wouldn't do it if I didn't just say it."

"That's understandable," he says, and there is an awkward silence that starts to appear between us.

"So, how did Angela react?" I ask, partly because I don't want the silence.

"She... She was surprised."

"Understandable."

"She wasn't taking it well. Not as well as I did." I wonder what he means by this. "Angela has never been very open-minded about..." He trails off, seeming uncomfortable saying it, but I know what he means. "She will get used to it though."

"It would be nice if she does, but either way, it isn't going to change anything about me."

He stares at me for a moment. "Okay," he says, seeming to understand. I am surprised by how understanding he is about all of this. "So," Aaron continues, apparently also not wanting the silence to start between us, "I got into an argument with Dad the day after I called you."

"You did?" I say, not sure what else to say, because I don't think he has ever argued with Justin about anything, at least, not as an adult.

"I didn't know what you told me. I didn't know everything that he did... I'm sorry I didn't pay more attention and learn more about what was going on before I acted the way I did."

"It's okay," I say, even though it didn't feel okay that long ago. *I won't say anything, it is better to forgive, and I am sure there are things I could have done bet*— I pause in mid-thought, and remember what Anna would say to me, thinking that this was my fault. "You know... it wasn't okay," I say and look over at him. He stares, looking more than a little surprised. "I always tried my best to keep your father happy. I was always faithful. I never did anything he didn't want to do. The same for you and your sister. I tried my absolute hardest to be a good mother. I supported both of you, no matter what. And when everything started falling apart around me... no one was there for me. How could you have known what actually happened... when you wouldn't even talk to me?" Aaron just stares at the floor, and this time I let the silence envelop us. I want him to think about this, to know what he and his sister did.

"Oh my God, I'm gone for like five minutes," Alesha says, "and you both look like fucking shit." She sits down in the seat between Aaron and me. She looks from me to Aaron, who is still looking at the floor. "Oh... You two had to go and talk about things, didn't you?" Alesha sighs. "Jesus fucking Christ, did you have to do that now?"

This makes Aaron look up at her. "Don't say that," he says to her.
"Really?"

"You can't say that," he says somewhat sternly.

Alesha looks around her, scouring the walls. "This doesn't seem like your house, is it?" she says, still looking around, and then looks at him. "Here's the deal... choir boy. No one tells me what I can and can't say. But you are always welcome to plug your ears, okay?" She smiles, and Aaron doesn't say anything, knowing that she would win any argument. I find myself feeling proud, but of Alesha.

"So, choir boy," Alesha says after a moment of silence.

"Don't call me that," he says.

"What do you do for a living?" she asks, ignoring his protest.

"I'm an engineer."

"Well, not as exciting as some things. But, so it goes."

"It's a good job—"

"More to life than a good job."

"What do you do, then?"

"Vlog, social media, social media manager for others, other video stuff, and whatever else pays for food and fuel." She says this with such pride, and not even a hint of regret.

"That's... interesting," Aaron says, seeming not so sure.

"Oh... I live in my van and travel the country while doing all of this."

"That must be fun," he says.

"It has its low points, but ninety-eight percent of the time it is great." He nods, seeming to understand that this could be nice.

"How is work going?" I ask Aaron.

"It can be a little stressful, but I like it," he says.

"How is Hailey? Do you have a wedding date yet?" I ask.

"What, you're engaged?" Alesha asks, and I remember that she doesn't know this. I have told her hardly anything about Aaron or Angela, or much about my family at all. I wasn't hiding it, but I also just didn't want to talk about it.

"Oh, umm... We broke up," he says. "I haven't told anyone else yet."

"What happened?" I ask in surprise.

"It just started to seem like a bad idea. We both realized that it just wasn't going to work."

"I'm sorry," I say.

"You broke up completely, or just the engagement?" Alesha asks.

He looks at her for a second. "I don't think changing when we get married later will change anything," he says, like she didn't understand.

"Okay," she says, and I know she is wondering why they would break up completely just because they didn't want to get married. I kind of agree with her. Aaron and Hailey seemed to always be very happy around each other, happier than Justin and I ever were, and it is a shame that it is over because marriage didn't feel right for them. "Was it a rough ending?" Alesha asks, and I am surprised at how forward she is.

"Not too bad. I think we had both seen it coming, so it was mutual."

"Cool, then you can probably still hookup when you're both feeling... Lonely," she says, elbowing him. I can't see, but I'm pretty sure there is a wink involved as well. Aaron stares at her, seeming unsure what he should say or do in response to this. "Shit, looks like the prude doesn't fall far from the prude tree." She laughs, looking at me.

"Hey." I protest. Then realize what I am saying in front of my son.

"Right, I forget," Alesha says, "I got you out of that lifestyle"—she turns to Aaron—"but it sounds like you're my next project," she says with a lot of mischief and insinuation.

"Can we not talk about this?" I ask, not liking where she is taking this.

"Okay... fine," Alesha says, lying over against me, hugging me from the side. "I lightened the mood though," she whispers into my ear, and she's right, she did lighten the mood. "Ooh!" She nearly yells directly in my ear, "The food's here!" I look and see Debra and Justin standing there with to-go bags.

"Thanks, Dad," Aaron says, taking the bags from him.

"Of course," Justin says, specifically avoiding saying this to me or Alesha.

"Um... this one must be yours. There is a big V on it," Aaron says, handing the bag to Alesha, and one of the others to me.

"Hotdog, they had them!" Alesha says.

"Hamburger," Aaron corrects her, joking.

"Veggie-burger," she corrects with a laugh.

"Thanks for picking these up," I say to Justin and Debra. I might hate them, but I won't be rude.

"No problem," Debra says. Justin doesn't even acknowledge me though, and I wonder if he is mad that I am a lesbian, or mad that I am happy and doing well.

"Oh, this is so good," Alesha says with her mouth full.

"I've never had a veggie-burger," Aaron says after swallowing a bit of his burger. "I always figured they wouldn't be any good."

"You figured it wasn't good without trying it? What the fuck kind of logic is that engineer boy?"

"Well, I jus—"

"Here, try it," she says, holding her burger up to his mouth.

"I'm not going to—"

"Try it, chicken!" she interrupts. He reluctantly takes a bite. "Good, right?"

"Yeah, it's good," Aaron says.

"Told you. Shit, you gotta stop judging everything before you try it. I mean, your life will be so boring if you continue like that," she says, with her mouth full of onion rings this time. I watch her with Aaron, and am amazed how she acts like a lifelong friend, and he acts like hers as well. They are such different people I never would have thought they would get along, but it seems that she can make anyone feel like her friend. Or have I been wrong about Aaron? Maybe he isn't the person I always thought he was. Maybe I have been blind, being caught up with being his mother first.

"Excuse me," a nurse says, walking up to us. "You aren't allowed to eat in here."

"Oh—" I start but am cut off by Alesha.

"It's my fault. They said we could see her as soon as she was back in her room, and I didn't know when that would be and I have been so worried about my Angela that I didn't want to leave... so they brought back the food to eat with me. I'm really sorry," Alesha says, starting to put her half-eaten burger back into the to-go bag.

"I can let it go for now... But if anyone asks, I didn't notice," the nurse says with a smile. "And I think you will be able to go back in about fifteen minutes."

"Oh thank God," Alesha says with a sniff and a few tears. "Thank you so much," she says as the nurse walks off.

We all watch as the nurse leaves and rounds the corner at the end of the hall. "Wow, that was some lie," I say.

"You were going to cave," she says to me, "And I hate for choir boy here to have to spend a week begging in church for forgiveness for lying. Not that he is capable of lying." She smirks at him.

"Hey, I can lie," he argues.

"Maybe... I mean, Lord knows your dad was good at it," she says, and I stuff the last piece of my burger in my mouth to keep from laughing. Partly because of Alesha's being so flippant about it, partly because Justin looks like he wants to kill her, and partly because Aaron almost laughed at this himself. "So, if you can lie so well. Give me an example. What do you think about me?"

"What?" he asks, laughing.

"Come on. Say what you think of me, but lie."

"Okay..." he says and thinks about it for a second.

"Nope, you lose," she says before he can say anything. I can't help but laugh at his expression.

"What? How?"

"Too slow. To lie, you have to be fast."

"I wasn't that slow," he disagrees.

"Yes, you were. And it isn't like you were actually thinking about what to say. You were actually only thinking about two things," she says matter-of-factly.

"And what would those two things be?" he asks.

"What I look like naked, and if my van has a waterbed in the back."

"What?" he says, looking as embarrassed as I feel.

"Answers," she continues. "Mind-blowing, and yes."

"Alesha!" I say, wanting her to shut up.

"Okay, fine. It's not a waterbed. But the shocks are crap in my van so it really gets rockin—" I slap her on the back of the head. "Ow!"

she says, rubbing the back of her head as she turns and looks at me. "Oh... Too far?"

"Yes, too far," I say.

"Right, sorry," she says. "But you still suck at lying."

"At least he knows how to shut his mouth," I say.

"True. But that's no fun." She smiles.

"You can see your partner now," the same nurse as before says to Alesha, and walks off.

We all realize that what Alesha said before made it sound like she was Angela's girlfriend. "Goddamn, I am the fucking queen of lying," she says with a smile, and it seems that she really is the best at it.

34

Change of Plans

I sit next to Angela's bed, waiting. She has already woken up once, but it was only for a minute or two before she fell back asleep. The nurse said it could be an hour or more until she is completely coherent and awake. So, Justin left because of something with work, Debra went to crawl back under her rock for some sleep, and Alesha and Aaron went to the cafeteria for ice cream.

My phone rings. I pull it out of my pocket and answer without looking at the name, just wanting to quiet it before it wakes Angela. "Hello?" I say, at just above a whisper.

"Hey," I hear a voice that I instantly recognize as Anna say.

"Oh, I wasn't expecting you."

"Yeah, I'm on my break... Is it a good time?"

"Yeah," I say.

"Are you sure? I can call back lat—"

"Please don't," I say, not sure why I sound so desperate when I say it.

"Are you okay?" she asks, concerned.

"Yes... It has just been a very long day. And I could use someone to talk to."

"Isn't Alesha there?"

"She went to get something to eat with Aaron."

"Your son and Alesha, that must be interesting," she says with a laugh. Anna is the only one I have ever really talked about my family with, the only one who knows it all. So she knows what an odd mix this is.

"Actually, they are like best friends."

"What!" Anna yells into the phone, laughing.

"I honestly don't know. But they are like old friends, joking, giving each other a hard time, sharing food—"

"Sharing food?" Anna says.

"Yeah. He tried her burger."

"And now they went to get something to eat."

"Yeah?" I say, feeling like I am missing something.

"Is Aaron's fiancée there?" she asks, and I am a little surprised she remembered he was engaged.

"No, they broke up."

"Oh, my, God!"

"What?"

"It sounds more like flirting than just joking."

"No. Alesha is actually being mean to him. I had to make her stop once."

"Pushing him down in the sandbox and dipping pigtails in ink?"

"Oh, come on," I say, laughing, and I love it... It feels like the way it was before things changed between us.

"Okay, how did he take it? Did he get mad? Did he insult her back?"

"Well..." I say, and think about it. Remember him laughing about it, or smiling, even about things I thought he would be insulted by. "Oh my God... They are flirting," I say in disbelief as Anna starts laughing.

"Fuck, you are slow at figuring these things out." She laughs, and I don't know what to think about them flirting right in front of me. But I laugh, because she is laughing, and I can't stop myself.

"Should I do something about it?" I ask.

"Why? They're adults."

"True..."

"Oh, one thing."

"What?" I ask.

"If they come back, and Alesha took him to see her van, don't ask anything about it."

"She wouldn't do that."

"Umm... you would have said that, and I would have said that. But what did we do in the sleeper of my truck?"

"Oh dear God," I say, and she bursts into laughter.

"Just don't ask questions, because you know Alesha will tell you," she says, and I cringe at the thought while laughing, because I know she is right.

We both go quiet after we stop laughing. The quiet seems to last just a second too long. "How have you been?" I ask abruptly, suddenly scared she might hang up.

"Oh... I've been good. It's been easy driving, nothing bad has happened. So, can't complain..." she answers, and the answer is too short, it's too... something.

"That's good. Glad it has been easy driving," I say, wondering why conversation has suddenly become so hard, and I realize it is because we are now talking about us. Everything is great as long as we don't talk about each other. As soon as we do, the fractures of our friendship become painfully clear.

"How long are you staying in Texas?" she asks.

"It might be awhile."

"Really?"

"Angela will need some help for a while, so I am going to stay and help her. She has a small house she rents, so I am going to stay there with her," I explain. Though I haven't told Angela this. But I'm not planning on making it an option for her.

"Well, it sounds like you are getting along with your kids better."

"Yeah, I am."

"Maybe you should keep an eye out for a job and just stay there." I almost feel sick when she says this. "I mean, it wouldn't take much to beat cleaning our crappy houses," she says with a small laugh. "And if you do move back to Texas, it is better you do it now before you have to endure the New York winters," she says, laughing again.

I force a little laugh. "You make a good point, I'll think about it," I say, getting the feeling that this is a hint for me to not move back into her bedroom in her house. "Hey, I gotta go. The nurse just walked in," I lie.

"Okay, talk later. Bye."

"Yeah, bye," I say and hang up, and I stare at the phone.

"Who was that?" a sleepy voice asks.

"Hey, Sweetie, you're awake," I say, smiling at Angela.

"I guess so... Anyone interesting?" she asks, referring to Anna again.

"Oh, that was... just a friend," I say, and it isn't a lie. She is just a friend, someone I will talk on the phone with, until it becomes just texts, then just memories of a handful of nights... Just someone I was once friends with.

I talk with Angela; who still seems half asleep as she talks for ten minutes or so when Alesha and Aaron walk in laughing about something. "Hey Aaron," Angela says groggily.

"Hey, you're awake," he says.

"Where have you been?" she asks him.

"I was having ice cream."

"Ice cream?" Angela asks, like she wants to know why they didn't bring her some.

"Want me to get you some?" I ask.

"Umm..." Alesha says. "I hate to fuck up your ice cream craving, but you should stick to clear liquid for a few hours. Ice cream might upset your stomach."

Aaron and I stare at her. "How would you know?" Aaron asks.

"My mom had a minor surgery last year, and anesthesia may give you an upset stomach for a while," she says. "But how about a clear soda?"

"Who are you?" Angela asks, confused.

"Oh, right. Sorry, forgot you haven't met me—"

"How do you forget something like that?" Aaron asks Alesha.

"Not sure. Your stupidity must be rubbing off on me," she retorts. "Anyway, as I was saying. I'm Alesha, your mom's friend."

"My mom's friend?" Angela repeats, clearly not fully together yet.

"Yes," Alesha says, "Just friends... like regular friends, not 'night-time lovers' friends."

"Why would you say that?" Aaron asks her.

"Just making it clear," Alesha says, like this is a perfect way to make sure there are no mistakes. "Want a soda? I'll pop out and grab it."

"Uhh... that would be nice, thanks," Angela says.

"I'll go with you," I say, standing, "and give you two a few minutes." Figuring that Aaron might want a minute with her alone, they have always been close.

"You seem to be getting along well with Aaron," I say, once we are out of the room and the door is shut behind us.

"He seems decent enough, not like his fucking dad. God, that guy has the biggest asshole vibe I have ever seen," she says, and then realizes what she said. "Oh, sorry. I didn't mean that he was like that when you married him, I know you wouldn't have—"

"I know what you mean, and you're right," I say, laughing a little as she tries to backtrack.

"But it seemed to me that Aaron is trying to be supportive... more or less, so I thought I would give him a chance."

"He is trying," I say, a bit proud that he is being more open-minded than I thought he might.

"I also thought that it might help you if he likes me," she says.

"Seems to be working," I say as we walk down the hallway. "So, did you have a nice dessert together? Seemed like you were gone a while."

"Yeah, it was great. I also thought you might want a bit of time alone, and he had been asking about how my van was set up, so I took him down for the grand tour."

"You were both down in your van most of that time?" I ask, staring at Alesha as we stop in front of the coke machine.

"What?" she asks, staring back.

"Nothing... nothing at all," I say, quickly looking away.

"Wait... you think we did it."

"I do not."

"Oh my God, you do." She laughs. "I told you I wouldn't do that."

"I know, I know—"

"But if you already think it happened, I already said I could give him a ride... maybe I will—"

"I didn't think so, and I never did. It was Anna who said it. I never did. And why would you say something like that to me?"

"Sorry, I couldn't help it," she says, laughing at my expense.

"Let's just get the cokes," I say with a sigh. I feed the machine the money and press the button for a Sprite, knowing it is the one Angela would want.

"So," Alesha says, pulling the bottle out of the machine, "how's Anna?"

"She's good," I say.

"Are you two... back together?" she asks with hesitation.

"We were never together like that—"

"Yeah, sure."

"We weren't... I'm sure."

"How?" she asks, prying. But I like her prying, because she doesn't pry for gossip or to be nosey, she does because she cares about me, and doesn't want me to be alone.

"She said, since I am getting along with my kids, I should maybe stay here and find a job." It hurts when I say it out loud.

"Oh, fuck..." Alesha says, and she sounds like I feel.

"It was just a nice time, but it's over... And I'm fine with that. I really don—" I'm interrupted by Alesha suddenly hugging me right in the middle of the hallway. "Really... I'm fine," I say, suddenly not feeling fine. It is like the reality of Anna saying I shouldn't come back falls onto me as I say this, and Alesha hugged me knowing its weight before I did. "I think I thought that maybe things would be more between us, even when things weren't going well." I admit, failing at keeping myself from crying.

"You can find someone better than her," she says with a tight voice and a loud sniff.

"I really don't care if I do or not," I say honestly, because I really don't care at the moment.

"Oh, like fuck," Alesha says, stepping back and looking me in the eye. "I will not let your newfound career as a lesbian end with just one woman. I am making it my mission to get you laid while I'm here—"

"Please don't," I interrupt, laughing.

"Maybe a nurse or doctor," she says, looking up and down the hallway, like some woman who is ready and willing would just be standing there waiting for me.

"I don't need that."

"Maybe a lesbian bar. That could be fun," she says excitedly. "I'll go with you!"

"You'll go with me to a lesbian bar?" I ask, raising an eyebrow.

"I don't have to fuck anyone, and it would be nice being hit on by a woman instead of some sleazy drunk guy."

"I don't drink—"

"You don't have to. You're just there for some good old rebound sex."

"No."

"You know you will like it. And you're fucking hot for your age. I bet you can bag several women there," she says with an evil look.

"Now you sound like a sleazy guy."

"Oh, you know the idea of rebounding with a harem of beautiful women is an exciting idea for you," Alesha says, and I know she is once again just lightening the mood. I wonder what her life was like growing up since she always feels that she needs to make people happy, always being the light.

"Well, if it is a harem of beautiful women, then I will do it," I say, joking.

"Excuse me," Aaron says, opening the door. "But, could you not talk so loud?" I look over, horrified.

"Oops," Alesha says. "I thought the doors were more sound-proof than that."

"I... I..." I try to say, but can't seem to find anything to say. I didn't even realize we were in front of Angela's room.

"I was just giving your mom a hard time," Alesha says with a smirk. "Hey, maybe I should take you to a bar and find you a... date," she emphasizes, and he just turns and walks back into the room without a word. "What?" Alesha says, throwing her hands in the air as she follows. "You just look like you could let off some steam."

Angela stares as we walk back in, clearly wondering what is going on, and probably wondering if I am her real mother. "How are you feeling, sweetie?" I ask, twisting the lid of the Sprite to loosen it for her.

"I'm feeling better. Thanks for the coke," she says, seeming much more together, not so sleepy.

"That's good," I say, sitting down on the edge of her bed, stroking her hair back out of her face.

"How long will you be here before you go back?" Angela asks me. I'm surprised she asks this so quickly, having figured it would be a little longer before this came up.

"I don't know. But I'm going to stay with you until you can manage on your own. I'm in no hurry to go anywhere, so I can stay close by even after that," I say with mixed emotions that are clawing to get out, and I notice Alesha look slightly away, understanding what my being able to stay here actually means.

Part of me feels like somehow I have circled and am right back where I started. And like the last time I was here, I'm not sure how to move on. It's like my old life with Justin just won't let me go, at least, not completely.

35

My Life

"Haven't talked to you much," Evy says over the video-call as I lie on my bed in Angela's guest room, which is technically her office. It is so small that it feels smaller than the truck's sleeper at times.

"Yeah, I guess we've all been busy."

"Yeah... How are things going there?" they ask.

I think of the past few weeks, and how much work it has been with not only the recovery from her surgery, but the whiplash, a few cracked ribs, and massive bruises all over her body. It has made things very hard for Angela. There has also been a lot of tension between me and her. It seems that she isn't as accepting as Aaron is about my sexual orientation. She hasn't said anything, but it is obviously something she doesn't agree with.

"Things are going great. Angela is doing a lot better, everyday she improves."

"That's great. But what about you?" they ask.

"I'm great," I answer too quickly.

"Okay..." Evy says, not convinced. "Well, if Angela is doing so much better, you must be thinking of a return date."

"Oh... I'm not sure yet," I say, not wanting to tell her.

"You better start thinking about it, unless you are going to stay there," they say, and start laughing, knowing how glad I was to leave and that I never wanted to come back.

"Well—"

"Holy fuck... Are you actually thinking about staying?"

"I'm getting along well with the kids, and there is a lot of work here so it will be eas—"

"You are fucking serious? You are actually going to stay?" They sound shocked, almost upset.

"I know this is going to cause you trouble," I say, feeling bad.

"No... No, it's fine. I can find someone else."

"I am sorry..."

"I understand that you need to be near your kids," Evy says, and I can feel the lie eating at me. "Have you told Anna?" This makes my heart jump as they stare at me intently through the screen, waiting for the answer.

"I haven't, but she won't be surprised." I don't tell them that the reason I haven't told Anna is because we barely even text now, only a few lines since we talked on the phone at the hospital that day.

"Why wouldn't she be surprised? I'm fucking surprised, for shit's sake."

"It was her idea..." I say quieter than I mean too.

"What?"

"It wasn't really her idea." I correct, "She said that maybe I should stay here if the kids had come around," I say, leaving out the part where she didn't seem to want me around her house anymore.

"What the fuck?" Evy says to themself. "It's your choice, of course. And you always have a place here, so... Yeah."

"I will visit. You aren't getting rid of me that easy," I say, trying to force a small laugh, but it doesn't work.

"So," Evy says, apparently not ready to hang up. "Are you going to hunt around for a girlfriend?"

"You're as bad as Alesha," I say, actually laughing this time. "She wants me to hit the lesbian bars."

"Not a bad idea," they say.

"Yes, it is a bad idea."

"Too bad deli lady is back here."

"I know..."

"Wait, what?" Evy says, and I realize what I just said. "Oh my fucking God. You are game to find a hookup."

"No... no, I just wasn't paying attention to what I was saying—"

"Which is why you told the truth. You want to fuck deli lady!" they say laughing.

"I do not," I say, pretty much whining.

"You so fucking do. Hey, I have an idea—"

"I don't want to hear it."

"You should text her, tell her what's going on."

"Why would I do that?" I ask, confused why I would ever do that.

"It lays some groundwork, you come and visit me during the day... and visit her in the night."

"Nope, I'm not doing that," I say.

"How about this? If you don't text her anything after being all friendly at the supermarket, and getting her number, it will be like you are completely ignoring her."

I sigh, knowing they are right. "I will do it—"

"Yes—"

"But only to say why I will not be able to meet up," I say, feeling like I am playing into Evy's plan of some kind.

"Well, I have to go. But let me know if anything happens between you and deli lady."

"What could happen? We are on other sides of the country."

"You know... You could use this video-call for other things. Just saying," they say with a grin that I don't trust.

"I am not doing that."

"I bet you once said something like that about having sex with a woman."

"Oh... shut up," I say, laughing.

"It's late here, though. So, I will talk to you later. Love you."

"Good night, love you," I say, and end the call. *Well, even though it may not have worked out for me and Anna, I am glad I have Evy as such a great friend*, I think with a smile.

Anna

It feels nice to set my feet on my own driveway. Something about this last run has just been shit. Every day... fucking shit. I look at the house, and stare up at my bedroom window, and wish Mary was in there waiting for me. But she isn't.

"You home?" I ask, closing the door behind me and kicking off my shoes.

"We're in here," Nathan calls from the kitchen. I'm not surprised he's here, he always is. But I'm just glad Evy has someone. I remember the days when they thought they would never have someone like him.

I walk into the kitchen to see Evy sitting at the table and Nathan cooking something on the stove. "Oh... It's good to see you," I say to Evy, hugging them from behind while they're still sitting.

"Nice to see you too, but sit your fucking ass down."

"Don't be too hard on her, sweetie," Nathan says, looking over his shoulder.

"Okay..." I say, pulling out a chair and sitting down. "What? Am I in trouble or something?" I ask, laughing a little, figuring that Evy is pissy about something dumb.

But Evy doesn't laugh or even smile, and neither does Nathan, who sits down next to Evy. "I talked with Mary earlier tonight," she says.

"Oh, how is she?" I ask, getting the feeling I know where this is going.

"She's managing. But did you know she is getting a job and staying in Texas?" they say, and I glance down at the table, feeling like a teen getting scolded for something.

"No, I didn't. But I am—"

"You didn't know?" Evy says, glaring at me. "That's odd, since she said you suggested it."

"What the fuck is this? Stop treating me like some goddamn child," I say, starting to really get pissed that Evy isn't minding their own business.

"Fuck, I'm not trying to treat you like a child," Evy says more calmly. "It's just... What the hell's going on between you and her?"

"I don't know... It's just hard."

"Really?" Evy says, clearly not letting me off that easy.

"I forgot," Nathan says, leaning over and kissing Evy's cheek. "I have some emails I have to send. So, I'm going to go get those done before dinner."

"Okay," Evy says to him, and I know he is just leaving, so it might be easier for me. Or maybe easier for Evy to get everything they want out of me. "So?" Evy says, looking back at me. "Tell me how it is hard."

I sigh, knowing I will have to tell them. But part of me wants to. I've never hidden anything from Evy, so I'm not sure why this is so much harder. "We were... I guess just the right place at the right time. We were just convenient for each other."

"So, you don't think she was serious about you?"

"We just hit it off when she was riding with me, and it was fun. But, she just came out, and from a bad situation at that. I know she should get a chance to experience more, and I'm not a long-term person."

"Fuck, stop saying that," Evy says with a sigh. "Why don't you ever realize that you are never happy when you are just sleeping around?"

"Sleeping around?"

"Do you have a better term for it?" they ask, and I don't say anything. "Yeah, that's what I thought. As for the rest of that, you seem to be making a lot of decisions for her—"

"I don't do that!" I say, angry at the implication.

"Why the fuck do you think she got so mad at you that night?"

"Yeah, I know. I shouldn't have been so surprised that she fixed a roof."

"No, you dumbass. She was pissed because you wrote off everything she had been fighting for."

"What?"

"She had been working so hard to be more than what she had ever been allowed to be, to do what she was never allowed, and you wrote off all of her work like it was a fucking joke. She loves you, and you acted like what she pushed herself to do was nothing," Evy says.

"I didn't think of it like that..."

"Yeah, so maybe you should let her make decisions for herself. You're treating her like that fucking ex of hers."

"You're right..."

"Have you ever told her you love her?" Evy asks abruptly.

"What?" I ask, looking up in surprise.

"Oh, you heard me."

"No..."

"Did you tell her you like her?"

"No..."

"Holy fuck... What is wrong with you?" they ask. "It's clear as day you fucking love her. You do, right?"

"Yeah... I think so," I say, looking back down at the table. "But I don't know how she feels about me," I admit. It is what I have been thinking for... too long.

"Holy shit, you're an idiot. I mean, the goddamn lamp in the corner knows she loves you. It's that obvious."

"Really?" I ask, not sure.

"Okay, tell me this. Who made the first move?" they ask.

"Like sex?"

"I mean first anything. Wait... was the first thing sex?"

"No... We were on the Ferris wheel at Magical Land, the fireworks were going off, and we kissed," I say, leaving some out.

"Great... Now, what are you leaving out?" I just stare at them. "Oh please, I know you far too well for that shit."

I sigh. "We were sitting there watching the fireworks when she said she thought she was falling in love with me—"

"Holy fuck! You have to be fucking kidding me... Did you seriously think that this was just some fun thing for her after that?"

"I don't know!" I say, feeling like I might suddenly have a panic attack.

"That isn't some normal 'it was convenient' fuck-buddy. That was Hollywood romance movie shit," Evy says, seeming like they might have a panic attack themself. "Oh God, no wonder she is so devastated."

"What?" I say, looking up at them.

"Yeah, she was devastated every time you left. She was miserable whenever you weren't around. And she said she was doing great when I talked to her tonight, but she looked like shit."

"Oh fuck," I say, knowing now I screwed up.

"So, what are you going to do?" Evy asks, staring at me.

"I'm not sure..." I say, my stomach feeling like it's in knots.

"You might want to decide quickly. Some lady at a deli gave Mary her phone number, and I told her to call her because she deserved better than the piece of shit you were being."

My heart stops. "You what!"

"I wasn't going to tell her not to. Plus, I thought it would be good for her to maybe... have fun with someone else," they say with a sly grin.

"You did that to screw with me."

"No, I did it because I was really pissed at you, and Mary needed encouragement," they say, and I know I have no right to act like Mary and I are a couple or something. "So, you going to do something?"

"Yeah..." I say, thinking.

"You know," Evy says, more gently than before, "Not all long-term relationships end badly. You were young back then. You need to realize that every time won't be like that."

I'm not really surprised that Evy knew this is what I was thinking about. "I know..."

"Then let's eat, and then maybe you should call her." I just nod.

I start my truck, the horizon just starting to glow orange with the morning sun. I think about last night as my truck warms up, and think about how I didn't call Mary. I tried, but just couldn't get myself to do it. I couldn't get myself to call and say, *"Hey, let's be serious girlfriends,"* something about it wasn't right. I wasn't ready for that call.

Releasing the brakes with a hiss of air, I pull out of my parking place and turn for the highway I have been down so many times. Alone, just like all the times before.

Mary

I chop onions for the soup as Angela sits at the table separating and buttering rolls to go into the oven. "So," Aaron says, looking at Alesha. "Why are you here?"

"Because I am bored and hungry. I also brought food."

"It's a package of cheap cookies," he says.

"And a twelve-pack of soda." Alesha points out.

"That still doesn't explain why you are here," he says.

"Okay, fine, I'm secretly dating your sister."

"Not funny," Angela says, not amused by the idea. She still isn't comfortable with my sexual identity, and doesn't like joking about it. While in the hospital, she asked how I knew I was a lesbian, and that I wasn't just mad at Justin. Alesha was there and responded for me by asking Angela if she *went around fucking women when she was mad"* and when Angela looked appalled at the idea, Alesha laughed at her. This seemed to have gotten the point across that it doesn't work like that, that being angry doesn't make you queer. But this also made her not like Alesha.

"Oh, come on, it's a little funny," Alesha says, pouring a can of coke into her glass.

"Will you stop causing trouble?" I say to her, feeling like she's my third child.

"But Aaron started it..." Alesha sulks, as she dips a cookie in her glass of coke.

"I did not," Aarons says. "You started it by showing up."

"You two are giving me a headache," I say, sliding the diced onion off the cutting board and into the soup.

"Oh right," Alesha says, glaring at Aaron. "Blame me, why not?" And I sigh to myself as I see the slight grin on both of their faces as they mess with each other, because I know this is leading to something I don't want to think about.

Being around Aaron more while he is with Alesha has made me realize that he isn't as religious or as invested in the church as I had been, that he might have been acting more so for my sake. That he wanted to make me happy, following what my expectations were of him. Until now, I hadn't realized how much of the same expectations that were placed on me. I placed on my own children without even knowing it.

"So, Mom," Angela says, clearly wanting to interrupt their back and forth. "Are you ready for your job interview tomorrow?"

"Ooh," Alesha interrupts. "Are you interviewing for that job opening I sent you at that... 'adult shop'?" She air quotes.

"No..." I say, a bit annoyed she would bring that up now. I thought it was funny when she sent it to me, and the starting pay is surprisingly high, but I would rather she not bring it up as a joke with my kids. It is like she forgets they're my kids, and not just friends of mine like she is.

"Why would you use air quotes? It isn't like you were that cryptic," Aaron says.

"Why am I not surprised you knew exactly what I was talking about?" she says, smirking at him. "I bet you know, exactly, what, store, I'm... talking about," she says, leaning closer to him.

"Will you please back up," he says, leaning back in his chair to get away from her.

"Oh, so you aren't denying you go to that store," she says, grinning bigger, only inches from him.

"Will you stop it," I tell her. "I would rather you not make things more uncomfortable than you already have."

She instantly stops and sits back down in her seat. "Sorry."

"Yes," I say, looking back to Angela. "I think I am ready for the interview."

"It will be nice working again," she says, seeming to think I had a job here before. But I never truly did. Cleaning the church wasn't a job. At least not like my full days of work for Evy.

"So," Alesha says, dipping a cookie in her coke. "You going to try to find a place next?"

"I think so," I say, noticing that Angela doesn't object to my moving out, but I don't blame her.

"Well, there ain't a lot of room, but you are always welcome to stay with me," Alesha says.

"You live in a van... How could she stay with you?" Aaron asks, and I notice he seems to start these little arguments more than Alesha does.

"You jealous?"

"No."

"Oh... You don't want to try it out?"

"Stop it," Angela says shortly, and I am getting the feeling she wants all of us out of her house. "But you can stay here as long as you want, Mom." Something about the way she says this feels more like she felt obligated after Alesha's offer.

"I would offer, but I don't think my roommate would be very happy," Aaron says.

"I will find a place soo—" I start to say.

"What the fuck was that?" Alesha interrupts, looking towards the front of the house.

"It sounded like a horn," Aaron says, as we all stand up; Angela using her cane, but standing with little trouble.

I am almost across the living room when; what I can now clearly hear is an air horn, sounds again with two long blasts. "It's a semi-truck," Aaron says, looking back from the window in the door, and my heart seems to stop for a second.

"Holy fuck," Alesha says, looking at me from the front window she is looking out. "It's Anna..." With these words my breath catches, but I pull myself together, knowing she might just be in the area.

"That's Anna?" Aaron says.

"She's getting out," Alesha reports from the window. "And there is some pissed-off neighbor dude walking towards her."

I open the front door to hear the neighbor ranting about how it is a residential street, and she can't drive or park a semi on it. "I'm going to call the police!" he yells.

"I'm picking something up, so call the fucking police, you pile of shit," Anna says back to him.

"Oh, I'm sure you are," he says.

"Just keep pushing me and you'll lose them, I have room on my rig for yours," she says, and he looks confused, but I can't help but laugh remembering the bumper sticker and row of fake balls hanging from Anna's trailer.

"Whatever," the man says, turning and walking away.

"Man, what a dick," she says as we meet in the middle of the yard.

"Why are you here?" I ask, just wanting to know, not wanting to waste time.

"I love you." I freeze in place. *This has to be a mistake, this can't be right.*

"Wh... what?" I stammer.

"I have been a fucking asshole, because I have all my own shit that I never seem to get past, and I am so stupid I don't even see what's going on in front of me and I don't know why it is always so hard but it seems to be, but I finally realized what you are to me and that I threw it away, and I know you deserve so much better than me but I had to try and make things right, so I drove here to say that I love you." Anna rattles this all off like she has been saying it the whole way down here.

"That... was, a lot."

"I'm just so scared that I will fuck up and not say it, so I didn't want to take a chance. But I really love you."

"How many times are you going to say it?" I ask.

"Until you know that I actually mean it, that I don't want some casual relationship. That I want you by my side every morning and every night."

I swallow down the lump. "I want that too..." I say.

"Really?"

"Yes, because... I love you, too."

"Really?" she says again, and I can't help but smile at how adorable she is, when she is this nervous.

"You want to stay for dinner? We're having soup. You can park the truck somewhere, and I will pick you up in the car."

"Nope, sorry!" Alesha interrupts, walking up, Aaron and Angela a short way behind her, seeming very standoffish.

"What?" I ask, confused on why she would have a problem with this.

"Sorry, but it is a small house and there is only room for one of each," Alesha says.

"One of each?" Anna says, as confused as the rest of us.

"One of each," she repeats. "We have a lesbian"—she waves a hand at me—"an idiot man"—she gestures at Aaron—"a prude"—she gestures at Angela—"and a gorgeous straight funny girl," she says with a flourishing hand movement at herself. "So you see, we already have a lesbian, and we can't have two in the house. You will both have to go somewhere else for dinner," Alesha says, waving her hand like she is shooing us away. I smile at her, making us go out.

"Okay..." Anna says and grins. "but I'm not a lesbian. I'm bi."

"I hate to have to tell you," Alesha says without hesitation. "But I am a bigot... It's true, I hate truck-driving bisexuals with funny bumper stickers and red shoes," she says, pointing at Anna's red shoes.

"Really..." Anna says.

"Yeah, can't stand being around them. So you will have to take Mary somewhere else for dinner."

"Wow," Aaron says, stepping a little closer. "That is very niche bigotry."

"I know. Isn't it weird?" Alesha says, looking at him with a smile.

"Oh," I say, "This is my son Aaron and my daughter Angela."

"Nice to finally meet you," Aaron says, stepping forward and shaking Anna's hand.

"Yeah, same," Anna says.

"Hi," Angela says, not stepping closer, but half waving.

"But," Aaron says. "I think I have been around Alesha too much lately. " Alesha looks at him, seeming caught off guard. "I think I have the same bigotry she does. So you will have to take my mom somewhere else for dinner. Sorry." I had to force the lump in my throat down again when he says this. I never expected him to say something like this.

"Yeah," I hear behind me, and I turn to see Angela step forward slightly, cane in hand. "I think I caught a little of that too..." I can't help but sniff back some tears. It isn't that I need their approval, but I also don't want to lose them.

"I guess I have to take you out for dinner, since this seems to be a house full of fucking haters," Anna says with a smile.

"Yeah, I guess so," I say. "I'll see you later tonight," I say to the three of them as Anna and I start walking towards the truck.

"Oh, don't do that," Alesha says. "We won't be waiting up at all, so no worries. We are just going to stay in, eating soup and watching pay-per-view porn."

"Really?" I hear Aaron say.

"I'm joking," Alesha says. "No one uses pay-per-view these days." She laughs. I don't have to look back to know the look Aaron is giving her. I hear the door of the house close as Anna and I reach the truck.

"You know that Alesha and Aaron are—"

"Don't say it," I say, interrupting Anna. "I'm trying desperately to ignore it." Anna laughs at this.

I open the door of the truck and pull myself into the cab. I sit down in my seat and realize how much I've missed the truck. Anna pulls herself into the truck and as soon as her door is shut, I pull her to me, kissing her with all the passion I have in me, and she does the same.

"So," I say as we pull a few inches apart. "I'm thinking a short dinner."

"Really?" she says, and I can feel her breath against me.

"Yeah, I've missed the sleeper," I say as she grins.

"We better enjoy it before it's gone."

"Are you buying a new truck?" I ask.

"Nope, I'm retiring from trucking."

"Why?" I ask, confused.

"It's too dangerous... and now I don't want to take those risks. I have a reason now," she says, smiling close to me.

"I love you so much."

"I love you too," she says, kissing me again.

Author Note

I got the idea to write this story while listening to the song Angel from Montgomery, by John Prine. It made me want to write a story about a woman coming to terms with who she was, which she kept hidden deep inside herself her entire life until she realized it wasn't too late to change. I also decided, for some reason, that a semi-truck was the perfect place for this.

Driving a long-haul semi has a certain amount of romanticism to it, at least from the outside looking in. In reality, it's a job of long, boring days, until it isn't boring, and that is when you realize how dangerous it can be. But I feel like it is the loneliness that truly is what eats away at you. And even though I have never driven truck, I feel like I might have also been happy to have someone riding along like Anna did.

I have always had a personal connection to semi-trucks because my grandpa, who had a small dirt construction company, loved semis. His truck was nothing special, but it was his pride and joy. When I was very young, we would sometimes go out to eat with my grandpa, and it was always at the truck stop—which was actually really good at the time. After eating, my siblings and I would walk around with him in the parking lot packed full of semis. We would then pick which ones we wanted.

Novels like this are always fun to write because you can add little bits of your own life experiences. Like when I made poor Mary climb onto a roof to fix it. I only thought of that because I was on the roof of a workshop painting sealant on it, and thought it was the perfect thing to move Mary out of her comfort zone. But there is also an empowering sense of accomplishment when you complete something like this when you have never done it, and she needed that. I did not plan on it being part of Mary and Anna's big fight; that just happened. I swear, sometimes I don't know why my characters get mad at each other, but they always work it out.

I don't know if any of you noticed, but there was also some crossover between this novel and my Love, Sorrow series. I thought most people who had read the Love, Sorrow books would notice, but then I found out that my editor didn't notice at all, even though she has obviously read all of these books many times. Maybe I'm not as obvious as I think, but I am not sure.

I'll stop rambling now. But I really did want to add something new to the world of Rom-Com novels, and a semi-truck seemed like just the ticket. Also, I couldn't help but stick two people with good chemistry, like Mary and Anna, into the tight living arrangement of a sleeper. It might not be the *one-bed* trope, but it's darn close.

If you wouldn't mind helping me out and enjoyed reading about Mary's journey, then please tell your friends and family about it and share it on your social media. Leaving reviews and ratings is the best way to help others find this novel, and I truly appreciate and am thankful for every review and rating.

Acknowledgments

This novel wouldn't have been possible without the loving support of my family and so many friends, who were always there to encourage me. This truly would not have been possible without the help of my mom. Who is my editor, copyeditor, and beta-reader. Her dedication to this task is truly amazing.

I would also like to thank everyone who has read *Anti-Aging Cream*, thank you so much for your support.

About Author

Gallagher Green was born and raised in rural Kansas, USA. with the freedom to learn and build whatever was interesting to them at that moment. They were encouraged to learn the skills needed to build or repair, to learn the knowledge to answer the questions, and to ask the questions.

After years of asking themself hypothetical questions that seemly had no answer, they started answering the questions in the only way that made sense... by writing the answers in the form of stories. With this, they started their career as an author. A career they had never intended on. But now hopes that their work will help answer the questions readers have in life, in the same way other authors have helped them answer some of their questions.

Instagram: @gallagher.green.author
TikTok: @gallagher.green.author

For news on our newest releases, other titles, and fun merch,
please visit our website!

GoldenArtPublishing.com

9 798330 336463